POCKETFUL OF DREAMS

**The queen of the East End saga returns with
a charming new wartime series**

It's 1939, and the Brogan family of London's
East End are ready to show Hitler what for. But
things don't seem so rosy when rationing,
evacuation and air-raids start to put this larger-
than-life family to the test. When a mysterious
young man arrives, he provides just the dazzling
distraction they need – and for eldest daughter
Mattie, the promise of more than she'd ever
wished for. But as the pair fall deeper in love,
they are drawn into secret dangers, rife on the
streets of London. As the young couple try to
protect the East End, can their dreams survive
the darkening backdrop of wartime...?

POCKETFUL OF DREAMS

POCKETFUL OF DREAMS

by

Jean Fullerton

Magna Large Print Books
Long Preston, North Yorkshire,
BD23 4ND, England.

British Library Cataloguing in Publication Data.

A catalogue record of this book is
available from the British Library

ISBN   978-0-7505-4603-4

First published in Great Britain in 2017 by Corvus,
an imprint of Atlantic Books Ltd.

Published in Large Print 2018 by arrangement with
Atlantic Books

Magna Large Print is an imprint of Library Magna Books Ltd.

Printed and bound in Great Britain by
T.J. (International) Ltd., Cornwall, PL28 8RW

To my darling husband of 40 years, Kelvin

Chapter One

Gripping the two Kirby grips tightly between her lips, Matilda Mary Brogan or Mattie as she was known to all and everyone, carefully slid the comb of her sister Cathy's headdress into place and then, taking each pin in turn, fixed it there.

'There you go,' she said, smiling at Cathy in the mirror.

Cathy, who at eighteen was two years Mattie's junior, had hair the colour of ripe corn and storm grey eyes, like their father's, while, in complete contrast, Mattie had inherited the dark chestnut locks and hazel coloured eyes of their mother.

'It's so pretty.' Touching the wax orange blossoms with the tips of her fingers, Cathy turned her head from side to side. 'I just hope it stays on in this wind.'

'It ought to, I've anchored it with enough pins,' Mattie replied. 'Besides, it looks like it's brightening up.'

Cathy gave her a wan smile. 'You mean it's stopped thundering.'

It was the first Saturday in September and instead of catching the 5.30 from London Bridge to Kent for the hop harvest, which is what they'd done on this day of the year ever since the girls could remember, the women of the family had been up since the crack of dawn preparing for Cathy's big day.

Mattie lived with her parents, Ida and Jerimiah Brogan, at number 25 Mafeking Terrace which ran between Cable Street and the Highway in Wapping, just a few roads back from London Docks. Their road was lined with Victorian workers' cottages and was just wide enough for two horse carts to scrape past each other. It had originally been called Sun Fields Lane but after Baden-Powell and his handful of troops were relieved at Mafeking, it was renamed in their honour.

With three upstairs rooms, a front and back parlour plus a scullery, the houses in the street were probably considered spacious when they were constructed a century and half ago but with seven adults and two children living under its roof, the ancient workman's cottage was straining at the seams.

Mattie's parents had the largest upstairs room, overlooking the street, her brother Charlie, who was three years older than her, and nine-year-old Billy-Boy squashed into the minute back room while Mattie shared the third bedroom with her sisters Cathy and Josephine. This was where she was now, standing listening to her mother and grandmother bustling around downstairs as they prepared plates of sandwiches for the wedding breakfast.

As the women had used the facilities at the Highway's public baths the evening before, they set to making plates of sandwiches still in their dressing gowns and curlers, to be taken around to the Catholic Club where the wedding breakfast was to be held.

While the women of the family worked on the

refreshments, Mattie's father and her brother Charlie changed into their Sunday togs and had left twenty minutes ago to sort out the transport. As chief bridesmaid, Mattie had been given the task of helping Cathy into her wedding dress while the rest of the family got everything ready.

There was a crash downstairs.

'For the love of God,' screamed her mother's voice from the scullery below. 'For once will you let up on your bloody fault-finding, Ma?'

'Fault-finding, is it?' trilled Queenie Brogan, Jerimiah's sixty-two-year-old mother. 'Sure, am I not just trying to stop you being the laughing stock of the street, Ida, with your–'

The kitchen door slammed.

In the reflection, Cathy smiled at her. 'They don't stop, do they?'

'When are they not?' Mattie rested her hands lightly on her sister's slender shoulders and smiled. 'You look so beautiful and every bit the blushing bride.'

A pink glow coloured her sister's cheeks. 'I just hope Stan will agree.'

'Of course he will,' said Mattie. 'In fact, I wouldn't be surprised if he fainted away at the very sight of you.'

Cathy giggled. 'Did you ever think I'd be married before you, Mattie?'

'I can't say I gave it much thought,' Mattie replied, poking a stray pin in a little firmer.

Cathy turned her head and fiddled with a curl. 'Because I'm sure you'll meet the right man someday.'

'I'm sure I will, too,' Mattie replied. 'Someday,

but I'm not in any hurry.'

Cathy spun around on the stool and took her hands.

'And I don't want you to worry that you might end up an old maid on the shelf, cos you won't,' she said, an earnest little frown creasing her powdered brow.

Mattie suppressed a smile. 'I'll try.'

Giving her hands a reassuring squeeze, Cathy turned back to admire her reflection again. 'It seems wrong somehow to be so happy what with everything else that's going on.'

'Nonsense,' said Mattie fluffing up the short cream veil again. 'A wedding and a good old-fashioned knees-up is just what everyone needs to take their mind off things.'

Cathy bit her lip. 'Do you think it will be war?'

Mattie sighed. 'I can't see how we can avoid it. And what with the blackout each night and trenches being dug in Shadwell Gardens, it's not as if we haven't been preparing for it for months, is it? I mean, we've had the Civil Defence up and running for over a year, the blackout curtains up since Whitsun and it must be costing the government a fortune in printing as every day the postman's shoving a new leaflet through the door.'

'But Stan says there is still a chance Hitler will think better of it and leave Poland,' Cathy said.

Mattie forced a bright smile. 'Perhaps he will. Now, you know how Rayon crumples, so if I were you I'd stand up for a bit to let the creases fall out.'

Cathy obediently got to her feet.

Mattie knelt down and tugged gently at the

14

hem of Cathy's dress to get the folds in the right place. The dress, with its padded shoulders, square neckline, cross-cut panels and high waist-line, suited her sister to perfection. Cathy had fallen in love with the design two years ago and cut it out from the Spring Brides special edition of *Woman's Own;* just after she'd turned sixteen and their father had agreed for her and Stan to start walking out properly. Mattie had sweet-talked Soli Beckerman, the elderly pattern-cutter at Gold & Sons where she worked as a machinist, to make it for her and he'd done a beautiful job.

Satisfied with the way the fabric was draped, Mattie rocked back on her heels and stood up, straightening the skirt of her own apple green bridesmaid dress. Bending forward, she checked her hair only to find, as always, several wayward curls had escaped.

The door burst open and their mother strode in.

Ida Brogan was halfway through her forty-fourth year and at five foot five could look all three daughters more or less in the eye. If the faded wedding photo on the back parlour mantelshelf was to be believed, two decades ago she would have comfortably fitted into any of Mattie's size twelve dresses but now, as mother to a brood of Brogans, her hips had spread accordingly. That said, she could still sprint down the road after a cheeky youngster if the occasion arose.

With the exception of Christmas Day, Good Friday and Easter, her mother usually donned a wraparound apron and hid her silver-streaked dark brown hair that was once the same rich

15

chestnut tone as Mattie's under a scarf, but today Ida wore a navy suit and a smart pink blouse with a fluted front and a bow that tied at her throat. In addition, she'd bought herself a new felt hat which she'd decorated with a vast number of artificial flowers. However, in keeping with the government's latest directive she'd enhanced her ensemble with the cardboard box containing her gas mask which was now hanging from her right shoulder by a length of string.

'How are you two getting on...?' She stopped as a rare softness stole across her rounded face. 'Don't you look a right picture?'

'Thanks, Mum,' said Cathy, smiling shyly at her. 'Mattie's done such a good job, hasn't she?'

Ida nodded. 'Turn around and let me have a gander at the back.'

Cathy did a slow turn on the spot.

'Beautiful,' said their mother with a heavy sigh. 'You've done your sister proud, Mattie.'

'Thanks, Mum,' said Mattie, enjoying her mother's approval.

Ida winked. 'Good practice for when you and Micky get wed, isn't it? I suppose he's meeting us at the church.'

Mattie gave a wan smile.

'Just as well,' continued her mother. 'The way Queenie's been lashing everyone with that tongue of hers, she'd have given the poor boy the rough edge of it if he'd been here this morning.'

She caught sight of her daughters' alarm clock on the bedside table and scowled. 'Eleven-thirty! Where's your bloody father?'

'It's all right, Mum, the church is only five

16

minutes away so we've got plenty of time,' said Mattie. 'I'll take a look to see if he's coming.'

Going to the window, which had been criss-crossed with gummed-on newspaper, she threw up the lower casement and looked out.

Heavy grey clouds still hung low over the London Docks just to the south of them but, mercifully, there were a few blue patches forcing their way through.

'Can you see him?' asked her mother.

'Yes,' Mattie replied as she spotted Samson, her father's carthorse, turn into the street. 'He's just coming.'

Her father, Jerimiah Boniface Brogan, sat on top of his wagon. He was wearing his best suit with a brocade waistcoat beneath, a red bandana tied at his throat. The wagon with Brogan & Son Household Salvage painted in gold along the side, which was usually piled high with old baths, bedsteads and broken furniture, had been scrubbed clean the previous day. It was now festooned with white ribbons and even Samson's bridle had bows tied to either side. As the cart rolled over the cobbles, the neighbours stopped their Saturday morning chores to watch the bride set off to church.

Ida bustled over and, pushing Mattie aside, thrust her head out of the window.

'About bloody time,' she called as the cart with Mattie's father sitting on the front came to a stop in front of the house.

Although Jerimiah was three years older than his wife, his curly black hair showed not a trace of grey and, with fists like mallets and forearms of steel, he could still wipe the floor with a man

17

half his age. According to Grannie Queenie, her one and only child had been born in the middle of the Irish sea during a force nine gale and had had the furies in him ever since. As boisterous as a drunken bear and with a roar like a lion, Jerimiah Boniface Brogan wasn't a man to mess with but his yes was yes and his no was no and everyone knew it. But to Mattie he was a loving smile and a safe pair of arms to cuddle into and she adored him.

He stood up and whipped off his weather-beaten fedora.

'And a top of the morning to you too, me sweet darling,' he called, sweeping his enraged wife an exaggerated bow.

'Never mind the old codswallop,' Ida shouted back. 'Where the hell have you been?'

'Just socialising with a few friends in the Lord Nelson,' he replied, setting his hat back at a jaunty angle. 'Is the bride ready?'

'Of course she's ready,' her mother replied. 'She's been ready for hours.'

Jerimiah jumped down. 'Then her carriage awaits.'

'Right, I'll take Billy with me and I'll tell Charlie when I see him to make sure he keeps an eye on Queenie,' said her mother, hooking her handbag on her arm. 'I don't want her nipping into Fat Tony's to place a bet on the two-thirty at Kempton Park on her way to church.'

She turned to leave, then stopped and gazed at her middle daughter...

Tears welled up in her hazel eyes.

'You look so lovely, sweetheart,' she whispered.

Ida hugged her to her considerable bosom for a moment then, taking a handkerchief from her sleeve, hurried out of the room.

'Ready?' Mattie turned to her sister.

Cathy nodded. Her gaze rested on the double bed the three sisters shared. 'It'll seem strange not snuggling up with you and Jo each night though.'

Mattie smiled. 'No cos you'll be snuggling up to your new husband instead.'

Cathy laughed.

'But at least after today you won't have to hear Ma and Gran arguing the toss from dawn to dusk,' said Mattie.

'Thanks be to Mary, for that,' Cathy replied.

They exchanged a fond look, then Cathy threw her arms around Mattie. With tears pinching the corner of her closed eyes, Mattie hugged her back.

'Let's be off then,' said Mattie, hooking both their gas masks over her shoulder. She picked up her sister's white confirmation Bible and rosary, then handed them to her. After all, you don't want to keep that groom of yours waiting.'

Shuffling past the buffet table with the other guests, Mattie picked up a meat paste sandwich and two sausage rolls and put them on her tea plate. Well, perhaps table was dressing it up a bit as Cathy and Stan's wedding breakfast was in fact laid out on three scaffold planks that had been placed over the snooker table with a double sheet serving as a table cloth.

She was in the Catholic Club's main hall which

had a stage at one end and a bar at the other. Situated around the corner from the church, it had been built fifty years ago and was a square, functional building typical of the Edwardian period. Its high windows let in light despite the fine mesh that had been fitted over them to protect the glass from the threat of being used as target practice by the local lads. The lower half of the room was covered in brown glazed tiles while the upper half was emulsioned in cream. Faded photos of past club presidents lined the walls in neat rows and there was a green flag with a golden harp at its centre hanging from a pole to the left of the stage.

The hall was the focal point of the community and hosted everything from the Brownies, Guides, Cubs and Scouts, who used it on Tuesdays and Wednesdays, to Irish-dancing classes on a Thursday and a baby clinic on Tuesdays. The East London Temperance League used to use the hall for their meeting on a Thursday evening but, after the police were called once too often, they had to move. It wasn't really the teetotallers' fault, but having them downstairs when the bar upstairs was crammed with dockers downing pints was asking for trouble. It was one of the few places that could accommodate a wedding party or a wake so the hall was always in demand.

Mattie added a pickled egg to her plate, then squeezed out of the fray and made her way back to her table in the corner and sat down.

The sun had shone as they'd arrived at St Bridget's and St Brendan's on Commercial Road. Her brother Charlie had met them as they arrived. After filling Samson's nose bag with oats, Charlie had tied up the horse and wagon in the alley behind the church and joined his family in the church. He'd slipped in alongside Queenie as their mother instructed.

The wedding service and a full nuptial mass had lasted just short of two hours after which the family quickly got themselves into the various groups for the photos before heading off to devour the spread awaiting them.

That was almost an hour ago and now the formal speeches were over, the buffet had been opened and the guests from both sides of the family were munching their way through it. Although, to be fair, the Brogans and their kindred made up most of the wedding party and the left side of the church had been packed, cheek by jowl, while the groom's family barely filled three pews.

Stan was an only child whose father had died when he was three so his immediate family was his mother Violet. She had chest problems and was more or less wheelchair bound. Being almost a decade older than Mattie's mother, Violet Wheeler favoured the low-waisted styles and pastel colours of the Edwardian age so she was wearing a lilac and grey two-piece trimmed with lace and seed pearls. Mattie spotted Violet sitting in the corner furthest away from the stage surrounded by the handful of distant relatives she'd rounded up for her son's nuptials and Stan's best man, an old school chum.

Mattie's gaze drifted onto the new bride and groom who were sitting, heads together, on the top table.

'I suppose you're dreaming it were you sitting up there,' a familiar voice behind her said.

Mattie turned and smiled up at her dad, who was standing with a pint of Guinness in his beefy hand behind her.

'I'm certainly not,' she said, as he turned the chair next to her and sat astride it.

He glanced around. 'So where is your young man, then?'

'Micky's not coming because we're not walking out any longer,' Mattie replied.

Jerimiah regarded her ruefully. 'But he's a grand chap and worships the ground you walk on.'

Mattie smiled. 'I know, but he thinks I should marry him and I think I should get my Higher School Certificate and go to college.'

Her father grinned. 'And so you should. You're too bright to waste your life in that blooming sweatshop. We'll be at war again tomorrow and, just like the last time, once the men start marching off to fight, women will be called upon to take over. And, sad though I am to say it, Mattie, this is a chance for you to make something of yourself.'

Mattie smiled. 'And I'm going to. The Workers' Educational Association are running matriculation classes in Toynbee Hall and I'm going to enrol when they open for the new term in two week. That's assuming the gas attacks the government has warned us about don't get us first.'

'Well, if they do at least you won't have the need to tell your mother about Micky,' said her father.

'No, I won't,' laughed Mattie.

Jerimiah's gaze shifted down to the far end of the

room and a sentimental expression lifted his heavy features. 'But she does look a picture, though?'

'She could be the fairy queen herself,' Mattie replied, feeling extraordinarily pleased to see her sister so happy.

'She done well for herself, has Cathy,' said her father. Mattie's eyes shifted from her sister to the young man sitting beside her.

At twenty-seven, Stanley Kitchener Wheeler was eight years older than Cathy with thick light brown hair and dark brown eyes under a low brow. At just five foot six he topped his bride by only three inches, which was why Cathy now wore flat shoes most of the time. He'd treated himself to a new suit for his wedding but, rather than a sober black or grey one, he'd chosen a square-shouldered American style in brown with a broad chalk stripe, a style frequently seen in snooker halls and at dog tracks.

'I'll tell you no lie, Mattie,' her father continued. 'I wasn't all that pleased when she brought him home, not after the shady reputation he'd got himself at the boxing club, but since he got that old lorry and set himself up as a market driver he seems to have put all that behind him, especially now he's on the committee in that there peace thingy malarkey.'

'You mean the British Peace Union that meet here on a Thursday night?' asked Mattie.

'That's the fellas,' her father replied.

'I suppose so,' Mattie conceded. 'But I can't say I'm not a bit surprised to hear he's a member as he's never struck me as being interested in politics.'

'With Hitler marching across Europe, there are a lot of people more interested in politicking now than they were a year ago,' her father replied. 'And, anyway, I don't mind what he's involved in as long as he looks after my little girl. If he takes care of her half as well as he does his old mother, I'll be more than happy.'

Raising his glass to take another mouthful, something caught her father's eye.

'For the love of Mary!' he snapped, placing his glass back on the table. 'Can they not give over just for one blessed day?'

Mattie followed his gaze to the refreshment table where her mother and Queenie were standing toe to toe and glaring at each other.

'I'll give you a pound to a penny it's Billy again. Isn't the boy the very Devil incarnate, but whatever it is your mother will be making excuses for him,' said her father.

Grasping his pint in his enormous hand, he started across the dancefloor.

Mattie popped the last piece of sausage roll in her mouth, licked the grease from her finger and then, picking up her empty glass, she stood up and walked to the bar.

Pete Riley, the club manager, was standing behind it polishing a glass. As children, Pete and Jerimiah had lived three doors apart and, if their stories were to be believed, had spent their days dashing barefoot around the streets and alleyways, up to no good. Pete was now father to nine and grandfather to three more. His hair, once black, was now a steely grey and his belt buckle strained on its last notch.

'Another G and T please, Pete,' Mattie said, setting her empty glass on the towelling mat with Indian Pale Ale printed on it.

Pete stowed the used glass in the rack above the counter and picked up a clean one from the shelf behind the bar. 'You know it's against club rules to serve women at the bar.'

'Of course I do,' said Mattie brightly, 'which is why my dad is asking you to put it on his slate as I'm collecting it for him.'

Pete pulled a face. 'Mattie...'

'Please.' She gave him a dazzling smile and batted her eyelashes. 'It is my sister's wedding.'

Pete sighed and flipped the tea towel over his shoulder. 'All right, just this once but don't let the committee hear about it or they'll have my guts for garters.'

Mattie blew him a kiss and leaned back on the bar.

Casting her eyes around the room, she spotted her friend Francesca. They had known each other since they'd been placed together in Miss Gordon's class aged four and a half. Francesca lived with her father and brother above their fish and chip shop on Commercial Road, next to Fish Brothers' pawnbrokers.

An inch or two taller than Mattie, Francesca had clear olive skin, almond-shaped ebony eyes and straight black hair so long she could sit on it, but today she'd whirled it into a plaited bun. She was wearing a navy felt hat with matching shoes and bag and her sky blue dress hugged her slender figure.

She was sitting in one of the side booths toying

with an empty glass and gazing across the room with a sad, faraway look in her eyes. The object of her affection, Mattie's brother Charlie, was standing with a handful of his mates on the other side of the room.

'Can you make that two, please, Pete,' she added, over her shoulder.

Having got her drinks, Mattie wove her way through the dancing wedding guests to join her friend.

'You looked like you needed a top-up, Fran,' she said, putting the glass in front of her friend.

Francesca looked up and smiled. 'Ta. I was just thinking you've all given your Cathy a right good do.'

'Yes, we have, haven't we?' agreed Mattie. 'I know Mum's pleased with the way everything's gone and there are even a few sandwiches left for Dad's lunch tin on Monday.'

'And everyone's enjoying themselves,' continued Francesca as the two fiddlers Jerimiah had hired struck up a familiar reel.

'Yes they are,' agreed Mattie, 'particularly Gran.' She indicated Queenie, who barely scraped four foot ten, had white candy floss hair, a face like a pickled walnut and a temper like a firecracker. Weighing no more than half a hundredweight soaking wet and just two years into her seventieth decade, she still did the family washing by hand in the backyard and put it through the mangle every Monday.

In her younger days, Queenie had been well known for storming into public houses along the Knock Fergus area of Cable Street to fetch

Grandpa Seamus away from the drink.

She had come to live with Mattie's family after Seamus was found face down in the Thames mud. Although Queenie had maintained that he must have been done to death by some foul felon, the coroner recorded accidental death due to excessive alcohol – a more likely verdict given that he'd been seen toasting the Irish Free State's tenth anniversary in every public house on the Highway for the three days prior to his death.

Queenie had marched into number 25 Mafeking Terrace with her portmanteau in one hand and a cage containing Prince Albert, her ancient grey parrot, in the other and had commandeered the front parlour. That was seven years ago and she had steadfastly resisted all of Ida's attempts to wrest it back ever since.

Mattie's gran, knocking back gin like there was no tomorrow since they'd arrived, had discarded her moth-eaten fur coat three sizes too big and had taken to the dancefloor. She was holding her skirt above her knees with one hand and was hopping from one spindly leg to the other and swinging a red handkerchief in the air with the other.

'Well, it is a party,' laughed Francesca. 'I thought your Aunt Pearl would be here?'

'I didn't,' Mattie replied. 'Since she's taken up with that new man of hers, she thinks she's too posh for the Catholic Club, but I know Mum's glad she hasn't shown her face.'

A roar of male laughter cut through the noise and Mattie looked across at her brother.

Having completed the formalities of his sister's

wedding, Charlie had dispensed with his jacket and now stood with his top two shirt buttons open, his tie loosened, his sleeves rolled up and Stella Miggles draped over him.

'I really don't know what he sees in her,' said Francesca with a catch in her voice.

'Nor do I,' agreed Mattie.

In truth, with her twenty-four-inch waist and a D-cup bra, Mattie could see exactly what her brother saw in Stella. Unfortunately, Stella's substantial bust and lenient attitude towards roving hands blinded Charlie to all else including, sadly, Francesca.

Mattie picked up her drink and knocked it back.

'Come on,' she said, grasping her friend's hand. 'This is a wedding not a wake so let's go and grab ourselves a couple of spare men.'

'And so as we contemplate the dark days ahead, we can draw comfort from St Augustine's words: "that others, subject to death, did live, since he whom I loved, as if he should never die, was dead",' Father Mahon said, his soft tones drifting over the congregation. 'Or was it St Francis who said that? I'm never quite sure. Or perhaps it was Pope Clement VIII. No ... no, I'm almost certain it was the saintly Bishop of Hippo who...'

Mattie shifted onto her other hip to relieve the numbness in her rear and stifled a yawn.

It was Sunday morning and she was sitting amidst the gothic splendour of St Bridget's and St Brendan's. With its plaster Stations of the Cross on the walls, a lady chapel complete with a life-size statue of the Virgin Mary and the painting of the Last Supper in the top chancery, it was a place as familiar to Mattie as her family's kitchen.

The family usually attended the 10 o'clock mass on Sunday but their mother had said that, just this once, they could go to 4 o'clock service instead, which was a blessing as Mattie's father had still been in full voice at half eleven.

Having seen the bride and groom off on their honeymoon – three days in Southend – Jerimiah had taken to the stage. He'd led the assembly through his usual repertoire of 'Danny Boy' and 'When Irish Eyes are Smiling' before moving on to the more traditional 'Wearing of the Green'. Not to be outdone as her son's deep baritone gave up the last note of 'Fields of Athenry', Queenie jumped on stage too and treated the company to a rendition of 'She Moves Through the Fair' that left not a dry eye in the room.

After the celebrations finally broke up just before midnight, Mattie, her mother and Jo had spent another hour clearing away the buffet debris and tidying away. Having successfully navigated their way home through the blacked-out streets by way of the white stripes the council had recently painted on the kerbs to prevent people walking out into the road, they finally fell into their beds as the clock on the mantelshelf in the back parlour chimed one.

'For the love of Mary, what is he blithering about?' said her mother, who was sitting in the pew to Mattie's right and wearing the same outfit as the day before.

'I'll thank you, Ida, to remember where you

are,' snapped Queenie in her loudest whisper. 'And not to be speaking of dear Father Mahon in such a way.'

Despite consuming half her weight in gin the night before, Mattie's grandmother had been up with lark. By the time the rest of the Brogan family had stirred, she'd already been to get fresh bread from the Jewish baker around the corner and had a pot of tea brewing.

She was currently sitting on Mattie's left wearing her fur coat, battered felt hat and, as it was the Lord's Day, her dentures, too.

'I know full well where I am, Queenie,' Ida replied. 'But I'm wondering if Father Mahon does.'

Queenie's lined face softened. 'The poor dear man has such a weight on his shoulders at the moment and it will surely be a blessing for him when the new priest arrives–'

'And when might that be, I ask you?' Ida rolled her eyes.

Someone behind them tutted loudly.

'Perhaps Father Mahon's going soft in the 'ead like Barmy Dick,' said Billy.

He was sitting on the other side of Ida and had spent the service alternating between kicking the pew in front and flipping through the hymn books.

Peppered with freckles, with pale blue eyes and russet hair, Billy was supposedly the 'face of' Ida's brother who had died at six after the sulphur used for fumigating bugs had leaked through the brickwork from the house next door and poisoned him. Thankfully, no one queried

30

their carroty cuckoo, so the family didn't have to explain further.

Like the rest of the family, Billy was kitted out in his Sunday best, which in his case was his new school uniform. To give him growing room, the blazer was much too wide across the shoulders and too long in the arms, which made him look as if he'd put on one of Charlie's jackets by mistake. His mother nudged him. 'Shush!'

'I only–'

'Mum, tell him to stop fidgeting,' murmured Jo, who was sitting beside him. 'He's rucking my dress up.'

Jo, who favoured Mattie's dark colouring, was just sixteen. Despite her blossoming figure she was dressed, as her tender age dictated, in a summer dress with a sash, white ankle socks and the sky blue cardigan Mattie had knitted her for her birthday. However, although Mattie's younger sister had the face of an angel, she also had a pair of green eyes that could cut you at fifty paces and a mind as crafty as a pixie's.

Jerimiah, who flanked his family at the end of the pew, cleared his throat and cast his gaze over them, stilling the muttering instantly.

Usually, mass was a predominantly female gathering. Like most of the men of the congregation, Mattie's father and brother Charlie preferred to spend the one day of the week when they didn't have to be up at dawn under the blanket for an extra hour or two which meant that while the family were at church, her father, after a welcome lie-in, mucked out the stable, cleaned the harnesses and made sure Samson was fit for another week's work. However, today he'd left Charlie to do that and, like dozens of others who hardly ever crossed the threshold, he had come to church.

Given that by the time the service finished the whole country would probably be at war with Germany for the second time in a generation, it wasn't surprising really that the ranks of the faithful had swollen to at least three times its usual size.

'*Laus tibi, Christe,*' muttered Father Mahon.

Mattie crossed herself and stood up with the rest of the congregation.

'*Credo in unum Deum,*' the congregation said in unison.

The double doors at the back of the church burst open and Pat Mead, who owned the paper shop opposite the church, ran in.

'It's war!' he shouted, as he puffed down the aisle.

'How do you know?' someone asked.

Pat lumbered to a halt in front of the chancery steps.

'Chamberlain's just told us on the wireless ten minutes ago,' Pat replied, taking a handkerchief from his pocket and mopping his crimson face.

'Bloody Hitler,' a man shouted.

'Bloody politicians, you mean,' called someone else. 'It won't be them going off to fight but our boys.'

A woman started crying as people either fell to their knees or covered their faces with their hands.

Ida clutched Billy to her considerable bosom. 'Holy Mother, bless and preserve us!'

She crossed herself awkwardly as her son

wriggled in her embrace and Mattie and Jo did the same out of habit.

'What shall we do now?' asked Jo.

Jerimiah glanced over the heads of the congregation at Father Mahon, who was standing in the pulpit, gazing helplessly down at his distraught congregation with his hands clasped together.

'Well,' he said, standing up and stepping out of the pew. 'As I don't think the good father will be continuing with mass, we might as well go home.'

'That's right,' said Ida, releasing Billy. 'You and Charlie can get our indoor refuge kitted out like the Civil Defence pamphlet says while me and the girls get the dinner on.'

Queenie huffed. 'You hide in your indoors refuge if you like, Ida, but those Hun buggers won't find me cowering under the stairs when they come.'

Ida and Queenie exchanged their customary acerbic look.

With a sigh, Mattie picked up the gas mask she'd been issued with three months before from the hymn shelf and hooked it over her shoulder. Jo did the same and, with Queenie bringing up the rear, they shuffled out of the row.

Slipping her arm through Jo's, Mattie and her sister followed their parents down the packed church towards the street outside.

Leading the family from the front like its commander, Jerimiah marched between the closed-up shops in Watney Street Market. As they passed the Lord Nelson they saw that someone had brought a wireless and set it on a table. There was a small crowd of drinkers standing around with their pints in their hands and perplexed looks on their faces.

'And, until further notice, all theatres, cinemas and similar establishments will be closed as a precaution,' a plummy BBC announcer informed the gathering.

'That puts pay to going to the Roxy with the girls next week,' said Mattie.

'Furthermore, it is every citizen's responsibility to observe the blackout and to carry their gas masks at all times,' continued the presenter, 'and to ensure they wear a label attached to their person at all times for identification purposes.'

'I don't see how a luggage tag tied to my vest will survive if I'm blown to pieces,' said Jo as they passed Fielding's the stationers on the corner of Chapman Street and turned into Mafeking Terrace.

Mattie laughed but Ida gave her youngest daughter a hard look.

'It might be a joke to you, my girl,' she said, as they reached the end of their street. 'But some of us remember when the Germans bombed the Isle of Dogs last—'

A piercing wail cut through the air and everyone in the street froze.

'What is it,' Jo shouted.

'Air-raid siren,' Jerimiah yelled back. 'We'd better head down to the shelter in Cable St—'

The door of 23 Mafeking Terrace burst open and Mr Potter, the area's coordinating air-raid patrol warden dashed out.

Cyril Potter was probably in his late fifties with a round apple-like face, short arms and, after thirty years sitting on his backside tallying the accounts in the council's rates department, a figure like a whipping top. He and his wife Ethel had lived opposite Mattie's mother and father for years but, unlike the Brogans, they had no children so poured all their parental talents into the local Scouts and Guides. On almost every night of the week either Cyril or Ethel, complete with their respective woggle or wide-brimmed hat, could be seen striding off to their various troop meetings.

As Hitler couldn't be bothered to wait until the Civic Defence personnel had been issued with their proper uniform before invading Poland, Cyril had improvised and was wearing his scoutmaster jacket, which was modelled on that of a Boer War officer's, with the addition of a white ARP armband and a tin hat.

'Don't panic! Don't panic!' he screamed as he ran up the street as fast as his podgy legs could carry him, banging on doors.

Having reached the top of the street, he crossed the narrow alleyway and did the same down the other side.

Mattie's neighbours came out, some carrying babes in arms, others tightly clutching toddlers. Some carried blankets and bags containing the picnics the government had instructed people to take with them to the shelter. Since the prime minister had flown to Munich after Hitler invaded Hungary the year before, the whole country had been placed on high alert and the council had been trying to persuade the population to be the same. That said, the promised ground-level air-raid shelter hadn't yet materialised and although people had been urged to buy Anderson shelters for their back gardens, no one had yet advised the residents of East London who didn't have back gardens how they should protect their families.

Cyril skidded to a halt in front of them. 'It's an air raid!'

'I know,' Jerimiah yelled back over the insistent wail.

'They'll be here any moment.'

'I expect so,' Mattie's father hollered. 'Gerry's not one for hanging about.'

The whites around Cyril's eyes shone bright for a second then, ripping his helmet off, he threw it aside and pulled the gas mask from its cardboard box. Shoving the moulded rubber over his face, he tore at the webbing until he'd secured it at the back of his head.

'Get your gas masks on,' he ordered them, his voice now muffled by the cork filter in the corrugated tubing affixed trunk-like over his nose.

No one moved.

Cyril's pale eyes regarded them wildly through the insect-like glass disks for a moment, then he spun on his heels.

Screaming something that sounded like 'Gum-yum-gum-mom-on,' he pelted up the street again.

With astonishment and disbelief on their faces, the sea of people parted as the man in charge with seeing them and their loved ones to a place of safety raced between them waving his arms crazily, his sparse hair flapping around his head like a ginger halo.

He'd just got level with number 12 when he

turned, swayed for a moment, clutched at his throat, then crumpled onto the cobbles.

There was a moment of stillness, then everyone surged forward. Pushing his way through the crowd, Jerimiah got to him in three strides and pulled off his mask.

Mattie arrived just behind her father and fell to her knees beside the warden. Slipping her hand under his ear, she felt for a pulse as she'd been taught in first-aid classes.

'Is he dead?' asked Ida, elbowing her way through.

'No,' said Mattie, detecting a faint beat with her fingertips. 'I think he fainted.'

Turning over the warden's mask in his massive hands, Mattie's father flipped open the bottom of the tin filter attached to the tubing.

'I'm not surprised,' he said, pulling out the cork within. 'Silly bugger didn't take the wax wrapping off and nearly suffocated himself.'

The monotonous wail grating on Mattie's ear suddenly changed to the two-tone howl of the all-clear. There was a collective sigh from those around them.

'Praise the saints above,' said Ida, placing her hand on the crucifix on her chest. 'It must have been a false alarm.'

'I suppose we'll have to get used to it,' said Mattie, rising to her feet and standing next to her gran.

Queenie took out a roll-up from beneath her Sunday hat and lit it. 'That we will, child, but it seems that you can be telling Hitler to save himself the trouble of sending his Waffetaffer to put the willies up us.' She drew on her cigarette and blew smoke upwards. 'Cos we've got our own fecking sirens to do that.'

Chapter Two

The Victorian ironwork glided by as the screech of the brakes brought the nine-thirty from York via Doncaster to a halt alongside platform five of King's Cross Station. Daniel stood up.

At six one and with a forty-two-inch chest, Daniel didn't consider himself to be too much above the average man, but after the three-hour journey from York to London, his back and shoulder joints were begging to be released from the confinement of his seat.

Unhooking the leather strapping, he dropped the window down and a gust of cool air rushed in.

Pushing his gold-rimmed glasses up to the bridge of his nose, Daniel took a deep breath.

'Thank Christ we've arrived,' said the cutlery manufacturer from Sheffield.

The elderly woman next to him, draped in a fox fur stole complete with head and dangling feet, tutted loudly.

The businessman's eyes flickered over Daniel. 'Your pardon, Father.'

Daniel smiled. 'That's quite alright and it is rather stuffy in here.'

Fortunately Daniel had reserved a seat in First

Class, which was just as well as the second and third-class compartments were heaving. Although Britain had only been at war for a week and a day, the whole country was mobilising as the plans the government had been making for almost a year were put into action. The train was packed with members of the armed forces heading for their respective camps and depots. There were so many servicemen crammed into the train that many had been forced to sit on their kitbags in the corridors for the entire journey.

Reaching through the window, the cutlery manufacturer opened the carriage door and left.

'The air would be much improved if some people had more consideration for others,' the elderly woman continued, glaring at the general with a chest full of Great War medals sitting opposite.

Clenching his pipe between his teeth, the general got to his feet and, grabbing his attaché case from the rack, blustered out of the carriage.

The two airmen who'd been snoozing beneath their caps since Peterborough sprang up, pulled their kitbags down and pushed their way towards the platform. One stopped at the carriage door and let out a loud wolf whistle which was answered some way away. They laughed and one of them shoved into Daniel.

'Really, just because there's a war on, that's no excuse to forget civilities,' snapped the older woman as the airman jumped down from the train.

'Just high spirits,' Daniel replied, pushing his wire-rimmed spectacles back up his nose.

Reaching up, he took his suitcase from the luggage rack and placed it on his seat, then took down the elderly lady's portmanteau and placed that alongside his own.

'Thank you, Father,' she said. Stepping down from the train, she disappeared into the throng on the platform.

Setting his hat firmly on his head, Daniel picked up his case and also stepped down from the train.

The crowd heading for the ticket barrier was awash with khaki, navy and air force blue, while the passengers surging down the platform to board the train were mostly less than three feet tall. They all had luggage labels tied to their coats and many were clutching teddies or raggedy dolls.

Mingled amongst the evacuees were mothers with too-bright smiles and jolly members of the Women's Voluntary Service, distinctive in their green coats and hats. Behind the great swell of children being sent out of harm's way was huddled a group of women who were either heavily pregnant or carrying tiny infants in their arms. For most their only experience of life outside London was a yearly trip to the seaside, so no wonder they looked desolate as they contemplated leaving their kith and kin for a stranger's hospitality.

Side-stepping several prams, Daniel walked through the steam bellowing from the stationary engine and, smiling gently as he passed the mass of scared, tearful children, he headed towards the exit. As he reached the end of the platform, a little girl of about four or five, with bright golden curls and wearing an oversized coat, dropped her golliwog. She screamed but her voice was lost in the echoing noise of a hundred other children, the hiss and clatter of the trains and the Tannoy announcements.

In two strides Daniel crossed the space and scooped the soft toy from the platform, then sprinted after the child.

'Excuse me,' he said, stepping in front of the two women and holding up the golly. 'I think you've left someone behind.'

'Mr Bobby,' the small girl shouted, stretching up for her precious toy.

Daniel handed her the golly, then hunkered down in front of her. 'If he's Mr Bobby, what's your name?'

The little girl hugged her golly and stuck her thumb in her mouth.

'Go on, tell the father,' said her mother, a blonde woman in her mid-twenties and dressed in a navy maternity dress with flat pumps.

'Gladys,' mumbled the child over her thumb.

'Well, Gladys, you need to keep an extra tight hold on him so he doesn't get lost again,' said Daniel. 'Can you do that?'

Gladys nodded and Daniel straightened up.

'Thank you so much,' said Gladys' mother, gazing in wide-eyed wonder up at him.

'My pleasure.' Daniel raised his hat and continued along the platform.

Handing his ticket to the collector, he made his way to the left luggage office. Glancing up at the arrivals board, he noticed that the 2 o'clock from Cambridge had just arrived so he waited a few moments until the passengers spilled out into the concourse, then pushed open the half-glazed door and walked into the office. As usual, the place was packed to the gunnels with impatient travellers.

Daniel joined the back of the collection queue as passengers from the Cambridge train surged in. After about twenty minutes of shuffling forward and a frantic search for a missing hatbox for a very distraught bride-to-be, Daniel stepped up to the mahogany counter.

'Good afternoon,' he said, smiling courteously. 'I left a bag in number 35 about four weeks ago.'

'I shall need a ticket, Father,' the clerk grunted.

'Of course,' said Daniel, putting his hand in his breast pocket. 'I have it here somewhere.'

He ferreted around for a minute or two, then shoved his hands in his side pockets. 'I know I pulled it out ready as we pulled into the station so it must be...'

Behind him people started grumbling and tutting.

He pulled his wallet from his inside pocket. 'I can't think where it could be.'

Mutters of 'get a move on' started behind.

Daniel returned to his pockets. 'I'm sure I have it here somewhere,' he said, depositing his handkerchief, half a packet of Fruit Pastilles, a rosary and penknife on the desk.

He rummaged a bit more, then turned to the people behind him. 'I'm so terribly sorry. I was sure I'd put my ticket in a safe place–'

'For gawd's sake,' shouted a man in a cloth cap from the back. 'Give him his bag.'

The clerk, who was now quite red in the face, drew a deep breath. 'The rules state that I have to have a ticket before–'

'Sod the bloody rules,' shouted someone else.

'Yeah, I've got a ruddy train to catch,' called another.

'He's only doing his job,' said Daniel as the door opened and more people pressed in.

'He's right. I'm only doing my job and he could be anyone,' said the beleaguered clerk. 'He could even be a Nazi.'

The office erupted in laughter.

'Ain't you got eyes?' asked the man in the cloth cap again. 'He's wearing a dog collar not a bloody swastika. Now, unless you want us all to suffocate, do us a favour and let him have his bag.'

The clerk threw his hands up and disappeared through the door behind him.

Daniel smiled at his audience.

'I am so sorry,' he repeated, repositioning his spectacles again.

As the end of the drama was in sight, the sea of faces had changed from irritation to indulgence.

'It's all right, Father,' said a middle-aged woman at the back, and others muttered their agreement.

The clerk returned with an expensive-looking caramel-coloured leather suitcase with contrasting dark-brown corners, thickset clasps and DJMC stamped in gold letters above the handle.

'There you go,' said the clerk sliding it over the counter to him. 'Rules and regulations, but as you're a man of the cloth...'

Clasping the handle, Daniel took it from him. 'I'm much obliged to you and apologies for causing you so much trouble.'

The clerk smiled. 'Don't mention it.' He glanced

at the dangling label. And you have a nice evening, Father McCree.'

Daniel drained the last of his over-stewed tea. Placing the cup back in its saucer, he smiled.

'Well, Mrs Dunn, I can honestly say that's the most welcome cup of tea I've had for a very long time,' he said, offering her the cup.

It was now just a shade before eleven and the day after he'd arrived in London. Having booked himself into a modest hotel around the corner from the station, Daniel had gone to a nearby restaurant and treated himself to beef stew and dumplings for supper, followed by jam roly-poly and custard before returning to the hotel and collapsing into bed. Even though the mattress was a little on the lumpy side, he'd fallen asleep the moment his head hit the pillow, waking only when the breakfast gong sounded at seven.

It had taken him an hour and a half to undertake the forty-minute journey to his destination due to a points failure at Moorgate station, which had left them stranded in the carriage for almost half an hour before the train moved off. He'd finally reached Stepney Green Station at ten-fifteen and it had taken him a brisk twenty minutes' walk to reach St Brendan and St Bridget's church and rectory.

The rectory was a double-fronted Victorian house that sat incongruously amongst the huddled two-up two-down workmans' cottages around it. The decor he'd seen so far was tired and faded, but the windows sparkled and a faint smell of beeswax was evidence of the housekeeper's diligence with the duster.

The room he was now in was the smaller of the two front rooms and in times past had been the lady of the house's morning room. Sitting opposite him in an upholstered easy chair was Father Mahon, the long-serving priest who he had come to assist in his parish duties. Although Daniel couldn't be sure, he'd put a pound to a penny that Father Mahon was nearer to eighty than seventy. The old man's closely cropped white hair was so sparse that from a distance he looked completely bald, and he was so stooped that the top of his head barely reached Daniel's shoulder. Daniel was therefore surprised that, when he offered his hand in greeting, the good father's grip was that of a man half his age. He also noticed that Father Mahon's coal-black eyes, although surrounded by finely etched lines and wrinkles, were both focused and sharp as they held Daniel's gaze.

'Can I get you another, Father?' the house-keeper asked.

Unlike the rector, who looked as if a strong wind could carry him away, Mrs Dunn his housekeeper looked like an Irish hurling striker in a wraparound apron.

'No, I'm fine, thank you,' Daniel replied.

'Or perhaps another piece of cake?' persisted Mrs Dunn.

'No, honestly.' Daniel patted his stomach. 'St Peter himself would have trouble saying no to such a morsel but, if I'm to do justice to the fish pie you've promised me for lunch, I need to keep space free. Father Mahon assures me your cooking is delicious.'

The housekeeper shot the elderly priest sitting opposite Daniel a hard look. 'And sure how would he know.'

'Soft now, Mrs Dunn,' said Father Mahon. 'You don't want to be scaring the lad on his first day with us.'

Not sure at twenty-eight if he still qualified as a 'lad', Daniel pushed his spectacles back up his nose and smiled politely.

'By that I suppose you mean I should be happy to see you waste away,' Mrs Dunn scolded. 'As the Good Lord is my witness, Father, himself barely eats enough to keep the breath in his body.'

The priest sighed. 'A man shall not live by bread alone, Mrs Dunn.'

'Nor by the stews, pies or pot roast I put before you either, it would seem,' she replied, taking the priest's cup from him and slamming it on the tea trolley. 'Still,' she smiled sweetly at Daniel, 'at least now you've come to join us, Father McCree, there will be someone in the house who will appreciate my hard work in the kitchen. And don't worry, Father.' She nodded at Daniel's luggage by the ancient bureau. 'I'll send Alf to carry your things to your room when he's finished stoking the boiler and I'll be serving dinner at one.'

Wheeling the squeaky trolley with the used crockery rattling on it, she left the room.

'You must forgive her,' said Father Mahon as the door clicked shut. 'She's a good woman, none better, but after nigh on thirty years of ordering poor Paddy about, God love and rest him, she has yet to break the habit.'

'Please, there's no need at all to be apologising,

Father,' said Daniel.

The old priest cocked his head to one side and regarded Daniel curiously. 'Where is it in Ireland you said you were from?'

Pulling the handkerchief from his top pocket and taking off his glasses, he replied,

'Donegal. My family lived in Meetinghouse Street across from the castle. Do you know it?' He made a play of polishing the lenses.

The old priest smiled and shook his head. 'I'm a Cork man meself from Kinsale but I just thought I heard a bit of Limerick in you.'

Daniel smiled but didn't reply.

Father Mahon sighed. 'Well, anyhow, in these uncertain times the flock is in great need of practical as well as spiritual guidance so, if you come from the moon, I'm glad to see you.'

'We are in testing times, to be sure,' said Daniel, happy to move away from his accent. 'And I'm wild keen to get started.'

'So the bishop's letter states,' said Father Mahon. 'In fact, he writes about you in glowing terms and you shouldn't have the trouble my last assistant had. Poor boy. Father Frobisher, a godly man, you understand, and fired with enthusiasm, was the fourth son of some minor aristocrat or another and spoke like a BBC announcer so you can imagine how well he went down around here. But I'm sure you'll get on marvellously, although your waistline will suffer for it.'

A wry smile lifted the corner of Daniel's mouth. 'I'll be sure to guard against falling into the sin of gluttony.'

'There is one thing about the bishop's letter

commending you to the parish that I'm perplexed about. The bishop stipulates you're not to
undertake mass or take confession.'

'Yes, I know that's unusual but it's part of a
penance he's laid on me.' Clasping his hands
together, Daniel bowed his head. 'I'm afraid to
say it dates back to my time in–'

'Whatever it is, it is between you and God, lad,'
interrupted the older man. 'It's of no matter and
of no mind to me.'

Daniel raised his head. 'Thank you, Father.'

'And although it might be difficult for you to
imagine now, Father McCree–' Father Mahon's
eyes twinkled mischievously – 'but I was a young
lad like yourself once upon a time and I know
well the temptations of such an age.'

There was a knock.

'Come!' shouted Father Mahon.

The door opened and an elderly man wearing
baggy light brown overalls, a roll-up dangling from
his mouth, shuffled into the room.

'Mrs D tells me you want somefink shifted
upstairs,' he said.

'Yes, Father McCree's belongings, if you don't
mind, Alf,' said Father Mahon.

The handyman lumbered towards Daniel's
luggage over by the window but Daniel beat him
to it.

'If you take the larger one, I can manage this
one,' he said, grasping the handle of the tan case
he'd collected at King's Cross.

'Right you are, guv,' said Alf, lifting Daniel's
battered old case with the P&O and White Star
passenger label stuck on the side. 'You're at the

top of the house at the back.'

He left.

Father Mahon got to his feet and looked at Daniel. 'There's an hour or so before lunch so why don't you settle in and we can talk more then.'

Daniel thrust out his hand but the rector raised a scraggly eyebrow.

Returning his case to the floor, Daniel knelt in front of the old man and, clasping his hands together in front of him, bowed his head.

Father Mahon placed his slender white hands lightly on Daniel's dark-brown hair.

'*Actiones nostras, quaesumus Domine,*' muttered the rector.

Studying the scuffed toe caps of the rector's brown shoes, Daniel let the words of his childhood wash over him until he heard 'Amen'. Father Mahon withdrew his hands.

Crossing himself, Daniel stood up and, with his hands still clasped in front of him, bowed his head. 'Thank you, Father, for giving me this opportunity to serve St Bridget and St Brendan's congregation.'

'And God,' he said.

Daniel forced a smile. 'Oh, yes, of course, God.'

Leaving Father Mahon's study, Daniel followed Alf up two flights of stairs and met the handyman just as he opened the door to the room at the end of the landing of what had once been the servants' quarters.

'There you go, Father,' Alf said, plonking Daniel's case on the floor. 'There's a bathroom with its own lav two doors along so you don't have to trudge down in the middle of the night. And you've got a clear view down to Greenwich from there.' He indicated the south-facing dormer window. 'Don't forget to pull the blackout curtains before you switch on the light.'

'Thank you,' said Daniel.

''Sright,' said Alf and, touching his forehead, he left.

Daniel locked the door and then stood in the centre of the threadbare rug that covered most of the floorboards. Reaching behind his neck, he unclipped the back stud, ripped off his dog collar and undid the top two buttons of his shirt.

Rolling his head to loosen the muscles in his shoulders, he took a deep breath and surveyed his new abode.

The good-sized room was furnished with a single iron-framed bed tucked in against the far wall; it was covered with a patchwork bedspread that, put him in mind of the one he'd had as a boy. Next to the bed was a small bedside cabinet with a lamp on top. There was a heavily carved Edwardian oak wardrobe on the opposite wall with a nineteen thirties chest of drawers along-side. In the recess, which he guessed had once been a built-in cupboard of some sort, there was a sink with a mirror and a light above it, while a striped towel hung from the supporting bracket beneath. A small desk with another reading light had been crammed in beneath the dormer window. The only decoration in the room was a single crucifix hanging on the wall above the bed.

The room was warm and there were tinder and coals in the modest cast-iron fireplace which, as the nights were drawing in, would be very welcome although he was sure the government would have to bring in fuel rationing as they stepped up the war effort.

Putting the tanned suitcase he'd retrieved from the left luggage store down, he grabbed his own battered case and swung it onto the bed. Flipping the catches, he quickly unpacked his clothes and shoes along with the handful of books he'd brought with him. Then, snapping it closed, he stowed the suitcase on top of the wardrobe. Having arranged his washing and shaving gear on the glass shelf above the sink, he went over to the window and, leaning on the desk beneath it, looked out.

Following the line of bloated silver barrage balloons running eastward above the capital's vital docks, he survived the view.

The odd-job man was right.

You could see clearly across the Thames to the south side and then along to where the river turned. In addition, just a couple of streets over the main Fenchurch Street to North Woolwich railway cutting through the crowded street on its raised track.

Daniel gazed at it for a few moments then, crossing back to the light brown suitcase, he picked it up and returned to the desk.

Laying it on its side he took his wallet and slid the skeleton key out. Having already picked the lock, it took only a couple of seconds of fiddling before both catches sprang open.

Replacing the key in his wallet, Daniel opened the case. He surveyed the Bakelite dials, headphones and glass gauges for a moment. A wire that had been fashioned into a figure of eight had a brown and green flex attached to it. Daniel hooked the wire on the window catch. Taking the blue and red wire, he quickly unplugged the desk lamp and then took out the bulb. Winding the bare wires around the prongs of the light bulb, he put it back then pushed the plug back into the socket.

Picking up the headphones, he put them on and flicked the red switch at the centre of the console. There was a crackle as the valve inside warmed. Slowly, Daniel turned the main dial, passing the various continental radio stations until he found what he was searching for.

Pressing the earpiece to his head, Daniel gazed at the silvery barrage balloons dancing above London's docks. A faint crackling sounded in his ear and he turned the dial again; there was a low wowing, then a voice. *'Dies ist Wiese Rambler, morgen Lerche. Dies ist Wiese Rambler, morgen Lerche. Kommen Sie am Morgen Lerche.'*

Daniel pressed his mouth closer to the microphone. *'Dies ist Morgen Rambler Wiese Lerche, hören Sie laut und deutlich.'*

'Good morning, Mrs Brogan,' said Eric Drayton, one of the church's longstanding sidesmen as he offered Mattie's mother a hymn and a prayer book. 'It's grand to see you and your lovely girls.'

'Good to see you, Eric,' Ida replied. 'And how's Mrs Drayton?'

'Keeping busy,' Eric replied, forcing a smile. 'You know, so she doesn't keep thinking about the boys.'

'I'm sure she's done the right thing, sending them to safety,' said Mattie's mother.

Eric forced a smile. 'That's what we keep telling ourselves, but the house is very quiet without them. I'm surprised you've not sent your Billy, Mrs Brogan.'

'I was going to evacuate him with his school, even had his bag packed, but he started one of his chests so I had to cancel it. I'm going to send him when his cough is cleared.' Ida took the books from him. 'Give May my regards and tell her she and the boys are in our prayers.'

Dipping her fingers in the holy water and crossing herself, their mother continued into the church.

Mattie and Jo exchanged a cynical look, knowing that there was more likely to be snow in Hell rather than their mother sign Billy's evacuation application.

After following their mother's example with the holy water, the girls trailed after her as she cleared a path through the rows of Sunday outfits and best hats.

'I see Cathy's not here again,' said their mother as they approached their usual seats. 'It's the second week in a row.'

'I think she said Stan wanted to go and see an old friend in Hackney who has just got his call-up papers,' said Mattie.

Although they'd only been at war two weeks in every post men were receiving letters telling them to report to their allotted processing centres immediately. It seemed the army wasn't going to make the mistake of relying on willing volunteers

53

to fight for king and country this time around.

'I suppose that's understandable,' said her mother. 'But I can't say I don't feel a bit let down after Father Mahon spent hours explaining to Stan that poor Cathy hasn't been to mass with us all since they were wed.'

'I know,' said Mattie, 'but what with their few days' honeymoon in Southend and everything, they haven't got into a proper routine yet.'

'Maybe so.' Her mother drew a handkerchief from her sleeve and blew her nose. 'But it don't seem right not to have all my girls beside me on a Sunday morning.'

'Perhaps Dad could have a word,' said Jo. 'You know, man to man.'

Ida's lips tightened again. 'I don't see how he could as he's never here either.'

They watched in silence as Peter Ryan, the church's oldest server, shuffled to the right side of the altar and lit the low mass candle. Holding the taper aloft, he staggered to the other side of the altar, almost toppling over as he halted in the middle to honour the crucifix before lighting the second candle.

'Where's Henry Wright today?' asked Ida, referring to the young man who was usually in charge of such duties.

'He's been called up.' said Jo. 'So it'll be Mr Ryan most weeks now, helping set up for Father Mahon.'

'Sweet Jesus.' Ida rolled her eyes before sliding off the seat onto the kneeler.

Mattie did the same. Stifling a yawn, she closed her eyes and said her usual prayers for the family

54

and friends.

'Well,' said Mattie's mother, as she sat back in her pew and surveyed the congregation. 'It seems numbers are picking up again.'

'It's probably because now that Chamberlain's declined Hitler's latest peace proposal and the Germans have moved to the Belgium border, people have finally realised that we're actually at war,' Mattie replied, arranging the folds of her red winter coat. 'But I think the increase in the congregation isn't so much to do with the Germans as the arrival of the new priest.'

Her mother swung around. 'You never told me!'

'I did,' said Mattie.

'She did, Mum,' said Jo. 'Just before you and Gran had that ding-dong about her using the scrubbing brush to clean out Prince Albert's–'

'Shhhhh,' hissed someone behind them.

Ida turned and glared for a second, then turned back and folded her arms tightly.

She pressed her lips together and stared ahead as the men and boys of the choir, dressed in their red cassocks and lacy surplices, came out from the vestry and took their places in the stalls.

The organist started to play.

'Who told you anyway?' her mother asked out of the corner of her mouth as the congregation stood.

'Mrs Dunn,' Mattie replied, matching her mother's hushed tone. 'I met her in Watney Market on my way home. He's called–'

The choir started singing the harmonic entrance chant as the procession started down the main aisle.

Picking up her hymn book, Mattie looked ahead as Peter Ryan hobbled down the aisle holding St Brendan and St Bridget's thick leather-bound Bible up high, or at least as high as the seventy-five-year-old's arthritic shoulders would allow.

Behind him came their Billy. He was carrying a candle and was dressed in a black choir robe covered by an unadorned white surplice. He looked the picture of boyish innocence – a notion which anyone who knew him would hotly dispute.

Following on, as always, came Father Mahon, his hands pressed together in supplication and his head reverently bowed as he approached the altar.

He glided past, followed by another, very much taller, figure. Mattie's eyes widened.

Mrs Dunn had described Father McCree as a lovely boy, but the man walking behind the parish priest was no boy.

In profile, the strong line of his jaw was evident, as were the sharp cheekbones and firm mouth. Unlike many priests, who favoured a close crop, the new priest's hair was less severely trimmed and showed a hint of curl. As he swept past, Mattie's eyes followed him, noticing his broad shoulders.

The procession genuflected and then continued into position around the dais. Father McCree took his place on the apostles' side of the church, ready to assist.

Father Mahon bowed and then hobbled around to stand behind the altar. He raised his right hand. *'In nomine Patris, et sp...'*

Crossing herself automatically, Mattie's gaze shifted to Father McCree's face and a tremor ran through her from head to toe.

If Father McCree looked good in profile, he looked heart-stopping full on. In fact, even the rimless spectacles perched on his nose did nothing to soften the tough, angular features of his face and as her eyes reached his well-defined mouth, she was definitely not thinking of anything remotely holy.

Father Mahon finished the greeting and Fr McCree stepped forward and raised his head.

'*Confiteor Deo omnipotenti,*' he exclaimed in a deep, vibrant voice, '*beatae Mariae...*' His dark eyes skimmed over the congregation and locked onto Mattie. '*Semper–*'

They stared at each other for several heartbeats, then Mattie forced her gaze down.

There was a pause and then Father McCree's powerful voice filled the church again.

'Lovely to meet you, Father McCree,' said a respectable-looking woman in a dog-tooth check coat.

'You, too, Mrs...?' Daniel offered his hand.

She took it. 'Willis. Deirdre Willis. I'm in Bigland Street, round the corner from the United Dairy.'

Father Mahon had given the congregation his final blessing about twenty minutes ago and Daniel was feeling more than a little pleased with his first performance, especially as he hadn't actively participated in the mass for almost a decade. Still, as they say, once a Catholic always a Catholic. Of course, there was that one momentary lapse, but ... he pushed aside the vision of the striking brunette in the red coat from his mind and smiled politely.

'I'm afraid I'm not yet familiar with the area.'

'It's three streets down from the market,' she explained. 'And you're always welcome to pop in for a cuppa.'

He extracted his fingers from her moist grip. 'You're very kind.'

Giving him a coquettish flutter of eyelashes, the middle-aged matron moved on and Daniel turned to the next parishioner.

'Good morning, Father McCree, it's so...'

Daniel shook another hand but a nearby flash of red caught his eye as the girl that had knocked him off his liturgical stride earlier moved a step nearer.

Forcing himself to stay focused on the parishioners passing before him, Daniel continued smiling, shaking hands and admiring babies until the vison in the red coat stood before him. Well, not quite before him because, just as he reached to take the girl's hand, a middle-aged woman in a long black coat and royal blue hat stepped between them.

'Good morning, Father McCree,' the woman said, giving him the once-over. 'I'm Mrs Brogan and lovely to meet you.'

'You too, Mrs Brogan,' said Daniel.

'Me husband and eldest son would have been here too,' she continued. 'But they had the horse to sort out.'

'Horse?'

'Samson,' she explained. 'He pulls the cart and my husband and Charlie, our eldest boy, give him a good muck out and gets his tack in order and ready for the next week on Sundays. My Jerimiah deals in discarded household items and has a couple of arches in Chapman Street by Shadwell station, round the corner from where we live.'

'Well then, I look forward to meeting with them both,' said Daniel, keeping his eyes from shifting on to the slim young woman to her right.

'This is my youngest daughter, Jo.' She indicated the fresh-faced girl to her left

'Hello, Jo,' he said.

She gave him a shy smile in acknowledgement and then moved off to look at the church's information table.

Mrs Brogan's eyes followed her.

'Such a clever girl,' she said. 'Always has her nose in a book.'

Jo Brogan seemed more interested in the young lad loitering under the west window out of Mrs Brogan's vision than the literature on the table in front of her, but Daniel smiled politely.

'And this is my eldest, Mattie,' said Mrs Brogan.

Daniel's gaze shifted to the young woman in the bright red coat and perky black felt hat.

Her abundant wavy hair was deep auburn and, although it was swept way from her face and rested in gentle waves around her collar, a stray tendril curled around her left temple. The face that had thrown him mid-sentence was well-proportioned with high cheekbones and a firm jaw, which gave her face strength, while the delicate nose and full lips were pure femininity. He'd met pretty girls before, and resisted them, but as she tilted her head and her eyes captured his, Daniel felt like an adolescent caught in his first crush.

He smiled. 'Good morning, Miss Brogan.'

'And to you, Father McCree,' she replied.

Her hazel eyes held his gaze and Daniel's mouth widened in response as a warm sensation spread through his chest. He offered her his hand and she took it; her palm slid across as his fingers wrapped around hers.

'Lovely service.' Mrs Brogan's voice cut through his thoughts. 'All the better it was that we could hear it for once.'

Mattie pulled her hand from his grasp and gave her mother a sharp look.

'Not ... not th ... that I want you to think I'd say a word against Father Mahon. The man's a living saint so he is and none would say other.' The older woman blustered on as a flush spread up her throat. 'But it's just, well you know–'

'You're a lucky woman to have two lovely daughters, Mrs Brogan,' Daniel interrupted her, not taking his eyes from Mattie.

'Three,' she corrected him. 'My other daughter, Cathy, is usually with us, but–'

'I expect she'll be here next week,' Mattie cut in before her mother could get started.

Daniel smiled. 'What a blessing for you, Mrs Brogan, to have three daughters named for St Martha, St Josephine and St Catherine.'

Amusement danced in Mattie's eyes. 'Actually, Father, I'm Matilda not Martha and my dad named us all after empresses, not saints, I'm afraid.'

'How inventive of him,' said Daniel.

'That's my dad,' Mattie replied. 'He says there are hundreds of saints but empresses are just one in a million. Just like his girls.'

Daniel smiled.

Mattie smiled back.

'That you will, Father, as I'll make sure he comes to mass with us next week,' said Mrs Brogan, cutting between them. 'Come on now, Mattie, as I'm sure Father McCree has other things to do than natter to you all day.'

Shifting her handbag to the other arm, Mrs Brogan headed for the church door.

'Good bye, Father,' said Mattie.

'Good bye, Miss Brogan,' he replied. 'And I hope to see you again next Sunday.'

'You will, Father,' she replied. 'And please call me Mattie. Everyone does.'

She gave him another little smile and then followed her mother.

Daniel's gaze followed her, running up her shapely legs and settling on her pleasing figure. His eyes lingered for a few seconds then, hooking his finger in his dog collar to ease it from his freshly shaved throat, he turned to greet the next parishioner.

Chapter Three

Jumping down from the blacked-out number 25 bus, Christopher Joliffe looked around to get his bearings. Although it was only just after four in the afternoon and the third week in September, what with the dense fog that had choked the capital all day and with the sun hidden behind a thunderous sky, it was more akin to midnight than the middle of the afternoon. He'd taken the three-hour train journey from Northampton to London many times over the past ten years, on bank business or to visit friends, and counted himself pretty familiar with the capital but now, without street or shop lights because of the blackout, it was devilishly easy to get lost, especially as the nights were drawing in so early. However, with the old Tudor row of shops at his back and Chancery Lane underground station across the road, Christopher worked out he was just a ten-minute walk from his destination.

Waiting until his eyes had adjusted to what little light there was, he listened for any oncoming traffic and crossed the road. Keeping close to the white lines painted on the kerb, he turned left and made his way west along Holborn until he reached Red Lion Street, where he turned left and then continued on until he reached the north side of Red Lion Square and the Conway Hall.

The hall was a grand art deco-style building with

German secret service to take his offer seriously to collaborate with the German plan in Europe in return for the six northern counties to Dublin. He's put it to Hitler who has sanctioned it because they also offered to turn a blind-eye to U-boats sheltering off the West coast and station spotters at strategic points along the high cliffs to report on merchant ships passing,' continued Drummond. 'To cement this alliance and as a gesture of good-will between them and Germany, the Republicans are sending us one of their radio operators to be your contact to Germany.'

'Who is it?'

'I don't know, all I know is he'll be contacting you soon,' Drummond replied.

'Bloody hell!' Christopher raked his hands through his hair. 'As if this isn't dangerous enough without having everything going back and forth through some bastard bog-trotter.'

'I'm sorry, old chap,' said Drummond. 'But it's out of my hands.' He slapped Christopher heartily on the back. 'But don't worry about all that now, you just get yourself another snifter and I'll introduce you to a few people.'

With his mouth pulled into a hard line, Christopher exchanged his empty glass for a full one and followed his mentor through the melee to where a tall man wearing an extravagant striped tie was chatting to a slender, dark-haired woman in a full-length blood-red evening gown.

They stopped talking and turned as Christopher and Drummond reached them.

'Evening to you both,' Drummond said.

The man nodded his acknowledgement.

'Christopher, I'd like to you to meet the honorary secretary of the British People's Party, Mr–'

'Beckett–' Christopher cut in, thrusting out his hand. 'And it's a pleasure to meet you, sir, and thank you for your many informative articles in the *New Pioneer*.'

The fascists' literary star smiled urbanely.

'That's music to a journalist's ears,' he said, giving Christopher a limp hand. And call me Sam, Mr…?'

'Mr Joliffe, Christopher Joliffe.'

'Christopher worked with me in Northampton.' Drummond slapped Christopher on the back. 'He did a marvellous job recruiting patriots to our cause and he's now in London to coordinate our efforts in East London. He aims to enlighten and mobilise the populace into seeing the folly of supporting this Jews' war.' He turned to the woman. 'And, Christopher, this is Countess Sophia Rožmberk of Bohemia.' The countess offered her gloved hand.

From a distance her carefully applied make-up gave the countess the appearance of a woman in her mid-twenties, but close up it was obvious that she was at least ten years older. She had a thin face with sharp cheekbones, a narrow chin and dark eyes. Her plunging neckline made it clear that she was not only very aware of her best feature but that she was happy to share what she had with anyone who cared to look.

Stepping forward, Christopher took her hand and raised it to his lips. 'Good evening, your ladyship.'

'Pleased to meet you,' she said, her eyes running boldly over him. 'And my, my, what a 'and-some fellow you are, Christopher, *liebling*, and so blond.'

Although he was naturally fair, Christopher had picked up a useful tip on his first trip to Germany. A chap in the Hitler Youth had shown him how to mix a dash of peroxide in with his shampoo to give the much sought-after white-blond shade.

Christopher ran his fingers through his hair and smiled. 'Thank you, and the pleasure's all mine, I assure you.'

The countess's eyes sparkled. 'We shall see but, tell me, have you read *The Protocols of the Elders of Zion?*'

'I certainly have,' said Christopher. 'And, in fact, I have already bought and given away several copies to those who don't yet believe that the Jews of the world are conspiring to control all the money.'

'Jews.' The countess's face contorted into an ugly expression. 'Vile, odious creatures, all of them.'

'They should all be put down as one would a rabid animal,' said Christopher.

The countess's red lips widened into a provocative smile. 'I can see you and I are going to get on very well,' she said, slipping her arm in Christopher's. 'Now, come vith me and I'll introduce you to some other like-minded people.'

With her arm through her husband's and her high heels clip-clopping on the wet flagstones, Cathy Wheeler turned into Mafeking Terrace and a smile spread across her face. It was just before

69

five and, as she'd hoped, every door had a woman standing in it so they could see her on the arm of her new husband. Even though the country had been at war for six weeks, other than the taped windows and missing streetlights, the thoroughfare looked very much as it always did at this time at night and Cathy felt a rush of affection at returning to her old home.

'Slow down a bit,' she said, patting her new wide-brimmed hat to make sure it was set at just the right angle.

'Sorry, luv,' said Stan, giving her an apologetic smile. 'I just don't want to be late for the meeting.'

'It doesn't start until eight so you've got bags of time,' said Cathy, waving at Rita who lived at number twelve.

Stan gave her a tense smile and then turned back.

Cathy studied his profile. He was a good chap was Stan, and he didn't have to be the brainiest because being solid and dependable was much more important. Plus, putting double what most women had for housekeeping on the table each Thursday evening, from his business hauling fruit and vegetables from Spitalfields to small greengrocers all over Bethnal Green and Hackney, was also in his favour.

Stopping in front of her mother's house, they were just about to knock when Ida opened the door.

'Hello, Mum,' said Cathy, noting that her mother had disposed with her wraparound apron in honour of their visit.

'Hello, luv,' Ida replied, enveloping her in a warm embrace.

Tilting her head to ensure the hat stayed in place, Cathy hugged her back.

'Evening, Mrs B,' said Stan, removing his fedora as they stepped through the door.

'Hello, Stanley,' her mother replied, shutting the door behind them.

Cathy slipped off her coat.

'Is this new?' asked her mother, taking it from her.

'Yes, Stan bought it for me in Bodger's last week,' Cathy replied, smoothing down her skirt and straightening the bow on her Peter Pan collar. 'The trim is real coney.'

Ida looked impressed, as well she might as Stan hadn't had much change from the five-pound note he'd handed over for it.

'Go on through,' said her mother, nodding at the back parlour door.

Her parents' main living room was a perfect reflection of her father's profession in that it was furnished and, for the most part, decorated with items he'd collected on his rounds. The three easy chairs were a mismatch of styles ranging from the elaborately carved wooden one with a padded seat, which her gran favoured, through to her father's button-back leather porter's chair with a wobbly arm which he'd procured as part of a house clearance in Bloomsbury. The mantelshelf, too, was cluttered with objets d'art including a Staffordshire dog with an ear chipped off, a Wedgwood bowl without a lid, a pair of silver-plate candlesticks with most of the top coat rubbed away and a Punch Toby jug with no handle. But pride of place, and dominating the whole room, was a tall mahogany bookcase which contained her father's prize acquisition: a set of eleventh edition *Encyclopaedia Britannica* that had been printed in 1913.

Mattie and her father had spent hours poring over its engraved illustrations of exotic mammals and nightmare-inducing tropical insects. Sometimes, when she, Mattie and Jo were sent to bed early because there wasn't a shilling for the meter, Mattie would take a volume with her and, snuggled under the eiderdown, she would read to them by the light of her Brownie torch about the romantic deeds of knights and kings from long ago. Unfortunately, volume twenty-five was missing so if you wanted to find out about salt or Schubert you were out of luck, but it didn't bother Cathy as she was more interested in reading about Mary Pickford and Douglas Fairbanks in *Cinema Goer* than Marco Polo and Genghis Khan in an encyclopaedia.

In truth, although walking into her parent's lounge now made Cathy feel warm, safe and comfortable, as a child, she'd been reluctant to bring friends home. Although no one would say it to their faces, the Brogan children were called the didicoy kids and Cathy knew inviting her classmates into her second-hand, shabby home would only increase the name-calling.

Billy sat crossed-legged in front of the fire reading this week's edition of *Hotspur* and he glanced up briefly as they walked in, but her father, who was sitting in his usual chair by the hearth, put aside his *Daily Sketch* and stood up.

He shook Stan's hand, then looked at Cathy.

'Hello, Dad,' she said.

A smile wrinkled his weather-worn face and he flung his arms wide. 'Ain't you got a cuddle for your old dad then, Cath?'

Smiling, Cathy walked into his arms and was rewarded with a tobaccoey bear hug.

'Where's Jo, Charlie, Gran and Mattie?' she asked.

'Your sister's doing her homework at Pam's house,' said Ida, settling herself back in the boudoir chair Jerimiah had salvaged from a fire some while back. 'Charlie's gone to a lecture at the town hall on fire-fighting and God in Heaven only knows where your gran is or what she's up too, and–'

'I'm making the tea,' said Mattie, emerging from the kitchen and coming over to give Cathy a peck on the cheek.

The kettle whistled.

'I'll come and give you a hand,' said Cathy.

Leaving Stan talking to her father, they went into the kitchen. Mattie pulled the blackout curtains and then Cathy switched on the light.

'You look tired,' Cathy said.

'I'm not surprised,' said Mattie, spooning tea into the pot. 'Aren't you, with blooming air-raid sirens going off the third night in the row?'

'A little, but we only have to go downstairs to our shelter,' said Cathy, setting out the cups on the tray. 'Stan's made it ever so comfy; with a carpet on the floor and even a couple of pictures. And, of course, now I'm not working I don't have to get up so early.'

'Lucky you,' said Mattie, pouring milk in each cup. She gave Cathy a wry sideward glance. 'So tell me, Little Sister, how is married life?'

Cathy gave her a bright smile. 'Just lovely. I've bought a whole new set of bed linen and ordered new eiderdown quilts for all the beds. On top of that, Stan's going to repaper the front room. I've finally mastered the cooker and–'

'And what about...' Her sister winked. 'It?'

'Oh, that.' Cathy felt her cheeks grow warm. 'It's lovely, too.'

Cathy lowered her eyes and, shifting the sugar bowl over a fraction, she put Billy's glass of milk on the tray, then picked it up.

'After you,' she said.

They went through to join the rest of the family. Leaving Mattie to hand out the drinks, Cathy went over and perched on the arm of Stan's chair.

The sound of BBC Theatre Orchestra drifted out from their old Murphy wireless as the family chatted for a bit about the shortage of sandbags and how the prices in the shops were going up already.

'It says here,' said Jerimiah, shaking out his newspaper, 'that we have to list everyone in the house on a new form that will be sent through soon. It's so we can all get our identity cards.'

'And for the call-up and rationing that starts after Christmas, too,' said Mattie.

'I hope they make sure that the children get enough.' Ida ruffled her son's hair. 'Our Billy's a growing lad.'

Billy pulled a face and shifted out of his

mother's reach.

Mattie rolled her eyes. 'Am I the only one who reads the government stuff shoved through our letterbox? Children will get more or less the same as us, but with extra milk, and you'll have to register Samson, Dad, so you can get his grub.'

'Rationing, call-up, sending the children away,' said Ida, swapping her knitting needles into the other hand as she turned a row. 'And when the bombs start, well ... I don't know what will become of us all.'

'Now, now, Mother,' said Jerimiah, peering at her over the top of his glasses. 'There's no need for that kind of talk.'

'They won't bomb us, will they, Stan?' Cathy chipped in.

'No they won't,' said Stan, puffing out his chest a little. 'Because Hitler doesn't want to go to war.'

Mattie raised a sceptical eyebrow. 'Well, he's going a funny way about it.'

'And Stan's not the only one who says we should talk to Germany,' continued Cathy. 'The Peace Pledge Union and the International Voluntary Service for Peace say so too.'

Her sister looked astonished. 'Do they?'

'Yes they do,' continued Cathy, feeling a little smug that, for once, she had one up on Mattie about current affairs. 'Even the prime minister is trying to find a way to start talks with Germany again so we can to stop the war before Christmas.'

'Well then, Stan, perhaps you can answer me this,' said Mattie, in what Cathy thought of as her annoying I-know-more-than-you tone. 'If Hitler and his Nazis are so keen to have peace why did they fire at the *Ark Royal* and sink HMS *Courageous* last week?'

Stan shifted in his seat. 'That was unlucky.'

'It was for the sailors,' retorted Mattie.

'That's why Britain and Germany should sort out a peace plan before anyone else is hurt,' Stan replied.

'Killed,' said Mattie, regarding him coolly. 'They were killed, Stan, over 500 of them.'

'Which is why my Stan's the chairman of the local Britons for Peace Union, aren't you, luv?' said Cathy.

'Yes I am,' said Stan, patting her knee approvingly.

To be honest, like many people, Cathy found the whole government thing boring but, as a good wife, felt obliged to show a bit of interest as it seemed to matter to Stan.

Putting her arm around her husband's shoulders, Cathy looked defiantly at her sister.

Mattie held her gaze for a moment, then sighed and stood up. 'I'll put the kettle on again.'

Stan looked at his watch.

'And talking about the Britons for Peace Union.' He rose to his feet. 'I ought to be off or I'll be late.'

'I thought they met on Thursday after the Irish dancing,' said Jerimiah.

'They do but I'm not going to the Catholic Club, I'm going up west to represent our branch at a meeting,' Stan replied. 'Thanks for the tea, Mrs B, and I'll see you all on the weekend.'

'Nice to see you, Stan, and give your mother

my regards,' said Ida.

Cathy rose to her feet. 'I'll see you out.'

Back in the cool hallway, Cathy retrieved her husband's coat from the rack and held it out for him.

'Thanks, luv,' he said, shrugging it on. 'Be careful on the way home and don't forget to shine your torch downwards as I don't want you arrested for breaking the blackout!'

'I'll remember,' said Cathy, handing him his scarf.

'And you know Mum likes to be in bed by the time the news comes on at nine,' he added.

'Don't worry, I'll have her tucked in snug by eight-thirty.' Cathy picked a speck of soot from his sleeve.

Stan's arm slipped around her waist. 'Wish me luck.'

Cathy smoothed his collar. 'Good luck, but you won't need it.'

His deep-set eyes ran slowly over her face.

'What time do you think you'll be in?' said Cathy.

'Late, I expect, and I'll try not to wake you.' He pressed his lips onto hers. 'Sorry.'

She gave him a peck on the cheek. 'That's all right.'

Switching out the light, she opened the door and her husband left.

She let out the breath she was holding. She hadn't lied to Mattie. 'It' was lovely; lovely but frustratingly infrequent.

Negotiating his way past the heavy black curtains

77

shrouding the door, Stanley Wheeler found himself in the lobby of Conway Hall just as the hall clock struck seven-thirty.

Walking to the reception desk, a Slavic-looking clerk directed him to his right. After showing his invitation to the bruiser on the door, he was ushered in for the inaugural meeting of the British Council for a Christian Settlement in Europe.

The main ballroom was set out with at least a dozen rows of chairs, all facing the lectern placed in the centre of the stage. The hall was filled with men dressed much as he was, in togs from fifty-shilling tailors like Hepworth's and Burton's, but there was a handful of women in cocktail dresses dotted amongst the suited men.

Nodding at acquaintances as he passed, Stanley made his way through the throng to the bar.

'Double scotch with a splash,' he said, reaching into his breast pocket for his wallet.

'Put your money away,' said a familiar voice. 'And I'll have the same.'

Stanley turned.

'Hello, Jock, good to see you,' he said, taking the man's offered hand.

Jock Houston, the London coordinator for the British Patriots' Union, was a man of middling height with a mass of crinkly brown hair, sunken cheeks and a Roman nose. In honour of the evening's guest speaker, Jock had spruced himself up and was wearing an expensive lounge suit, matching waistcoat and bow tie, which wasn't bad for an ex-bookmaker with a criminal record.

'Decent crowd,' said Stan.

'I'd say 'bout ton or so, I reckon,' Jock said, in

a voice that could grind glass.

The waiter set their drinks before them and Jock handed over a ten-bob note.

'Although I did think there'd be a couple of party banners,' said Stan, picking up his Scotch.

'MI5.' Jock tapped the side of his nose. 'The buggers are everywhere these days.' Jock took a sip of his drink.

'Of course, we have to be on our guard.' Stan grinned. 'Until the boot's on the other foot, that is.'

Jock grinned back. 'How's your little lot out east?'

'Growing,' said Stan, taking a sip of very acceptable single malt. 'Although because we've had to call ourselves the Britons for Peace Union, we've found ourselves chockablock with Fabian do-gooders, four-eyed liberals and loopy highbrows, plus some long-haired chap who calls himself a vegetarian. Have you ever heard the like of it?'

'Well, there's more out than in,' Jock replied.

'Still, that lot of lunatics screaming and shouting about peace is the answer at the meetings as the police don't look too closely into what's going on behind the scenes,' said Stan.

'With the patriots on the committee, you mean?'

'Yeah! Our people who really run the show.' A cynical smile lifted Stanley's heavy features. 'All solid chaps and ready for the call.'

'Good.' Jock grinned and slapped him on the back. 'Now, grab your drink and come with me, there's someone who wants to meet you.'

Jock led Stan towards a young man of about

Stan's age, who looked as if he should be standing on the prow of Viking longboat wearing a horned helmet; on his arm was a skinny woman with her tits all but hanging out.

The man looked up as they approached. 'I wondered where the Devil you'd got to.'

'Looking for this bugger,' said Jock, thumbing at Stan beside him.

The young man's ice-blue eyes shifted onto Stan. 'Is this the chap you've been telling me about?'

Jock nodded. 'Christopher, this is Stanley Wheeler, the warden of East London. Stan, this is Christopher Joliffe.'

Christopher offered his hand. 'Good to meet you, Stanley. This is Countess Sophia Rožmberk of Bohemia.'

'Charmed, I'm sure,' she said.

'Good evening, your countess,' blustered Stan, trying to stop his eyes straying to the plunging neckline of her satin gown.

Amusement flickered over her face. 'It's your ladyship.'

Stan frowned. 'Beg pardon?'

'You address me as your ladyship.' The countess held out her gloved hand.

Stan shook it. 'Good evening, your ladyship.'

'You English.' She gave a tinkling laugh and Stan felt sweat prickle under his tight collar.

Christopher raised a hand and clicked his fingers. A waiter scurried over.

'I've been hearing about all your tomfoolery in East London,' he said, taking drinks for himself and the countess.

'You mean the lark we had in Brick Lane?' asked Stan, feeling more than a little pleased that his initiative had filtered tip to the top of the organisation.

'Smart move, breaking the main water pipe to the shop,' said Christopher.

'Thanks,' said Stan.

'Now, I don't know if Jock has mentioned it yet, but I'm going to let you into a little secret, Stan. I'm officially not listed on Right Club's membership or have anything to do with the hosts of this little shindig because my real job is to coordinate loyal patriots like you, Stan, so need to be kept under the wire because it involves me dealing directly with our friends across the sea. However, now this Jew-loving government has declared war on those who share our ideals, it's too risky for us to have direct contact with the Germans, but we have friends in other places, Emerald Green places, if you follow me, Stan.' Christopher winked.

Stan frowned. 'I'm not sure I–'

'The Irish Republican Army,' whispered Christopher. He gave Stan a comradely wink. 'Are you following my drift now, Stan?'

A tingle of anticipation rippled up Stan's spine.

'I certainly am,' said Stan, squaring his shoulders and standing a little taller.

'Ladies and gentleman,' a voice called over the hubbub of the room. 'If you could take your seats.'

People around them started to make their way towards the rows of chairs.

'But we can't talk now.' Christopher handed him a card. 'Ring me on this number and we'll

81

meet soon.'

With the countess in tow, Christopher headed for the reserved seats near the stage.

'Come on, Stan, or we'll end up at the back,' said Jock.

Elbowing their way down the side of the hall, they stepped into the nearest line which was just four rows from the front and sat down. Stan tucked the card Christopher Joliffe had given him in his inside breast pocket, his mind whirling. The compère, a slightly built individual with slicked-back hair, rapped his knuckles on the pedestal.

All noise in the room ceased and Stan fixed his attention on the stage.

'Thank you for coming to this auspicious gathering,' said the man on the stage. 'This is the start of a momentous crusade to help our country, the country we all love so much, join hands with its historical, cultural and, more importantly, its Aryan ally, Germany. Therefore, without any further ado...'

The special guest speaker stepped onto the stage and Stan's heart beat wildly.

'...I give you our visionary, our leader and the country's next prime minister.'

The compère stepped aside to rapturous applause and, as the people in the hall rose to their feet as one and raised their right arms in salute, Stan did the same.

With his fingers stretched to their limits, he looked in wonder as, dressed in a tailored black suit with a black shirt and tie beneath, the guest speaker, Oswald Mosley, stepped up to the rostrum.

Shouts of 'Heil, Mosley,' filled the room.

Taking a deep breath, Stan shouted the same at the top of his voice.

From his situation just in front of the podium, Christopher smiled and resisted the urge to look at his watch.

'And so, in conclusion, patriots,' Mosley exclaimed in his well-rounded upper-class accent.

At last, thought Christopher.

Although clearly a gifted orator, Sir Oswald did tend to ramble on a bit and what had been billed as a twenty-minute speech was already double that.

'We know the answer for we have felt this thing within us. Our divine purpose is conquest and to be the glory of the ages. In that high fate, tomorrow we live.'

Along with every other person in the room, Christopher rose to his feet to give the obligatory five minutes' standing ovation.

As he was within the great man's line of vision, Christopher shouted 'bravo' and 'well said' while maintaining a frenzy of clapping.

Mosley's pencil-thin moustache lifted at the corner as he acknowledged the crowd's appreciation, then, surrounded by his hand-picked sentries, he strode off the stage.

'Brilliant, wasn't it,' said Drummond as the hubbub in the hall started to die down.

'It was,' Christopher agreed. 'He'll go down in history as our greatest prime minister.'

'Only if we get rid of the bunch of clowns in the House of Commons,' laughed Drummond.

'Surely you mean when?' said Christopher.

His mentor smiled. 'Indeed I do.'

There was a rustle of silk as the countess, who was sitting on Christopher's other side, shifted around.

'Wasn't that marvellous?' she drawled, her hand travelling up the inside of Christopher's thigh as she spoke.

'It certainly was,' he replied, his gaze straying down her ample cleavage.

An amused smile lifted the corner of her mouth. She looked into his eyes for a second or two and then she sat back.

'Oh it's been a very long day.' She feigned a yawn and stretched her arms. 'Christopher, *liebling,* vould you be an absolute angel and arrange for a cab to take me to Knightsbridge?'

'I will,' Christopher replied. 'But perhaps you'll allow me also to escort you?'

'How gallant you are,' she said, running her hand gently down his face.

Christopher rose to his feet. 'I'll get your wrap.'

Leaving her talking to Drummond, Christopher strolled towards the cloakroom.

'Christopher!'

He looked around to see Jock hurrying towards him. 'I'm glad you're still here. You know about the IRA chap.'

'Yes, Drummond told me earlier,' said Christopher, his anger flaring again.

'Well, I've just been told he's arrived in East London and will be making contact soon,' said Jock. 'So you need to get Stan's little bunch in shape as soon as possible as the call from Germany could come any day.'

Looking across to where the leading lights of the Right Club, the British Council for Christian Settlement in Europe and Militant Christian Patriots were gathering around Mosley, Christopher imagined himself, surrounded by black and red banners with a white lightning emblem, being counted in their number.

'Don't worry, we'll be ready,' Christopher replied. 'I'm in charge and it'll be the worse for Stan's motley crew if they don't toe the line.'

Jock nodded and turned to leave, but Christopher caught his arm. 'Tell me about the countess?'

Jock laughed. 'That's what she calls herself, but if she really is some toff then she's got no money. She had a fling with Lord Greyhall a few years back and, since then, she's been sleeping her way through the male members of the Right Club, looking for someone to pay her bills.'

'I'll be perfectly fine now,' said the countess, letting go of Christopher's arm as they reached the top of the dozen steps to the first floor of her apartment block.

'No, I said I'd escort you home and what sort of gentleman would I be if I shirked my duty to see a beautiful woman safely home?' said Christopher as they rounded the top of the banister. 'Now, let me have your key.'

'Very well,' she gave him a playful smile then, after fishing around in her handbag for a moment or two, she produced a key with a fat silk tassel attached.

Smiling, Christopher took it and opened her somewhat shabbily painted front door.

'Thank you, my pretty blond Sir Galahad,' she said, giving him a lavish smile as she swept past him.

She went to close the door but Christopher put his hand on it. 'I thought perhaps you'd offer your knight in shining armour a drink.'

She gave him a look of deepest regret. 'Perhaps another time.'

She pushed on the door but Christopher held it firm. 'That's not very friendly, now is it, *liebling*.' He shoved it open and the countess stumbled back.

Stepping through, Christopher closed the door firmly behind him and slammed the bolt across.

'Not very friendly at all,' he repeated.

Panic flashed across her face and she dashed through to the lounge, trying to slam the door behind her, but Christopher shoved his foot in the gap and pushed it open.

As Christopher marched across the room, the countess retreated until she found herself with her back against the sideboard. Not taking her eyes from his face, she searched for something to defend herself with. Grabbing the empty fruit bowl, she flung it wildly at him.

Christopher batted it aside and it spun across the floor. She picked up the lamp but he ripped it from her hand and threw it aside, hitting her across the mouth with his fist on the backward swing.

The countess staggered and was about to fall but Christopher caught her by the throat and pinned her to the wall.

'No!' she gasped as his finger tightened around her windpipe.

'I'm sorry, countess.' Christopher's mouth stretched back into an icy smile. 'But I don't take no for an answer.'

Holding her there, his hand went under her skirt and he ripped away her flimsy undergarments, then he threw her face down on the floor. Kneeling between her legs, he anchored her to the floor with his left hand as he unbuttoned his trousers.

Chapter Four

As the bus slowed towards the junction of Cannon Street, Mattie grabbed the handrail on the back platform and, seeing the light was red, jumped down.

She didn't usually bother with the bus as it was only half an hour's walk along Commercial Road from Watney Street to where she worked, but she was late.

In truth, it didn't really matter what time she arrived at work as she was a pieceworker so she got paid per item, but if she arrived late she missed the pick of the work. The first in got the easy bundles like straight skirts and sleeveless blouses, which meant you could make them faster and so earn more. The latecomers would be left with fiddly garments like pleated dresses and blouses with frills.

Dodging between the lorries and vans, Mattie hurried across the road then turned into New Road. The road, which ran between Whitechapel and Commercial Road, was lined on both sides by three-storey mid-Victorian townhouses with steps up to their front doors and wrought-iron railings protecting passers-by from falling into the basement space below street level.

When they'd been built a hundred years ago, the solid red-brick dwellings were designed to be spacious homes for wealthy merchants with businesses along the river nearby. Sadly, as the traders and their money moved east to the Edwardian suburbs of West Ham and Forest Gate, the once comfortable residences, like much of the area around, fell on hard times. Now, instead of their front parlours echoing to children's laughter or the pleasant melody from a pianoforte, the family rooms on the ground floor had been gutted to make shops, storerooms or factory showrooms.

Waving to Sadie, who was opening up the front shutters of her wholesale haberdasher's business, Mattie dashed across Nelson Street and headed for the middle house with the Gold & Sons Costumes sign above the open door. The arched window to the right of the entrance displayed a couple of battered shop dummies with painted smiles on which the company's newest designs were displayed. Well, not actually their designs, because Gold & Sons got their creative inspiration by buying garments from places like Bourne & Hollingsworth and Selfridges in Oxford Street or Pontins and Barkers in Kensington, dismantling them and then using the patterns to make cut-price copies.

It was only the second day of October and there was a decidedly autumnal nip in the air, but because the fashion industry was always a season in front, Gold's and every other factory in White-chapel, Aldgate and Spitalfields were already manufacturing summer dresses, skirts and blouses.

Passing the cutting room, with its layers of fabric piled up on the bench for cutting, Mattie continued along the hallway to the yard at the back.

Bouncing down the back step, Mattie entered the brick-built hut housing the two dozen treadle sewing machines that were already clattering away. Squeezing her way past her fellow workers, Mattie slipped behind her machine, opposite her friend Iris.

Iris was a year older than Mattie and had already been working at Gold's for a couple of years when Mattie started. She had short blonde hair and a rosy apple face which reflected her cheery disposition.

She, like Mattie, was wearing a wraparound apron and a scarf looped into a turban to keep her hair out of her face while she worked. Stopping mid-stitch, she looked up.

'I got you this,' she shouted, pushing a roll of cotton fabric with bright yellow and red flowers printed on it and tied up with an offcut strip. 'It was the last one.'

'Thanks,' yelled Mattie, taking it from her.

It wasn't just the last bundle, it was the last garment, as the bench against the wall where the cutters stacked the work was completely empty. There were ten garments in every bundle and she and Iris had been splitting bundles all week, but their pay packets would be light again this week.

'There's supposed to be something coming in later,' said Rose, another girl who had joined around the same time as Mattie.

'They said that yesterday,' said Iris. 'And then we sat here all afternoon twiddling our thumbs. If it carries on like this, I'm going somewhere else.'

'It's the same everywhere since the government told us food rationing was coming in after Christmas, but there's rumours going around that they will be rationing clothes as well,' said Mattie, 'which is why the shops are holding back on their summer orders.'

'Well it's not fair,' said Rose, lowering the machine foot on the fabric.

'It's war,' Mattie replied with a heavy sigh. 'And it's going to get a lot worse than no new clothes in the shops.'

'I don't know why we have to get involved at all,' said Rose. 'Someone said in the pub last night that if the Poles hadn't dragged their feet squaring things with Hitler, we wouldn't be in this mess now.'

'It's not the Poles you want to blame but the bloody Yids,' chipped in May, sitting on Rose's other side. 'Everyone knows we're only fighting so they can keep hold of their bloody money.'

'But what about what it says in the newspapers about the Nazis smashing up their homes and taking all their belongings?' asked Mattie.

'It's a load of old codswallop, if you ask me,' May sneered. 'Ask yourself who owns the newspapers? A bunch of grasping Jew boys like Gold, that's who.'

Mattie opened her mouth to reply, but as if he'd heard his name, Isaac Gold appeared in the doorway.

Somewhere in his late fifties, Isaac Gold was only an inch or so taller than Mattie and probably weighed only a pound or two more. Always three days away from his last shave, what was left of his hair under his kippah was so weighed down by Brylcreem that it looked as if it were painted on his head rather than growing there. Although it was rumoured that, along with his family home in Stamford Hill, he was a wealthy man and owned properties throughout Stepney and Bethnal Green, Mattie had never seen him wearing anything other than baggy grey trousers, frayed shirt and oversized waistcoat with a tape measure draped around his scrawny neck.

He surveyed them over his half-rimmed glasses. 'And how are all my lovely ladies this fine morning?'

'We'd be better if we had some work on the table, Mr Gold,' replied Mo, one of the two machinists working the overlocking machines in the corner.

'Well, my dears,' he said, as a slow smile spread across his face. 'I have some good news for you in that regard because this very morning I got a call from the Ministry of Labour with an order that will keep us all busy until Christmas.'

'What is it?' asked someone.

'Uniform skirts for the RAF,' Mr Gold replied. 'A three gross of them for starts.'

A mutter of approval went around the workshop as Mr Gold's benevolent gaze moved over them.

Mattie rose to her feet. 'How many panels and sundries?'

'Three, with a waistband, two buttons and a zip,' the owner replied.

'How much?'

Mr Gold's eyes shifted from her face for a second. 'Well, now, what with the shortage of cloth and getting thread and–'

'Now, how much?' asked Mattie again.

'Thruppence a piece,' he replied flatly.

There were gasps all around.

'But that's half the going rate,' said Mattie.

'I know, I know,' said Mr Gold, raising his hands and eyes towards the nicotine-stained ceiling. 'But there's a war on, you know. And, besides, you girls will be able to knock 'em out ten to the dozen so you'll earn just as much–'

'For doing double the work,' snapped Mattie. 'At that price we'd be lucky to scrape 17/6 a week.'

'We all have to tighten our belts.' Mr Gold's haggard face contorted into a regretful expression. 'It's the same all everywhere. *Oy gevalt.*' He looked imploringly Heavenwards. 'Such times we live in. Such times.'

Mattie gave him a cool look. 'So the ministry's paying you half as much too, are they?'

The women in the room started grumbling.

Mr Gold's eyes and lips narrowed. 'So do you want that I should bankrupt myself? A business has overheads and expenses–'

'And so do we,' said Mattie. 'Especially now the men have gone.'

'At least you've got regular work,' said Mr Gold.

'That's not work; that's slavery. If it's not bad enough that the roof leaks, that the one bog is blocked more often than it's working and we have to put up with Mosher the cutter's wandering hands, now we're supposed to work our fingers to the bone, too. Well, as far as I'm concerned, if you want three-panelled WAF skirts with a waistband, two buttons and a zip, you'll have to sew them yourself, Mr Gold, because I'm off.'

'So am I,' said someone else.

'Me too.'

'I'm coming with you,' said another.

The machinists stood up and, throwing their half-completed garments onto their idle machines, started collecting their seam-rippers and cotton-snippers together.

'Alright, alright,' said Mr Gold, sweat glistening in the light from the bare bulb swinging from the ceiling above. 'Although it'll beggar me, I'll make it four pence apiece.'

Mattie picked up her satchel and, placing it on her chair, dropped her shears inside. 'It's too late, if you offered me ten bob a piece, I'm not staying.'

Taking her coat from the back of her chair, Mattie put it on and slung her satchel over her shoulder but, as she was about to walk out, Rose caught her arm.

'See, I told you,' she said in a low voice. 'It's the bloody Jews' war and they'll be the ones making money out of it. You can lay a pound to a penny that Gold's two fucking sons won't be fighting the Germans, it'll be our husbands and brothers.'

'So, Queenie, what odds is Fat Tony offering on Happy Molly in the two-thirty at Kempton to-morrow?' asked Georgie Tugman, as his close-set eyes studied her from beneath his cloth cap.

Flipping over to the next page in her pocket book, Queenie scanned the page. 'Two to one on.'

It was just gone 3.30 in the afternoon and Queenie was standing in the alleyway alongside the Lord Nelson in Watney Street. As sunset was just over two hours away, many of the shops had already put up their shutters to comply with the blackout regulation so the unlit street couldn't even benefit from the golden light shining from the shop windows. Women huddled around the fruit and veg stalls in the market hoping to grab a last-minute bargain as the stallholders sold off their perishable goods.

Although her feet were aching fit to murder her, Queenie had had a good day.

Having seen the family off to work by eight, she'd had the week's laundry done and strung across the scullery by eleven so she'd strapped her money bag under her fur coat, crammed her old felt hat on her head and, shoving her note-book in her pocket and her pencil behind her ear, she'd headed out

After a lunchtime stint in the Old Rose along the Highway taking lunchtime bets from the workers from Tobacco and St Katherine's Docks, followed by a cuppa and a spam sandwich in Kate's cafe, she'd arrived back in Watney Street just as the early factory whistles were starting at 3 p.m. For the past hour she'd alternated between the Nelson, which was halfway down the market, and the House at Home at the bottom end of the street, catching the dockers and factory workers as they made their way home. It had been a good day and, even with just a halfpenny commission on each bet, she'd chalked up two bob for the day's work.

'That's a bit short,' said Tom Packer, standing next to his friend Georgie.

Queenie smiled up at the two lads. 'You're at liberty to find better and, if you do, give them my regards.'

Georgie and Tom exchanged a quick glance then, diving deep in their pockets, produced a few coppers.

'We'll have thruppence each to win on Happy Molly and the same on Flaming Heart in the one o'clock at Haydock,' said Georgie.

Casting her eyes up and down the street, Queenie tucked her right hand behind her.

The boys dropped their coins in her palm and her fingers closed around them. The two boys hurried away.

Retrieving the pencil from behind her ear, she opened her dog-eared notebook and started writing.

''ello 'ello 'ello,' said a gruff voice behind her. 'Wot's all this then?'

Queenie jumped and dropped her book on the floor.

She spun around.

'Jesus, Mary and Joseph, you nearly frit the

95

ghost right out of me,' she said, pressing her hand to her fluttering chest. 'What the feck do you think you're playing at, Mattie Mary Brogan?'

'I could ask you the same, Gran,' laughed Mattie as she picked up Queenie's tote book. 'It could easily have been Sergeant Bell instead of me catching you running bets for Fat Tony.'

'Well, it wasn't,' said Queenie. 'And, even if it was, I doubt old Digga Bell will want his missus to know he's been taking his refreshment breaks in Sutton Street with her at number seven.'

She winked and Mattie laughed again.

A little bubble of happiness squeezed Queenie's old heart.

She loved all her grandchildren something fierce, of course she did, and although she'd cut her own tongue out rather than tell her, she had to admit Ida had done a grand job raising them, even if Billy did need to feel a hand around the back of his legs more often. But of all of them, her marrow ran the strongest through Mattie. Sometimes, when Mattie flashed a smile or laughed, Queenie saw a glimpse of the wild-haired, barefooted girl from Kinsale she'd once been.

'Even so,' Mattie continued. 'You'll hear it from Mum if she finds out.'

'When do I not?' said Queenie. 'You'd think she'd have a bit of compassion for a poor widow but no, just lashes me day and night with that sharp tongue of hers.'

Amusement lifted the corner of her granddaughter's mouth. 'Well, if you ask me, Gran, you're both as bad as each other and Mum did have a point when Prince Albert escaped into the kitchen and shat all over the draining board.'

Queenie tried to look contrite but couldn't keep a smug smile from spreading across her face.

'Are you coming home?' asked Mattie.

Queenie scanned down the tattered page of her notebook and then nodded. 'It'll do for today.'

Hooking her arm in Mattie's, they crossed the road.

'Actually, Gran,' said Mattie, as they turned into Chapman Street. 'I'm glad I bumped into you because I've had a bit of a day of it myself.'

'What happened, child?' Queenie asked, looking anxiously up at her granddaughter.

'I got into an argument with Mr Gold and, to cut a long story short, I told him to stick his job where the sun don't shine,' Mattie replied.

'Did you now?' Queenie chuckled.

'Yes I did, and it's all right for you,' continued Mattie, 'you haven't got to tell Mum she won't get any housekeeping this week.'

'She'll manage,' said Queenie. 'And with every factory needing help, you'll be walking into another job soon enough, for sure.'

'If I wanted just to move to another damp factory, I could,' said Mattie. 'But I've been mulling it over and, no matter what Stan says, I'm sure the balloon's going up soon and if the men can do their bit for king and country, us women can too. I was only going to stay at Gold's until I got my Higher Certificate anyway but now I suppose I could use the opportunity of putting myself out of work by signing up for war work to give me some more experience.'

'And grand you'll be at it, I'm sure,' said

Queenie as they turned into Mafeking Terrace. 'But don't you go taking anything in a munitions factory, I've heard they're right dangerous. I heard some poor woman sneezed and blew her own head off.'

Mattie laughed. 'Don't worry, Gran. I'm not intending to walk out of one factory straight into another.'

Going down the narrow alley to the back of the house, she and Mattie went in through the open side gate. Yesterday's roast had been shoulder of lamb so tonight's supper was Irish stew and the smell of it filled the house.

Surprisingly, given that without fail Ida set the meal on the table each night as the six o'clock pips started, her daughter-in-law wasn't standing over the stove stirring the pots, nor was Jo laying the kitchen table.

She and Mattie exchanged a puzzled look.

'Only me and Gran,' Mattie called, shutting the door behind them.

'In here,' called her father from the main part of the house.

Shrugging off her coat, Queenie handed it to Mattie who hooked it with hers on the back of the door. They walked through to the back parlour. Ida, who was wearing her cooking apron, was sitting in her fireside chair clutching a handkerchief in her hand while Jo, still in her school uniform, was perched on the arm beside her and had a comforting hand on her mother's shoulder.

To Queenie's surprise, not only was her son home from work but so was her grandson Charlie. However, when she saw Stella Miggles hanging on his arm, Queenie's eyes narrowed and her thin lips pulled into a hard line.

'I'm glad you two are back,' said Charlie, as she and Mattie walked in. 'Cos we've got some news. We're–'

'Engaged,' cut in Stella, thrusting her left hand forward.

Queenie glanced at it and then back to the woman wearing it. 'Engaged, is it?'

'Yes, Gran,' said Charlie, looking at her expectantly.

'Is she in the family way then?' Queenie asked.

Jerimiah scowled and Ida shot Queenie a look that could have killed.

A red flush burst onto Stella's cheeks. 'No I'm not, Mrs Brogan.'

Charlie patted his new fiancée's hand. 'It's all right, luv, people are bound to ask.'

'Especially, as it's very sudden, Charlie,' said Mattie.

'It might seem that way, but truth is it's all very quick because...' Stella snuggled up closer to Charlie and looked adoringly up at him. 'Tell 'em, Charlie.'

Charlie looked at Queenie. 'It's because ... because I've signed up.' He smiled. 'What do you say to that, Gran?'

Queenie's gaze ran over her six-foot one grandson, from the tousled dark hair to his size eleven boots who, with his broad cheekbones and coal-black eyes, was so like his father at the same age it tugged at her heart every time she looked at him.

She drew a deep breath and was about to tell the great lummox exactly what she thought but then she caught Mattie's eye.

They exchanged a meaningful look and Queenie sighed.

Didn't she know well enough that men thought with their cods and it would seem Charlie was no exception. He would find out soon enough that the woman who was going to take his name was known to have had two trips already to Old Mother Connery in Ensign Street to get her out of a bit of trouble. It would serve no purpose other than to send him off to defend king and country unhappy and she wouldn't do that, not to her lovely boy.

Going over to him, Queenie stretched up and placed her gnarled hands on either side of his face. 'You're a good boy, Charlie,' she said, pulling his face down to hers and kissing his cheek. 'And, as I have been since the day I helped you into the world, I'm so very proud of you, me darling.'

'I'm guessing Mum wasn't too happy then to hear Charlie's news,' said Cathy as she poured tea into the row of cups on the counter.

'What, about the engagement or that he'd signed up?' asked Mattie, sliding a Ginger Nut onto each saucer.

'Both,' said Cathy.

'Well, she wasn't too happy about him getting hitched but cheered up a bit when she was told that Stella's father wouldn't give his consent so they'd have to wait until next year when she was twenty-one, but as to him signing up.' Mattie shook her head. 'She tried to put a brave face on it but, as soon as Charlie left, she was in tears.'

'I can imagine,' said Cathy. 'My heart leaps into my throat every time the postman shoves something through the letterbox thinking it might be Stan's call-up papers. Hopefully it'll all be over before the army get to him.'

Mattie didn't comment.

It was four days after Charlie dropped his double bombshell. She and Cathy were helping out at the Darby and Joan Club, which was held every Thursday lunchtime in the small church hall at the back of the building.

The hall had been built at the turn of the century and had green tiles halfway up the wall with cream emulsion above and a solid beamed ceiling. There were oblong windows on either side, covered by wire mesh on the outside to stop bricks or bottles from shattering the glass. As was evident from the pictures of Bible stories around the walls, it was where the Sunday school was held. The familiar pictures of Jesus turning water into wine, walking on water and divvying out bread and fish were all scenes Mattie remembered fondly from when she'd attended the weekly lessons. The large picture at the far end of the hall, however, was one she was less keen on. It featured a life-sized image of Jesus with his chest split open to reveal his bleeding heart dripping crimson blood and had been a recurrent image in many of her childhood nightmares.

The small infant chairs were now stacked in the corner and in their place were a dozen square tables, their surfaces bleached white from regular scrubbings with bleach. Around the tables sat elderly men in misshapen trousers, collarless shirts and wide braces accompanied by women wearing faded dresses, wrinkled lisle stockings and with their white hair scooped into various whirls and knots.

Like most of the churches in the area, St Bridget and St Brendan's ran a lunch club for the elderly members of the congregation. It gave the older parishioners a chance to get together for a hot meal and talk about how much better it used to be when they were young. They also liked to discuss who had been rushed into hospital and to compare the abundance, or otherwise, of the spreads at the funerals they'd recently attended.

Mattie and Cathy had cleared away the last of the pudding dishes ten minutes ago and were now behind the hatch in the kitchen pouring out the teas while they waited for Father Mahon to arrive and give them some wise words to ponder on in the coming week.

'Any chance of those teas, ducks,' shouted Micky Jarvis from the table nearest the hatch.

'Just coming, Mr Jarvis,' Mattie shouted back.

Lifting the tray full of cups and saucers, Mattie carried it through the door and into the hall.

''Bout time,' said Pat Gilbert, as Mattie set the tray down on the table. 'Me mouth's as dry as a nun's–'

'Help yourself to sugar,' Mattie cut in, placing a cup in front of each of the four old men sitting around the table.

Leaving them to stir their tea, Mattie headed back to the kitchen to reload the tray but, before she got there, one of the double doors at the other end of the hall swung open and Father McCree walked in.

Mattie's heart did a little double step at the sight of him. Unlike Father Mahon, who always wore his cassock, Father McCree wore an off-the-peg black suit with just his dog collar to indicate his calling, which meant his broad shoulders and the snug fit of his trousers were all too evident.

'Good afternoon,' he said, looking through his wire-rimmed spectacles at the assembled elderly of the parish and smiling warmly at them.

'Good afternoon, Father McCree,' the gathering replied.

His gaze reached Mattie and he stopped.

Something changed in his expression for a second, then his benevolent smile widened and he strolled over.

'And good afternoon to you too, Miss Brogan,' he said, stopping just in front of her. 'What a pleasant surprise.'

'And yourself, Father,' Mattie replied, avoiding his gaze, 'although we were expecting Father Mahon.'

'He was up half the night with his cough,' Father McCree replied. 'So I told him I'd talk to the club while he caught up on some shut-eye.'

'I'm surprised he didn't argue,' said Mattie.

'He did.' Father McCree winked. 'But I called for reinforcement in the shape of Mrs Dunn.'

Mattie laughed.

Father McCree joined in and then gave her a puzzled look. 'I hope you don't mind me asking, but why are you here serving tea in the church hall and not slaving over a sewing machine.'

'Well, as it happens slaving is the right word

because...' And Mattie told him about her argument with Mr Gold.

'Well, good for you,' he laughed when she'd finished. 'I wish I'd been there.'

'I'm glad you weren't,' Mattie replied. 'Or you'd have given me a dozen Hail Marys on the spot for my temper.'

Father McCree's rich laugh rolled over her again. 'I doubt it. But what are you going to do now?'

'I'm going to sign on for war work,' Mattie replied. 'In fact, I would have done so a couple of days ago but all the Civil Defence services are having a mock exercise this week so they've closed the recruiting office at the town hall until Monday but I'll be there first thing.'

'I'm sure they'll sign you up on the spot.' He rubbed his hands together. 'Well, I'd best do what I'm here for.'

'Me too,' said Mattie. 'I've got a pile of dishes in the sink that won't wash themselves.'

Dragging her eyes from him, Mattie turned away and, collecting a couple of stray pudding bowls as she passed, headed back to the kitchen where Cathy was already up to her elbows in the sink.

'Sorry,' she said, piling the used dessert dishes on the side ready for washing. 'I was just talking to Father McCree.'

'So I saw,' said Cathy, shaking the suds from a plate and stacking it on the rack. 'Although I'd say flirting with Father McCree is nearer the mark.'

'Cathy! I was doing no such thing.'

'If you say so,' her sister laughed.

Lowering her eyes, Mattie picked up a tea towel and took a wet plate. 'If you must know, he was telling me that Father Mahon's chest has been troubling him again.'

'Poor man,' said Cathy, taking another plate to drain.

Relieved that she'd managed to distract Cathy, Mattie started to dry another plate but her gaze drifted towards the open hatch.

Father McCree was standing with one hand in his pocket and a decided twinkle in his eye as he talked to the parish's older generation.

'Although life might seem uncertain, we should remember that.' He cast his gaze over the audience and then looked straight at her. 'Sometimes we find ourselves travelling down a road we didn't know was there.'

There were mutters of amen and nods of agreement.

Father McCree smiled and replied to a couple of comments. 'You're going to rub the pattern off those plates soon, Mattie,' said Cathy, cutting into her jumbled thoughts.

Stacking her dried plates on the pile, Mattie scooped them up and went over to the cupboard.

'I thought I might exchange these for a cup of tea if you have one, ladies,' said Fr McCree as he walked into the kitchen carrying a tray of used cups and saucers.

'Thank you, Father,' said Cathy, as he set it on the central table.

'This is my sister, Cathy,' said Mattie, smoothing the drying cloth around the inside of a cup.

'Yes, your mother mentioned she had another

daughter,' he said. 'I'm pleased to meet you at last.'

'Likewise, I'm sure,' Cathy replied, with a nervous smile. 'And I'm sorry I haven't been to mass as often as I should but my mother-in-law's in poor health and needs a lot of attention in the morning so I can only get away when my Stan gets back.'

Father McCree looked concerned. 'Would she like a priest to call?'

'She's C of E and not very religious,' said Cathy, looking a little awkward. 'But it's very kind of you to ask.'

He unhooked a tea towel from the side of the draining board. 'Let me help.'

Reaching across, he took a plate from the rack.

A faint smell of sandalwood drifted into Mattie's nose and her heart did a little flutter again.

'Someone was telling me that your husband is the chairman of the Britons for Peace Union, Mrs Wheeler,' said Father McCree as he dried the plate.

Cathy nodded. 'Yes. He says the war is a mistake and we should do everything we can to get the government to take Hitler's new offer seriously. There are about fifty of them in the branch now and they meet in the Catholic Club hall every Thursday.'

Father McCree put the plate on the pile and picked up another. 'He sounds very dedicated. Perhaps I'll drop in and say hello one night.'

'Ah, there you are, Father McCree,' said a woman's voice.

Mattie turned and saw Mrs Thorpe, the despot in charge of the church flower committee, standing in the doorway.

The wife of the local funeral director, Miriam Thorpe didn't have to work, so instead she poured her considerable energy into the church. Today she was wearing a tweed coat with a fox fur, complete with head and claws, around her shoulders and her steely manner suggested she was on a mission.

'Mrs Dunn said I'd find you here and...' Her gaze flickered onto the tea towel he was holding. 'What on earth are you doing?'

'Mrs Thorpe, how nice to see you,' said Father McCree, putting the dried plate on the top of the stack. 'And I'm wiping up. Now, what can I do for you?'

'It's the flowers for Sunday,' said Mrs Thorpe. 'Can you come and have a word with Mrs Cornwell about her display?'

'Of course,' said Father McCree, picking up a cup from the draining board. 'I'll be along presently.'

'It's rather urgent, Father McCree.'

He smiled coolly.

'I can't finish the display until...'

Father McCree's polite expression didn't waver.

Mrs Thorpe lowered her eyes. 'I'll wait for you in the church, Father.'

She hurried away.

He turned and offered Mattie his tea towel. 'I'm afraid duty calls.'

'I understand,' said Mattie. 'The Germans are one thing but the St Bridget and St Brendan's flower committee is another matter.'

As she took the towel from him, his fingers touched hers, sending a little fizz of excitement up her arm. His gaze searched her face for a moment and then he looked at Cathy.

'Nice to see you, Mrs Wheeler.'

'You too, Father,' Cathy replied.

Father McCree's dark eyes returned to Mattie's face. 'Will I see you on Sunday?'

'Yes. Yes, you will,' said Mattie, suddenly mesmerised by the shape of his mouth.

'Good. I look forward to it.'

Pushing his glasses up to the bridge of his nose with his index finger, Father McCree stared down at her for a couple of heartbeats, then he turned and walked out of the kitchen.

Mattie stood staring after him for a moment then, pulling herself together, she turned and smiled brightly at her sister.

'Right,' she said. 'What should I do? Get the cups from the hall or take out the swill bucket?'

An amused expression spread across Cathy's face and she raised an arched eyebrow. 'Find yourself a boyfriend.'

Two hours later, Daniel let himself back into the rectory. Although there was still another hour until the blackout came into force, he closed the heavy curtain around the door as he entered. As it was mid-afternoon, Mrs Dunn was out collecting the weekend meat from the butcher and picking up a fresh loaf from the baker for their Friday supper of scrambled egg.

Although the Friday menu was a little sparse,

Mrs Dunn, who was an excellent cook, managed to keep a very full table the rest of the week with a full-cooked breakfast each morning, a meat, and two veg dinner with lashings of gravy at midday and a hearty soup or hotpot for supper. Thankfully for his waistline, Daniel had found the St George's swimming bath, which was a short walk along the Highway. A dozen fast lengths three times a week had so far managed to keep his weight hovering around the twelve-stone mark. However, he was toying with the idea of dropping in on the Monday-night boxing club to pound the punchbag for an hour.

Shrugging off his coat, Daniel hooked it on the hallstand alongside Father Mahon's. He picked up the afternoon post from the hall table and thumbed through it. There was a postcard addressed to him with a picture of Ely Cathedral on it. He shoved it in his pocket and then walked through the house to the kitchen.

As always, the rectory's housekeeper had left a tray set out with a mug, sugar and a small jug of milk in case he or Father Mahon wanted tea. Lighting the gas under the kettle, Daniel opened the dresser cupboard and took out the tea caddy. Careful to avoid spilling leaves on Mrs Dunn's spotless work surface, Daniel added two generous spoonfuls into the small teapot, then popped the tin back.

Leaning back against the sink, Daniel took out the postcard and flipped it over.

Dear Daniel,
I hope you are well and are getting to know people

in your new post. Uncle Vernon and I look forward to hearing all about it soon. We are having a lovely time with the Worsleys but unfortunately Billy isn't any better and is confined to his room. Uncle Vernon is sure it won't interfere with your plans too much. I'm coming up to town on the first of next month and will be catching the 5.25 train from Waterloo, so perhaps we could meet for tea.

Love Aunt Fanny

'I thought I heard you come in!'

Thrusting the postcard into his jacket pocket, Daniel looked around and smiled. 'I was just making a cuppa, Father, would you like me to pour you one?'

'I would thank you greatly if you did, son,' said Father Mahon. 'And as herself isn't back yet, I'll have three sugars.'

Daniel laughed and the old priest joined in, setting off a bout of coughing.

'You get yourself back in the warm, Father, and I'll bring it through,' said Daniel.

Father Mahon nodded and shuffled out.

Daniel made the tea. He added a couple of Mrs Dunn's butter biscuits to the old man's saucer, then he left the kitchen.

Father Mahon was already sitting back in his easy chair next to the fire by the time Daniel entered his study. Putting their drinks down on the table beside the older man, Daniel went to the window and closed the blackout curtains.

Switching on the standard lamp behind Father Mahon's chair, Daniel picked up his tea and headed for the door.

'Won't you stay and keep me company for a bit, lad?' said Father Mahon.

'If I'm not intruding,' said Daniel, indicating the scribbled note for the coming Sunday's homily.

Father Mahon shook his head. 'No, you'd be doing me a kindness and you'll be better company than St Francis of Assisi.'

Daniel took the chair opposite.

'So,' said the good father as Daniel settled back. 'What have you been up to today?'

'I popped in to Mrs O'Conner this morning to see her new baby, then spent an hour or so with Mrs Morris,' he said.

'How is she?' asked Father Mahon.

'On the mend, although Mrs Morris still looks very pale,' Daniel replied. 'And then I prevented a murder in the church.'

'Mrs Riley?'

'She would have been the victim,' said Daniel. 'But you wouldn't need Miss Marple to sniff out the culprit as Mrs Thorpe's secateurs would probably be embedded in her chest.'

The old priest chuckled. 'I don't know why we're bothering sending our boys to fight the Germans when, to be sure, the flower committee of any church in the land could rout them.'

Daniel laughed. 'She found me in the church hall chatting to Miss Brogan and Mrs Wheeler.'

A fond smile spread across Father Mahon's wrinkled face. 'Such lovely girls.'

An image of Mattie's shapely legs flashed through Daniel's mind.

'They are,' he said.

'And the apples of their father's eye,' Father

Mahon continued. 'Have you met Jerimiah?'

'Yes a couple of times,' Daniel replied. 'Mostly in the bar at the Catholic Club.'

Actually, he'd run into Mattie's father the week after he'd arrived in the parish and although by his own admission Jerimiah Brogan had dipped out of school at twelve to help his father on the cart, after an in-depth conversation with him about the machination of Chamberlain's newly formed war cabinet, Daniel could see where Mattie and all the Brogans got their spark. Jerimiah also reminded him of someone but, although he'd met him several times since, he was still scratching his head to remember who.

'Well, the sisters were making short work of the washing up when I arrived.' He took a sip of tea. 'I understand Mrs Wheeler married outside the church.'

'Yes,' said Father Mahon. 'I had my misgivings, but her husband's a communicant at St Philip's and took full instructions and the oath to raise the children in the Catholic faith so I spoke to the bishop and he gave his permission.'

'He's Stanley Wheeler, isn't he?' said Daniel.

'That's him,' said Father Mahon. 'Runs that peace group, which is a bit of a surprise seeing what a ruffian he was.'

'Really?'

'Oh yes, forever in trouble with the police,' continued Father Mahon. 'But never so much that he found himself up before the beak like the rest of his gang but, since he's met Cathy, he seems to have settled down. I can't judge him too hard for weren't we all a bit of a handful before we learned to shave?'

Daniel smiled but didn't comment.

'Seems only the other day that Mattie, Cathy and young Jo were walking beside the statue of Our Lady in their white dresses and veils and now they're women full grown.'

'I'm surprised Mattie's not been snapped up by some young man before now,' said Daniel, before he could stop himself.

'So am I. She's had her share of likely fellas but … Mattie's set on making something of herself. I'll confess I have a bit of a soft spot for her as she reminds me of her grandmother at the same age.' A soft expression crept over the old priest's face. 'I can see young Queenie now, running barefoot through the long grass with the summer sun lighting her hair.'

'Were you her parish priest in Ireland then?'

Father Mahon laughed. 'No, my family lived two streets down from hers in Kinsale and we went to school together. She married Seamus Brogan a few months after I entered St Patrick's College in Thurles.'

Daniel smiled and tried to imagine Queenie Brogan, in her fur coat and battered hat, as a foot-loose young girl.

'And, as I say, Mattie is just like her,' continued Father Mahon. 'I just hope I'll still be around to marry her when she finally decides to settle down.'

An image of Mattie in a bridal gown started to form in Daniel's mind, but he forced himself back to the task at hand. War and romance didn't mix. He knew that but, troublingly, he needed to remind his heart of that fact again each time he ran into Mattie Brogan.

'And I think you'll all agree that Teddy here did a pretty good job in Old Montague Street last week,' said Stan.

Christopher, who was sitting in the place of honour at the top of the table beside the chairman, smiled politely as the men seated around the card table on the stage nodded their approval.

It was Thursday 6th October and somewhere close to ten o'clock in the evening and it was Christopher's first visit to the weekly meeting of the Stepney branch of the Britons for Peace Union.

The meeting had finished half an hour ago and had been particularly tedious. Hitler's new peace proposal, put to the government, had had them all flapping their hands like nuns in a knocking shop, after which there had been interminable discussions about strong-worded letters and getting signatures on some sort of petition to present to the prime minister. Anyway, the loonies and limp-wristed pansies had gone now, leaving Christopher to get on with the real business.

He, Stan and a handful of men were sitting behind the heavy velvet stage curtain in the main hall of the Catholic Club. Stan had referred to his so-called committee as 'his three musketeers' but, truthfully, with stubby necks, low brows and intellects to match, Christopher thought the three stooges would be closer to the mark. Not that it mattered, after all, *Kristallnacht* wouldn't have been as successful if Röhm hadn't recruited such men into his brown-shirted *Sturmabteilung.*

'You should have seen the old Jew-boy and his family carrying on as they watched their business go up in smoke,' said Teddy, a scruffy individual who by the look of his ink-blackened hands worked in a printers somewhere.

'Pity you didn't roast a couple of 'em,' said Roger Willis.

Teddy winked. 'Next time, mate.'

'So, Mr Joliffe,' said Harry Unwin, a bovine chap with deep-set eyes. 'What do you think of our little operation?'

'You have all done a grand job,' Christopher replied, casting them a benevolent smile as he took out another cigarette and lit it.

Stan puffed out his barrel chest. 'I'm glad them up top appreciate it. So what's next?'

'Well, firstly, let me give you this.' Delving into the pocket of his raincoat, which was draped over the back of his chair, Christopher pulled out a small book. 'It's *The Protocols of the Elders of Zion.*'

'I've heard of that,' Stan said.

'I should hope so,' Christopher replied, blowing a stream of smoke towards the stage lights above. 'It sets out clearly how the world's Jews are systematically plundering international finances and I expect you all to read it.'

The men around him, whose reading matter probably stretched no further than the racing and football results, regarded the slim volume unenthusiastically.

'Secondly, there's the matter of the call-up,' Christopher said.

There were grumbles of discontent.

'There are ways around it but it costs,' continued Christopher.

'How much?' asked Stan.

'Five guineas,' Christopher replied.

'Bugger that,' snorted a whey-faced man with a pockmarked face. 'I don't earn that in a bloody month.'

Christopher shrugged. 'It's up to you, but just tip me the wink and I'll point you in the right direction. Now, the Irish Republican bunch in Dublin have thrown their lot in with us and our German brothers and are sending one of their agents to join us soon.'

'What for?'

'He's going to be our contact with the Abwehr–'

'The who?'

'German intelligence, Fred,' said the man next to him. 'Don't you listen at meetings?'

'Not if I can help it,' Fred replied, his chair creaking as he leaned back on it.

The men sniggered.

'This is serious, you know,' Stan said, looking a little red around the collar. 'I don't want this IRA bloke to think we're a bunch of bloody idiots.'

Teddy shrugged. 'I don't give a bugger what this bog-trotter thinks, he's on our turf now and if he knows what's good for him he'll remember it.'

'And when's this Paddy arriving?' asked a thin-faced individual with a day's worth of stubble.

'Soon,' said Christopher, flicking ash on the floor.

'Well he'd better get his skates on,' said Teddy. 'Or the Germans will have landed and we won't–'

A plank squeaked to the right of the stage and

the scenery hangings fluttered.

Christopher gave them all a hard look and made a sharp, cutting movement across his throat with the flat of his hand.

The half a dozen men around him clamped their mouths together and fixed their eyes on the long stage curtains. The floor creaked again as a tall man wearing a dog collar strolled out from between the drapes.

'Evening, gentlemen,' he said, with a friendly smile.

Christopher smiled back. 'Evening, Father...?'

'McCree,' the priest replied. 'Father McCree. I'm helping Father Mahon out for a few months and I'm looking for Stan Wheeler.'

Stan rose to his feet. 'I'm Stan Wheeler.'

Father McCree strode forward and offered his hand. 'Well, hello and nice to meet you.'

Stan looked perplexed, but took it. 'And you, Father. My wife has mentioned you a couple of times.'

Father McCree smiled and, pushing his wire-rimmed glasses back on his nose, looked through them at Christopher.

'And you must be Christopher Joliffe,' he said, extending his hand in Christopher's direction.

Uncrossing his legs, Christopher rose slowly to his feet.

'I am,' he replied, shaking the priest's hand.

'Good to meet you, I met your wife the other day, too,' Daniel replied, gripping his hand firmly.

'I don't have a wife,' said Christopher.

'I met your wife the other day,' the priest repeated, looking expectantly at him. 'She'd got

117

caught in the rain!'

The men around the table shifted in their chairs.

Christopher stubbed out his cigarette in the overfilled ashtray in the middle of the table. 'Look, Father, I don't know what your game is, but–'

'I say: "I met your wife the other day and she'd got caught in the rain",' Father McCree cut in. And you're supposed to reply: "I told her to take her new umbrella." Do I have to spell it out?'

'Spell what out?' asked Christopher, feeling as if he had missed something along the line.

Father McCree looked Heavenward and the light from above reflected on his spectacles. 'For the love of Mary, I'm your bloody contact.'

The men around the table stared dumbly at him.

Christopher's mouth pulled into a hard line. 'That's not the password.'

'My people told me to give you the whole "wife in the rain" story,' Father McCree shrugged. 'If your superiors haven't passed it on to you then we're not going to get very far, are we?'

'No, you're not,' said Christopher.

Chairs scraped back as the men around the table stood up and crowded around Daniel. Roger grabbed the priest's arms and pinned them behind him while the pox-scarred individual drew a short-bladed knife.

'Shall I gut him?' he asked, jabbing the point into Daniel's throat.

Despite the blade at his windpipe, Father McCree looked coolly past his assailant at Christopher. 'Now, killing me isn't really the brightest idea, is it? Apart from having to make sure the blood's scrubbed off the floorboards before the Mothers' Union meeting starts in the morning and disposing of a body, how do you think Admiral Canaris and Mosley are going to react if, after months of careful planning to get me here, you slit the throat of their ally's go-between? And all because either Jock Houston forgot to tell you or you got so drunk at Sir Oswald's little soirée in Conway Hall a month ago that you can't remember it. Plus, who do you think Tom Barry, my chief in Dublin, will blame when his radio operator is found floating face down in the river?'

All eyes shifted from the priest onto Christopher, who chewed the inside of his mouth.

Jock had babbled on about passwords at the meeting but, as the countess had had her hand on his cock at the time, he'd had other things on his mind. And if this Father McCree was who he said he was, then Christopher's career in the Right Club and the British Union of Fascists would be finished before it started, not to mention what Himmler and the SS would do to him when they arrived. Add to which, none of those Jew-loving nancys at MI5 had the balls to just stroll in like this bugger had, so he must be the IRA contact.

The church clock across the road started to chime out the hour.

'Let him go,' Christopher said.

Roger, who was holding the knife to Father McCree's throat, didn't move.

'But what if he's from MI5–'

'I said, let him go,' Christopher repeated.

Roger gave him a grudging look and relinquished his hold on the priest.

Father McCree brushed down his lapels. Taking a chair from the pile stacked in the wings, he placed it so the back was facing them.

'Now we're all acquainted,' he said, swinging his leg over the chair and sitting astride it. 'Perhaps we can get down to some serious business.'

The men looked uncertainly at each other, then resumed their seats around the table.

Kicking his chair back, Christopher did the same. Shooting the newcomer a belligerent look, he took a packet of Rothmans from his pocket and lit a cigarette.

'Right, firstly, let me say I've been told to pass on German High Command's congratulations and thanks for the grand job you boys have been doing,' said Father McCree. 'But now they want you to help them in other ways.' Putting his hand in his pocket, Father McCree pulled out four sheets of paper and spread them on the table in front of them. 'As you can see, this is a map of East London which I've divided into quarters. German Intelligence wants you to choose one of the areas and mark up all the gas works, electricity substation grids and water pumping stations, plus all the rail lines and stations.'

Christopher's mouth pulled into a hard line.

'Well, McCree, you seem to have it all figured out,' said Christopher, blowing a stream of smoke skywards.

'Not me, German Intelligence,' the priest replied pleasantly. 'I'm just passing on the message.'

With some difficulty Christopher forced himself to hold the priest's hard gaze for a second.

'Anything else,' he asked, making a play of

stubbing out his half-smoked cigarette in the overspilling ashtray in front of him.

'Yes,' said Father McCree. 'They want you to find out about the Civil Defence preparations in the area.'

'And how am I supposed to do that?' Christopher asked, putting another cigarette in his mouth and lighting it. 'I work in a bank.'

'I know,' the priest replied, with more than a hint of amusement. 'But you could volunteer like thousands of others. I'd suggest the police force. I understand they're looking for auxiliary officers.'

'Are they?'

'So I hear,' replied Father McCree.

'Anything else you want us to do?' asked Christopher.

'Not at the moment, but...' Father McCree glanced over his shoulder and leaned across the table. 'I don't have to tell a bright bunch of fellas like you that things are starting to get dangerous.'

'Yeah, for the stinking Yids,' said Roger.

The others sniggered their agreement.

'And us if we don't tread carefully,' the priest said. 'Especially you, Stan.'

'Me?' Stan's heavy features pulled into a disgruntled expression. 'I hope you ain't saying I'm some sort of squealer–'

'Because I'm your wife's priest and we're likely to run into each other from time to time,' Father McCree replied, as if explaining to a five-year old why he should eat his greens.

'Oh yes,' said Stan. 'It goes without saying.'

'Well, I'm saying it nonetheless so there's no misunderstanding.' Father McCree stood up and

121

turned to Christopher. 'Can I have a word?' he asked, cocking his head towards the stage stairs.

Christopher rose to his feet and followed the priest as he slipped between the curtains and trotted down the side steps of the stage to the back of the hall.

'So you're the man in charge, are you?' Father McCree asked, as Christopher stopped beside him.

Christopher raised his head and smoothed back his hair. 'Yes I am.'

'Well it's bloody lucky for you I wasn't MI5, isn't it?'

'Well, I–'

'My commander in Dublin told me that I was to assist a group of highly disciplined British patriots,' cut in the priest. 'Instead I find a bunch of idiots who are supposed to be mild-mannered pacifists behaving like extras in a gangster movie and shouting their mouths off so loudly I'm surprised the desk sergeant in Wapping police station couldn't hear you.'

Biting back the urge to smash the jumped-up Mick in the face, Christopher forced a laugh. 'The boys were in high spirits–'

'Now, you listen to me,' Father McCree cut in, jabbing his finger at him. 'I don't like you or what you fascists stand for, but the Ruling Council in Dublin has decreed that we are in alliance with Nazi Germany and that's why I'm here, but I'll tell you this. My fellow countrymen have bled and died since 1690 in order to wrest Ireland from the grasp of the English bastards. The conquest of Britain by Germany is the best chance we've had

122

in two hundred and fifty years to do that and I'm not letting you or your bunch of brainless gorillas sabotage that. Do you understand?'

Christopher tried to reply, but the priest's flint-like stare stopped his words.

He nodded.

'Good,' said Father McCree. 'I'll be back when I get further orders.'

He turned to leave, but Christopher caught his arm. 'What if I need to speak to you?'

Repositioning his spectacles back on the bridge of his nose, Father McCree smiled. 'My dear chap. I am a priest, am I not? So feel free to drop into St Bridget and St Brendan's at any time.'

Casting another scornful glance over Christopher, Father McCree opened the hall door and left.

Christopher stared blindly at the door for a long moment as he struggled to control the surge of fury threatening to engulf him then, taking a deep breath, he turned and retraced his steps back to the stage where Stan and his men were still sitting around the table.

'Cor, he was a bit hard, for a priest I mean,' said Stan, as Christopher re-emerged from behind the curtains. 'I thought they were supposed to be meek and mild buggers, not bloody bruisers.'

'Yeah,' agreed Roger. 'I wouldn't want to get on the wrong side of him.'

Grabbing his packet of Rothmans from the table where he'd left them, Christopher took out a fresh cigarette. Putting it between his lips, he took his lighter from his pocket.

'Don't you worry, chaps.' Holding the flame to

the end of the cigarette and hoping only he could see it trembling, Christopher inhaled. 'I told him straight I wouldn't put up with him coming in here throwing his weight around, and if he wants to live a long and happy life he'll have to watch his bog-trotting step.'

Chapter Five

The wind passing through the wire mesh of the barrage balloon above made a low humming noise as Mattie shook out her umbrella and trotted up the half dozen steps leading to the main entrance of Stepney town hall.

The late-Victorian building with its grand façade of mock classical columns leading into the illuminated front foyer was the hub of the council's business for the borough. That was until war was declared. Now the whole of the ground floor, basement and the yard at the back had been given over to Civil Defence. In addition, as with every other building in the area, the ornate iron railings outside had been removed already to be melted down for ammunitions, the windows had been criss-crossed with glued paper to prevent flying glass in the event of a bomb explosion and sandbags were piled up against the lower windows and doors.

It had been a whole week since she'd stormed out of Gold & Sons and Mattie was anxious to find work again; her mum had made it clear that she needed to pay her way. As a scrap metal and general goods dealer her father's income had always been uncertain, but the family's weekly income had been squeezed further by the newly introduced Price of Goods Act, which meant he could only sell to a government-licensed dealer at a fixed price. As a cleaner, her mother's wage was constant but it was pitiably low and was being stretched by rocketing food prices.

A man in a grey boiler suit and wearing a tin helmet walked out as Mattie reached the top step.

'There you go, luv,' he said, holding the door open for her.

'Thank you,' said Mattie, noticing the letters ARP stitched in red on the breast pocket of his overalls. 'Can you tell me where I sign up for war work?'

'Straight down to the green door on the right,' he replied.

'Thanks again,' said Mattie as he carried on his way.

Unlike the outside of the town hall, which was a stone homage to the glories of the classical age, the inside of the building reflected the Victorians' love of all things medieval. Every glazed door and skylight had stained-glass motifs of heraldic symbols and in every alcove there was a pedestal displaying a statue of either a knight or a fair damsel. The entrance area was dominated by the two sweeping stone staircases.

Walking across the floor with its mosaic of St George slaying a fire-breathing dragon, Mattie headed down the main corridor. Behind the curved mahogany reception desk to her right were

125

a couple of women in the distinctive forest green uniform of the Women's Voluntary Service. One of the women was showing a mother how to fit her baby with a new cocoon-like infant gas mask, while on the long bench against the opposite wall, three lads, the PM on their armbands indicating that they were police messengers, lounged about smoking.

Side-stepping the group of workmen loading the council's ceremonial silverware into straw-filled tea chests, Mattie reached the green door, turned the handle and entered.

Sitting behind a long table at one end of the room was a middle-aged woman and two men in grey suits, who Mattie guessed were the Civil Defence recruiting officers. Against the wall was a row of filing cabinets, above which an enormous map, covered with coloured markers, had been pinned.

Even though it was only just 9 o'clock, the three rows of seats were already half full of people waiting to be interviewed. Tucking her skirts beneath her, Mattie took the third chair in the first row and crossed her legs. One of the volunteers who had completed their interview stood up to leave and the woman behind Mattie left her seat and walked towards the recruiting officers.

A couple of people arrived and sat down while others were called forward. Mattie was next but one in the queue when she noticed the door open and a young man, wearing an expensive-looking suit and club tie, strolled in.

Slim and with very blond hair and clear blue eyes, he glanced around the room. Spotting

Mattie, he took the chair next to hers.

'Is this where we volunteer for war work?' he whispered.

'Yes it is,' Mattie replied.

He gave her a little smile and she looked ahead again.

'These are a bit of a nuisance to carry around, aren't they?' the young man beside her said, indicating the brown cardboard box sitting on his knee.

'Yes, they are,' Mattie replied. 'And I've noticed that a lot of people don't bother carrying them around any more.'

'I know,' he replied. 'But I suppose we'll be glad we've got them if the Germans do gas us.'

Another interviewee left and the woman behind the recruitment desk called 'next' and a thick-set man with badly nicotine-stained fingers ambled up to the counter.

'Been waiting long?' the young man asked.

'About fifteen minutes,' Mattie replied

'Next,' bellowed the middle-aged woman from the far end of the room.

Mattie stood up. 'That's me. Nice to meet you.'

'And you.' He offered her his hand. 'Christopher Joliffe.'

She took it. 'Mattie Brogan.'

Giving him a quick smile and hooking her gas mask over her shoulder, Mattie stepped forward.

'Take a seat, miss,' said the middle-aged grey-haired woman.

Smoothing her skirt under her, Mattie sat down.

The woman smiled. 'I'm Miss Lewis, the deputy recruiting officer for the Stepney, Wapping and

Limehouse Civil Defence zone and you are?'

'Mattie Brogan.'

'Which is short for...?'

'Matilda Mary.'

Dipping her nib in the inkwell, Miss Lewis started writing. 'Now, if I can take a few more particulars...'

Having made a note of Mattie's address, date of birth, marital status and employment history, Miss Lewis turned to the column headed educational attainment and, without asking, scratched a line across it.

'I've actually passed my school certificate examination,' said Mattie.

The woman's substantial eyebrows rose. 'Have you?'

'Yes,' Mattie replied. 'I passed with a distinction and I'm just starting my higher school examination which I'm hoping to take next May.'

Miss Lewis looked impressed and made a note of it. 'So, Miss Brogan,' she said, looking up again. 'What sort of work are you looking for?'

'Something full time and paid,' Mattie replied. 'I'm able to start immediately.'

Picking up the clipboard alongside her, Miss Lewis scanned down it. 'Well, they are looking for assembly workers in Tyler's Metal in Silvertown for 6d a day and they need packers at Canning Town munitions works. That one pays £1 15s a week for a fifty-two hour week for twelve hours on and twelve off.'

'I was hoping for something more directly to do with the war effort,' said Mattie.

'You could sign up,' said Miss Lewis.

'I've thought of that,' said Mattie. 'But my brother's just enlisted and my mother would skin me alive if I did too.'

'Can you drive?'

Mattie shook her head.

'Pity,' said Miss Lewis. 'They're looking for tanker drivers at the fuel depot in Hackney.'

'What about the ambulance or fire service?' asked Mattie.

'Again, if you could drive we could slot you into the ambulance service but, other than drivers, all they're asking for at the moment is part-time volunteers,' said Miss Lewis. 'Even the police force only want women for clerical work and to answer the telephone but, again, it's on an unpaid basis.'

'Surely there must be something other than factory work,' said Mattie.

'Well, there is something,' Miss Lewis said, scanning the list again. 'You're a bit young and it's a lot of responsibility, but...'

'What is it?'

'There's a full-time air-raid warden needed for part of the North Ratcliffe Ward. It's £2 a week with an extra 3d a day when you're on night duty. It covers from Sutton Street along the Commercial Road to Butcher Row and then back along Brook Street. The air-raid precaution controller has included a dozen residential streets, the public baths, two halls, a dozen public houses and both the Methodist chapel and the Roman Catholic church, rectory and social club in the list of the area. Plus the Tilbury to Minories railway runs right through it so it's likely to be targeted when the bombing starts,' said Miss Lewis. 'I don't know the area myself, but–'

'I do,' interrupted Mattie. 'In fact, I know it like the back of my hand. It's just a walk away from where I live and I went to Highway School, which is in the middle of that area.'

'It's long hours, often at night, and you'll have to do a lot of training.'

'I don't mind,' said Mattie, eagerly. 'The training, I mean, or the long hours and I'm willing to learn.'

The recruitment officer didn't look convinced. 'We were looking for someone with experience–'

'I've got as much experience of war as most of the people you'll interview today, Miss Lewis, don't you think?' Mattie cut in, looking the older woman squarely in the eyes.

The elderly woman opposite her considered her for a moment, then her managerial expression softened. 'Well, I suppose we could give you a try.'

She took a card and a form from the stationery rack between her and her fellow officer and, after scribbling in the boxes, handed it to Mattie. 'Use the table at the back and fill this in, then drop it in over there.' She pointed at a box at the end of the counter with 'Applications' stencilled on it. 'And then take this form down to the control room below and they will tell you what to do next.'

Taking the form and card, Mattie stood up. 'Thank you so much, Miss Lewis, for giving me the chance.'

'My pleasure, Miss Brogan.' The older woman gave a sad smile. 'As you say. This is a new experience for all of us.'

Two hours later, having filled in the application form, and been allocated a start date, Mattie strolled home and let herself into the house by the back door just as the first spots of rain, which had been threatening to drench her all the way home, landed on the paving stones in the back yard.

Closing the door on the storm, Mattie lit the gas under the kettle, then went over to the kitchen dresser to find her mug with the transfer of a bouquet of pink and blue flowers on the side for her much-needed cup of tea.

Like every other stick of furniture in the house, the dresser on which her mother stored her mismatched crockery was something Jerimiah had collected on his rounds.

After fixing the broken drawer, replacing the brass handles and the missing panel at the back, Jerimiah had painted the dresser white and now it looked as good as new. He'd never said where he'd got it but it must have been from a well-to-do household as it only just fitted against the far wall of their small kitchen. This meant that you had to turn sideways to get into the larder.

As always, her gran had left the kindling ready in the grate so, while the kettle boiled, Mattie lit the fire. By the time the kettle whistled, the room was beginning to warm. Mattie made her tea, grabbed a couple of Digestives and took them through to the parlour. Switching on the wireless, she sank into her mother's chair and put her feet up on the pouffe. Cradling her cup in both hands, Mattie let her head drop back and she closed her eyes as the strains of the BBC Light

Orchestra soothed her.

She must have dozed off for a few minutes because she woke with a start as the back door opened.

'Anyone home?' called her gran.

'Just me,' Mattie called back.

Finishing off her now lukewarm tea, she swung her legs down, stood up and carried her empty cup into the kitchen. Queenie had already shed her fur coat and had hooked it on the back of the door; she was now standing in front of the glowing fire.

'Hello, Gran. I'm making another, do you want one?' Mattie asked, holding up her empty cup.

'I could murder for one,' Queenie replied, blowing on her hands and rubbing them together. 'It's fierce weather out there.'

'I just missed it,' said Mattie, adding another spoonful of tea to boost the pot.

'How did you get on?' her gran asked.

Mattie told her about signing on as an ARP warden while she made the tea.

'Stan's gone off to one of his meetings so I think Cathy's coming over later,' said Mattie, popping the cosy on the pot to let it brew.

Putting the plug in, she poured the rest of the boiled water into the sink. Reaching into the earthenware pot on the windowsill, Mattie grabbed a handful of grated carbolic soap and threw it in the steaming water, then she placed the used crockery her mother had left on the draining board into the sudsy water.

'Meeting!' Queenie pulled a face. 'Thinks too much of himself by half does that one.'

'Stan's a bit slow on the uptake sometimes but he's not that bad,' said Mattie. And he thinks the world of Cathy.'

'So he should. She's a darling girl and too good for the likes of him. I don't like the shape of his head.'

'Oh, Gran,' laughed Mattie. 'Say what you like but Cathy's happy with him and I just hope that, one day, I'll find someone who thinks the world of me, too.'

'You will,' said Queenie, softly.

Mattie looked round. Her grandmother had picked up the mug of tea that Mattie had just drained and was holding it up towards the light so she could peer inside at the tea leaves left behind.

'In fact, he's already here,' continued Queenie in a voice that sent a chill up Mattie's spine.

'If you're trying to get me to give Micky another chance like Mum, then–'

'No, it's not Micky, it never was,' said Queenie, turning the cup on its side. 'But I can't see your man clearly. It's as if he's there but not.'

'Well, when he comes out from behind the tea leaves and makes himself known, I'll give him due consideration, Gran. Until then, perhaps I'd better get on with making the tea.' She held out her hand and Queenie handed over the cup.

A knowing look crept into her gran's eyes. She opened her mouth to say something, but thought better of it and stood up.

'The tea leaves never lie, me darling.' Placing her gnarled hand on Mattie's arm, she squeezed gently. 'If I don't take these boots off, me feet will

133

take root so I'd be obliged if you could bring my tea through when you're done.'

Mattie smiled and exchanged a fond look with her gran before the old woman ambled off to the parlour.

Mattie took the front half of her father's vest, which was now the washing rag, from the nail above the sink, then plunged her arms into the warm water.

She laughed quietly.

The tea leaves might not lie but they weren't always that clear either. How can the love of her life be there but not there? A chill ran up Mattie's spine again and she shivered.

She stared blankly at the blackout curtain for a second, then pulled her mind back from its futile wandering and swilled the cloth over the first plate.

For goodness sake, Matilda Mary Brogan! She shook off the bubbles and stacked it on the draining board. You'll be seeing blooming leprechauns next.

Chapter Six

'And finally this, as you can see, ladies and gentlemen, is the Wapping Area Reporting and Control room,' said Mr Granger, the area controller.

It was just before twelve on the third Monday in October and Mattie was attending her Civil Defence introduction day at the town hall. She and the half a dozen newly selected Civil Defence novices walked into the basement of the town hall.

Mr Granger was a rotund man in his late fifties with thinning light brown hair and a ruddy complexion. Until the Germans moved into Poland he'd been the council's senior clerk but now his role had changed from overseeing the council's roads, housing and schools to organising the means by which to defend them.

He was dressed in a navy military-style jacket with a wide white stripe on the left upper arm that denoted his Civil Defence rank.

It was now somewhere close to midday and Mattie's stomach threatened to rumble again. She'd arrived at 8.46, a quarter of an hour before she had to report for duty, but other than a quick cup of tea at 10.30 she'd had nothing since breakfast. Thankfully, having suffered a morning of mind- and bum-numbing talks from the local police commander, the Civil Defence area chief, an ex-brigadier with a handlebar moustache and an inability to pronounce his 'r's properly, followed by the heads of the fire, ambulance and gas decontamination services, the tour of the control centre was the last thing on the list before a much-needed midday break.

'As you can see,' continued Mr Granger, with a sweep of his arm, 'on this wall we have a map of the whole area on which are plotted all the air-raid shelters, first aid and information posts along with the fire and rescue detachments, which you will notice are at regular points so that every citizen can report an incident or casualty as soon as possible.'

Mattie and those around her duly studied the map which was covered with coloured pins with thread strung between them.

'And over here...' All of them turned their heads towards the dozen or so blackboards covered with neat rows of stencilled letters. 'You will see we have every road and street listed alphabetically under the senior ARP warden's name with the name of the local full-time warden's name and their part-time street warden written alongside.'

Mattie ran her eyes over the array of place names and was caught somewhere between alarm and excitement to see M Brogan had already been painted next to a great number of them.

'And, finally, this is the messaging centre.' He walked forwards to where four young women in civilian clothes were seated in front of a bank of telephone exchanges. 'This is the nerve centre of the whole area's Civil Defence. As soon as an incident is reported, either by telephone or by one of your ARP station messengers, these lovely ladies will immediately pass on the details to the senior controller on duty who will, in turn, dispatch the required service.' He cast a cool eye over Mattie and her fellow Civil Defence trainees. 'Are there any questions?'

The young man standing to Mattie's right raised his hand.

Mr Granger smiled graciously at him. 'Yes?'

'There's a couple of us here who are full-time air-raid wardens, so how long am I expected to be on shift and who covers when I'm not?'

'Like the control room, you will be expected to be on duty for a ten-hour shift, including night

136

duties, for five days a week. You will also be required to do additional duties when necessary. It will be on a rota basis which your supervising warden will give you when you report to the Civil defence depot.'

A well-made-up blonde wearing a pair of tight-fitting trousers and uncomfortable-looking high heels put her hand up.

Mr Granger turned his attention to her. 'Yes, Miss...?'

'Blewit,' she replied. 'Patricia Blewit, but everyone calls me Trixie.'

'Well, Trixie,' the controller replied, 'What would you like to ask me?'

'When do we get paid?'

The group gave a polite laugh which Mr Granger joined in with.

'You collect your wages every Thursday from the cashier's office on the second floor, my dear,' he replied, giving the young woman a boyish smile.

'Thank you, Mr Granger,' said Trixie.

The controller looked at the group again. 'Anything else?' Everyone shook their heads. 'Then I think it must be dinnertime.'

There was collective sigh of relief which Mattie and her grumbling stomach whole-heartedly agreed with.

An hour later, sitting in a corner of the town hall's overcrowded first-floor canteen, Mattie popped the last portion of sponge pudding in her mouth and turned the page of the book which she'd propped against her glass on the table in front of her.

'Hello again.'

Mattie looked up.

Standing next to her, wearing a similar navy jacket to Mr Granger and holding a tray, was the young man she'd met at the recruiting office.

'Hello.' She smiled. 'It's Colin, isn't it?'

'Christopher,' he replied. 'And you're Mattie. Mind if I join you?'

'No, of course not.'

She closed her book and he set his tray down and took the seat opposite.

'I see you've plumped for the steak and kidney pie and crumble,' said Mattie as he sprinkled salt on his dinner.

'I did. What about you?'

'The same but with jam roly-poly and custard,' Mattie replied.

'So I'm guessing, as you're wearing a navy uniform and have a tin helmet with ARP painted on the front, you're an air-raid warden somewhere,' he said, spearing a chunk of potato.

'For the North Ratcliffe Ward, God help them,' she said. And I'm guessing from your white armband with APS stencilled on it that you're working with the police.'

'Yes indeed. Christopher Herman Joliffe, auxiliary police constable reporting for duty.' He saluted. 'All I need to do is get my bearings so I don't get lost when I'm out on patrol as I can't very well ask a policeman if I do.'

Mattie laughed. 'I suppose I should be thankful then that I know my area pretty well, unlike a couple in the group with me who have been allocated areas miles away from where they live.'

'So you're one of the new recruits in today.'

'Yes, there are eight of us,' said Mattie.

'Where are they now?'

'A couple of the chaps have gone for a swift half around the corner while a few of the girls have popped down the market and Miss Blewit is over there.' Mattie nodded towards the corner table where Trixie and the controller were sitting. 'With her new friend.'

'Your book?' He turned his head and read the cover. *'No Other Man.'*

'It's my sister's,' said Mattie. 'I'm more of a Georgette Heyer fan, really, but I'm studying *The Woodlanders* in English classes at night school so needed some light relief.'

Christopher pulled a face. 'I did Thomas Hardy for my higher cert so know what you mean.'

'What do you do now?' asked Mattie.

'I've just been promoted to deputy head of Credit and Mortgages at the City and Country Bank on Commercial Road,' he said. 'I started five weeks ago. They, like everyone else, are keen to support the war effort so have offered all employees the chance to volunteer for part-time Civil Defence duties.'

He smiled and Mattie smiled back.

Out of the corner of her eye she saw Mr Granger stand up and she glanced at her watch.

'I ought to get back,' said Mattie, gathering her dirty crockery together.

'Leave it,' Christopher said. 'I'll take it back with mine.'

'Are you sure?'

'Of course, it's no trouble. I don't have to be

back at Bow Station for another hour.'

'Thanks.' Mattie stood up. 'And good luck with–'

'Look.' He shifted forwards in his chair. 'I hope you don't think I'm being too forward but now they've reopened the flicks they're showing that new film, *The Lion Has Wings,* at the Odeon this week, so what about I take you? Shall we say Friday at seven-fifteen outside the cinema at Mile End?'

Mattie cast her eyes over him.

Although he wasn't as tall as Father McCree and his jaw was not quite as square, with his wavy blond hair and clear blue eyes, Christopher was really quite handsome.

She stood up and hooked her gas mask over her shoulder. 'Thank you, Christopher. That would be lovely.'

Some hours later, Christopher scribbled in his police notebook as he sat at the corner table in Bow Road police station's third-floor canteen:

Fire Station for the St George's section located at the west end of Cable Street.

With bottle-green tiles halfway up the wall and cream emulsion above, it was very much like every other canteen he'd ever been in except it was populated by loud, beefy policemen, which, given that he'd been forced to join their number in order to gather details of the local Civil Defence capability and installations so that bastard McCree could send them back to Abwehr headquarters in

140

Berlin, was more than a little troubling. He'd toyed with complaining about the Irishman's high-handedness to Drummond, but thought better of it. Having just gained the trust of the leaders in the British Council for Christian Settlement in Europe he didn't want to scupper his chances of moving up their ranks by refusing to carry out a direct order from German Intelligence. Besides, he'd be robbing himself of the enjoyment of paying the priest back in kind, which he'd sworn to do.

It was also some six hours after meeting that pretty ARP warden again at the town hall and she'd agreed to a date which took away some of the sting of having to trudge around the streets all afternoon.

Actually, he'd been oddly happy to see her. He was puzzled by this until it dawned on him that, unlike most women he ran into who he instantly forgot about as soon as they were out of his eyeline, he'd realised that he'd been thinking about her quite a bit, even when he'd been studying the centrefold of his new *Eyeful* magazine.

He'd just crossed the last 't' when the chair opposite him was pulled out and Sergeant Evans, A Relief's section sergeant, sat down.

Christopher went to stand up, but his senior officer waved him down.

'As you were,' he said, undoing a couple of buttons on his tunic for comfort.

'You look wet through, constable,' said the sergeant, taking out a packet of Players and offering him a cigarette.

Christopher took one. 'I was in Roman Road when the heavens opened an hour ago.'

Sergeant Evans shook his head dolefully. 'A good policeman never gets wet.'

'Doesn't he?'

'No, the first rule of policing is that a good policeman knows every hidey-hole. The second thing you should always know is when there's a cuppa being brewed,' said the sergeant, flicking a flame with his lighter and drawing on his cigarette. 'There are some other things about being a proper copper and I'll tell you them as you go on but, needless to say, you won't find any of them written in Police Orders.' He blew a stream of smoke towards the refectory's nicotine-stained ceiling. 'How are you getting on?'

'Not too bad,' Christopher replied, lighting his cigarette.

Taffy Evans was a ruddy man with closely clipped sandy-coloured hair. He was nearer fifty than forty and he had been a sergeant in the redbrick Victorian police station located on Bow Road for twenty years. Because of his extensive knowledge of the area and its villains, the superintendent had tasked Taffy to keep the volunteer auxiliary police officers, like Christopher, in check and out of trouble.

'So,' said Sergeant Evans. 'What have you been up to?'

Christopher turned back a couple of pages in his notebook and ran through the local riffraff and old ladies worried about Nazis under their bed he'd spoken to that afternoon.

'And, lastly,' he said, as he got to the bottom of the second page, 'I advised a Mr Gower who lives in Antill Road to make sure he fixes a proper handle on the inside of the door to his Anderson Shelter so he doesn't get himself trapped again.'

'Well done,' said Taffy Evans. 'I wish some of my regular men put themselves around as much.' His gaze flickered onto the notebook in front of Christopher. 'Although you are a one for taking notes, aren't you now?'

Christopher smiled. 'Well, as I'm new to the area and the force, I thought I'd jot stuff down until I got a better feel of things.'

'I'm a bit of a "learn it as you go" sort of chap,' said Sergeant Evans. 'But I suppose in your case it makes sense.'

'I was the same at school,' continued Christopher, 'always writing things down.'

'Ah well,' said the sergeant, leaning back and making his chair creak. 'I suppose it takes all sorts to make a world.'

'True,' said Christopher. 'And ... and...'

'Go on, boy, spit it out.'

'And I just want to thank you for helping me to find my feet,' said Christopher. 'I mean, supporting you boys in blue as a volunteer auxiliary officer is a world away from what I do each day in the bank.'

Sergeant Evan's heavy features lifted in a benevolent smile. 'That's all right.' He winked. 'You just stick by me and you won't go far wrong.'

Christopher closed his notebook. 'I'm due to book off soon, sarge, but is there anything you want me to do?'

'Well there is a kindness you could do me before you go.' Taffy grinned and patted his dome-like stomach. 'Ask Mavis behind the counter to dish me up some pie and two veg and fetch it over.'

Christopher nodded. 'Of course, and I'll see you on Wednesday.'

'You certainly will, boy.'

Rising to his feet, Christopher turned to leave.

'But mark you, now.'

Christopher turned back.

'You keep tight hold on those notes of yours,' said the sergeant, stubbing out his spent cigarette. ''Cause those Nazi bastards would give their Hitler-saluting right arms to get hold of that sort of information.'

Christopher smiled and continued on his way.

With the evening fog swirling around her legs and clogging her nose, Mattie placed her hand on the metal plate and pushed open the door of the Empress Fish Bar at the west end of Cable Street.

'Evening, Mr Fabrino,' she called across to Francesca's father, Enrico, who was standing behind the counter.

It was his grandfather, Alfonso Mario Enrico Fabrino, who had opened the chip shop the same year that Queen Victoria was made Empress of India. Hence the shop's name and the faded portrait of the monarch on the wall behind the counter.

The interior of the shop had white tiles to halfway up the walls, industrial lino covered the floor and the curved glass-screen fryer with a marble counter was situated to the right of the door. On the large wall opposite the entrance were three paintings of the Arno, Uffizi Palace and the Ponte Vecchio in Florence, where the Fabrino family originated. All three paintings were set within a classical oval frame and had been skilfully executed by Giovanni Fabrino, Francesca's older brother. As it was Monday there were only a few customers in the shop so there was only Enrico serving behind the counter. He looked up and a smile lifted his thin face.

Enrico Fabrino was no more than five foot nine, with sallow skin and thinning grey hair. Although he was probably a year or two younger than her father, he looked ten years older. He'd always been slight but losing Francesca's mother, Rosa, some six years ago had stripped the flesh from his bones.

'Watcha, Mattie,' he called out as he wrapped a customer's fish supper in newspaper. 'How's your family?'

'Very well, thank you for asking,' said Mattie. 'Is Francesca out the back?'

Enrico nodded.

'Go through,' he said, plunging a long metal utensil into the boiling fat to agitate the sizzling chips. 'And say hello to your parents from me.'

Slipping through the narrow gap at the far end of the counter, Mattie moved the curtain aside and went through to the back of the shop.

The Fabrinos' living quarters comprised a parlour immediately behind the shop. This was where the family spent their time when the shop was closed. It was a reasonable-sized room with a large cast-iron range that Francesca lit each morning and which supplied the family with the almost unheard-of luxury of hot water on tap and made the room warm and snug. Grandpa Alfonso's sofa and chairs were still used but Francesca had softened the old-fashioned Victorian oak furniture with chintz curtains and colourful cushion covers. However, what really warmed the room was the portrait of Francesca's kindly mother, Rosa, that Giovanni had painted a year or two before she died.

Francesca, needle and thread in hand, was sitting on the sofa and turning her brother's collar. She looked up and smiled as Mattie walked in.

'Goodness,' she said, setting aside her sewing. 'You look frozen.'

'I am,' said Mattie, unwinding her scarf and hooking her coat behind the door. 'In fact, I'm frightened to blow my nose in case I snap it off.'

Francesca laughed.

Moving the kettle onto the heat, Francesca reached for the caddy on the shelf above as Mattie sank gratefully into the sofa.

'I was beginning to think you weren't coming,' said her friend, spooning tea into the pot.

'Sorry,' said Mattie. 'There was a signal failure on the district line at Upney so Vera, the warden on night shift who had been to see her daughter in Barking, was late.'

'Well, you're here now,' said Francesca, handing her a steaming mug of tea. 'So tell me how your ARP training went?'

'Alright, I suppose,' Mattie replied.

Cupping her hands around the mug and savouring the warmth, Mattie told her friend about her day.

'Maybe it's because I'm new, but the training does seem a bit overly complicated to me,' she concluded. 'Most of it is common sense. "If you hear the siren, direct people to the nearest shelter."' She pulled a face. 'Well, what else would I do?'

Francesca laughed. 'Trouble is, some people haven't got any sense.'

'That's true,' said Mattie. 'So what have you been up to?'

Sipping her tea, Mattie listened as her friend ran through the political machinations in the wholesale tobacconist where she worked.

'But I tell you, Mattie, if Miss Huggitt tells me one more time to make sure I double-check the boxes before sending them off on the van, I'll scream,' Francesca concluded. 'In fact, I'm seriously thinking of leaving and getting a job in a munitions factory. They pay double what I'm getting now and provide a proper midday meal.'

'What about your dad?' said Mattie, unable to hide her surprise.

Although Francesca's father had been keen on his children getting a good education and displayed all their end-of-year certificates and educational commendations on the wall, he still held very traditional views. One of which was that, until they married a suitable, preferably Italian, young man, daughters should spend their time at home helping to look after the family. It had taken several weeks of refusing to speak on Francesca's part and considerable pressure from her brother on her behalf before their father finally gave in and she applied for her present job.

Francesca shrugged. 'There's a war on and at least I'm not–'

The back door into the scullery clicked open bringing a gust of cold air and Francesca's brother, Giovanni, came into the parlour rubbing his hands.

'Ruddy tatas out there.' He spotted Mattie and smiled. ''Ello, lovely lady,' he said in an exaggerated Italian accent.

With jet black hair and with the same liquid brown eyes as his sister, Giovanni Alfonso Fabrino was never short of female company, and the Empress's profits doubled on a Thursday and Friday night due to his presence behind the counter.

Mattie laughed. 'Ciao, Giovanni.'

He looked at his sister. 'Any chance of a cuppa, Fran?'

'I've just made a pot,' said Francesca.

He gave her a quick peck on the forehead. 'You're a love. I suppose Father's in the shop.'

'Yes, and asking for you,' Francesca replied. 'You'd better let him know you're back.'

Sighing, Giovanni went to the curtain leading to the shop and went through.

Mattie opened her mouth to speak, but Francesca held her hand up. There was a pause, then the curtain flew back and Giovanni stormed back in.

He stood glaring at the floor with his hands clenched for a moment, then shouted something at his father in Italian.

Enrico replied in the same tone and language, which brought forth another torrent of furious Italian from Giovanni before he slammed the door.

He muttered something under his breath that

made Francesca blush to the roots of her hair, then he stormed off upstairs.

Mattie gave her friend a questioning look.

'Giovanni wants to sign up,' said Francesca. 'He told Dad it was his duty to fight and Dad told him it's his duty to obey his father.'

'So is Giovanni joining the army?' asked Mattie.

Francesca shook her head. 'Not yet. After a lot of bellowing and roaring at each other, Giovanni has agreed to wait until he gets his call-up papers, which he's hoping, as his surname begins with an "F", won't be too long. I hope so too, as it's like living with a couple of enraged bears.' A sorrowful look crept into her friend's large brown eyes. 'Talking of the army, have you heard from Charlie?'

'Mum had a letter a week ago saying his feet were sore from square-bashing and the grub was horrible but, reading between the lines, he's having a whale of a time,' said Mattie.

'Just like his fiancée then,' said Francesca. 'I saw Stella in the Regal at Stratford last week, dancing and giggling with anyone who'd buy her a drink.'

Mattie gave her oldest friend a sympathetic smile.

For Francesca's sake, Mattie hoped that absence wouldn't make Charlie's heart grow fonder and instead of marrying Stella he would open his eyes to see the beautiful woman who had loved him since she was five.

Putting down her cup, Mattie stretched across and placed her hand over her friend's. 'Whatever happens, I do know if he can't see you're worth a hundred Stellas then it's his loss.'

Chapter Seven

Grinding his cigarette butt under his heel, Christopher pulled the Old Globe's bar door open then stepped back.

'Thank you,' Mattie said, giving him a little smile as she walked by.

'There's a table in the corner,' he said, following in behind her. 'Why don't you grab it while I get our drinks. What are you having?'

'A G&T, please,' said Mattie, shaking the water from her plastic rain cap.

Leaving her to weave her way through the crowded saloon, Christopher went to the bar. The clock behind the bar showed that it was quarter to ten, which gave them plenty of time to have a leisurely drink before last orders at ten-thirty.

The Old Globe was situated near the bridge that spanned the Regent's Canal, just a five-minute walk from the Odeon cinema in Mile End.

With a horseshoe mahogany bar, bare floorboards and a piano in one corner, the pub was much like any other in the area but, whereas only a few short months ago the bar would have been filled with workmen in donkey jackets and cloth caps, now both the main bar and the saloon bar were full of men and women in uniforms. Some wore the navy of the ARP warden while others sported the grey overcoats of the Auxiliary Fire Service or the khaki battle jacket and green hat of the WVS. In fact, he and Mattie were amongst only a handful of people who were wearing civilian clothes and even in the cinema, they had been outnumbered twenty to one by uniformed members of the audience.

The barmaid, a strawberry blonde with an attention-grabbing cleavage and lush-red lips, ambled over.

'Hello, handsome, what can I get you?' she asked, giving him a lavish look.

'A double G&T and a pint of Best,' he replied, taking a packet of Rothmans from his inside jacket pocket.

She wiggled off again to get their order.

Lighting his cigarette, Christopher leaned on the bar and looked across at his date.

In her tartan pencil skirt and cream lacy twin set, Mattie looked very sophisticated which surprised him a little given she was a factory girl. Not that the outfit didn't suit her, it did. In fact, her understated attire only highlighted her curves.

He was also surprised that, unlike his landlady whose mangled vowels could burn paint from a door, Mattie's Cockney accent, although noticeable, didn't grate on his ear. Added to this, her clear skin, minimal make-up and unbound hair gave her an air of vitality that was very enticing.

'There you go,' said the barmaid.

Christopher turned and smiled. 'Thanks. What's the damage?'

'One and six,' she replied. 'And sorry, we ain't got no lemons.'

'I know; there's a war on.'

She laughed and Christopher handed over a

151

florin. 'Get yourself one with the change.'

'Don't mind if I do,' she replied, giving him a dimply smile. 'Out with yer girlfriend?'

'Date,' he replied. 'First date, actually.'

'Oh, well,' she said with a loaded sigh. 'Maybe I'll see you another time.'

Christopher smiled. 'Maybe.'

Picking up his two drinks, he sauntered back to where Mattie was sitting.

'There you go,' he said, placing Mattie's drink on the Double Diamond coaster in front of her. 'Sorry, there're no lemons.'

'Don't worry, I haven't seen one for weeks,' said Mattie. 'And thank you again for the chocolates, they were a lovely surprise.'

'Well, you can't sit in the best seats in the house without them,' he replied.

Mattie laughed in a sort of muted way that was very appealing too.

'So,' he said, sipping the head off his pint. 'Tell me more about your family.'

She ran through the various and peculiar-sounding Brogans, both living and dead, and Christopher hoped he didn't show his disdain when he heard her mother was a skivvy and her father was an Irish rag-and-bone man.

When she'd finished, he told her he was twenty-seven, which wasn't a lie, followed by a slightly less-truthful account of his family circumstances.

As they spoke, he caught the barmaid casting the odd glance in his direction but, other than meeting her gaze a couple of times, Christopher kept his attention on Mattie.

Naturally they moved on to talk about the war.

152

Christopher listened as she regurgitated the Jew-loving press's propaganda that the Nazis were evil and the situation Europe found itself in now was somehow Hitler's fault. Mattie then told him about getting her Higher Certificate at evening classes.

'And what will you do once you have it?' he asked, a little impressed by her determination in spite of himself.

Mattie shrugged. 'I don't know, perhaps I'll sign on for the Auxiliary Transport Service or work at the War Office.'

'Perhaps you could take over organising the Civil Defence at the town hall,' laughed Christopher, noticing her skirt had slid up to reveal half an inch of stocking-top. 'Honestly, how do they expect to win a war if they don't know how many ambulances and recovery trucks they have in each depot?'

Adjusting her skirt, Mattie frowned. 'I know we're not as well organised as we should be, but–'

'The town halls need to pull themselves together,' said Christopher, taking a cigarette out and lighting it. 'For instance, when I asked last week, someone said there were three fire engines stationed at the Royal Docks depot but there are only two marked up in the control room board.'

'That's because the auxiliary fire team manning one of them hasn't completed all their training so they can't be shown as an operational crew until they have,' said Mattie.

'Oh, I see,' said Christopher, blowing a stream of smoke nonchalantly upwards. 'And what about at your post? How many fire engines do you have

153

on standby, for instance?'

Mattie gave him a curious look. 'Doesn't careless talk cost lives?'

Christopher paused for a split second, then he gave her his most charming smile.

'Oh, Mattie, you've discovered my secret.' He placed his hand on his chest theatrically. 'I am really a German spy!'

A becoming flush coloured Mattie's cheeks. 'I'm sorry, Christopher, I know I'm being silly, but–'

'No, I'm sorry,' he said, taking the opportunity to shift nearer so their knees touched. 'And you're quite right not to say. It's just being new to the area I'm trying to make sure I don't let anyone down just because I can't remember if Cannon Street Road runs east to west or north to south.'

'Well, it's north to south and don't worry,' she laughed, relaxed again. 'Even those of us who know the area like the back of our hands find ourselves turning up the wrong street because of the blackout.'

He smiled and then noticed she'd finished her drink. 'Can I get you another before I walk you home?'

'That would be lovely but I'm on early shift tomorrow so I ought to get home,' said Mattie, gathering up her handbag and gas mask from under her chair and standing up.

Stubbing out his cigarette, Christopher rose to his feet, too. Taking her coat from the back of her chair, he held it out for her.

'Thanks,' she said as he slid it over her shoulders, catching a hint of gardenia as he did. 'You're only a short walk from your digs so it seems unfair for me to ask you to walk me home when you have to come all the way back.'

'I don't mind,' he said, catching a glimpse of the barmaid looking his way again.

'No honestly,' she said. 'I'm fine.'

Purposely running his forearm along the outside of her breast, Christopher took Mattie's arm. 'Well then, I insist on waiting with you until the bus comes.'

She smiled her assent and, arm-in-arm, they walked out of the pub. Listening for unseen traffic, they crossed the road to the bus stop.

They'd only been there for a few moments when they saw a number 25 coming towards them.

Mattie let go of his arm. 'I've had a lovely evening, Christopher.'

'I'm glad,' he said. 'So how about you let me take you dancing next week?'

'What, to the Regency?'

'I was thinking perhaps the Lyceum or Trocadero.' He dusted down the lapels of his jacket. 'I'm a bit of a Fred Astaire on the old dance floor, you know.'

Mattie laughed. 'You know, self-praise is no recommendation.'

'That's true but why don't you see for yourself and let me take you dancing?' he replied.

'Perhaps I will.'

'Splendid, Friday week it is then,' he said, taking advantage of their move forward to glance his groin against Mattie's hip. 'I'll meet you at Stepney Station at eight, if that's all right with you?'

The number 25 bus rumbled to a stop beside them and Mattie stepped on the platform and smiled down at him. 'Eight would be fine.'

He waved.

She waved back and the bus pulled away.

Christopher watched it disappear into the gloom. He reached into his pocket for his cigarettes and lit one. He took a long drag, then recrossed the road and went back into the Old Globe.

The barmaid looked up as he came in and gave him a seductive smile. Christopher smiled back.

He knew he'd eventually get Mattie between the sheets but, until she yielded to his charm, he was happy enough to sate his appetites elsewhere.

'Anyone at home for a cuppa?' Mattie called, walking through Mrs Wheeler's back door.

It was the Monday after her date with Christopher and, after a busy weekend on duty, she'd finally finished her last shift for three days.

She'd booked off at Post 7 twenty minutes ago so, as she'd missed Cathy at church the day before, she'd decided to pop in to see her sister on her way home.

'In here,' her sister called back from the front room. 'I'll just finish this row.'

'I'll put the kettle on,' Mattie called back, hooking her coat on the door peg.

The meaty smell of the evening stew filled her nose. Unlike their kitchen in Mafeking Terrace, which was cramped with a low, sloping roof, the Wheelers' kitchen was large enough for a full-size table and chairs and had a double-sided dresser on which Mrs Wheeler's matching dinner set was displayed. There was also, in addition to the cold water tap, an Ascot gas heater which Mattie's mother would probably have given her front teeth to own.

Mattie took the kettle to the sink, held it under the tap and, as she waited for it to fill, gazed idly at the matching set of pans hanging from a row of hooks on the wall.

'Hey!' Her sister's voice cut through her wandering thoughts. 'You'll flood the place.'

Mattie blinked and quickly turned the tap off.

'Sorry,' she said. 'I was miles away.'

'I can see that,' Cathy replied, 'and I expect it's because you were thinking about your lovely evening out with your new young man.'

'I was,' Mattie lied.

Actually, it wasn't Christopher she was thinking about. Instead she was remembering how well Father McCree's tailored black cassock had fitted across his broad shoulders at yesterday's mass.

Cathy's eyes stretched wide. 'And has he got a name then?'

'Christopher,' she said. 'Christopher Joliffe.'

'And?' squealed her sister.

'And we went to the pictures and then had a drink in the Old Globe. I had a G&T and he had a pint of bitter.'

Cathy's pretty face screwed up into a frown. 'Mattie!'

Mattie feigned confusion for a second, then smiled. 'Oh, and we're going to a dance next Saturday.'

'I'm so pleased for you,' said Cathy, strolling over to the larder to fetch the milk. 'I know Mum thought he was wonderful but I never did think

157

Micky was good enough for you. You need someone brainy like yourself.'

'Don't get your wedding hat out yet, Sis, we're just going on a date,' said Mattie. 'And you've got brains, too, Cathy.'

'I don't feel like it these days.' Pouring their tea, Cathy sighed. 'I know it's my job but once I've done the house from top to bottom and prepared the evening meal, well,' she gave a rueful smile, 'I'm exhausted. I'm also a bit bored.'

'I'm not surprised,' said Mattie, spooning in two sugars. 'I'd be crawling up the wall by now. Why don't you go back to work?'

Cathy shook her head. 'It wouldn't be fair on Stan because people would think he couldn't provide.'

'All right, but what about volunteering at the town hall for something part time,' said Mattie, 'like manning a first-aid station or an information post.'

Again Cathy shook her head. 'I suggested that to Stan but he wouldn't hear of it as he said it was against his principles to aid the war effort.'

Mattie pulled out a kitchen chair and sat down. 'What on earth is he going to do when he's called up?'

Cathy shrugged. 'I think he's banking on the government finding a peaceful solution before he gets his papers.' She picked up the other cup. 'I'll just pop this through to Stan's mother in the other room and check she's all right. Won't be a mo.'

Cradling her cup in her hand, Mattie blew across the top of her tea. As she waited for her

158

sister to return, she starting running through the various premises she had to ensure complied with the blackout. Walking the streets in her mind's eye, Mattie checked off the leather factory and public baths in Whitehorse Lane, then added in the old Memorial hall, Stepney Causeway's Boys' Home and the Methodist chapel to her list before coming to the largest building – St Bridget and St Brendan's, its adjoining rectory and, of course, its newest addition. Inevitably the image of Father McCree standing on the chancel steps sprang into her mind. She tried to push it aside but, instead, the echo of his laugh flowed through her.

'If your face is anything to go by, this Christopher must be a real dish,' said Cathy, cutting through her thoughts as she returned.

Mattie smiled but didn't reply.

'Do you want to stay for supper?' asked Cathy.

'Thanks, but Mum will be keeping something hot on the pot for me,' she said. 'What time's Stan in?'

'Six.'

'Then I'll keep you company until he comes home,' Mattie replied.

Collecting three plates from the dresser, Cathy put them on the oven's warming rack. 'Now, tell me about Christopher.'

'Well, he's a bit taller than your Stan with very blond hair and slim...' As her sister peeled the potatoes and chopped cabbage, Mattie told her about her evening with Christopher.

'He sounds a bit of a catch,' said Cathy when she'd done.

Mattie had to agree. With a rag-and-bone man for a father, a mother who cleaned and a gran who was a bookies' runner, Christopher, with his blond good looks and lucrative career, was indeed quite a catch. And a few short weeks ago Mattie wouldn't have thought otherwise, except now it seemed that she'd developed a preference for taller, dark-haired men with brown eyes.

'Mum's right. You're too fussy. Good-looking young men with salaried jobs don't grow on trees, you know,' her sister said, sounding unnervingly like their mother. 'If you go on like this you'll end up an old maid.'

Mattie smiled. 'I'm twenty not thirty, Cath. And perhaps I don't want to get married. Perhaps I'll become a nun instead.'

Her sister's jaw dropped and she stared incredulously at her.

Mattie held her serious expression for as long as she could, then burst out laughing and Cathy did the same.

'All right,' said Mattie, wiping her eyes. 'I'm not really thinking of taking holy orders but nor am I marrying a man just because he gets a monthly cheque instead of a grubby brown envelope each week.'

The sound of the six o'clock pips drifted through from the front room.

'I thought Stan was in at six,' said Mattie.

Cathy smiled and, as the last pip sounded, the back door opened.

Stan strode in.

'Evening, love, I…' He spotted Mattie sitting at the table. 'Mattie, I didn't expect to see you, and all kitted out in your new uniform, too.'

'Hello, Stan,' Mattie replied. 'I've just dropped in on my way home.'

His pencil-thin moustache lifted in a pleasant smile and he walked over to Cathy.

Slipping his arm around her waist, he kissed his wife's cheek. 'Smells lovely.'

She giggled. 'Me or the dinner?'

He gave her another peck. 'Both.'

Letting her go, Stan shrugged off his Crombie. 'How long until you're dishing up?'

'About thirty minutes?'

'Sorry, sweetheart, but could you make it twenty?' asked Stan, hanging his coat over Mattie's. 'Someone dropped a note around to the market office for me. They've called an urgent area meeting and I have to be at Finsbury by seven-thirty.'

Cathy sighed. 'I suppose so.'

He grinned. 'Thanks, darling.'

'Goodness, Stan, didn't you have three meetings last week?' said Mattie.

'I did, but with Churchill and his war-mongering friends in the cabinet mobilising the army, the chance of peace is hanging in the balance.'

Mattie smiled.

Even though no bombs had actually dropped as yet, given the reports of German troop movements on the French border and the constant stream of refugees arriving at Dover, Mattie couldn't help feeling that negotiating peace with a fanatic like Hitler was just wishful thinking on Stan's part.

She stood up. 'I'll leave you to it.'

161

'And I ought to say hello to Mother,' said Stan. 'Nice to see you, Mattie.'

Loosening his tie, Stan strolled out of the kitchen.

The cabbage simmering on the back gas ring suddenly boiled over and Cathy swore under her breath.

Mattie picked up her gas mask, handbag and ARP helmet, then stood up. 'See you down home on Saturday.'

Dragging the pot off the heat, Cathy nodded. 'And I'll want to hear all about your next date with Christopher when I do.'

Leaving Cathy grappling with the vegetables, Mattie reached up to unhook her coat but, as she did, she knocked Stan's overcoat off the peg. Retrieving it from the floor, she was just about to hang it back when a book dropped out onto the coir door mat.

The book had fallen open on the title page which had the inscription:

To Stanley, a true patriot

The exaggeratedly flowery initials, CHJ, were signed beneath. Picking it up, Mattie was just about to slip it back where it came from when she saw the title. There, printed in solid black letters, were the words:

The Protocols of the Elders of Zion

Casting a quick look at her sister, who was straining the cabbage in the sink, Mattie quickly put the book back and hooked Stan's coat on the peg. With a hasty goodbye, Mattie slipped through the blackout curtains and out of the back door.

Chapter Eight

'There we are, Mrs Wiseman,' said Mattie, rocking back on her heels and dusting soot from her hands. 'That should keep you both snug.'

'Thank you, my dear,' said the old lady, huddled in shawls and sitting in her fireside chair.

It was just before eight o'clock on the last Saturday in October and Mattie was in the back parlour of Morris and Alma Wisemans' house in Luke Street, the road that backed onto Mafeking Terrace, to light their Sabbath fire. It was something she's done each Saturday as a child to earn a copper or two but now she did it out of affection for the old couple.

The Wisemans lived in the two ground-floor rooms and entered the house through the scullery door while the Ellis family, mum, dad and seven children, lived in the rooms upstairs and used the front door. The Wisemans' parlour was always spotless, thanks to their daughter who lived across the Commercial Road in Prescott Street and visited every Thursday to give the house a good clean.

Mattie had known the Wisemans for as long as she could remember. Dressed in traditional black garb with a black sheitel over her own sparse grey hair, Alma looked exactly the same as she always had.

'Shall I make you a cuppa?' asked Mattie, easing herself up from the rag hearth rug.

'You're an angel to ask,' said Alma. 'But only if you have time.'

'Tons,' Mattie replied. 'I'm on day patrol and don't have to report to the ARP control centre until nine.' She grinned. 'And I could do with a cuppa myself.'

'And help yourself to some apple cake while you're about it,' Alma called after Mattie as she went through to their tiny lean-to scullery at the back.

The kitchen, as always, was in tidy order with six plates set out on the rickety table, each of which was covered by a napkin.

The Wisemans kept kosher as best they could. With one small kitchen comprising an ancient butler sink and a handful of crockery it was difficult to keep milk and meat separate, but they always kept the Sabbath. However, this meant that until the sun set on Saturday no work was permitted so everything they ate needed to be prepared the day before, hence the cold meals laid on the table.

The Sabbath was also the reason that Mattie knew the Wisemans as they had been one of her Saturday morning regulars when she, like most of the children in the area, lit fires for Jewish families observing the Sabbath.

Filling the kettle from the corroded cold water tap over the sink, Mattie lit the back gas ring on the old couple's stove, which should have been

164

consigned to the scrap heap three decades before. Scrubbing out two mismatched cups from the old dresser, Mattie took the milk from the stone keep on the window sill just as the kettle started to whistle.

After making the tea, Mattie filled the couple's ancient Thermos flask with boiling water for them to use for a hot drink later. Finding the battered tray with its faded image of Southend pier, she set the teapot, the milk bottle, bowl of sugar and two cups on it, then returned to the lounge.

'You look like a million dollars in your uniform,' said the old woman as Mattie stirred the pot.

A million dollars was probably a bit of an exaggeration but Mattie's uniform certainly fitted better now than it had when it was first issued. She'd spent two days tapering the waist seams while letting out the fabric over her bust. She'd also shortened the jacket sleeves and sewn the ARP badge on straight. Despite her mother's tight-lipped disapproval, Mattie had also bought herself two pairs of cotton drill trousers and, after taking off the waistbands and adding darts, they now fitted comfortably over her hips while leaving her free to move.

'Thanks,' said Mattie, handing Alma Wiseman a cup. She picked up one of the straight-backed chairs and moved it forward so she could sit next to the old woman.

Cradling the cup in her hand, Alma blew across the top of her drink and raised her watery eyes.

'You always were a good girl, Mattie,' said Alma, her wrinkled face lifting in a fond smile. 'And it seems only yesterday you came here in pigtails to light our fire.'

'And you used to always give me a fairy cake or oat biscuit when I did,' Mattie replied.

'Well, you were always such a bag of bones,' said Alma. 'A strong wind and you would have been taken away, for sure.'

'Well that's not the case any more,' laughed Mattie.

The old woman looked her over. 'No and I bet there's many a fellow who'd say the same, I can tell you. I'm surprised you haven't got a ring on your finger like your sister.'

'Simple, because I haven't met anyone whose ring I'd want,' Mattie replied.

'Pish,' said Alma, waving Mattie's words away. 'As I live and breathe, I can't believe there isn't some man who hasn't caught your fancy.'

Before Mattie could stop it, the familiar image of Father McCree smiling at her flashed across her mind.

'There is someone, isn't there?' laughed Alma. 'I can see it on your moosh.'

Mattie looked away. 'No ... no there isn't–'

'He's not ... married?'

Mattie raised her eyes to see a look of horror on the old woman's face. 'No, he's not married,' said Mattie. 'I mean, there isn't anyone–'

'I tell you this as I live and breathe,' continued Alma, pressing both hands to her chest. 'Don't get yourself tangled up with a married man.'

'I'm not and I won't,' Mattie replied.

The door opened and Morris Wiseman walked in.

A tailor by trade, he was now retired, but he still

did the odd bundle of piecework to supplement their meagre state pension, as the parcel of fabric tucked against the arm of his chair testified. He was probably just a year or two short of his seventieth year and also looked much the same as when Mattie had first met him. However, today, instead of the usual baggy trousers and shapeless jacket, Mr Wiseman was dressed in a black suit with a tie and a velvet kippah on his bald head.

'Hello, Mr Wiseman, have you been to synagogue?'

'Hello, Mattie,' he replied. 'No, I've been sitting shiva with Ruth Bronstein in Planet Street.'

Mattie looked surprised. 'Mr Bronstein died!'

Morris nodded. 'It was very sudden. Poor Bernie.'

'It must have been,' said Mattie. 'I only saw him in Watney Market on Tuesday and he looked well enough then.'

'It was the shock to his heart,' said Alma.

'What shock?'

Tears sprung into the old man's eyes.

'What shock she asks!' He raised his hands. 'I'll tell you what shock. The shock of having a petrol bomb smash through your window—'

Morris mumbled something in Yiddish and then his face crumpled as he covered it with his hands.

The old woman looked at Mattie. 'Forgive Morris, my dear, he's upset. His family and Bernard's came over from Poland together some eighty years ago. Bernard and Ruth were asleep in their beds when they realised a fire had broken out downstairs. Ruth called the fire brigade and they managed to put it out but poor Herman's heart gave out with the shock of seeing his home and business go up in smoke.'

Standing up, Mattie went over to the old man and placed her hand on his arm. 'I'm really sorry, Mr Wiseman.'

He looked up, his face wet with tears, and gave her a sad smile.

'I know you are, my dear.' He patted her hand. 'You have a good heart, not like some around here. And it wasn't just Bernie who was attacked that night but Liberman's at the corner of New Road was as well. And, last week, the basement of Isaac's retail store was torched and him and his two children ended up in hospital because they breathed in too much smoke.'

'And then there are the beatings,' added Alma. 'Two in Cable Street last week and another in Turner Street.'

'Yes, I'd heard,' said Mattie. 'It's not right.'

'It isn't,' agreed Morris. 'And some are saying it's getting as bad as Germany.'

The clock on their mantel started to chime and Mattie glanced across at it.

'I'm so sorry, I must go or I'll be late,' she said. Picking up her gas mask, she hurried towards the scullery. 'I'll see you next week.'

'God bless you,' Alma shouted after her as Mattie unhooked her coat and helmet from the nail hammered into the back door.

'And you,' Mattie called over her shoulder as she stepped out into the cold morning.

Hurrying across the yard and down the narrow alleyway between the houses, Mattie soon found herself back on the main thoroughfare. Picking up her pace, she turned towards the river but, as she approached the railway arch, she stopped and stared. Sprawled under the parapet, in crudely painted letters, was written:

This is the Jews' war, let them fight it.

Scribbling the headings Solid, Liquid and Gas at regular intervals along the top of her notes, Mattie turned her attention back to the open textbook propped up on her gas mask case.

'I'm making a cuppa, do you want one, luv?' asked Brenda, who was sitting at the other side of the table.

Mattie looked up. 'You're a chum.'

Brenda Willis was a year or two shy of thirty and an inch or two short of five foot. She had a rosy apple-like face and light brown hair cut into a short bob that stopped just below her ears. Like Mattie she was dressed in a navy uniform but, whereas Mattie had enough room to move comfortably, Brenda's generous curves were squeezed into a skirt at least a size too small and a jacket that couldn't be fastened across the bust.

'Don't mention it.' Brenda closed the *Woman's Realm* she'd been flicking through and stood up. 'It's not as if there's anything else to do, is there?'

Scooping up the cups from their last round of tea, she wiggled her way across the wooden floor towards the kitchen at the far end.

It was now mid-afternoon and Mattie and Brenda who had lived across the road from Mattie for years, and a couple of other women were sitting around a teacher's desk on the ground floor of Shadwell School's infants' hall. The school itself was a bog-standard late-Victorian school built over three floors with staircases in each corner and a half-tiled hall on each floor with classrooms running off it. In addition, surrounding the school, there was a high brick wall with wrought-iron spikes running along the top to keep pupils in, strangers out and the lead on the roof.

However, as the pupils had been evacuated, the building had been commandeered by the local authority and designated as Post 7 in the Wapping and Shadwell sub-division of the Stepney Civil Defence area. To reflect its new role, the hall had been stripped of its educational displays and now, in place of posters with images of British trees and flowers and lists of the times tables, there were blackboards with the telephone numbers of the hospital, fire stations and undertakers scrawled across it. Outside, instead of boys kicking balls and girls swinging skipping ropes, the asphalt playground was now home to the various modes of Civil Defence transports. These included two ancient lorries that were manned by the Heavy Recovery Teams. It was the HRT's job to dig people out of the rubble in the event of a bomb but, as the vehicles rattled and shook alarmingly every time they drove out of the yard, Mattie was convinced they would fall apart long before they reached the actual incident. Alongside them was an old GPO van and a 1930 Ford Model Y with mismatched wheels, both of which had been hastily painted white to aid visibility in the blackout. The red cross daubed on their sides

170

indicated that they were Post 7's ambulances.

As well as Mattie and the other ARPs, there was also an electrician and a gas fitter on duty, ready to make safe damaged houses, and a handful of spotty youths who were the Post 7 messengers, who spent most of their time smoking and sniggering over health and fitness magazines.

They had all been on duty since nine and although a couple of women, like Mattie, were spending the idle hours in productive pursuits such as reading or knitting balaclavas for sailors, the majority of the men and women who were the first line of defence against Hitler were killing the time by playing cards, catching up on the neighbourhood gossip or participating in a noisy knock-out darts tournament accompanied by the strains of the BBC Light Orchestra, which was blaring out from the school radio.

'There you go,' said Brenda, placing a mug in front of her. 'A nice cup of rosy lee wiv two sugars.'

'Thanks,' said Mattie.

'Don't mention it,' said Brenda, taking a pack of ten Silk Cut from her top pocket.

Mattie took a sip of her drink and was just about to get back to her studies when Cyril Potter, her neighbour and the post's chief warden, strode in with a clipboard in one hand and silver-topped swagger stick under his arm. Brenda looked over at Mattie and rolled her eyes.

Unlike the rest of the ARP contingent in the hall who were wearing a hotchpotch of whatever the Ministry of Home Defence could lay their hands on, Cyril had somehow acquired a brand-spanking-new and complete chief warden's outfit. If this

171

wasn't surprise enough, the fact that the battle jacket fitted as if made for him and the trousers were the correct length for his dumpy legs was nothing short of a miracle. Added to this was a sparkling white helmet with a bold W painted in black at the front, a broad yellow flash on his arm, a white lanyard and an expensive leather gas mask case which was strung across his rotund body.

Having quickly marched to the headmaster's desk which had been dragged into the hall, Cyril stopped and surveyed the assembled company. He rapped the top of his stick on the desk to ensure everyone stopped what they were doing and looked at him.

'Attention, wardens!'

The two dozen men and women with the red ARP badge pinned to their chest stopped talking.

'As always, I received the weekly report from HQ in the post this morning,' he said in a strident tone. 'And although I normally wait until Monday to inform you of the ministry's directives, there are a few things that need our urgent attention. First, there has been a report that a great number of civilians have been spotted minus their gas masks and HQ wants us to remind people of the vital importance of carrying their respirators with them at all time. Secondly, there is a new leaflet on its way from the Ministry of Home Defence–'

'What, another bleeding one?' said Wilfred Burton, the Cable Street warden who was a veteran of the Somme. 'We've only just got rid of the last lot.'

'Wot's it about this time?' called Mavis Norris, the Turner Street warden who was busy filling in

172

her Littlewoods pools coupon.

'Some ruddy nonsense about wearing warm clothes in the shelters, no doubt,' replied Hattie Smith, the Shadwell Basin warden who was sitting in the old armchair by the stove and knitting. 'Like we couldn't work that one out for ourselves.'

Everyone laughed.

'Lastly,' continued Cyril, 'and the reason why I've had to bring this to your attention immediately, is the blackout.'

There was a collective groan.

'Yes, I'm sorry I have to bring it up again,' continued Cyril, repositioning his spectacles on his nose. 'But people are becoming lax so HQ wants us all to be doubly vigilant and tackle those who aren't complying with regulations.' He looked at his watch. 'It's two-thirty now so the blackout will be starting in just over thirty minutes so I want all wardens out and about on their rounds checking that people aren't carelessly showing a light. And if they are, remind them that–'

'There's a war on!' chorused Mattie and her fellow wardens.

A rosy flush spread across Cyril's fleshy jowls. He surveyed the scene for a second or two then, jamming his baton under his arm, he spun on his heels and stomped out.

As the buzz of conversation resumed, Brenda lit another cigarette and picked up her magazine.

Mattie yawned and turned her attention back to the book.

'Burning the candle at both ends, are we?' asked Brenda, blowing a stream of smoke skywards.

'Only if studying the properties of solids

qualifies,' Mattie replied.

'You w'at?'

'It's my chemistry homework,' Mattie explained.

'Well, I'm sure it's all very useful to someone, luv, but if you ask me, you should be out enjoying yourself with some nice young man.'

'Well, as it happens, I have met someone,' said Mattie.

'Have you now?'

'Yes,' Mattie replied. 'His name's Christopher and he's something in the City and Country Bank on Commercial Road.'

'And?'

'And he's five ten or so with very blond hair, blue eyes and comes from the West Country, some-where where his mother still lives.'

Brenda looked impressed. 'Where did you meet him?'

Mattie told her.

'He sounds like a catch,' her friend said when she'd finished. 'Is he a good kisser?'

Mattie pretended to be shocked. 'Honestly, Brenda, what *do* you take me for?'

Brenda laughed. 'Just asking! When you seeing him again?'

'Next Saturday,' Mattie replied. 'We're going dancing up west.'

'Well, if he can dance too you'd better hang onto him,' said Brenda, 'as they're getting thin on the ground 'round here.'

She gave Mattie a considered look. 'Nice, is he?'

A slow smile spread across Mattie's face. 'Not bad.'

'And course him being good with figures means

he can help you with your homework.' Brenda winked. 'If you get my drift.'

Mattie laughed. 'Now all I have to do is decide what to wear.'

'I wouldn't worry, duck.' Brenda looked her over. 'With your figure and legs, you'd look good in a sack.'

Closing her books, Mattie slipped them in her satchel under the desk and stood up.

'I ought to head off on my evening blackout round,' she said, hooking her gas mask over her shoulder. 'See you next Saturday.'

'God willing,' Brenda replied. 'But if I don't see you before, have a good time on your date.'

Picking up her gas mask and tin hat, Mattie headed for the door.

'And remember,' shouted Brenda, as Mattie unhooked her overcoat, helmet and ARP equipment knapsack hung on the row of children's pegs. 'Don't do anything I wouldn't do.'

'So you understand what you need to have standing by in case of an air raid?' Mattie asked Miss Braithwaite, standing in the old lady's dimly lit scullery.

'I think so, dear, but it's such a lot to remember,' replied the elderly spinster, 'especially with all that dreadful noise going off and everyone running about.'

'I know but it's all on the London County Council leaflet,' said Mattie.

After an hour and a half of walking the streets, Mattie had more or less finished her blackout patrol. So far she had been forced to knock on at

175

least a dozen doors to inform people that they hadn't sufficiently blacked-out their windows and doors, which was several more than last week. Although the blackout had come into force over three months ago, other than the odd German aircraft, which Mattie was sure Gerry sent just to disrupt the population's sleep by setting off the Civil Defence sirens, nothing much had happened.

Unfortunately, because of this, people were developing a false sense of security, which to Mattie's mind was all part of the Führer's plan to make the British complacent before he let loose his Luftwaffe.

Miss Braithwaite looked troubled.

'Leaflet?' she said, tugging her crocheted shawl a little tighter. 'I'm not sure if...'

Mattie reached into her ARP haversack. 'I have another.' She handed it to the older lady. 'It lists everything you need to have ready, but don't forget your warm clothing and your gas mask.' Mattie turned it over. 'My name is on the back if you need me and I'm stationed in the Highway School.'

Miss Braithwaite looked down at the handout, then back at Mattie. 'You're Ida's girl, aren't you?'

'Yes, I am,' said Mattie.

The old woman's face lit up. 'I thought I recognised you. How's your mother?'

'She's well,' Mattie replied. 'Now, keep this close by, Miss Braithwaite, and I'll call back and see how you are in a few days.'

The old woman smiled. 'Thank you, dear, and give my regards to your mother.'

Turning off the light, Mattie slipped out of the

176

back door then, as she didn't want the old lady falling in the dark, she flipped the switch again as she closed the last few inches of the door. After all, she reckoned, even the sharpest-eyed Messerschmitt pilot would be hard-pressed to see a sliver of light from a forty-watt bulb at 5,000 feet.

Leaving Miss Braithwaite to her supper, Mattie crossed the back yard and, after a short walk down the alley behind the house, was back on Lucas Street within a few minutes.

She reckoned she only had to do a quick walk up Lucas Street around St Bridget and St Brendan's and then back down Sutton Street and she'd be done. Switching on her blackout torch with its smoked glass to dim the light, Mattie pointed it at the ground and walked towards Commercial Road.

Of course, there was nothing wrong with Christopher, nothing at all, and he clearly wasn't put off by her playing hard to get. Quite the opposite, in fact, so perhaps Babs was right and she should be having some fun.

With that thought in mind, Mattie turned into the main road. She walked past the darkened church, turned into Sutton Street and saw a light showing from one of the windows on the top floor of the rectory. It wasn't bright, in fact, had the moon been more than just a curved shard in the sky, she probably wouldn't have noticed it but, all the same, she'd have to knock and say something.

Walking up the rectory pathway, Mattie reached the front door and pulled on the bell.

There was a long wait then, finally, just as she was about to go, the door creaked open.

177

A little fizz of excitement tingled through Mattie but, instead of seeing Father McCree's tall, athletic frame filling the darkened doorway, it was Father Mahon who stood there, rubbing his eyes.

'Father, it's me,' said Mattie, as she turned her muted torch upwards so he could see her face. 'Can I come in?'

'Of course, Mattie, me dear.' He moved back behind the curtain.

She stepped in and closed the door and the drapes before he turned on the hall light.

Although he had his dog collar on, Father Mahon was wrapped in an old paisley dressing gown and had a pair of worn slippers on his feet. He'd clearly been asleep because there was a red mark on his left cheek and his wispy white hair was sticking up on the same side.

'Good evening, Mattie, I hope there's nothing wrong with your family?' he said.

'Not as far as I know.'

He crossed himself. 'God be praised.'

'I'm sorry to disturb you,' she continued. 'But I'm afraid I'm here in an official capacity as your ARP warden because you're showing a light.'

The old priest looked alarmed. 'I was certain I'd drawn the study curtain properly.'

'No, Father, it's on the top floor at the front,' said Mattie. 'It's not much, probably just a hall light left on and an uncurtained window, but I have to–'

'That's Father McCree's room,' said Father Mahon. 'I expect he forgot to close the curtains before he went off to visit his aunt.' He smiled. 'I'm sorry to ask, but this damp weather's playing

178

murder with me old knees so I'd take it as a kindness if you would pop up to his room to close the curtains. Would you mind?'

Mattie smiled.

'Of course not,' she said, as her heart did an unexpected little double beat. 'I can see myself out so you get yourself back in the warm, Father.'

'You're a darling girl, so you are,' he said, then shuffled back into his study.

Leaving her knapsack and hat on the table, Mattie started up the stairs to the first floor. Turning the corner at the top of the stairs, she headed for the narrower set of stairs at the back of the house which led to what had once been the servants' quarters. The solitary light with a fringed shade hanging at the top of the stairs wouldn't have even been seen if the door at the end of the bare-boarded landing had been closed, but now the open door meant that it was in direct view of the window beyond.

Mattie headed for the door to what she guessed was Father McCree's bedroom and grabbed the brass knob. She pulled it shut but, as she let go of the handle, the door slowly started swinging open again. She tried shutting it for a second time but the same thing happened. Unable to see any way of making the door stay shut, Mattie decided the best thing to do would be to close the curtains.

She walked in and the faint smell of sandalwood aftershave drifted into her nose.

Mattie couldn't help looking round the simply furnished room. Her gaze took in Father McCree's suit, which was hooked over the top of his wardrobe, the white shirt on the back of the chair

179

and the bed with its patchwork cover and crumpled pillow.

She dragged her attention away and, with her lips pressed firmly together, she marched towards the window.

Reaching across the desk, she grabbed the curtains and tugged them sharply close. However the right curtain got stuck halfway across so she climbed up onto the desk to free it but, as she did so, her torch slipped from her pocket and rolled under Father McCree's bed.

Jerking the curtain closed, Mattie climbed down and switched on the table lamp. Crouching down, she peered under the bed hoping her torch would be within easy reach. It was, but it was half-hidden by a tan suitcase.

Grasping hold of the handle of the case, she pulled it out and was just about to squeeze herself under the bed when the room flooded with light.

She turned to find Father McCree standing in the doorway.

He was holding a towel and his hair was damp. His face was freshly shaven and he was wearing just his trousers, which hung low on his hips.

Although sprawled on the floor, her eyes were working overtime as they took in everything from his wet, tousled hair down to the honed muscles of his torso and the dark curls spreading across his chest and tracking down his stomach.

His eyes fixed onto the tan suitcase for a second before returning to her face.

'What are you doing?' he asked in a voice that could have sliced glass.

'A light! You were showing a light! A light through the window,' she babbled as she scrambled to her feet.

His mouth pulled into a tight line. 'I mean, what are you doing nosing around under my bed?'

'I dropped my torch,' said Mattie, feeling like a five-year-old caught pinching sweets from a jar. 'Father Mahon said you'd gone out and he asked me to close the curtain because of his knees but I didn't know you were in–' Her gaze flickered over him again and back to his face – 'the bathroom.'

His eyes bore into her for a moment, then he smiled and Mattie's heart did a complete backward flip.

'Then let me fetch it for you,' he said, his familiar pleasant tone returning.

Leaving damp footmarks on the floor, Father McCree threw his towel on the chair, then ducked under the bed and retrieved her torch.

Sliding the tan suitcase back out of sight, he stood up.

'There you are,' he said, stepping forward a couple of steps and offering it to her.

Compelling her eyes to stay on his face, she took it from him. An emotion she couldn't interpret sped across his face and something rather nice coiled deep within her.

Then he smiled. 'I'm sorry about the light.'

'The light?' said Mattie, the heady scent of coal tar soap and fresh male stealing her thoughts.

'The blackout,' he explained. 'It won't happen again.'

'Good.'

Their gazes locked again for several heartbeats then, with thoughts that should have sent her straight to the confessional racing through her mind, Mattie fled the room.

''Twas a lovely service, as always, Father Mc-Cree,' said Mrs Shaw, leaning on her stick for support as she left the church.

'Thank you, Mrs Shaw,' he replied. 'I hope you're fully recovered.'

'Thank you, Father,' she replied, giving him a gummy smile. 'The doctor on the Marie Celeste ward in the London said he'd never known anyone have so much water drained from their lungs and survive.'

It was close to eleven o'clock and the main mass of the day had finished just ten minutes before. As always, Daniel and Father Mahon were standing at the back of the church to greet the congregation as they left.

'Three pints they drained,' continued the old woman, taking the roll-up from behind her ear. 'Before I could catch me breath again. A miracle the quack called it, but to be sure wasn't it yours and Father Mahon's prayers to the Virgin Mary on my behalf that pulled me through.'

Daniel crossed himself. 'Our Lady, be praised.'

Before he could stop himself, he yawned.

Mrs Shaw chuckled. 'I suppose you've been up since dawn.'

'Before,' said Daniel. 'We were at prayer in the church at six.'

Mrs Shaw's gnarled fingers grabbed his arm with surprising strength. 'Blessed we are at St

182

Bridget and St Brendan's to have such holy men as yourself and Father Mahon.'

Daniel gave a wan smile.

Father Mahon was certainly destined for sainthood, not least for the daily lashings from Mrs Dunn's tongue, but himself: probably not. Rather than concentrating on the Almighty and his works, Daniel had spent the whole time forcing his attention not to stray to Mattie Brogan, who was wearing her very fetching red coat and sitting in the seventh pew on the left, so much so he'd lost his place twice during mass, which had earned him an odd look from Father Mahon.

Although it was almost six hours since he'd got out of bed it was also seventeen hours and thirty-five minutes or, as near as damn it, since he'd walked half-naked into his bedroom and found Mattie there.

However, when he'd realised the reason she'd dragged the suitcase out from under the bed wasn't because of the transmitter inside it, his mind had relaxed and his body had taken over.

As his fear had receded, every male cell in his body had acknowledged its interest which, given all that was at stake, was bloody distracting, to say the least.

Mrs Shaw moved on. Daniel went to greet the next parishioner but a flash of red caught his eye and he saw Mattie skirt around the back of the crowd and head for the door.

Daniel made his excuse and dashed after her.

She was almost at the church's stone gateway when he emerged into bright October sunlight.

'Miss Brogan!'

183

She stopped and turned to face him.

'Father McCree,' she said, smiling warmly. 'I'm sorry, I was just–'

'I'm glad I've caught you, Miss Brogan,' he blurted out. 'I want to apologise for being sharp with you yesterday, in my room with you and–'

'No, it was my fault, I–'

'You were only doing your job,' he said, his attention caught by an escaped curl dancing on her cheek. 'I was just a bit surprised to find you there, that's all.'

'And I was surprised to see you too,' she replied.

She looked up at him and Daniel's gaze ran slowly over her upturned face as his lips imagined the feel of every spot his eyes alighted on.

They stared at each other for several heart-beats, then she smiled.

Daniel smiled too and an odd stillness descended.

Gazing into her eyes, the urge to take her in his arms rose up but, just as it threatened to overwhelm him, someone coughed.

Dragging his eyes from her, Daniel turned.

Standing next to them stood a policeman in full uniform, with bushy mutton chops sideburns and a distinctly uncomfortable expression on his face.

'Good morning, Father,' said the officer. 'I wonder if I might have a moment of your time.'

'Of course, constable,' said Daniel, pulling himself together. 'How can I help?'

'I'm wondering if you could point me in the direction of a member of the...' Pulling his notebook from his breast pocket, the constable flipped it open. 'Brogan family.'

'I'm Miss Brogan,' Mattie said. What's happened?'

'It's your gran, miss,' said the constable. 'She's been arrested.'

The cell hatch squeaked open and an eyeball appeared. Hurrying over to the door, Queenie gripped the metal crossbeam of the door and stood on tip-toes.

'Aw, may God and all his saints bless you, sir,' she called up to the unseen officer. 'Didn't I know you wouldn't be so heartless as to lock a poor widow in a cell to catch her death.'

There was a bit of muttering outside.

'That new young constable of yours, fine lad and a credit to his mother that he is, must be mistaking me for some other old woman,' she continued, throwing in a couple of pathetic coughs for good measure.

The flap slammed shut.

Queenie let go of the ironwork and stepped back.

'Devils you are and no mistake,' she bellowed, shaking her fist at the metal door. 'I hope your mother never hears of how you locked up an innocent old woman who was doing nothing to nobody.'

There was no reply except the sound of size-ten hobnail boots marching away.

'I've got a bloody dicky heart, too, you know,' Queenie screamed at the top of her voice. 'I might be dead the next time you come by.'

A door slammed and there was silence again.

Queenie went back to the wooden bed fixed to the wall.

Shaking out the itchy grey blanket, she wrapped it around herself then, swinging her legs up, she purposely put her muddy shoes on the bed and rested back to glare furiously at the closed cell door.

Of course she could have put a fairy curse on every policeman in the station but that wouldn't be fair or kind with most of them not being bad lads and having wives and children and all. And, if the truth be known, it was her fault she was now freezing her arse off in a cell. All because she'd had her nose too low in her Guinness for her eyes to see the copper. In the past, any old-time copper worth their salt would have been stuffing their face with bacon and egg by ten Sunday morning, but most of them had gone. This new lot of rozzers were all shaving rash and half-broken voices and, in truth, looked more like choir boys than coppers. They were all for arresting you rather than accepting a pint or two to turn a blind eye.

She laughed.

Mind you, twenty years ago she'd have had it on her toes and they wouldn't have seen her for dust. When she was a wee un you had to be swift on your feet to fill your belly with a pinched apple or to outpace the butcher's dog when you'd swiped a chicken from the display. Even ten year past she would have given the coppers a run for their money but not now. Still, the game was ever as it was and there was no point crying for it to be otherwise. If she was going to be here for a couple of hours, she might as well make the best of it. Tucking the blanket around her a little tighter, Queenie hunkered down and closed her eyes.

She'd just nodded off when the cell door opened and Mattie walked in, followed by a sour-faced officer with a brass pip on his shoulder.

'Is this your grandmother, Mrs Breda Marie Brogan, also known as Queenie?' he asked, in the rounded tones of a BBC announcer.

'Yes, it is.' Mattie rounded on him. 'And she's over sixty, you know, inspector, and shouldn't be in a damp cell.'

'Shouldn't she?' he asked, looking down his long nose at Mattie.

'No, she shouldn't, not at her age,' Mattie replied. 'It would have been a kindness if your officers could have put her in the collator's office as you usually do instead of locking her in a cell like some sort of criminal.'

'Well, miss,' said the inspector, flicking a speck of dust off his uniform sleeve. 'As your grandmother has been arrested for soliciting bets in a public place in contravention of section 4, subsection 3a of His Majesty's 1906 Street Betting Act and the fact she is *"usually"* put in the collator's office, indicating that she is a frequent visitor to Arbour Square, I think that very much makes her "some sort of criminal". However.' He raised his hand just as Mattie's face flushed. 'As your parish priest has pleaded your case and testified to your grandmother's otherwise good character, I have decided not to press charges – this time. Your grandmother will be released when I've completed the paperwork, until then you can wait here.'

187

'Thank you, inspector, I'm very grateful,' said Mattie. 'And so is my grandmother.'

The officer gave them both a sceptical look and left.

'Oh, Mattie, me darling, thank goodness,' said Queenie as the cell door closed again.

Her granddaughter raised an eyebrow. 'What, that they're dropping charges or that the officer found me before Mum?'

Queenie grinned. 'Both, but how did you get Father Mahon to come to the station with you?'

'I didn't,' laughed Mattie. 'I bought Father Mc-Cree.'

As if he'd heard his name, the cells door opened and Father McCree strode in.

Mattie stood up and walked across to meet him.

'Right, they've finished off the paperwork so Inspector Torrance says we're free to take Mrs Brogan home,' he said. Queenie stood up, ready to go.

'Thank you, Father,' said Mattie, gazing up at him.

He smiled down at her.

The room shifted as images of another bright young girl and handsome young priest swirled through Queenie's mind.

'Holy Mary, Mother of God,' she said, clutching her hands together tight on her chest and sitting back on the bench.

'Are you sure you're all right, Gran?' asked Mattie.

Putting his arm lightly around her, Father McCree guided Mattie forward as they went to help Queenie.

Mattie didn't seem to notice his touch but Queenie did.

The memory of a sunny day in Kinsale, almost half a century before, flashed vividly through her mind before returning to its rightful place in the past.

All the light and love in the universe melted together and Queenie stood up again.

'Thank you, my dears,' she said. 'I'm grand, so I am, just grand, like your two selves.'

Chapter Nine

Daniel watched the railway official with an armful of destination signs side-stepping along the gantry in order to change the Waterloo departure board.

It was Wednesday the first of November and just over seven weeks since he had arrived in Stepney. The weather had taken a turn for the worse but, despite the temperature outside hovering just around freezing, the inside of the station was almost tropical. This was due not just to the engines belching scalding steam on every platform, but also because the entire concourse was so crammed you could barely see the floor. Even the Tannoy announcing arrivals and departures was barely audible over the volume of noise.

Daniel was standing below the station's famous four-dialled clock in the centre of the main concourse with the ticket office to his left and the flower stall behind him. To his right, by platform eleven, three military trucks were having what looked like tents loaded onto them.

Around him city types, in bowlers and pin-striped suits, pushed between men in khaki and airforce blue as they dashed to catch their home-bound trains to Brixton and Battersea. To add to the early evening confusion, in addition to the armed forces personnel carrying kitbags and other equipment, there were a great number of smartly dressed young women in high heels and with bright red lips, who all seemed determined to send their menfolk off to war with vivid memories of what they would enjoy when they got back.

Taking the *Evening News* from his pocket, Daniel shook it open and skimmed down the second page. He'd just reached the bottom when someone shoved him from behind.

'Sorry, mate.'

Daniel turned to see a sailor with a loaded knapsack over his shoulder and a curvy blonde on his arm.

The sailor snatched his flat cap from his head. 'I mean, Father.'

'Please, there's no need to apologise,' said Daniel. 'We seem to have the whole of London waiting with us.'

'Too blooming well right we 'ave,' the blonde chipped in.

'This is Dolly,' said the sailor, shuffling her forward. 'My fiancée.'

Daniel shifted his gaze onto the young woman. 'Nice to meet you.'

'Char-harmed I'm sure, Father,' she replied,

giving him what could only be described as a lavish look. 'I've come 'ere to wave off my Frankie so he can do 'is bit like wot every other fella is doing.'

Daniel smiled. 'And I'm sure he appreciates it.'

The sailor raised his eyebrows at her.

'Oh,' she said, letting go of his arm. 'I ought to go and powder my nose before your train arrives.'

Giving Daniel the once-over again, she trotted off towards the ladies' on the far side of the concourse.

Daniel turned his attention back to the departure board.

Shrugging the kitbag off, the sailor plonked it on the floor between them. 'Can I check the results?'

Daniel handed him the newspaper.

'I thought you preferred red-heads with rich fathers, Francis,' said Daniel without shifting his gaze from the board.

'I most certainly do, old chap,' the sailor replied, studying the racing results on the back page.

'And your fiancée needs to work on her cockney accent,' said Daniel.

'I know,' said Francis. 'But she was only transferred to us from Section VII last week. I have to say, the glasses make you look quite intelligent.'

'Bloody pain to have to wear them though,' Daniel replied, 'especially as I keep forgetting to put them on.'

Francis suppressed a smile. 'Any problems settling into St Thingys?'

An image of Mattie Brogan sitting in the pews, wearing her familiar red outfit, flashed through

Daniel's mind.

'None at all,' he replied, pushing aside the unbidden thought of her full lips. 'All those years as an altar boy are standing me in good stead. You know, once a Catholic and all that.'

'What about convincing the chaps in the local fascist cell that you were the real Father McCree?' Francis asked, studying the departure board again.

'It was touch and go,' Daniel replied, remembering the feel of the knife blade against his windpipe. 'But I talked them around.'

'Good,' Francis replied. 'Uncle Vernon knew you'd do the job.'

Daniel raised an eyebrow by way of reply.

It was all very well for Uncle, or Sir Vernon Kell as he was listed in *Debrett's*, to be all play-the-ball-old-man about it but it wasn't the director of MI5 who'd had to blag his way into a group of Nazi sympathisers without the correct password.

'So are they playing ball?' Francis continued.

'With enthusiasm,' Daniel said. 'Naturally, I'm sending the completely wrong coordinates back to Meadow Rambler so if the Germans try to bomb the Old Ford gasworks, they'll end up hitting a field in Epping.'

'Are they using the usual system?' said Francis.

'Yes, random numbers,' said Daniel. 'And the Old Testament is the code book.'

'What frequency were they on?' asked Francis.

'1500 kHz, so I'm guessing they're in northern Germany somewhere,' said Daniel, pretending to check his watch. 'Any more on this Christopher Joliffe who seems to have suddenly popped up?'

'Yes, the chaps in the back room have dug up a few things.' He folded the newspaper and offered it to Daniel.

He took it and felt something solid within. Holding it close, he slipped the object from between the news sheets and into his inside pocket.

'As far as we can make out from our other agents who have infiltrated various fascist organisations, Joliffe has taken over the local groups in East London and intends to get them onto the streets to stage a popular uprising when Hitler starts the invasion,' Francis continued. 'Nasty piece of work, by all accounts.'

Daniel took off his glasses and pretended to inspect the lenses. 'Aren't they all?'

'Quite, although this one seems particularly brutal,' Francis replied.

Averting his gaze, Daniel brushed a speck of dust from his sleeve. 'In what way?'

'There's a few rumours linking him to some vicious rapes when he was in Germany and there's even a whisper about him having a hand in a murder or two,' said Francis.

A cynical smile raised the corner of Daniel's mouth. 'So he's just your ordinary everyday Nazi then.'

'Indeed,' his friend replied. He shifted his weight onto the other leg. 'You know, I'm not into all this God and religious stuff but, I have to tell you, I'm not the only one in the Big House who was shocked to discover that the IRA's man was a real priest.'

'No doubt the Church was a bit shaken too,' Daniel replied.

'They bally well were,' said Francis. 'I think that's why their top brass were so eager to co-operate with our operation.'

'I'm sure,' said Daniel. 'But if you think about it, in his eyes, the real Father McCree, patriot Irishman that he is, is only doing what those Spanish priests were doing aiding and abetting the International Brigade as we fought Franco's bunch of fascist thugs.'

'That's a very objective way of looking at it,' said Francis.

'Perhaps,' Daniel replied. 'But one of the best ways to convince people I am the real Father McCree is to know how he ticks. And, remember, if we don't win this war, you and I will go down in history as a pair of renegades who tried to prevent the glorious conquest of England by the Nazis while Joliffe and men like him were lauded as heroes.'

Glancing at him, Francis raised an eyebrow. 'God forbid.'

The corner of Daniel's lips lifted a fraction. 'I thought you didn't believe in all that.'

His friend shot him a long-suffering look, then a sea of navy blue and white caps surged forwards as the railway official shuffled along the gantry again and put up the signs for the seven-fifteen to Portsmouth.

'This is a bit different from fighting our way out of Bilbao two years ago,' said Francis softly.

The image of bodies lying mangled in the rubble of the Basque region's main port flashed through Daniel's mind. He turned and looked at his old comrade.

'Different country but the same enemy,' he replied in the same hushed tone.

They exchanged a comprehending look and then Dolly burst between them.

'All done,' she said, hooking her arm in Francis's again.

'About bloomin' time, gal,' said Francis, a bright expression instantly replacing his sombre one. 'I thought you'd bleedin' fallen down the hole.'

He offered Daniel the newspaper back.

'Keep it,' Daniel said. 'And good luck.'

'You, too, Father,' his friend replied. 'And watch out for yerself.'

'Don't worry.' Daniel tapped his waxed dog collar. 'I've got friends in high places.'

A ghost of a smile flitted across his friend's face then, with his arm linked with the MI5's newest recruit, Francis Lennox, Daniel's brigadier in the British Battalion of the International Brigade, disappeared into the throng.

'So, as you can see,' said Miss Gilmore, tapping the blackboard behind her with the pointer. 'While iron and copper are classified as transition metals, tin and lead are listed as post-transition metals.'

Stifling a yawn, Mattie made a note beside the list of elements in the right-hand column of her blue Woolworth's exercise book.

It was just before eight o'clock and, as was usual on a Wednesday, she was sitting in one of the classrooms on the second floor of Toynbee Hall in Commercial Road. Well, really it was a small committee room but as Brick Lane School, where the Higher Certificate evening classes usually ran, had been taken over as a first aid and casualty station, the Workers' Educational Institute had had to move its operations to Toynbee Hall.

Tackling the complexities of chemistry were two dozen or so men and women who, like Mattie, paid three shillings a week to study for their Higher Certificate and were attending class after a full day's graft.

Shaking off her tiredness, Mattie looked up at the teacher.

Miss Gilmore was stick thin and her dead-straight steely grey hair was cut into a severe bob that only just reached the bottom of her ear. Always in tweeds and sensible brogues, she was probably the same age as Mattie's mother and was one of the first women to graduate from the newly recognised Institution for Higher Education for Women; not a lesson went by without some reference to the 'jolly gals' at Girton. A founder member of the suffragette movement, she'd been up before the magistrate twice in that regard but now she taught Chemistry, Mathematics and Physics.

'Now, be warned, class,' said Miss Gilmore, surveying them over her half-moon spectacles. 'I will be testing you on all the symbols for transition metals before we move onto the rest of periodic table, so I suggest you knuckle down and memorise them for next week's class.'

'Yes, Miss Gilmore,' said the labourers, factory hands and shop girls perched on the school desks and chairs around her.

Satisfied with her pupils, Miss Gilmore laid the

pointer on the desk in front of her. 'Then class dismissed.'

Gathering her books and pens together, Mattie picked up her old school satchel from beneath the desk. She tided her equipment away and stood up.

Having said goodnight and see you next week to her fellow students, she unhooked her overcoat from the peg by the door and, shrugging it on, made her way down the stairs to the front door.

Slipping behind the blackout curtains, Mattie opened the door and walked out into almost total blackness, the occasional downturned car lamp and bus headlight providing the only illumination. Turning her collar up against the chilly night air and treading carefully along the paved path, she made her way to the street.

Waiting until she was sure there were no trams looming silently out of the darkness, she crossed Commercial Road and made her way to the bus stop on Whitechapel High Street opposite Aldgate garage. Taking up her place at the back of the small queue waiting for the bus and running through the chemical symbols for gasses in her head, Mattie looked eastwards to watch for a bus.

'Excuse me, is this the stop for the number 15 going to Limehouse?' asked a familiar-sounding voice.

Mattie turned. 'Father McCree?' she said, her heart beating ridiculously fast.

He looked across. 'Is that Miss Brogan?'

'Yes, it is,' Mattie replied, side-stepping to give her place to the woman standing between them. 'What are you doing here?'

197

'Waiting for a bus. And you?'

'The same.'

He gave a rumbling laugh and Mattie's heart did a little double step.

'Hence us both standing at a bus stop,' he said.

'Yes,' said Mattie. 'The stop for the number 15, I mean. I'm waiting for it myself.'

A number 25 drew up and most of the queue shuffled forward. Although blacked-out, small slivers of light escaped from the edges of the bus's concertinaed leather blinds, showing Mattie the strong planes of Father McCree's face. She could see that he was looking at her, the darkness of his eyes driving all thoughts from her head.

Mercifully, another bus honed into sight.

'This is ours,' said Mattie as it stopped beside them.

She went to reach for the upright handrail but Father McCree held out his hand. Mattie took it and stepped onto the platform footplate.

'Upstairs, if you please,' called the conductor, pulling the bell cord.

The bus jolted forward.

'After you.' Daniel said with a casual smile.

Tucking her skirt in behind her to save giving her parish priest an eyeful of stockings and suspenders, Mattie climbed up to the top deck.

There were a couple of people already seated, including a young couple necking on the back seat who jumped apart as if on fire when they saw Father McCree.

As the vehicle veered right around Garner's Corner, Mattie slipped into a vacant seat and Father McCree sat beside her.

While he made himself comfortable, Mattie stole a look at him.

Her eyes flickered over his profile, noting the end-of-day stubble on his cheek then the neatly trimmed sideburn in front of his right ear before drifting down to the line of bristles that stopped in an orderly fashion just above his dog collar.

'I hope I'm not squashing you too much,' he said.

'No, no, I've plenty of room,' she replied, acutely aware of his long, muscular thigh so close to hers. 'So have you settled into the parish now?'

'Yes I have,' said Father McCree. 'In fact, everyone's been so friendly I feel like I've been here forever.'

The bell rang and the bus ground to a halt for a few moments, then started off again. The conductor came up and Mattie opened her purse.

'I'll get them,' said Father McCree, rummaging around in his trouser pocket. 'Two to Watney Street.'

He handed over a couple of coppers and took the two 6d tickets in return.

'So have you been somewhere nice, Father?' Mattie asked, as he handed her one.

'I have,' he replied. 'I went to see my Aunt Fanny.'

'Where does she live?'

'Around the corner from Waterloo,' he replied. 'What about you? Have you been out having fun?'

Mattie rolled her eyes. 'Not with the elements of the periodic table.'

He gave her a questioning look.

'I'm studying for my Higher Certificate.'

'Are you now?' he said, looking astounded.

'You don't have to look so shocked, Father,' Mattie replied, trying not to feel deflated. 'I passed the entrance test for Raines School but I couldn't go because...'

'I'm not shocked, Mattie, I'm in admiration of you,' he replied.

'Are you?'

'Of course,' he continued. 'And I am sorry if I gave you the impression otherwise.'

'And I'm sorry for snapping your head off like that, Father,' she said.

'After a long day it takes a lot of determination to spend your free time studying,' he added. 'What do you want to do after?'

'I'm not certain yet, but...' Mattie bit her lower lip and gave him a pensive look.

His dark eyes searched her face. 'But what?'

'I know it's a bit of a fanciful dream for an ordinary girl like me,' she said, hooking her finger through her hair and twisting it. 'But I'd like to go to university and study History.'

'That's marvellous,' he said.

'Do you think so?' she asked, basking in his approving gaze.

'Of course I do,' he replied. 'It's a really useful subject as it can be used to join the Civil Service or to become a teacher or a solicitor. You could even consider a career in politics.'

'Could I?' asked Mattie.

'Yes, that's why I read European History at York University. I had a vague notion I might run for parliament one day.' A sour thought twisted his mouth. 'It's easy to dream of changing the world when you're just arguing the pros and cons with your fellow students, but it's a bit different when you get into the real world.'

'So I suppose that's why you went to the seminary instead,' she said.

He looked puzzled. 'The seminary?'

'To become a priest?'

'Oh yes, the seminary.'

The bus stopped and the young couple got off and three factory girls, in trousers and with their hair tied up in turban headscarves, took their places.

'You must have had a complete change of heart when you decided the Church not parliament was the way to change the world,' Mattie said as the conductor rang the bell and the bus rolled on.

He gave her a wan smile then, taking his handkerchief from his pocket, Father McCree took off his glasses.

'So tell me,' he said, breathing on the lens. 'When do you take your exam?'

'Next May, which seemed like a long way off when I started but we're almost at the end of the autumn term already,' Mattie replied. 'And it wouldn't be so bad if the blooming Shadwell siren hadn't gone off at midnight.'

'Yes, I could have done without a midnight visit to the rectory cellar myself,' he replied.

'We had to trudge all the way to Cable Street shelter and sit in the cold for hours before the all-clear went at two and then we trudged back,' said Mattie. 'Half the street didn't even bother this time, just stayed tucked up in bed.'

Father McCree looked grim. 'That's not very wise of them, now is it?'

'No, it's not,' Mattie replied.

The conductor rang the bell again.

'Watney Market!' he shouted from below.

'That's us,' said Mattie, rising to her feet and slinging her satchel over her shoulder.

Father McCree did the same. Stepping out of their seat they made their way down to the lower deck and off the bus.

Standing in the dim light of the shielded Belisha beacon, they listened for any cars approaching. When they were certain it was safe, they crossed Commercial Road.

When they got to the pavement on the other side, they turned to face each other.

'It was nice to run into you, Father McCree,' said Mattie.

'You too, Mattie,' he replied, smiling down at her. 'And thanks for making sure I got on the right bus.'

She laughed. 'Well we couldn't have you heading towards Oxford Street by mistake now, could we?'

He smiled and Mattie smiled back.

'Well, I'd better get home,' she said, not making a move to do so.

'It's pretty dark so perhaps I should walk with you–'

'No, I'll be fine, thank you, Father,' she said.

He gazed down at her. 'If you're sure?'

She nodded.

There was a pause.

'Well goodnight then, Father,' Mattie said, wondering why on earth she was imagining throwing herself into his arms.

'Goodnight.' He walked away from her.

'Oh, Father?' she shouted.

Barely visible in the gloom, he stopped and turned back.

'You won't tell my mum I snapped your head off a while back, will you?' she asked.

A flash of white told her he was smiling. 'No I won't, Mattie, as long as you stop thinking of yourself as an ordinary girl.'

With a flick of his arm, Christopher swirled Mattie around as the Ritz Orchestra played the final bars of 'Dancing in the Dark'.

He let go of her hand and they, along with the two dozen or so other couples on the dancefloor, clapped loudly to show their appreciation.

The conductor, a rotund chap with oiled hair, acknowledged their applause with a quick bow, then turned back to face his musicians. Raising his hands, they struck up the opening bars of a Viennese waltz and the dancers took their places.

'Shall we sit this one out?' said Christopher.

'Yes, let's,' Mattie replied.

Slipping his arm around her waist, Christopher led her off the dancefloor and back to their table.

It was the first Saturday in December and she and Christopher had been going out as regularly as their respective Civil Defence duties allowed for a couple of weeks and tonight they were in the ballroom of the famous hotel on Piccadilly.

'Are you having fun, sweetheart?' he asked, as she tucked her skirt under her to sit down.

'Yes I am,' Mattie replied, slipping her minute

evening bag off her wrist and placing it alongside her empty tea cup and plate.

He smiled. 'I'm glad. I'm sorry that I had to change our date to an afternoon tea dance but H Division has just had another dozen policemen volunteer so they are very short at the station and they need the auxiliary officers to cover patrols.'

'That's all right, I quite understand,' Mattie laughed. 'And really, Christopher, you don't have to apologise for taking me for tea at the Ritz.'

He grinned. 'I wanted to make our sixth date something special.'

'Well I think this certainly qualifies as special,' said Mattie, casting her eye around the beautiful room with its sparkling chandeliers and gilt mirrors. 'And it's our fourth date.'

He looked surprised. 'Really?'

'Yes.'

'Well I suppose that's because I feel as if we've known each other much longer than just a month.' Pulling his seat closer, Christopher's arm wound around the back of her chair. 'Have I told you that you look absolutely stunning in that dress?'

Mattie smiled and gave a silent prayer of thanks that she'd borrowed Francesca's water green silk chiffon dress for the afternoon.

'Makes a chap think of things,' he said, in a low voice.

'I thought that's all a chap thought about,' Mattie replied, countering his hot gaze with a cool one.

'They do, especially these days when none of us know what tomorrow will bring.' His smile widened. 'But don't pretend women don't have wicked thoughts too.'

'I'm not saying they don't,' said Mattie, trying to stop an image of a bare-chested Father McCree forming in her mind. 'But I'm–'

'It seems to me that in these uncertain times we should grab the chance for a bit of happiness while we can.' Looking deep into her eyes, Christopher rested his hand on her thigh. 'What do you say, darling, to having a weekend in the country at a nice little hotel so we can get to know each other a bit better?' He squeezed her leg. 'Come on, Mattie, say yes and I'll make sure you have some fun.'

'I'm not–'

'Say you'll think about it,' he persisted.

'All right.' Mattie removed his hand. 'I'll think about it.'

Christopher grinned and, raising his hand, clicked his fingers.

One of the waiters, dressed in the hotel's livery and with a small tray under his arm, hurried forward.

'Yes, sir,' he said, standing to attention.

'Clear this away,' Christopher said, indicating their used crockery with a flick of his finger. 'And bring us some fresh tea and another plate of cakes.'

The waiter bowed and, placing the tray on the table, started stacking the crockery. As he picked up Mattie's cup it toppled over and some tea splashed into the saucer.

'Have a care,' Christopher barked. 'The young lady doesn't want it in her lap.'

'Yes, sir, sorry, sir.'

'And bring us two glasses of champagne,' Christopher said.

'Certainly, sir.'

Lifting the loaded tray onto his shoulder, the waiter hurried off

Christopher scowled after him for a moment, then he looked surprised.

'I'm sorry, Mattie, my dear,' he said, looking earnestly at her. 'I've just spotted someone I know, do you mind I pop over and say hello?'

'Not at all,' said Mattie.

Giving her a peck on the cheek, Christopher rose to his feet.

'You can decide where you'd like to go for our weekend in the country while I'm away.'

Mattie smiled but didn't reply.

Christopher strolled over to a table on the raised dais at the far end of the room to greet a bald-headed middle-aged chap with a blonde snuggled against him who must have been at least half his age.

After his initial surprise, he shook Christopher's hand vigorously and offered him a cigar. Christopher said something and the older chap laughed heartily and slapped him on the back. He offered Christopher a chair at their table but Christopher shook his head and looked across at Mattie. The older man followed his gaze and, giving Mattie the once-over, he nudged Christopher, who nodded. They shook hands again and then, with the cigar clamped between his teeth and a grin on his face, Christopher strolled back.

'Who was that?' asked Mattie as he resumed his seat.

'Lord Bedlington, has an estate somewhere in Essex,' Christopher replied.

'How do you know him?' asked Mattie.

'We have some mutual friends,' Christopher replied, puffing smoke circles and watching them drift upwards. 'He's invited me to spend New Year with him and his wife.'

'What did you say?' asked Mattie.

Christopher turned and smiled. 'Well I should have said "I'd rather be with my beautiful girl-friend than be stuck in a draughty old pile with you and your frightful wife", but...' He took her hand. 'If I play my cards right, he could put in a good word for me with his friends in very high places so I'm afraid I had to say "yes".' He formed his expression into one of abject misery. 'Will you ever forgive me?'

'I expect so,' laughed Mattie. 'Especially as I'm on warden duty so will be seeing in 1940 wearing my ARP uniform anyway.'

He pressed his lips to her fingers again and then let go as the waiter returned.

Setting the tray on the table, the young man unloaded the clean crockery, tea service and laden cake stand, then set two tall glasses of champagne in front of them.

'Thank you very much,' said Mattie, looking up and smiling at the young man.

He acknowledged her with his eyes, then bowed and left.

'You know, Mattie,' said Christopher, tapping the ash from the end of his cigar into the ashtray. 'They're getting paid to serve you so you don't have to thank them.'

'But it's just politeness to thank someone who does something for you, isn't it?' she replied.

'Perhaps, sweetheart,' Christopher replied. 'But you wouldn't find people like Lord Bedlington thanking his servants.'

Picking up the drink in front of him, he took a large mouthful.

'Mmm, wonderful.' He smiled at Mattie. 'Try it, sweetheart.'

Taking her glass, Mattie lifted it to her lips.

It tasted fruity but not too sweet and the bubbles seemed to keep the taste on her tongue for longer.

'Nice?' asked Christopher, looking expectantly at her.

'Very,' said Mattie, raising her glass in appreciation.

'Good.' He had another mouthful, then glanced around at the luxurious grandeur surrounding them and smacked his lips. 'I could get used to this, couldn't you?'

Mattie smiled.

He laughed and threw the last of his drink back.

Taking another sip, she studied him over the rim of her champagne flute. Yes, who couldn't get used to drinking champagne at the Ritz, but not if it required her to not have the common decency to thank people.

Reaching out, Christopher grasped the door handle of the Walters & Sons hardware store at the corner of St Stephen Street and gave it a pull. The bar securing it inside rattled, showing the premises were secure.

It was now probably close to midnight and he'd arrived at the station for his evening patrol at six to find they were another three officers down. This meant that instead of being paired up with one of the regular constables, Christopher and a couple of other auxiliary officers had been sent out to patrol adjoining beats.

Before setting out, Taffy Evan had given them strict instruction to meet every thirty minutes at a given point so he could check on them and not to tackle anything suspicious themselves but to summon help by blowing their whistles.

So far for a Saturday evening, other than the odd drunk and two women in Antill Road almost coming to blows over a communal toilet, it had been a quiet night, which was hardly surprising given that the temperature was hovering close to freezing.

Despite the biting cold wind whistling between the frames of the market stalls, Christopher felt warm and decidedly bright even though he still had six hours of trudging through the empty street ahead of him.

This was due to two quite unrelated things. Firstly it had been a stroke of luck running into Drummond's close friend Lord Bedlington at the Ritz, especially as it had secured him an invitation to the earl's country estate. The second thing making him smile was Mattie.

Of course she hadn't actually agreed to slip away for a dirty weekend but, given the money he was lavishing on her, she couldn't in good conscience say no. He was confident that, sooner or later, preferably sooner, Mattie would fall for his fatal charm. Women had to because he wouldn't take no for an answer.

At first, given her common background, he'd thought she'd be an easy conquest but now he'd realised she was playing hard to get he'd found himself more keen to get her into bed. It was clear he would be the first and he hadn't had that sweet experience for a few years, not properly anyway. That young Jewess in Munich might have been a virgin, but tying her up and forcing a rag in her mouth wasn't what he had planned for Mattie.

Turning up his collar and tugging on his leather gloves, Christopher took his dimming torch from his pocket. Shining it on the pavement a few feet in front of him, he set off again on his patrol. Running through the various country pubs he'd been to that might suit his purpose, he'd just got level with Schapiro's the jewellers when the siren on Old Ford Road school started to wail.

The nearest shelter was in St Bartholomew Church's crypt, about half a mile west of him and as it was within his allotted beat he was supposed to report there to give assistance. However as he didn't relish the thought of being squashed in for hours with a bunch of sweaty cockneys, Christopher stepped into the doorway of the butcher's and waited as the stream of tired-looking residents carrying bundles of bedding and sleepy children trudged past him. After about five minutes the siren ceased and the street fell silent. Reaching into the pocket of his greatcoat, Christopher took out his cigarettes.

He'd just lit one when the front door of the

jeweller's opposite burst open.

''Urry up!' he shouted over his shoulder.

'But what about the old man?' the second thief asked from inside the shop.

'Sod 'im,' came the reply. 'If he gets a gander of our mooches we'll be up for a ten-year stretch.'

The first man grabbed his friend and dragged him down one of the alleyways between the shops.

Taking a draw on his cigarette, Christopher flicked it onto the pavement then crossed the road and pushed the door of the jeweller's open with his gloved index finger.

It swung back and Christopher shone his torch around. The half-glazed display cases which lined one side of the small shop had been smashed and their contents scattered on the floor. The drawers beneath the glass cabinets had also been pulled open and ransacked.

As the beam of light hit the back wall and glinted off the wall clocks and commemorative plaques, there was a groan.

'Help,' wheezed a voice from behind the shop counter. 'Please ... someone help me.'

Crunching over the shards of glass, Christopher walked around to the other side of the counter and shone his torch on the floor.

There, crushed beneath the four-foot-long polished mahogany counter-top which had been wrenched off to expose the jewellery display under it, was an elderly Jewish man, his features contorted in pain.

'T'ank Gott,' he panted, his hands gripping the edge of the heavy slab of wood. 'Quick, quick get dis off me.'

A cruel smile twisted Christopher's mouth.

Fixing the beam from his torch onto the old man, he studied him coolly for a second, then pulled out his packet of cigarettes from his pocket again. Putting one in his mouth, he lit the end and took a long drag.

'Please help, please,' whispered the old man, a faint bubbling sound accompanying his words.

Stepping forward, Christopher placed his right foot squarely on top of the dark wooden counter, pinning the shopkeeper to the floor.

The old man's eyes, already bloodshot from the pressure, darted frantically around for a couple of seconds.

'I ca … can't bre…' the old man gasped.

He coughed as blood trickled out of the corner of his mouth and down his wispy white beard.

Taking the cigarette from his mouth, Christopher flicked the ash from the end, then inhaled another lungful of smoke.

'Pity,' mouthed the shopkeeper, his shrivelled features flush with the mounting pressure. 'Have pity.'

Christopher took a long draw on his cigarette then, holding it between his thumb and second finger, tapped ash on the old man's face.

Holding the old man's terror-filled gaze, he watched while his weight slowly squeezed the air and life from the old man. The board under his feet shuddered as the Jew's feeble body summoned its fading strength for a last push against the crushing pressure but then his eyes fixed on a point above Christopher's head and all movement ceased.

Christopher stood motionless for a moment, then stepped off. The body beneath gave a groan as air was sucked back into the collapsed lungs.

Shining the torch beam onto his victim's motionless face, Christopher noticed something twinkling amongst the old man's dishevelled grey hair.

Crouching down, he picked it up. It was a brooch in the shape of a bow, made in gold with small diamonds traced around the stiff, stylized ribbon and with a large red stone as the knot.

He stood up and, holding it under the light, turned it over in his hand a couple of times. He slipped it into his inside jacket pocket.

Making his way back through the shattered remains of the shop, Christopher walked out of the front door and back into the street.

Flicking his cigarette away in a high arc, he pulled his whistle from his breast pocket, drew a breath and blew a long, shrill blast.

Before the note had faded, Sergeant Evan's stout figure materialised out of the dark, jogging towards him.

'What's happened?' panted Taffy, as he came to a halt in front of Christopher.

'I was just on my way to the shelter when I stumbled on this,' Christopher pointed to the door swinging off its hinges. 'I can't hear anything inside so whoever did it must have fled but you said we were to call for assistance.'

'Good lad,' said Taffy. 'Stay here and I'll have a quick shufty.'

Christopher nodded. He'd just lit another cigarette when his duty sergeant re-emerged with a sober look on his face.

'Has it been screwed, sarge?' asked Christopher.

'That it has,' said the sergeant. 'But I'm afraid this is more than a straightforward burglary, it's murder.'

'Murder?' gasped Christopher.

''Fraid so,' said Taffy. 'The shopkeeper's dead.'

Christopher forced a look of anguish onto his face. 'Perhaps if I'd gone in I could have–'

'Now, look you, lad,' cut in Taffy. 'Don't get yourself all inside out, there was nothing you could have done. Now you trot down to the police box on the corner and phone the station while I take some notes.'

Christopher saluted. 'Yes, sarge.'

Christopher turned and marched off.

'And don't you worry, son,' Sergeant Evan called after him. 'You did a good job here.'

In the shadow cast by the peak of his police helmet, a smile crept across Christopher's face.

Chapter Ten

It was just after eight on the third Friday in December and Mattie's first day off in over three weeks. Instead of being left to catch up on some much-needed sleep, her mother had prodded her awake at six that morning and insisted she come with her to get a 'few bits' down the market ready for Christmas.

Two hours later, and despite her and her

mother arriving at Watney Street Sainsbury's in good time, there were at least two dozen women in front of them, all waiting for the shop to open. If this wasn't bad enough, the temperature was close to freezing and the dense fog from the river meant their chilly wait was accompanied by a chorus of hacking coughs. However, while they waited for the shutter to be lifted, Mattie's mother was taking the opportunity to catch up on any gossip she might have missed.

Watney Street ran from Commercial Road in the north to Cable Street in the south. The old mock-gothic Victorian Christ Church was at the top of the street and Shadwell Station at the bottom, with the old East End market running between. According to Mr Grossman, the local librarian, a market had been held on the site for centuries; the shops and public houses alongside it being later additions. Like markets up and down the land, it sold the usual fare of meat, fish and vegetables, along with other items rarely seen outside East London such as gefilte fish, bagels and challah bread. Situated under the old Tilbury to Minories railway line that ran on a viaduct above the market were a series of arches housing a couple of workshops, a wholesale fishmonger and Gerty Winkler's second-hand clothing and rag-sorting yard.

Some of Mattie's earliest memories were of being dragged along after her mother while she looked for late bargains for tea or being sent around to Fielding's to get her father half an ounce of old Holborn and a packet of greens. Now, just two weeks before Christmas, the stalls were doing their best to bring their customers a bit of festive cheer by decorating their awnings with bunting cut from last year's wrapping paper. However, whereas in years gone by the fruit and vegetable stalls would have had artistically arranged pyramids of tangerines and packets of dried dates dotted amongst the spuds and carrots, this year there were none, and there wasn't a packet of paper chains or a Chinese lantern to be had for love nor money.

'I was saying to Madge,' continued her mother, 'that that Rita Colman's been seen arm-in-arm with some chap and her Fred not yet cold in his grave.'

'He's been dead six months, Mum,' said Mattie. 'And weren't the police forever around their place most Friday nights because he laid into her when he'd had a few?'

'True,' said Madge Crowther, a wiry woman with springy brown hair and a wandering left eye. 'But that was just his way.'

'And even if Fred was a bit handy with his fists, it don' mean she should be swanning around with some other man as bold as brass before his headstone's got a bit of moss it,' her mother replied.

'That's going to be difficult seeing how he was cremated,' said Mattie.

Her mother gave her a sharp look. 'You know what I mean.'

'She shouldn't even think about letting another man get his feet under her table for at least a year,' chipped in Madge. 'It ain't respectable.'

'No, it ain't,' agreed her mother.

Mattie sighed and returned to her contemplation of the tins of pilchards arranged in a pyramid in the shop window and her mind drifted off again.

The small door in the shutter covering the grocer's shop opened and one of the junior lads, dressed in his long apron with his white cotton half-sleeves covering his forearms, stepped out and started winding up the night shutter. Her mother shuffled forward with the rest of the queue and Mattie trudged after her.

'About bloomin' time,' Ida grumbled, shoving the battered pram she used to carry her shopping into the woman in front.

The woman turned. 'Oi!'

'Well, you wanna pay attention,' her mother retorted.

They exchanged a glare and the woman turned back.

'And tell your bloody kids I'll fetch the police on them if they start playing knock-down-ginger in our street again,' her mother added.

'I don't know why you had to bring that old thing,' said Mattie, as they moved forward again. 'I'm sure we could manage to carry everything between us.'

Her mother shook her head. 'I want to get a few things for Christmas.'

'Why?' said Mattie, her eyes wide with astonishment. 'We're already knee-deep in the Christmas stuff you've bought.'

'Why?' said her mother. 'With rationing starting in January and Charlie coming home for the last time before he sets off to put paid to these bloody Nazis and their tricks, I want to make

217

sure we have a proper family Christmas with all the trimmings this year.'

A couple of extra bits!

As far as Mattie could tell, her mother had been squirrelling away jars of pickled onions, gherkins and piccalilli as well as tins of peaches, evaporated milk and Old Oak Ham since she'd made her Christmas pudding in August. She'd even managed to buy two crates of brown ale with scorched labels from the cellar fire in Old Rose. They, along with the ironed wrapping paper saved from last year and the box of glass tree ornaments wrapped in cotton wool, were now stored under her parents' old brass bed.

'After all,' continued her mother, drawing one of Jerimiah's handkerchiefs from her overcoat pocket and blowing her nose loudly. 'We might as well enjoy our last family Christmas together cos who knows if we'll all still be alive this time next year.'

'Too right, Ida,' said Madge, returning to their conversation having assured the anxious young mother behind her that there was no harm in putting a drop of brandy in her baby's last feed to settle her infant.

The door opened and the crowd of women surged forward.

'Right,' said Ida, her bargain-seeking eyes scanning the various counters to see what was on offer. 'You get over to the cheese and eggs while I see what they have on the general counter.'

'What do you want me to get?' asked Mattie as she and her mother parted company in front of the surge of shoppers.

'A bit of ham for your dad's supper, a dozen

218

eggs, half a sliced tongue and anything that will keep,' her mother called back, elbowing her way to the front of the grocery line.

Fifteen minutes later, with a full shopping bag in one hand and a tray of eggs balanced in the other, Mattie regrouped with her mother outside the shop.

'Good,' Ida said, inspecting the three jars of mincemeat and two tins of sterilised cream alongside the wrapped meat and tongue in Mattie's shopping bag. 'But's what that round thing?'

'It's cheese,' said Mattie.

'Is it?' said her mother. 'I can't say as how I've heard of red cheese before?'

'That's just the wax covering,' Mattie explained. 'It comes from Holland.'

'So do tulips but I wouldn't eat them,' her mother replied.

'The section supervisor said if we kept it in the cool it would stay fresh and it was on special offer so I thought it would help Christmas tea go further if someone pops in,' said Mattie.

'I'm not sure about having foreign food on the table on Our Lord's birthday,' said her mother, regarding it suspiciously.

'I think I read in *Titbits* that the royal family have it for tea sometimes,' said Mattie.

'Well then, if the king thinks it right and proper then that's a different matter altogether,' said Ida. Taking the bag from Mattie, she deposited it alongside her own shopping in the pram. 'I'll put it in the cold keep.'

Her mother's cold keep sat against the wall of the yard that never got the sun. It was, in fact, a

219

marble butler's sink that her father had acquired years ago. It was double the size of any sink Mattie had ever seen, bigger even than the sinks at St George's Baths, where the women did their weekly laundry. Its lid, which was half of someone called Sven Kristiansen's gravestone, had to be pushed back when you were depositing something. Even in the height of summer it could keep milk fresh for two days.

'Right,' said her mother, kicking the brake off the pram. 'All I need to do is drop in at the butchers to get me weekend meat and then see what Doug's has by way of vegetables.'

'While you're doing that I might pop down to Shelton's and get myself a pair of nylons for tonight,' said Mattie as they stepped out into the road to walk around the brewery lorry unloading at the Lord Nelson.

'You out with that bank manager chap again?' her mother asked.

'Yes I am,' Mattie replied.

'You've been going strong with him for a while now, haven't you?'

'A couple of months, but I wouldn't say it's serious,' said Mattie.

'Not serious!' Her mother's eyebrows rose. 'Most of your young men don't make a couple of weeks, let alone months, so you must be keen on this Christopher.'

'He's quite nice,' conceded Mattie.

'I'd say he's more than quite nice, after all the swanky places he's been taking you these last few weeks!' said her mother. 'He must have spent a fortune.'

'He probably has,' admitted Mattie.

A suspicious look crept into her mother's eye. 'I hope as how he ain't thinking he's going to get it back in kind from you.'

'He can try,' said Mattie. 'But he'll be mighty disappointed.'

Her mother patted her hand. 'I know, you're a good girl and I'm sure he'll respect you for it.'

Mattie gave her mother a wan smile and decided it would be better not to mention Christopher's suggestion they have a weekend away somewhere.

All blokes tried it on, of course, but a hand up the skirt was quickly slapped away and, by and large, men didn't expect anything else. In fact, in the topsy-turvy way that blokes thought, they were pleased to have a girlfriend who wouldn't allow them to take any liberties as it meant she wouldn't allow any other fella either. However, in Christopher's case it wasn't so much that he tried to get in her blouse all the time, it was more that when his hands did stray, it was in such a way that it seemed accidental or unintentional, which made it difficult for Mattie to block or avoid.

'Then why don't you invite him for Christmas dinner?' her mother said, cutting through her uncomfortable thoughts.

Mattie bit her lip. 'I'm not sure.'

'If you're worried about Queenie being a bit whiffy,' said her mother. 'I'll make sure she goes to the baths and changes her underwear.'

'No, it's not Gran,' said Mattie. 'But asking him to "meet the family" is really asking him if he wants to walk out with me as a couple.'

'Well, what's wrong with that?' said her mother.

'I've always thought you were a bit too fussy when it came to men but now you've got a chap with good prospects you'd do well to keep hold of him. And didn't you say he was in digs?'

'Yes, in Bow, but–'

'Well,' cut in Ida. 'What sort of miserable Christmas do you think he's going to have without his family around him?'

An image of Christopher sitting alone at a stranger's dining room table, staring down at a shrivelled slice of beef, a couple of over-boiled potatoes and a handful of undercooked Brussel sprouts, sprang into Mattie's mind.

'His landlady does sound like a bit of a dragon,' she said.

'Well then, it's no more than your Christian duty to invite him,' said Ida. 'It'll give us a chance to get to know him and it might stop you and your father talking about politics all through Christmas dinner like last year.'

Mattie sighed. 'All right, I'll ask him.'

'Grand,' said her mother as they stopped outside the butchers.

Mattie gave a wan smile. 'I'll meet you at Doug's.'

'I shouldn't be too long, if young Harry stops giving her from Tarlin Street the eye and gets on with it,' her mother replied.

Repositioning her handbag on her arm, Mattie turned and headed towards Shelton's the haberdasher's at the bottom end of the street.

'And don't worry,' her mother called at the top of her voice to ensure the maximum reach. 'We'll all be on our best behaviour when your young

222

man who works in a bank comes to call.'

Slotting her time card in the rack, Mattie turned up the collar of her overcoat and wound her scarf around her neck to keep out the December chill. Yawning, she pushed the door open and, leaving the warm fug of Post 7's control room, walked out into Shadwell School's playground.

It was the Friday before Christmas and just before two in the afternoon. It was also the shortest day of the year so, as she walked through the school gates, she turned the hands on the noticeboard clock to ten past two so that people would know what time the blackout came into force that day.

Adjusting her knapsack on her shoulder, Mattie turned along the Highway and headed home. However, as she emerged from the railway arch at the bottom on the market, she noticed the gate to her father's yard was open. Waiting until the Maguire & Son coal wagon passed by, Mattie crossed the road but, instead of turning into Mafeking Terrace, she continued on.

Slipping between the half-open wooden gate, Mattie walked into the yard and noticed that, whereas a few months ago she'd have to weave her way between old bedsteads, prams and household furniture to get to the enclosed area under the railway arch which served as a stable and office, now she had an almost clear path.

Cracking the newly formed ice on the puddles as she walked, Mattie made her way to the back of the yard and opened the door.

The empty cart stood with its shafts up at the

rear of the space and Samson was munching hay in his stall, a warm haze of moisture visible about his solid piebald flanks. Her father sat hunched in his donkey jacket at his desk, his gloved hands cradling a steaming cup. He looked up as Mattie walked in, a wide smile lifting his tired face.

'Hello, luv,' he said, standing up. 'You done for the day?'

'Yes, thank goodness,' Mattie replied. 'Looks like you are too.'

He nodded. 'No point me and Samson trudging around the street in this weather for nothing.'

'I thought you usually picked up lots this time of year with people clearing out their old stuff before Christmas,' said Mattie.

'I do,' said her father. 'But not this year. Everyone is hanging on to what they've got and...' He waved his words aside. 'Anyway, forget that for now, you just come over here and warm yourself by the stove.'

Mattie did as he said. Taking her gloves off, she held her hands out towards the paraffin stove alongside his desk.

'Better?' he asked.

Mattie nodded.

'So what have you been up to?' he asked.

As the warmth crept back through her, Mattie ran through her day on duty, starting with the delivery of new stirrup pumps in the morning and finishing with the standup row between Cyril and one of the ambulance crew who'd turned up for late duty very much the worst for wear after a lunchtime Christmas drink-up.

'So, all in all,' said Mattie in conclusion, 'another day hanging around doing nothing very much.'

'Well, me darling, I'd be making the most of it if I were you because I'd lay a pound to a penny Hitler will be on the move in the New Year and then we'll all be busy,' her father replied. 'Right, you take yourself a pew while I finish off and then we can walk home together.'

Pulling out the decrepit buttoned-back leather chair from the desk, Mattie sat down.

'Your mother tells me you're bringing this bank manager young man of yours home for Christmas dinner?' said her father, stacking a set of chairs on each other.

'He's in charge of loans, not a manager,' said Mattie. 'But yes, he's coming for dinner.'

Her father's dark eyebrows raised a notch.

'He's just a friend,' she added. 'So don't get any ideas.'

'It's your mother you need to tell that to,' Jerimiah replied. 'It's her that's been telling the whole of Watney Market that you'll be marrying the governor of the Bank of England.'

Mattie didn't reply.

After his suggestion that they slip away for a weekend in the country, Mattie didn't think marriage was what Christopher had in his mind and, truthfully, even if it was, try as she might, Mattie couldn't imagine herself as his bride. Unfortunately, the man who seemed always to take that role in her dreams had already made his vows to a higher power.

'I've just got to stack this with the others and I'll be with you,' her father said, cutting into her

225

uncomfortable thoughts.

Heaving a mattress up from the floor, he leaned it against three others and turned back to face her. 'And then we can head off...'

He stopped and his attention shifted from Mattie to something behind her.

She turned to see her brother Charlie, in full battle dress with his field service cap slipped through his epaulets and his canvas kitbag over his shoulder, standing in the doorway.

The curl had been clipped from his dark hair and there was a barely healed scar on his right cheek. He was bigger, older and tougher, but Mattie could still see the big brother who'd smacked Willy Mace in the nose when he'd pushed her in the playground and who had bought her a red ribbon with his last thru'pence for her fourteenth birthday.

'Hello, Dad,' said Charlie.

'Hello, boy,' their father replied.

They all stood motionless for a moment, then Charlie dropped his kitbag on the floor.

Jerimiah crossed the space between them and put his arms around Charlie. He slapped his back a couple of times before letting him go.

Charlie looked at Mattie. 'Hello, scrawny.'

'Hello, knobbly knees.'

They grinned at each other, then he gave her a hug too, and kissed the top of her head.

Jerimiah closed his book. 'Let me give Samson some fresh water and then we can walk home to surprise your mother.'

Mattie picked up her ARP bag as her brother grabbed his kitbag and they walked out into the yard to wait for their father to lock up.

'How's it going, Charlie?' Mattie asked, her breath making small puffs in the cold air.

'Not bad,' he replied. 'Of course the drill sergeant is a bloody masochist and the top brass are all barmy but I've made a couple of good mates. And we're shipping out soon.'

'Where?' Mattie rolled her eyes. 'Sorry, I forgot. I shouldn't ask.'

'It don't matter, Sis,' said Charlie. 'The army don't tell us poor buggers in the infantry nothing but there's a whisper going around that we're going to be issued with arctic uniforms so we might be being sent to keep Hitler from invading the North Pole.' He pulled an admiring expression and looked her over. 'And what about you; all dressed up in your ARP warden gear.'

'Well we've all got to do our bit,' said Mattie. 'I saw Francesca the other day and she asked how you were.'

'Did she,' said Charlie.

'Yes, I told her that despite all your moaning you were having a whale of a time,' said Mattie.

Charlie laughed but didn't deny it.

'She's signed on for war work,' Mattie continued. 'She wanted to volunteer as an auxiliary policewoman but her dad didn't like the idea of her working with all those men.'

'Yes, Fran always did turn heads so I'm not surprised her dad wasn't keen to have all those men chasing after her,' said Charlie. 'In fact, I'm surprised some bright chap hasn't swept her off her feet already.'

Mattie raised an eyebrow. 'Are you, Charlie?'

'Yes, she's very pretty,' he replied. 'And she's got a lovely smile.'

'Perhaps she's already given her heart to someone,' said Mattie.

Charlie smiled. 'Well, I hope he appreciates her, whoever he is.'

Their father walked out and turned to secure the padlock across the door.

'By the way,' said Charlie, dropping his voice a tone. 'Have you seen Stella about?'

'From time to time,' Mattie replied, as an image of her brother's gin-filled fiancée staggering around the Regal's dancefloor flashed across her mind. 'Why?'

'It's just I've written a couple of letters and didn't get a reply.' He smiled. 'I expect she's been busy.'

'Probably,' Mattie replied.

'Well, never mind.' He patted his breast pocket and there was a faint jingle as he grinned. 'I promised to bring her a little present to cheer her up.'

Having locked up for the night, their father strolled over.

'Right,' said Jerimiah, rubbing his hands together. 'We'll say hello to your mother, have a quick cuppa and then head down the club for a few pints with the lads.'

'That's sounds grand,' said Charlie. 'But only a couple of pints as I've got to go and surprise Stella.'

'Good lad.' Jerimiah slapped him on the back. 'It always pays to keep the little woman happy.'

Charlie grinned and then fell into step alongside his father.

Mattie stared after her brother and wondered, not for the first time, how Charlie, who could divide and multiply six-digit numbers in his head and work out fractions and percentages in the blink of an eye, could be so bloody stupid.

The BBC concert orchestra played softly in the background as Mattie wrote down Amazon and then scored a line through the last clue of her crossword puzzle. She threw last Friday's edition of *The Times* on the pile with the rest of the saved paper.

It was four forty-five on Christmas Eve and, like every other Sunday afternoon, the Brogan family was having a few hours' relaxation, and Mattie needed it.

For the past week, between patrolling the streets to check for careless householders showing a light, being woken up in the small hours by air-raid sirens and keeping up with her studies, Mattie had helped their mother get the house ready for the big day. It had started on Monday when, after a busy nightshift, Mattie had arrived home only to have all the bed linen thrust into her hands and told to take them to St George's washhouse. Tuesday, before she went to work, she had hung every rug in the place out on the line for a beating while her mother and Jo swept the house from top to bottom. Wednesday was a relatively light day of polishing every stick of furniture. Mattie was at work for a double shift on Thursday so it had fallen to Jo to help put up the Christmas decorations, including the somewhat lopsided Christmas tree her father had picked up cheap on his travels.

Friday, Queenie was up and out before even Mattie's father was about. She had returned as they were locking up for the night carrying a turkey that looked to be half her own body weight. She didn't say, and no one asked, where she found it. Saturday morning was spent drawing and plucking the massive bird, followed by a mass assault on the greengrocer stalls in the market.

After getting back from church at eleven that morning, Mattie's mother had shooed Jerimiah and Charlie off to the pub, taking Billy with them to sit in the snug with a bottle of pop, while the women prepared dinner. They'd returned at the allotted time of two, just as Ida and Mattie were dishing up the spuds. Having cleared and washed the plates, Queenie, Jo and Mattie had set about preparing the vegetables for tomorrow's festive feast. Now, with water-filled saucepans of potatoes, cabbage and carrots all ready for tomorrow, Mattie and her family were having a few moments to themselves.

Her father, having slipped off his braces and unbuttoned his trouser waistband for comfort, was resting in his fireside chair and engaged in his usual Sunday afternoon pursuit of reading the Sunday papers and was steadily working his way through the *News of the World* and the *People*.

Having visited every market in East London and successfully gathering in enough provisions to feed a small army, Ida was now slouched in the armchair opposite her husband with her eyes closed, mouth gaping and emitting a soft nasal whine with each indrawn breath.

Queenie, sitting on the sofa under the window,

was supposedly crocheting a blanket for Mrs Doyle's new baby, but the hook and yarn in her hand lay motionless on her lap as she too was in the land of nod.

Jo was at her friend's house having tea and Charlie was having Sunday dinner with Stella's family, but he'd promised he would be back later to join them for midnight mass. Billy, who didn't know the meaning of the word quiet, had been sent upstairs to play and could be heard thumping back and forth overhead.

The five o'clock pips on the wireless heralded the news but, as the last one faded, there was a knock on the front door.

Ida gave a loud snort and woke up.

'Who's that banging on our front door and on a Sunday?' Queenie asked.

'Florrie in the baker's was saying there's been a spate of forged identity cards so it might be the coppers checking door to door,' said Ida, re-arranging her skirt as she sat up.

'On Christmas Eve? Don't be daft,' said Queenie. 'Sergeant Bell and D Relief were already downing pints in The Boatman when we came back from church so they'll be lucky if they can find the door, let alone dodgy documents.'

'Take a look, Mattie,' said her father, slipping his braces back up.

Rising to her feet, Mattie went over to the window. Looking through the net curtains, she saw a familiar figure standing on the front door step.

'Is it trouble?' asked her mother, battering the cushions into order.

'Yes,' said Mattie. 'It's Aunt Pearl.'

Leaving her family to put the front room in order, Mattie went into the hallway and opened the door.

Pearl was dressed in a three-quarter-length musquash coat, high-heeled ankle boots and a wide-brimmed felt hat with a long feather sweeping back. As ever, her face was painstakingly made up, heavily powdered and with an expression that suggested she was standing over a broken sewer. She was holding a large present wrapped in green and red Christmas paper.

'You took your time,' she said, her thickly mascaraed eyes giving Mattie the once-over.

'And good afternoon to you too, Aunt Pearl,' said Mattie with a pleasant smile. 'Won't you come in?'

Sweeping past her, Pearl stepped in and strode into the parlour.

Mattie closed the door and followed her.

As expected, her father had already made good his escape through the backyard and was probably already propping up the Catholic Club's members' bar. Ida had straightened her hair and Queenie had popped her teeth back in. They both regarded their unexpected visitor suspiciously.

'Hello, Ida,' said Pearl. 'I hope you don't mind me popping in like this.'

'Not at all,' her mother replied. 'Can I take your coat and offer you a cuppa?'

'I'd prefer coffee,' said Pearl, slipping off her coat and handing it to Mattie. 'As long as it's not that horrid Camp stuff.'

Mattie threw the coat over the back of the nearest chair, which earned her a sharp look from her aunt.

'That's all we've got,' said Ida, folding her arms across her bosom.

'Oh well,' said Pearl with an exaggerated sigh. 'I'm not staying long. Lenny will be back soon after he's seen Reggie Sweete about a bit of business.'

'Business,' said Queenie. 'Is that what they're calling stuff that falls off lorries now? And sure, isn't he a bigger eejit than I thought he was if he's having anything to do with that crook Sweete?'

'Well, if you want to talk about crooks, Mrs Brogan.' Pearl gave her a sugary smile. 'I heard you'd been nicked again. I was afraid the shock might have killed you, but no such luck.'

'Queenie speaks as she finds, Aunt Pearl,' snapped Mattie. 'Your Lenny's a crook and everyone knows it.'

'And it's common knowledge that he's got a wife in Southend so you've no right to wear that wedding ring either,' added Queenie.

Pearl sniffed. 'Well, I'll do what I've come for and go.'

'I suppose you're after seeing Billy?' said Ida flatly.

'Course, now seeing how you ain't exactly giving me a warm welcome I'd be obliged if you'd fetch my lovely boy down,' said Pearl, untangling a couple of trinkets from her overloaded charm bracelet.

The colour drained from Ida's face. 'What do you mean *your* boy?'

'Well, he is mine, ain't he?' Pearl replied.

'He wasn't "your lovely boy" when you left him

in the workhouse three days after you birthed him,' said Queenie.

Pearl shot her a venomous look. 'That was different, I–'

'And if it weren't for Ida, your "lovely boy" would have been raised in some orphanage somewhere,' Queenie continued.

'Yes,' added Mattie. 'It was Mum who sat up with him all night when he had croup and nursed him through whooping cough. She's his mum, not–'

'Just fetch him, luv,' her mother cut in wearily.

Giving her aunt a hateful look, Mattie went back into the chilly hallway.

'Billy!' she shouted up the stairs.

A door opened.

'Wot?'

Aunt Pearl's here.'

The door slammed as Billy, still wearing his school uniform from his visit to church that morning, thundered down the stairs.

''As she got my... Ow!' he whined, as Mattie grabbed him by the arm.

'Listen,' she said in a low voice. 'When Aunt Pearl hands you your present she'll tell you you can open it now.'

'I know, she always does,' said Billy.

'But this time I want you to thank her and say you're going to wait until tomorrow and open it after Mum's present.'

Billy's lower lip jutted out. 'Why?'

'Because if you don't, I'll tell Brian McGuire it were you who unbuckled his horse from the coal wagon and left it in the rector's garden while he was in the Bell and Compasses,' said Mattie.

He looked terrified. 'But he'll slaughter me.'

'He won't if you do what I say,' said Mattie.

Her brother scowled at her for a moment, then nodded.

He tried to pull away but Mattie held him firm. 'And when you've put your present under the tree, go over and give Mum a cuddle.'

'Oh, Mattie...'

She gave him her stoniest look.

He glared at her but didn't argue.

Satisfied that her will would prevail, Mattie let him go. Billy gave her a murderous look and thumped into the parlour.

With the gold threads on his nativity robe twinkling in the glow from the altar candles, Father Mahon stepped forward and stretched out his arms.

'*Domine Jesu Christe, qui Mariae et Joseph,*' he sang in a thin, reedy tone, and those gathered in the church replied with one voice.

The choir started to chant. Holding the platter of wafers, Daniel stepped forward to take his place at the communion rail alongside the old priest.

Keeping his head bowed, Daniel raised his eyes to look out as the congregation started to file forward to take communion.

Well, in truth, he was looking at one member of the congregation. Mattie.

He'd seen her as she'd walked in with her family, dressed in her new Christmas clothes: her royal blue coat trimmed with a black fur collar and cuffs, a smart wide-brimmed black hat and ankle boots with the same fur trimming as her coat. She looked stunning, but then he'd long come to the conclusion that she'd look good in a potato sack or even with just a towel wrapped around her, an image that had embedded itself in his brain since their encounter in his bedroom.

Wherever she was, his eyes sought her out. That was understandable because she was by far and away the most devastatingly attractive woman he'd ever met. And if it was just that she had a gorgeous figure, cracking legs and a face that an artist would have crossed oceans to capture on canvas, he could have handled that. After all, it wasn't as if he hadn't met the odd beauty or two in his time; it was an occupational hazard in his line of work, but Mattie was more than just a pretty face, much more. However, one of the problems with living in the rectory was that everything you did and said was scrutinised and discussed. Not too much of a problem if you were just drinking tea, petting babies and smiling at old ladies, but if his growing feelings for Mattie Brogan were to break through, God only knows what danger he'd land himself and others in.

Mattie raised her head but, before her gaze rested on him as he knew it would, Daniel looked down.

By feelings he didn't mean he was just fond of her, had affection for her or even that he desired her, although he certainly did. He meant love; total and overwhelming.

In any other time and place, he would have simply courted her until she agreed to be his wife, but this wasn't any other time or place, it was Christmas 1939. If he didn't want to be singing 'Silent Night' in German next Christmas he would have to put Mattie and what might have been from his mind.

People filed forward and he saw the blue of her coat as she stepped up to receive the host from Father Mahon. Even though he could feel her eyes on him, Daniel forced his attention to remain on the patterned tiles beneath his feet.

Distribution continued until the sidemen came forward, signalling that all those who wanted to receive communion had come forward. Father Mahon said the prayer of thanks, then tidied the altar before the choir and servers walked back down the nave. Daniel and Father Mahon brought up the rear before taking their positions by the church door.

Determinedly not looking at Mattie as she made her way towards him, Daniel wished everyone a blessed Christmas as they filed out until she was the next in line.

As the woman he was talking to moved on to speak to Father Mahon, Daniel turned and smiled at Mattie.

'Blessings be upon you on this holiest of nights,' he said, as the very nearness of her sent his pulse racing.

'And to you, Father,' Mattie replied.

Ignoring his pounding heart, Daniel kept his gaze pleasant but cool. Her dark eyes, shining in the candlelight, locked on his for a moment, then she looked away and moved on.

Daniel let out a long breath and turned to see Mattie's mother, Ida Brogan, standing before him.

'It was a lovely mass,' she said.

'Thank you, Mrs Brogan.'

'If you don't mind me saying, Father, you're looking a mite thin,' she said.

Daniel looked surprised. 'Am I?'

'Yes,' said Mrs Brogan, looking him up and down. 'It's no surprise to me though as Bridget Dunn never did know how to put meat on a man's bone. You must come around to ours, in fact, why don't you have your Christmas dinner with us tomorrow?'

Out of the corner of his eye he saw Mattie talking to Mrs Kemp, who held her six-week-old infant, swaddled in a pink blanket, in her arms.

'That's very kind of you but I wouldn't want to intrude and Mrs Dunn has already prepared dinner and I wouldn't want to upset–'

'Well, come for tea then,' continued Ida.

He heard Mattie laugh as the baby reached out to her.

Daniel's eyes flickered past Ida onto her daughter and a pang of longing gripped his chest.

Mattie had taken the baby from the young mother and was gazing lovingly down at it as she cradled it in her arms. Ida turned to follow his gaze and a sentimental look spread across her face.

'Sure, I expect such a sight puts you in mind of the Blessed Mary, doesn't it, Father?' she said.

Daniel didn't reply but, after watching Mattie for a moment, he turned back to her mother. 'Would four o'clock be too early?'

Chapter Eleven

'Your Christopher seems to be getting on well with your dad,' said Mattie's mother as the sound of male laughter burst out from the kitchen.

'Yes, he does,' Mattie replied, feeling the warmth from the hearth as she rested back in her father's fireside chair.

It was three-thirty on Christmas afternoon and the blackout curtains were already tightly drawn. The twinkling tinsel on the Christmas tree in the corner, the dim light of the forty-watt bulb overhead and the soft glow from the fire made the parlour homely and snug.

Despite the fact it was Christmas Day, as always, the older members of the household had been up early. Her father had trudged out as dawn broke to muck out Samson, leaving her mother to get the turkey in the oven. Queenie was up before them all for no reason other than she always was.

Billy had been awake from some unearthly hour, too, demanding to open his presents. For the sake of peace and quiet, her mother had agreed, which meant that once he was busy downstairs ripping wrapping paper, Mattie could catch a precious couple of hours under the covers.

She needed them too. The Germans had discovered that the sight of even a single aircraft would set off all the sirens along the length of the Thames. Therefore they'd decided in the lead up to Christmas to send some old bi-plane left over from the last war to wake the whole of East London at least once a night which meant Mattie, and the rest of London's population, was exhausted. But, to be truthful, there had been other things keeping her awake for the past few nights.

Even though her gran had promised not to fart or take her teeth out, Mattie was convinced that inviting Christopher to meet her family would be a complete disaster. However, after presenting himself on the dot of eleven, freshly shaven in a suit, collar and tie, he'd bowled her mother over by giving her a box of Jelly Fruits, complimenting her on her 'lovely house' and asking if he might be of some help in the kitchen. Seeing her mother warming to him, Mattie had started to relax.

Her father and Charlie had returned just before noon and, after being introduced to Christopher, the Brogan men had stripped to their vests at the kitchen sink to get the worst of the stable off before donning a fresh shirt. Having made themselves respectable, and because the Catholic Club was closed, they'd decanted to the Old House at Home in Watney Street to have the traditional swift half or two, taking Christopher with them.

That was almost three hours ago and now, having demolished a turkey, six pounds of sprouts, carrots, cabbage and at least double that in roast potatoes, followed by a great dollop of Christmas pudding and custard, the women of the household were putting their feet up while the men of the family, with Christopher swelling their number by half again, were in the scullery doing the mountain of washing up accrued by six adults and two children.

Jo had gone upstairs to read while Billy sprawled across the floor pushing the Hornby train Aunt Pearl had given him around a circular track on the fireside rug at Ida's feet.

'He's very nice is Christopher, Mattie,' said her mother, quietly, swapping over her knitting needles to start a new row. 'And so well spoken.'

'Yes, I suppose he is,' said Mattie, feeling the warm glow of her lunchtime sherry.

'I should say so,' said Ida. 'A young man who works in a bank, who's been to college, is saving to buy his own house and good-looking, too. And what a lovely present he gave you.'

Mattie put her hand on the bow-shaped brooch pinned to her jumper. 'Yes, it is pretty.'

To be honest, given that she'd only got him a pack of linen handkerchiefs with his initials embroidered on them and a bottle of Ascot aftershave, she was a little embarrassed when she'd opened his gift to her.

About the size of her palm, with the ribbon made of twisted gold, twinkling white stones around the edges and a huge red gem as the knot, her present was very pretty and, she guessed, very expensive.

'It's more than pretty,' said her mother. 'Those are real diamonds. You've done well for yourself there, my girl.'

'Don't start getting your hat out yet, Ida,' chipped in Queenie. 'Diamonds or not, she ain't marrying him.'

'Not yet she's not,' Ida winked. Who knows what might happen–'

'There we are, ladies,' said Mattie's father as he marched back in the room with Charlie and Christopher a step or two behind. 'All done and I've put the kettle on so we can have a cuppa after we listen to the king.'

Mattie stood up and relinquished her chair to her father. Christopher sat at one end of the sofa with Charlie at the other. As all the other chairs were taken, Mattie squashed in between them. Under the cover of her skirt, Christopher took her hand and gave it a little squeeze. They exchanged a smile.

'Right, let's have some hush for his majesty,' announced her father as he twiddled the dial on the wireless.

It crackled and buzzed for a moment, then the sound of Big Ben striking the hour rang out and everyone turned their attention to the old Bush radio sitting on the sideboard.

As the king's hesitant tones urged the country to remain strong and resolute in the face of evil and to trust wholeheartedly that God would come to England's aid in her time of need, Mattie shifted in her chair and looked at Christopher. As she studied his profile, she had to agree with her mother's assessment that she'd done well for herself. He was indeed a bit of a looker and he did have both an education and a salaried job, but unfortunately every time she looked at him he seemed to be in the shadow of a taller, darker man with a strong jawline, compelling eyes and a dog collar.

The king blessed his nation and, as the BBC orchestra blasted out the opening bar of 'God

Save the King', everyone in the room stood up to affirm their loyalty to the crown.

'Poor, luv, sounds tired,' said Ida as they resumed their seats. 'I'll never forgive that brother of his for swanning off with that American hussy and leaving the country to face the Nazis. The old king must be turning in his grave to see how his son and heir turned out.'

There was a blast of cold air across Mattie's feet as the back door opened.

'Oh oh, only us,' called Cathy's voice from the scullery.

Her sister walked in with Stan just a step behind.

He spotted Christopher and looked alarmed. 'What–'

'I'm Mattie's boyfriend, Christopher Joliffe,' said Christopher, leaping to his feet and thrusting his hand out. 'You must be Stan.'

Stan stared at him for a moment. 'Oh, yeah, yeah, I see, Mattie's boyfriend.' He took the offered hand. 'Nice to meet you, Christopher.'

Christopher smiled. 'You, too, Stan.'

They exchanged an odd look.

Cathy nudged him and Stan looked at his wife. 'And this is my Cathy.'

'Pleased to meet you, too,' said Christopher. 'Mattie's told me so much about you.'

'Call me Cathy,' she laughed. 'And don't believe any of it.'

Stan frowned. 'I'm sure she didn't say anything bad, luv.'

'She's joking, Stan,' said Mattie, taking their coats.

Ida heaved herself from her chair. 'I'll make the tea and cut us a bit of Christmas cake.'

Throwing the coats over her arm, Mattie nipped into the cold hallway and hung them on the rack. When she returned, Cathy and Stan were still standing in the middle of the room.

'Mum, Dad, we've got something to tell you.' Cathy slipped her arm in Stan's. 'We're expecting.'

'A baby!' screamed Ida, hugging Cathy. She turned to Jerimiah. 'Did you hear, Jerry? Cathy and Stan are having a baby! Our first grandchild.'

'I certainly did.' Mattie's father rose from his chair. 'Well done, Stan,' he said, shaking his son-in-law's hand.

Mattie embraced her sister. 'I'm so happy.'

Cathy smiled. 'Me too.'

They hugged again and then their mother barged between them. 'How far gone are you, luv?'

Leaving her mother extolling the benefits of a half of stout each day, Mattie went into the kitchen to make the tea instead. She filled the kettle and was just setting it on the stove when Christopher strolled in.

'That's a nice Christmas present for your mum,' he said, leaning against the doorframe.

'Yes, it is,' said Mattie, walking past him to collect the crockery from the dresser.

'Talking of presents.' He slipped his arm around her waist. 'What about yours?' Reaching up, he hooked his finger under the brooch, brushing her breast with his knuckle as he did. 'Do you like it?'

'Yes, Christopher, it's really lovely,' said Mattie.

He smiled down at her. 'I'm glad. Perhaps when we have that weekend away in the country you can show me how much.'

Mattie forced a light laugh.

'Now, now, Christopher,' she said, twisting out of his embrace. 'I promised to think about it, nothing more.'

She reached across to pick up the sugar bowl, but Christopher caught her hand.

'I know, sweetheart,' he said, drawing her back to him. 'But I'm an ordinary man with a man's desires.'

'I understand that, but I'm not that sort of girl,' Mattie replied.

Shock flashed across Christopher's face.

'Oh, Mattie, you don't think I was...' An expression of pain twisted Christopher's features. 'I'm sorry, my darling, if you got the impression that I thought you'd go with anyone. I think you're the sort of girl a chap like me dreams about settling down with and having a family.' He drew her back into his embrace. 'What about you, Mattie? Do you dream about having a home and children?'

'I do,' she replied. 'But I dream about lots of other things too, like gaining my advanced matriculation and then passing the Civil Service entrance test.' Damping down the panic in her chest, Mattie forced a light laugh. 'And, of course, before I think about getting wed I will need to find the right man.'

Christopher's arm tightened around her as his blue eyes looked deep into hers.

'Perhaps you already have.' He lowered his lips onto hers for a brief kiss. 'Or maybe he's found you.'

Mattie's mouth went dry. 'Christopher, I'm not–'

He stopped her words with another kiss as her heart raced in her chest.

'I know it might seem a bit sudden but I've fallen for you in a big way.' A tender smile spread across his face. 'I can see you as a bank manager's wife, in a house of your own–'

'But how can we ... anyone make plans?' said Mattie, freeing herself from his arms and taking a step back. 'You know, with everything being so up in the air and uncertain – because of the war, I mean,' she blurted out.

'Well, lots of people are,' Christopher replied. 'In fact, lots of chaps are keen to tie the knot before they get their call-up papers or report to their army bases. The number of people getting married since September has doubled.'

Mattie's mouth dropped open. She tried to gather her words but, before she could, Christopher's gaze shifted from her face to something behind her and a wry smile spread across his face.

Mattie turned and something akin to ice water washed over her as she saw Father McCree standing in the doorway, an unreadable but extremely unsettling expression on his face.

Daniel's mind didn't believe what his eyes were seeing through the plain glass of his spectacles. Mattie, the woman he dreamed of awake and asleep, the woman his aching heart needed with every beat, was standing there in Christopher Joliffe's arms.

A jagged sword of pain cut him to the marrow

and it took every ounce of Daniel's willpower not to stride across the small kitchen and snatch her from the Nazi bastard's embrace. With his fingernails digging painfully into his palms, Daniel forced himself to focus on anything other than the hands of the man touching her.

Mattie looked as lovely as ever with her auburn curls scooped back from her face and falling in waves over her shoulders. The brown pencil skirt and a cream cable jumper she was wearing clung to her womanly figure while the tan-coloured belt which separated them emphasised the trimness of her waist.

'Father McCree!' she said, springing back. 'I didn't hear the front door.'

'Your gran spotted me arrive through the window and let me in before I knocked,' said Daniel, hoping she couldn't hear the tightness in his voice.

Mattie stared wide-eyed at him for a couple of heartbeats, then blinked.

'Father McCree, this is–'

'Father McCree and I are already acquainted, sweetheart,' said Christopher, a wry smile lifting the corner of his mouth.

Mattie looked astonished. 'Are you?'

'Yes, when he came and asked for a donation for the church,' said Christopher.

'And very generous you were too,' said Daniel, somehow forcing his face into a pleasant expression.

Christopher offered his hand. 'Good to see you again, Father.'

Daniel forced himself to take it. 'And you.'

They regarded each other coolly.

'I won't be a tick,' Mattie said, opening the back door and hurrying out into the yard.

'What the hell are you doing here?' hissed Daniel as the door closed.

'Having Christmas dinner with my girlfriend's family,' Christopher replied in the same tone.

'And Stan?'

Christopher's poised expression wavered a little. 'I didn't know Stan was married to Mattie's sist–'

The back door opened and Mattie stepped in, carrying two bottles of milk she'd collected from the front step.

'Sorry, we'd run out,' she said, smiling at them both.

Repositioning his glasses back on the bridge of his nose, Daniel cleared his throat. 'I was just saying to Christopher how surprised I was to see him.'

'I bet,' said Mattie. 'Mum thought it would be a good idea to invite him for Christmas dinner.'

'Plus it gives me a chance to meet the family,' added Christopher, smiling urbanely at Daniel.

He slipped his arm around Mattie's waist and squeezed. She smiled up at him as Daniel fought to control his anger.

Wriggling out of Christopher's embrace, Mattie went over to the larder.

The door opened and Ida Brogan walked in.

'You'll never guess, Mum,' said Mattie, emerging from the pantry carrying the Christmas cake. 'But Father McCree and Christopher already know each other.'

'Well fancy that,' said Ida, looking from one

man to the other and back again.

Daniel forced a smile, then repeated the cock and bull story about the bank's donation.

'What a small world,' said Ida when he'd finished.

'Now, Father, you must be gasping for a cuppa,' said Ida. 'So why don't we leave Mattie and Christopher to fetch, it through.'

'The papers are saying that now Hitler has the Sudetenland, Czechoslovakia and Poland, he's reached the limits of his ambition,' said Jerimiah. 'But, if you ask me, now the Soviets have invaded Finland, I wouldn't be surprised if the Führer doesn't start eyeing up Denmark or Belgium. What do you think, Father?'

Although Mattie's father echoed his own thoughts on the German's next move, Daniel smiled piously and wondered again, as he looked at the older man's face, who Jerimiah reminded him of.

'I'm afraid I don't concern myself too much with politics, Mr Brogan,' he replied, watching Mattie out of the corner of his eye.

She was perched on the arm of Christopher's chair and had been since they'd finished distributing the tea and cake some forty minutes ago.

Thankfully, Christopher sat on the other side of the room from Stan, who looked both baffled and alarmed as his mother-in-law recounted in detail each of her long, arduous and flesh-ripping labours. With himself posing as the IRA go-between and Christopher the undercover area coordinator for all the fascist groups in East London, sitting around making chitchat over Christmas tea was fraught enough without adding Stan, the chairman of one of the said organisations, into the mix. Of course, anyone with an ounce of wit would realise this but unfortunately Stan's understanding of the situation was somewhat lacking.

Although Daniel should have been concentrating solely on jumping in to stop Stan inadvertently dropping them all in the shite, infuriatingly he couldn't keep his attention from Mattie, who was smiling at Christopher a great deal too much for his liking.

Jerimiah nodded sagely. 'To be sure, Father, you would have your mind taken up with God's greater plan.'

'Amongst other things,' said Daniel, as his eyes flickered briefly onto Mattie's crossed legs. 'But I'm sure whatever the Germans decide to do next, your son Charlie will make you proud wherever he's posted.'

Mattie's low laugh drifted across the room and caught Daniel in the pit of his stomach.

'So, Mr Brogan,' he said, willing his eyes not to stray to her again. 'How are things at the yard?'

'They could be better and my back fair aches at the end of the day having to hump everything on the wagon by meself.' Jerimiah replied. 'I was going to take on the Cox's boy but he got his call-up papers, too.'

Out of the corner of his eye, Daniel saw Christopher slip his arm around Mattie's waist.

'What with the price of feed for my old Samson and the government fixing the price for scrap metal–'

'Has Mattie been walking out with her young man long?' Daniel cut in.

'A month or two, now I think about it,' Jerimiah replied, looking a little puzzled.

'So fairly recently then?'

'So her mother tells me. Mattie's never had much time for courting.' Jerimiah tapped the side of his nose and grinned. 'Ambitious see, Father, but this Christopher's the first chap she's ever asked home to meet the family proper, so he must have something.'

Anxiety gripped Daniel's chest.

'But she hardly knows him,' he blurted out

'True,' said Jerimiah. 'But I met and married her mother in three months so I know that sometimes it just hits you out of the blue.'

It bloody well does, thought Daniel.

Christopher moved his free hand to rest lightly on Mattie's thigh.

Daniel swallowed the last of his tea and stood up.

The talking ceased as everyone turned their attention on him.

'Thank you for inviting me to join your family, Mrs Brogan, but I've just noticed the time,' he said, feeling Mattie's lovely hazel eyes on his face. 'And I promised Father Mahon I'd be back in time to join him for Vespers.'

'My pleasure, Father,' Mrs Brogan replied, rising to her feet and taking his cup from him. 'But can I prevail upon you for a blessing before you go on your way?'

'Of course,' he replied.

With the whole room looking expectantly at

him, Daniel scraped the Sanctae Familiae out from the back of his mind.

He raised his hand and everyone except Christopher bowed their head.

'*Domine Jesu Christe, qui Mariae...*' he intoned, ignoring the Nazi's cynical expression. Daniel's gaze-swept over the Brogan family as he recited the prayer but, as he came to the last incantation, his eyes rested on Mattie's head and he added, '*Adoro Te Devote*'.

With his head resting back on the lacy antimacassar, Christopher let the melancholic strains of the orchestral piece by Debussy, which was drifting out of the Brogans' ancient domed wireless, wash over him. He would have preferred something more robust by Strauss or Wagner but, as the BBC was reluctant to play German music, he'd have to suffer this effeminate offering.

It was just after ten-thirty on Christmas night and, in the kitchen beyond, Mattie was making them both a cup of cocoa before he went home.

Stan had been worried about his mother so he and Cathy had left after tea and Mattie's elder brother was still at his fiancée's house, but the rest of the family had turned in for the night. The old biddy and the younger children about an hour ago, followed by Mattie's parents after the ten o'clock news.

Christopher sighed and cast his gaze around what could only be described as a Dickensian junk shop. He doubted the Brogans had two articles of furniture or china that matched and certainly none that hadn't been owned by someone else before. He'd barely been able to eat the over-cooked dinner placed before him for wondering what uses the plate might have been put to before. And if that wasn't enough to sour his appetite then the deranged old bat Queenie fixing him with a piercing stare throughout the meal certainly had. She was a ripe candidate for being classified as a member of the gypsy sub-race. The rest of the family were just as bad, including that brat of a boy who'd flicked custard on his tie, her sulky sister and her father, who seemed to have not a jot of shame about earning his living as a tinker. Given their poor situation, it was hardly surprising that every time Mattie left the room her mother told him what a 'wonderful wife' Mattie would make.

A smile lifted the corner of his mouth. Of course, the day did have one amusing moment, the one when McCree walked in and caught him smooching with Mattie.

Although he had taken a vow of celibacy, it was clear from the look on the priest's face his cods were in working order, and baiting the holy man by caressing Mattie had helped turn what would have been a tedious afternoon into a diverting one.

The door opened and Mattie came back into the lounge carrying two mugs.

'Sorry, I've been so long the gas was low and the kettle has taken forever to boil,' she said, setting their drinks on the coffee table in front of him.

'Don't worry,' he said. 'I've been enjoying the music.'

Tucking her skirt under her, Mattie sat down

next to him. 'Have you enjoyed today?'

'Very much so, you have such a warm and lovely family, I felt like part of the family.' Christopher gave her his most adoring smile. 'And, who knows, maybe I will be soon.'

Mattie smiled and then buried her nose in her drink.

Christopher picked up his packet of Rothmans from the table.

'And perhaps if Father McCree is still around,' he continued, flicking a flame from his lighter. 'We could ask him to perform the ceremony.'

A becoming blush coloured her cheeks. 'I don't think that's–'

'Fair,' interrupted Christopher. 'I suppose not, given he's got a bit of a soft spot for you.' He drew on his cigarette. 'Bit like rubbing salt in a celibate wound.'

Mattie's flush deepened and she laughed. 'Really, Christopher, I'm sure Father McCree's thoughts about m ... me are pa ... pastoral ... no ... nothing more, just like Father Mahon's.'

Stubbing out his half-smoked cigarette in the ashtray, he put his hand on her knee. 'I'm just teasing you, sweetheart, but I can't say I blame him if he did fancy you,' he said, in a low tone. 'Because I certainly do.'

Shifting around, he took her in his arms and pressed his mouth on hers in a hard kiss. She responded by winding her arms around his neck and kissing him back. Pressing his tongue into her mouth, Christopher's hand shifted down to caress her cheek and throat before sliding down over the brooch he'd given her to capture her breast.

254

She shifted under him and, in response, Christopher rammed his crotch into her hip so she could feel his erection. Sliding his hand down and under her skirt, Christopher thrust his fingers up past the elastic of her knickers.

She tried to wriggle out of his grip so he pinned her between him and the back of the sofa. Holding her there, his fingers reached the soft moistness between her legs. She punched him in the shoulder.

'Christopher!' she hissed, shoving him away.

He held onto her and, with his crotch tight in readiness, he tried to get his hand back up her skirt but she knocked it away.

'No!' she said.

Raising his head, Christopher's mouth pulled into a tight line. 'Come on, Mattie, just a quick–'

'I said no,' she repeated, giving him a glacial stare. Brutal thoughts and images flashed through his mind as the pulse in his temple pounded.

Christopher held her gaze for a long moment then, with a curse, he sat up.

Snatching his cigarette packet, he took out a fresh one.

'I thought you liked your present,' he said, holding the cigarette between his lips.

'I do,' Mattie replied, adjusting her skirt, 'but if you only gave it to me to get your hand up my skirt, you can have it back.'

Christopher inhaled a lungful of smoke as the intensity of his sexual ferocity abated a little.

'No, I didn't, sweetheart,' he said, looking earnestly into her eyes. 'I bought it because I thought the diamonds would show off the twinkle in your eyes and the ruby matched your lips, nothing more.' He forced a contrite smile. 'But it's not easy for a man.'

Mattie's disapproving frown lifted. 'I know, but—'

'I can't help it if my feelings get the upper hand.' He took her hand and kissed it.

Mattie lowered her eyes and picking up her mug, she took a mouthful of her cocoa. Christopher did the same.

A spring boinged as someone in the room above shifted in their bed and he glanced up.

'When are you going to Lord Whatshisnames?' asked Mattie, cutting into his unedifying thought.

'Friday evening,' he replied, flicking the ash into the ashtray. 'I'm catching the seven-ten from Liverpool Street to Colchester and Lord Bedlington's car is picking me up at the other end.'

'Sounds very posh,' laughed Mattie.

'Believe me, it'll be totally tedious,' Christopher squeezed her hand. 'And I'd much rather see the New Year in with you, sweetheart.'

She smiled and tucked a stray auburn curl back behind her ear. 'Well, if it helps you in the bank you'll just have to suffer it.'

'I suppose I will,' he said, grinding his cigarette into the over-flowing ashtray.

He was just about to take her in his arms again, but Mattie held him off. 'It's getting late.'

Holding his annoyance in check, Christopher stood up. 'I suppose it is. I ought to go.'

Mattie rose to her feet too.

Opening the door to the hall, she unhooked his Crombie from the stand and brought it in.

She held it out for him and Christopher slipped it on, then they walked into the chilly hallway.

'Are you free on the Friday after New Year?' he asked, buttoning his coat.

'I think so,' said Mattie. 'But I'll ring you at work if I'm not.'

'Well, if I don't hear from you I'll pick you up at the usual time and we can go for a drink,' said Christopher.

She nodded.

Taking her hand, Christopher drew her into his embrace. 'You know it's your fault I got carried away earlier.'

She raised her eyebrows. 'My fault?'

'Yes, your fault for being so beautiful.'

She laughed, then opened the door into the icy December. He kissed her but, as he stepped over the threshold, he turned.

'And, Mattie, my sweetheart, just so you know,' he said, as her big brown eyes gazed up at him. 'I rarely take "no" for an answer.'

'I'll have two G&Ts, a lemonade and three packets of crisps, please!' Mattie shouted at the barman, a thick-set man with a glistening forehead and damp patches under each arm.

'You'll be lucky, luv,' he shouted back as he took down the glasses from the rack above. 'There ain't a packet to be had for neither love nor money in the whole of London.'

It was about eleven o'clock on New Year's Eve and she was in the Three Compasses pub with Francesca and Sally, another friend from school. However, unlike her friends who were dressed in smart dresses with their curls pinned up, Mattie was dressed in her ARP warden's uniform as she was in the middle of her second blackout enforcement watch of the night and would be on duty long after the revellers around her were tucked up in bed. Mattie and her friends weren't the only ones out tonight; the whole place was packed to the gunnels with people determined to forget the imminent threat of gas attacks and mass bombings and to see 1940 in with gusto.

Many of the pubs clustered around London Docks, Shadwell Basin and along Wapping High Street were centuries' old and traditional workaday watering holes, but the Compasses, which was built the same year as Prince Albert died, was considered slightly posher with its lofty yellowing Victorian plasterwork and high ceilings.

As the pianist in the corner struck up the opening bars of 'I've Got a Lovely Bunch of Coconuts', the barman returned.

'That'll be 1/6d,' he said, setting the drinks in front of her.

'1/6!'

He shrugged and held out his hand.

Mattie gave him two bob and he gave her a tanner in return.

'Don't blame me; blame Hitler,' he said, as she picked up her drinks.

Holding the drinks in a triangle formation and going the long way around to avoid the dancers swirling beneath the dartboard, Mattie made her way back to the table tucked in behind the draught screen where her friends were sitting.

'Good health, everyone,' said Mattie, placing

them on the table.

'Thanks, luv,' said Sally, tucking a strand of hair back into the tight roll at the nape of her neck.

Sally Naylor had golden hair, a ready smile and the longest legs between the Aldgate Pump and Bow Bridge. Her great-gran had been a music hall star back before the turn of the century. Sally's ambition had always been to follow her ancestor onto the stage, but she'd ended up working on the assembly line in Kelly's pickle factory instead. Like Francesca, who was wearing a snug-fitting mulberry gown with beaded detail on the square shoulders, Sally was dressed in her best frock which, in her case, was a dark green satin wriggle dress which clung to her lithe figure.

Tapping their feet in time with the music, Mattie and her friends sang along with the rest of the pub as the pianist hammered out 'Pennies from Heaven' on the old upright in the corner.

The pianist moved seamlessly into 'I've Got My Love to Keep Me Warm' and the revellers followed.

'It's a pity you're on duty or you could be out with your new fella tonight, Mattie,' said Sally, applauding with everyone else as the song finished.

'I wouldn't be as he's spending the weekend with some friends in the country,' said Mattie.

'Whoooo!' said Sally. 'Sounds posh.'

'Well, he wears a suit and works in a bank, so he is and…' Francesca raised an eyebrow. 'He's met the family.'

Sally looked impressed. 'I bet your mother got the best china out.'

'I'd put money on it,' laughed Francesca.

'I have to admit, she did push the boat out a bit,' said Mattie, and her two friends giggled and nudged each other. 'But she'd also invited Father McCree for tea.'

Francesca and Sally sighed in unison.

'Such a dish,' said Francesca.

'Such a waste,' Sally replied. 'Almost makes me want to convert to being a Catholic.'

'Not that Mattie cares now she's got her Christopher, eh?' said Francesca, nudging her and winking.

Mattie forced a smile and tried to summon an image of Christopher to mind.

She managed it briefly until McCree's mesmerising smile, dark eyes and muscular figure crowded it out. As always, the very thought of him sent her pulse galloping off, with her less-than-pure imagination close behind.

The pianist struck the chord for his next medley and a male voice blared out the first line of 'You Must Have Been a Beautiful Baby.

'For gawd's sake,' said Sally, pulling a pained expression. 'He's in the wrong key.'

With the pianist trying to keep time with the singer's tempo, the chap belted out three verses and choruses before he finally finished. People applauded and, after taking a bow, he sat down.

'We've got time for one more turn before Big Ben,' the man at the piano said as he ran through the scales.

'Over here!' shouted Mattie and Francesca, pushing their friend forward.

Sally took a large mouthful of drink and then, accompanied by shouts of encouragement and applause, she made her way over to the piano.

'How did Christopher and your family get on?' asked Francesca.

'Like a house on fire.' Mattie ran through the highlights of her Christmas Day. 'He complimented my mum on everything she put in front of him, chatted to Dad about some Roman exhibition and talked to Stan about West Ham's last away game. He even helped Billy glue together the balsam-wood airplane Jo bought him. The only one who didn't seem to warm to him was Father McCree.'

'Why?' asked Francesca.

'I don't know,' Mattie replied. 'But he was definitely put out when I introduced them, although it might be because he walked in on me and Christopher having a smooch in the kitchen.'

Francesca's eyes stretched wide. 'Mattie!'

'It wasn't anything really, but...' The unsettled look in Father McCree's eyes as he stood in the doorway flashed through her mind.

Mattie pushed it away. 'I suppose it must be because Christopher isn't a Catholic.'

'Probably, especially if he thinks you and Christopher are thinking about getting married.' Francesca grinned. 'That or he fancies you himself.'

Mattie's heart thumped in her chest as the pianist ran through the opening bars of 'Blue Moon' and the room quietened.

'She's wasted in that pickle factory,' said Francesca as their friend's clear soprano voice ran out around the bar. Sally sang her way through the popular song, finishing to wild applause.

'Let's have some hush!' called the landlord as

he turned on the wireless behind the bar.

The noise ebbed away.

There was a pause and then the first bong from Big Ben sounded out. Everyone rose to their feet and, as the last chime sounded, the pub erupted.

'Happy New Year,' screamed everyone.

Mattie hugged Francesca, who hugged her back, then they both hugged Sally who had elbowed her way back to them.

'Oi, blondie, give us another tune, darling,' shouted someone from the other side of the room.

'Yeah, something jolly,' called someone else.

'In a minute,' Sally shouted back.

'Come on,' yelled someone else. 'Before George starts up again.'

'Go on,' said Francesca, nudging her friend playfully in the ribs. 'Your audience is waiting.'

'And I ought to be on my way,' said Mattie, drinking down the last of her lemonade and picking up her patrol bag. 'And don't forget, you two, if you see my mum, don't you dare mention I was here.'

'Your secret's safe with us,' laughed Francesca.

Sally hugged them both again and then she turned to head back to the small stage at the far end of the pub.

Mattie was about to leave when the door swung open and her brother's fiancée, Stella, strolled in with her arm through that of a thick-set chap wearing a Crombie.

The man barged his way to the bar.

'Scotch and a brandy,' he shouted over the noise, waving a five-pound note at the barman.

'Make mine a double,' Stella called, stopping in

front of Mattie.

With her back to her and her bracelets jingling as she moved, Stella pulled a compact and lipstick from her handbag. She opened it and was just about to reapply Crimson Crush to her lips when she caught sight of Mattie in the reflection.

She spun around.

'Happy New Year, Stella,' said Mattie, regarding her coolly.

'And you,' she said, struggling to hold Mattie's gaze.

'Pity Charlie had to go back to camp on Boxing Day,' said Francesca, coming over to Mattie.

Stella's attention shifted to Mattie's friend and a smug look crept across her face. 'Yeah, wasn't it?'

'Oi, sweetheart, come on before my arms drop off,' Stella's companion called from the bar, holding their drinks aloft.

'Coming,' Stella called back, still looking at Francesca and Mattie.

She gave them the once-over, then turned to make her way through the revellers to join her date.

'She doesn't deserve Charlie,' said Francesca, hurt and desolation etched across her beautiful features.

Looking at her friend's stricken face, Mattie wondered what was worse. Being in love with someone who loved someone else or being in love with someone who had vowed not to love anyone else but God.

With his stomach full of locally shot venison, estate-grown vegetables and plum duff, Christopher swirled his drink around in the bulbous lead-crystal glass in his hand as the Ambrose Orchestra blasted out the opening chords of 'I've Got You On My Mind', which was playing on Lord Bedlington's gramophone in the ballroom beyond.

It was just after midnight on the first day of 1940 and he was comfortably ensconced in one of the three Chesterfield sofas in Bedlington Abbey, Lord Bedlington's country house some twelve miles from Colchester.

The Bedlington's chauffeur, in full livery, had collected him from the station two days ago on and after a half an hour drive through winding country lanes, he'd arrived at the family estate. The house itself was a hotchpotch of styles, starting with the original red-brick Tudor house through to the Classical columns of the façade and the solid Edwardian style of the new west wing. As Christopher was swept up the driveway in the back of the Bentley towards the Bedlington family's sprawling ancestral home, he couldn't help but think about the contrast between Christmas in the Brogans' squalid hovel and New Year celebrations in the splendid Bedlington Abbey.

Lord Bedlington and the rotund Lady Hermione Bedlington had greeted him personally and introduced him to their other house guests, who included a couple of MPs, a baron and an American who seemed to own the best part of Argyll. There was also an assortment of minor aristocrats who'd been displaced by Stalin's march across eastern Europe.

They'd all gushed with praise about the efforts

he and others like him in the Right Club, the British Council for the Christian Settlement of Europe and British Fascist Union were making to bring an end to the war. They were also at pains to tell him that although they hadn't been as vocal as some in their praise of Mosley, they had always admired him and what he stood for. Christopher had smiled and, out of respect for his host, hadn't queried if this sudden surge of fascist patriotism had anything to do with the fact that, having taken possession of half of Europe, Germany was now setting its sights on England.

Christopher took another sip of his drink and looked around him. His fellow guests were dotted about the lounge, dressed in dinner suits and with ostentatious medals pinned to their lapels, reminiscing about the good old days when the lower class knew their place.

With the log fire glowing in the grate beneath the carved marble mantelshelf and with his feet resting on the thick pile of a Turkish rug, Christopher couldn't help but be satisfied with his lot.

Of course it would have been much better if his mother's Weimar-Lippe crest sat above the fireplace rather than Lord Bedlington's, but perhaps next New Year, after Hitler rewarded those Englishmen who had smoothed his path to the conquest of England.

'Can I get you another?'

Christopher turned to see Lord Bedlington, who'd been talking to the prince of somewhere or another on the other side of the room, holding the decanter aloft.

Somewhere in his late sixties with a ruddy face

and a figure like a whipping top, Lord Bedlington wasn't a man to stint at the table or at the bar.

Christopher swallowed the last of his drink. 'Don't mind if I do.'

Gripping the soft leather of the sofa's arm, he started to rise.

'Stay where you are, old chap,' said Bedlington, ambling over.

Christopher sank back and his host refilled his glass. 'I'm glad you could join us, Joliffe,' said Bedlington as he sat down at the other end of the sofa.

'Thank you for asking me,' said Christopher. 'It's been most enjoyable.'

'For us, too,' Bedlington agreed. 'Pity Drummond and his crowd couldn't come.'

'Yes, but he was hosting his own famous, or should that be infamous, New Year shindig,' Christopher replied.

'So I've heard,' Bedlington chuckled, setting his jowls trembling. 'You know, you don't have to head home tomorrow. Stay as long as you like. Do you ride?'

'Not really,' Christopher replied.

'What about shoot?'

'From time to time,' Christopher replied.

'Well then, stay for a few more days at least and we can see if we can bag us a few brace. My keeper tells me there're plenty of pheasants to take a pop at.'

'Perhaps another time,' said Christopher.

'If it's the bank, I play golf with Sir Edward and I could have a word–'

'No, it's my other interests that need my attention,' said Christopher.

'Oh, I see.'

Christopher glanced around conspiratorially and then leaned towards the other man.

'I can't say too much,' said Christopher in a low voice. 'But things...' He winked. 'May be happening and I have to be ready to get my men on the streets at a moment's notice, Lord Bedlington.'

'I see. And call me Algie. All my close friends do.' The portly lord's face took on a sombre expression. 'I wish I could do more to help but, what with my dicky heart and gout, well, I'd be no use to a young buck like you in the rough and tumble and–'

'I quite understand,' said Christopher smoothly.

Picking up the silver cigar box from the coffee table in front of them, Bedlington offered him it.

Christopher selected one of Lord Bedlington's Cubans and clipped the sealed end with the cutter on the side of the box.

'Of course,' said Bedlington as he held the table lighter for Christopher. 'If there's any other way I could help the cause, then just–'

'Well, now you mention it,' cut in Christopher, drawing on the cigar to ensure it was alight. 'I could do with my own transport.'

Bedlington looked puzzled. 'Transport?'

'A car.' Christopher said. 'I happened to notice when you showed me around the estate yesterday you had quite a few stashed away in your garage.'

'Well, I–'

'Don't worry, Algie, I'm not after your Silver Ghost,' Christopher laughed. 'After all, I don't want to draw too much attention.'

'Well, I suppose we could spare the Austin 7,' said Bedlington.

Christopher flicked cigar ash into the elephant leg ashtray at his elbow 'I was thinking more of that nice green Daimler Consort you have tucked away at the back.'

Beads of sweat sprang onto Bedlington's forehead. 'Well, I suppose I … I … co … could–'

'You did say anything for the cause, did you not, Algie?' cut in Christopher, regarding his host coolly.

'Of course.' Taking out his handkerchief, Christopher's host mopped his glistening brow. 'Anything for the cause.'

Bedlington took a gulp of his drink.

Christopher smiled and blew lazy smoke rings upwards towards the crystal-cut chandelier above.

'Daddy!'

Christopher looked up to see Lord Bedlington's horsey daughter, Cecily, bounding towards her father.

Christopher rose to his feet as she approached, smiling at her.

There could be no doubting her paternity. Lord Bedlington's only offspring looked much as Christopher imagined her father would if he ever decided to don a pink chiffon dress and fix a feather clasp in his hair.

'Yes, my precious,' said Bedlington, as she dipped down to give her father a peck on the cheek.

'I'm very cross with you for keeping our guest of honour from the dancing,' she said, casting a simpering glance at Christopher from under her stubby lashes.

'It's my fault, Lady Cecily,' said Christopher, giving her his most endearing smile. 'We were talking about cars but I promise I'll be there to spin you around the room in a couple of jiffs.'

'Very well, I'll forgive you this time.' She thrust out her lower lip, which made her appear haddock-like rather than coquettish. 'But only if I can have the first dance.'

Christopher placed his hand over his heart. 'I swear to dance all and any dances as my lady commands.'

He gave her a flourishing bow.

'All right but don't be long,' she giggled, then giving him another lascivious look she lumbered off.

'I have my orders,' said Christopher, downing the last of his brandy.

'You do indeed,' said Lord Bedlington.

Taking a last draw on his cigar, Christopher ground it out in the ashtray and then, putting his hands in his pockets, started towards the ballroom, but after a few steps he stopped and turned back.

'You could just do me one more favour,' he said, smiling at his host.

'Name it, old man,' Bedlington replied.

'That maid of yours who served the puddings,' said Christopher. 'You know, the pretty one with the red hair.'

'Little Polly?'

'Yes, Little Polly.' A lazy smile spread across Christopher's face. 'I'd be obliged if you could send her to my room to turn my bed down when I retire.'

Bedlington's jowls quivered and he blinked rapidly. 'Well, I–'

'I will, of course, be sure to mention you by name to Mosley and Ramsey when I next see them and impress upon them, and my friends in German High Command when they arrive, that you are one of our most loyal supporters.'

A small muscle at the corner of the old aristocrat's right eye started to twitch as several emotions flashed across his face.

'Of course,' Bedlington replied, in a tight voice. Anything for a guest.'

Christopher gave him a warm smile, then turned again and strolled over to join the dancing.

Chapter Twelve

With her scarf wrapped around her face and cocooned in her seaman's coat to keep out the bitingly cold wind from the Thames, Mattie considered popping home for a quick cuppa to thaw out before she completed the rest of her rounds.

It was the second Sunday in February and Christmas seemed a distant memory, mainly because it had been close to freezing both day and night ever since. If that wasn't enough, there had been a bout of flu going around, which had laid low half the neighbourhood including the ARP personnel, which meant everyone had been rota-ed for double shifts for the whole of January.

Her mother had been laid up with it for ten days while Jo and Billy had been off school for two weeks. She and her father had been feverish for a week. The only person who hadn't succumbed was Queenie. Thankfully, the disease had abated and they'd returned to normal duties.

Mattie had been on night duty all week but this was her last one and she was now looking forward to three days off to catch up on her sleep - air-raid sirens permitting, of course.

Angling her dimmed torch at the ground, Mattie was just about to turn down Jutland Alley to check the old cottages for stray light when the sound of scuffles and excited male laugher echoed from under railway arches a hundred yards or so in front of where she stood.

There had been some nasty rumours about female wardens being set upon and even raped in the blackout, so Mattie thought it prudent to let them pass. Switching off her torch, she stepped into the shadows of a shop doorway.

Even in the moonlight, Mattie could see from the way they were careering about the road that the gang of half a dozen men had been drinking, but their high spirits seemed the result of more than just one too many ales.

'Where next?' shouted one as they drew closer.

'That grubby tailor's gaff in Olive Street,' came the reply, in a voice that Mattie recognised but couldn't place. 'Then the Kosher baker's around the corner.'

'Yeah,' sneered another. 'Give 'em something to put on their toast.'

Everyone laughed and hooted.

From the shadow of the doorway, Mattie leaned forward slightly to get a better look at the men lumbering down the street. She counted seven in all and, although in the dark she couldn't see any faces, the shape and gait of the man in front seemed familiar.

'What about doing the Yids in Hessle Street?' asked someone else.

'Yeah, it'd be a right lark stuffing–'

'Crafty buggers have got look-outs so it's Olive Street like I said, and keep your bloody voices down, will you?' the man in front barked at the rest of the gang.

A cold shiver ran through Mattie. Stan!

'Police! Call the police!' yelled a man's voice from the other end of the street.

'Scarper!' shouted her brother-in-law.

The men around him sprang into action and pelted off down the street towards the docks.

As they shot past her, Mattie took out her whistle and, stepping out of the doorway, blew it with all her might. The piercing blast cut through the still night, setting off dogs in the surrounding streets. It was answered by the distant whistles of the Wapping police station beat officers.

Tucking her whistle back inside her coat and shining the beam of her torch on the cobbles, Mattie hurried up the street. As she reached the commotion, she saw Morris Wiseman standing in his nightclothes and slippers, holding a sheet of newspaper in his outstretched hands.

He looked up as she approached.

'Oh, Mattie, it's you. Thank God,' he said.

'Mr Wiseman, what's happened?' she asked, as neighbours appeared and gathered around.

'What's happened! I'll tell you what's happened, Mattie, This!'

He thrust his hands forward and the stench of dog faeces wafted up.

There were cries of 'disgusting' and 'bloody animals' from those people close enough to see.

Fumbling in her pocket, Mattie pulled out a handkerchief and covered her mouth.

'And that's not the worst of it.' Discarding the revolting parcel in the gutter, Morris pulled a sheet of paper from his dressing gown pocket and gave it to Mattie.

'Benedictus Deus in Angelis suis, et in Sanctis suis,' said Father Mahon, his wheezy prayers echoing in the vastness of St Bridget and St Brendan's church.

It was the second Monday in February and Daniel had crunched through icy puddles as he crossed from the rectory to the church some half an hour ago. Although it must be almost half-past seven now, the sun had only just raised itself over the horizon but the February sunlight lit the interior of the sanctum with a warm red glow.

Daniel stifled a yawn and, blinking the sleep from his eyes, wondered if he'd ever have a full-night's sleep again. And it wasn't as if he was unaccustomed to disrupted nights; God knows, during the siege of Madrid he'd never had more than an hour or two's snatched shut-eye for almost ten weeks and he'd still been able to lead a company of men to safety when the Nationalists

273

swept in.

Stifling another yawn, Daniel genuflected towards the crucifix a second after the aging priest.

'Amen,' he said, crossing himself, a puff of breath escaping as he spoke.

With his hands pressed together, and trying to emulate his mentor's saintly expression, Daniel turned from the altar. Resisting the urge to stamp blood back into his feet, his gaze travelled over the dozen or so people braving the icy weather for morning prayers. He spotted Mattie Brogan, in her ARP uniform, tucked in the corner of the back pew and warmth spread instantly through Daniel's body.

Father Mahon gave the blessing and then tottered off the dais towards the vestry. Inside the small room to the side of the church, Daniel disrobed as quickly as he could. Having assured Father Mahon that he was quite happy to tidy their vestments away by himself, Daniel quickly hooked their robes back in the cupboard and the old priest left by the side door to head back to the warmth of the rectory. Daniel returned to the church to find Mattie still sitting at the back with her head bowed in prayer.

With his steel-tipped heels clicking on the tiles, Daniel walked down the aisle towards her. She raised her head. She looked exhausted but as her lovely eyes rested on him, gladness shone from them, squeezing Daniel's heart with both pleasure and pain.

She was swathed in her oversized navy coat with her ARP warden hat on the back of her head and a scarf wrapped around her neck. Daniel thought she looked even more beautiful than she had the last time he'd seen her. But then, to be honest, he thought that each and every time they met.

'Good morning, Mattie,' he said, smiling down at her and wishing he could plant his lips on her cheek. 'We don't often see you for early prayers.'

She gave him a wan smile. 'I was just passing on my way home so thought I'd just drop in.'

She lowered her eyes and bit her lower lip.

Daniel slid into the seat beside her. 'You seem a little troubled,' he said, 'not your usual self.'

'I'm just a bit tired and...'

She bowed her head.

Daniel took her hand.

'Whatever it is, you know can tell me, Mattie?' he said in a low voice, enjoying the feel of her skin against his.

Her eyes searched his face for a moment, then she took a deep breath. 'I've got a problem.'

Several awful possibilities flashed through his mind, none of which would stop him loving her but would impact greatly on Christopher's well-being.

'Is it Christopher?' he asked, already looking forward to pummelling the Nazi's face with his fist.

She took back her hand. 'It's Stan.'

'Your brother-in-law?'

'Yes,' she replied. 'I think he's one of those despicable thugs who've been firing Jewish houses and daubing vile slogans on the walls everywhere.'

'Are you sure?' he asked, knowing now her views on Hitler weren't the same as Christopher the band of barbed wire constricting his heart instantly disappeared. 'I can't believe that,' said Daniel, forcing an incredulous expression onto his face. 'Not of Stan.'

'Neither could I until last night,' Mattie replied. 'He's never had a good word to say about Jewish people so when he kept spouting on about having to stop the Jews taking over the world I thought it was just Stan being Stan and I didn't take him seriously, but last night I ran into a gang of men talking about "doing the Yids" in Hessle Street and I recognised Stan's voice. Then, a few moments later, a Jewish couple living around the corner called the police because they'd had some dog dirt and this...' She rummaged around in her pocket and pulled out a leaflet. 'Shoved through their letterbox, Father.'

Daniel took it from her.

It was a crudely drawn picture of an overweight man with a long nose, pound notes bulging out of the pocket of his expensive coat. The man had his hand up the skirt of a very young woman, her two terrified children sheltering behind her. The slogan across the top summed up the Nazis' message in four words: 'Death to all Jews'. Daniel had seen similar caricatures before but that didn't stop the bile rising at the back of his throat.

'My sister's married to Stan and all that,' continued Mattie, cutting across the thoughts racing round in his head. 'And I don't want to get him in trouble, but–'

'Have you told anyone else?' he asked.

She shook her head. 'Not yet, but–'

'Did you actually see him or his friends putting the dog dirt or the pamphlets through this couple's door?' Daniel cut in.

'Well, no, I was at the other end of the street but he and the gang passed by just after it happened,' said Mattie.

'That could just be a coincidence,' said Daniel. 'The perpetrator could have headed off in another direction and Stan and his mates were just making their way home from the pub. And you didn't actually see any of their faces clearly in the dark, did you?'

'I suppose not,' said Mattie. 'But I recognised Stan by his walk and voice.'

'It's pretty circumstantial evidence and I don't see a magistrate accepting that as proof positive in court,' said Daniel.

'But surely if he didn't do it then he'll be able to prove to the police that it wasn't him,' she replied, thoughtfully.

'Yes and open a whole can of worms in the process,' said Daniel.

'You're right,' said Mattie. 'And I don't suppose Mum would be very impressed if I got Stan arrested, not with Cathy in the family way.'

'I imagine not,' agreed Daniel.

Resting her head back, Mattie sighed and closed her eyes for a moment. Then her head snapped back.

'But don't you think I ought to tell someone, Father?' she asked, her eyes like liquid pools in the dim light of the church. 'Christopher, perhaps? After all, he is an auxiliary police officer–'

'Could you swear on the Holy Bible that it was Stan?' Daniel asked.

Under her greatcoat, Mattie's shoulders sunk.

'No, Father. I couldn't.'

'Then truthfully, Mattie, for everyone's sake, I suggest that until you have irrefutable evidence, perhaps it's better not to accuse your brother-in-law of something that could get him locked up as a traitor,' said Daniel.

Mattie considered his words for a moment or two and then nodded. 'Perhaps you're right.'

She yawned.

Feeling an utter swine for manipulating her so, Daniel reached across and closed his hand over hers again. 'And perhaps you should be away to your bed, miss.'

She gave him a tired laugh.

'You're right.' Rising to her feet, she picked up her haversack and hooked it over her shoulder. 'And thank you, Father.'

Standing up, Daniel stepped out of the pew to allow her to pass.

'All part of the job,' he said, pressing his arms to his side to keep them from wrapping around her. 'And I look forward to seeing you on Sunday.' Gazing down at her lovely face, Daniel smiled and she smiled back.

Their eyes locked for a heartbeat, then she turned and walked down the aisle, leaving a hint of gardenia in her wake.

Signing the letter in front of him, Christopher placed it on the small pile to his right then, picking up his cup, he swallowed the last dregs of tea and pulled a face.

He returned the cup to the saucer and flipped down the middle switch on his desk intercom.

'Yes, Mr Joliffe,' his secretary Veronica's tinny voice replied.

'Can you come in?' he said.

He let the switch spring back and there was a tap at the door.

'Come!'

It opened and Veronica hurried in.

Today his secretary was wearing a rather fetching little blouse with a frill down the front, which drew attention to her ample breasts, and a tweed skirt. Christopher cast an appreciative eye over her. Of course she didn't hold a candle to Mattie, but he couldn't help feeling more than a little disgruntled that, despite lavishing such an expensive present on Mattie, he seemed no nearer to getting her knickers off.

Of course, Lord Bedlington's little maid had taken the edge off his desire for Mattie, but only just. Quite annoyingly, the more Mattie held out, the more it fired him to have her. Perhaps it was time to show her that he meant what he said and that he would not take no for an answer.

He smiled at his secretary.

'There, my dear,' he said, indicating the half a dozen sheets of paper. 'And they need to go in the midday post.'

'But it's eleven-thirty already,' she said.

'I know, it'll only take you fifteen minutes to get to the main post office in Salmon Lane once you've typed the envelopes, and,' Christopher put on his helpless little boy expression. 'I would be very grateful.'

She gathered up the signed letters. 'Very well, Mr Joliffe.'

'Good, and get me a packet of Rothmans while you're out,' he said.

'Yes, Mr Joliffe.' Hugging the correspondence to her, she turned. 'Oh, silly me, I almost forgot, Father McCree is outside and he wonders if you could spare a moment to see him.'

Irritation fizzed through Christopher, but he smiled pleasantly nonetheless. 'Of course, send him in.'

Veronica disappeared back to her office, only to reappear almost instantaneously with Father Mc-Cree a few steps behind.

Christopher stood up.

'Father McCree,' he said, walking out from behind the desk and offering his hand. 'What an unexpected pleasure.'

'Good morning, Mr Joliffe,' said McCree, taking his hand.

Christopher tightened his grip but, annoyingly, the priest's hold was firmer.

'It's good of you to see me at such short notice,' said Father McCree.

'My pleasure,' Christopher replied.

'Can I get you a cup of tea, Father?' asked Veronica, giving the priest a coy smile.

McCree smiled. 'Thank you but no. Mr Joliffe's time is precious so I won't impose on his good nature by taking more of it than I really have to, Miss...?'

'Milligan,' she replied, fiddling with the ruffle at her throat. 'Veronica Milligan.'

'Named after the saint who wiped Our Lord's face on the way to the cross, no doubt,' McCree said.

Veronica looked puzzled. 'No, me dad's sister.'

Father McCree's lips lifted in an indulgent smile.

'The post office, Miss Milligan,' said Christopher, giving his secretary a meaningful look.

'Sorry, Mr Joliffe.'

She hurried out.

'So,' Christopher said, resuming his seat without bothering to offer the priest one. 'To what do I owe this great pleasure, McCree?'

'It's Father McCree, if you don't mind,' Daniel replied, regarding Christopher coolly. 'Stan and his so-called Britons Peace Union committee is the reason I've called.'

A prickle of apprehension fizzed up Christopher's spine, but he maintained his urbane smile.

'What about them?'

'They've been out causing trouble again,' said McCree.

Christopher shrugged. 'So a few Jews get roughed up and their businesses torched, so what?'

'Well, I hope you can be as blasé about their antics when the police pull you in for questioning,' the priest said.

A cold hand seemed to grab at Christopher's vitals. 'The police!'

'Yes, the police. Stan and his merry thugs were seen running away from a house that had just had dog excrement posted through the letterbox, and this–' He pulled out a crumpled sheet of paper. 'Shoved through the door.'

Christopher glanced at one of the leaflets he'd

281

given to Stan to distribute a few weeks before.

'Who reported this?'

'Fortunately for you it was a member of my congregation,' continued McCree. 'So they came to me instead of the police.'

Christopher felt panic rising in his chest.

'What Stan and his gang get up to has nothing to do with me,' he said, annoyed to hear the quiver in his voice.

'Hasn't it?' A chilling smile spread across Father McCree's face. 'Do you really think if Stan is pulled in on a charge of conspiring with the enemy, he won't spill his guts to the Secret Service about you and your friends at the Right Club to avoid having his neck stretched?'

An icy shiver ran through Christopher but, before he could reply, McCree stepped forward and placed his hands on the desk.

'Now you listen to me,' he said in a low, menacing tone quite at odds with his calling. 'You might tell your chums Drummond and Ramsey you're the big man in East London but last night Stan and his bloody gorillas very nearly brought this whole house of traitorous cards down around our ears. Now, I don't give a damn if you and all your Nazi chums end up dangling at the end of a rope, but I'm not having Irish Independence, the cause I've worked to achieve for over a decade, jeopardised because of your bloody men. So take them in hand or I'll do it for you.' He jabbed his finger at the blond man. 'Do you understand?'

Fury flared in Christopher. 'How dare you speak to me—'

'And you want to consider something else while you're about it, Joliffe,' McCree continued as if he hadn't spoken. 'I'm guessing you're hoping that when Hitler arrives in glory on these shores you'll be in line for a medal and some sort of position in the new regime.'

'The thought hadn't crossed my mind,' Christopher replied casually.

'I suppose that's just as well, under the circumstances.' A cynical smile lifted the corner of the priest's mouth. 'After all, I doubt the Führer will be doling out rewards to so-called area coordinators whose followers have been arrested for arson and assault instead of gathering information about the local defences and the docks and jetties along the river – as they were ordered.'

The image of himself on a podium sitting alongside Mosley, Ramsey and Greene as one of the leaders in England's glorious new order evaporated at McCree's word.

'All right, you've made your point,' Christopher said. 'I'll have a word with Stanley Wheeler.'

'Make sure you do,' continued Father McCree, still looming over him.

There was a knock at the door.

Father McCree's flint-like eyes remained on Christopher's face for a moment, then he straightened up and gave a sharp nod.

'Come,' called Christopher.

The door opened and Veronica put her head around the edge.

'Sorry to interrupt,' she said. 'But you asked me to tell you when Mr Groves was free.'

'And I'm sorry for taking up so much of your

time,' said Father McCree, an artless expression replacing his menacing one in an instant. 'And bless you, Mr Joliffe, for your most generous donation towards the church's annual Sunday school trip.'

'Aw,' said Veronica, giving the priest a doe-eyed look. 'Where are you taking them?'

'To London Zoo now, thanks to Mr Joliffe's generosity,' Daniel replied.

'Very good, Miss Mulligan,' said Christopher. 'And tell Mr Groves I'll be along presently.'

Veronica nodded and, after giving McCree another shy smile, she left.

Picking up his hat, Father McCree turned his attention back to Christopher.

'Remember,' McCree told him, as he set his fedora back on his head. 'When the German army goes on the offensive, the Abwehr will expect you to play your part and I wouldn't want to be in your shoes if the SS arrive and find you or your peace committee wanting.'

'It's very quaint,' said Mattie, taking a sip of her drink and gazing around at the olde worlde surroundings of the Eagle public house on Woodford Road.

Christopher glanced around unenthusiastically. 'I suppose it is, if you like that sort of thing.'

Although her conversation with Father McCree that morning had made her question whether she had actually seen Stan while she'd been on patrol the night before, by the time she woke up later in the day she was certain. She might not have seen his face but she knew that Stan had been at the head of that gang of thugs. She was equally certain that they were responsible for putting the dog mess through the Wisemans' door, and probably a whole lot more, if the truth were told. However, as Father McCree pointed out, she didn't have any concrete or, as he put it, irrefutable, proof.

Taking a sip of her drink, Mattie forced her mind to stay on the actual man sitting beside her and not the man she wished she was with. Glancing over the rim of her glass, she studied Christopher, who sat hunched beside her with a Rothmans filter tip in his mouth and an expression like thunder on his face.

'The barmaid told me the pub dates back to the sixteen hundreds and it was one of the major stops for the London to Cambridge stage coaches,' Mattie continued.

Christopher didn't reply.

He stubbed out his half-smoked cigarette and stood up. 'I'm getting myself another, do you want one?'

'No, I'm fine,' said Mattie. 'But don't you think you've had enough?'

He glared at her. 'What do you mean?'

'Well, you've had three double scotches to my two gin and tonics,' Mattie replied. 'And you've got to drive back.'

He gave her a sour look. 'I hope you're not criticising my driving.'

'No I'm not, I'm just–'

'If you knew anything about the subject,' he cut across her. 'You'd know that it's been proven that you drive better when you've had a couple.'

'I'm surprised to hear that,' said Mattie. 'Especially as the government has now banned workers from drinking at lunchtime in case they–'

'I've come out for a quiet drink not a bloody lecture.' Christopher threw the last of his drink back. 'Now, do you want another drink or not?'

'No thank you,' said Mattie, matching his harsh expression. 'I'm perfectly fine.'

Giving her a frosty glare, Christopher lumbered off.

Mattie took another sip of her drink and waited.

Being an hour from closing time on a Monday evening, there was only a handful of drinkers in the bar, mostly locals.

Having got his change from the barman, Christopher pocketed it and strolled back with another double scotch in his hand. Throwing himself in the chair beside Mattie, he took out a gold cigarette case and flipped it open.

'Is that new?' she asked, hoping a change of topic might lighten the mood.

'It was a present from a friend.' Flicking his lighter, Christopher lit his cigarette. 'The people I stayed with at New Year.'

'Lord … Lord Bidderford?'

'Bedlington,' he snapped. 'Lord Algernon Bedlington, seventh Earl of Harwich, who owns half of North Essex, to be precise.'

'Well, you obviously made a good impression,' said Mattie. 'A car and a gold cigarette case.'

'I did,' he replied, flicking his ash on the pub floor.

Tilting her head, she read the inscription:

To Chris from–

'Ciss. Lady Cecily, only child and heir to Lord Bedlington's estate.' Snapping it closed, he slipped the case back in his pocket. 'She was very taken with me.'

'I'm sure she was,' said Mattie. 'If she gave you such an expensive present.'

Reaching across, Christopher placed his hand on her thigh. 'She probably would have been even more generous if I hadn't told her I was serious about someone else.'

Mattie forced a smile.

Under the cover of the table, Christopher's fingers started to inch up her leg. 'You know they have rooms upstairs.' He winked. 'What do you say?'

Regarding him coolly, Mattie removed his hand. 'The same as I did the last time you made the suggestion.'

'Oh yes, I forgot. "I'm not that so'a gal",' he replied, mimicking her accent in a falsetto voice. 'No, you're the sort of girl who's quite happy for me to pay for the best seats or pick up the bill for a slap-up meal at a fancy restaurant, or stuff your face with expensive chocolates and take expensive gifts, without paying me back with a bit of the other.'

Mattie stood up.

He looked puzzled. 'Where do you think you're going?'

'Home.'

'I haven't finished,' he said, raising his glass and splashing scotch on his trousers.

'No, but I have.' Taking her coat from the back

287

of the chair, Mattie shrugged it on. 'You arrive late without an apology, down liquor like there's no tomorrow and then start on at me because I'm not some tart who'll go with anyone.'

'I'm not anyone,' he said, stubbing out his cigarette. 'I'm your boyfriend.'

'Not after tonight, you're not.' Opening her handbag, she took out her purse. 'And here's the money for my two drinks.' She threw a florin and two six-penny pieces on the table. Christopher stared at them for a moment, then flicked his cigarette ash vaguely towards the ashtray on the table.

'If that's the way you want it.'

Closing her bag, Mattie hooked it on her arm. 'Goodbye, Christopher.'

She turned to walk away.

With fury searing through him, Christopher watched Mattie as she strode across the half-empty pub and out of the door.

Who the bloody hell does she think she is?

He downed the last mouthful of his scotch and stood up. Dropping his half-smoked cigarette, he stepped on it and headed for the door, knocking into a couple of customers as he passed.

The air was chill on his face and he took a deep breath to clear the stuffiness of the pub. However it did nothing to cool the heat spreading through the pit of his stomach or his tight erection.

Bugger it! He'd already booked a room in the Eagle as he was certain she'd be so impressed by the Daimler that she'd finally surrender to his charms and sleep with him.

Still, she couldn't have got far and once he got

her back in the car he'd show her he really wouldn't take no for an answer, especially not from a girl whose father drove a bloody horse and cart for a living.

Taking his keys from his pocket, Christopher started towards his newly acquired vehicle parked in front of the public house but, as he stepped out the door, the ground seemed to shift under his foot and he stumbled. He grabbed the wrought-iron railings running in front of the hotel and cursed.

Recovering his balance and placing his feet carefully as he went, Christopher made it to his car and, after a couple of attempts, managed to get the door open. Sliding in, he pulled out the choke and pumped the clutch a couple of times before turning the ignition.

The car purred into life. Christopher put it into gear and pulled away. As he headed down the hill, a smile spread across his face as he contemplated a very satisfying end to the evening, well for him at least.

Swerving left into Station Road, he slammed the car back into fourth gear, narrowly missing the bollard on the corner as he roared up the slip road to Snaresbrook Station.

Screeching to a halt outside, Christopher jumped out and dashed through the unmanned entrance. In the light from the muted station lamps he saw Mattie on the other platform for a split second before an eastbound train puffed into the station.

There was a hollow bang as a door slammed shut, then the driver tooted twice and the train chugged out of the station, leaving the smell of coal in its wake.

Christopher stared across at the empty platform for a moment then, with the blood pounding in his temple, he kicked the plyboard side of the ticket collector's empty booth, shattering the wood in an instant. Breathing hard through his nose, he grabbed the chalk noticeboard and, ripping it from its hook, threw it on the track.

Taking a deep breath, Christopher surveyed his handiwork for a second, then, spinning on his heels he stormed back out to his car.

He yanked the door open and was about to get in when a young girl trotted across the street.

'Was that the Stratford train?' she asked.

'Yes it was,' said Christopher. 'I've just waved my friend off on it.'

'Drat,' she said, rubbing her upper arms and stamping her feet. 'That means I've got half an hour's wait in this weather.'

Christopher's eyes slid over the girl's bouncy blonde hair, her heart-shaped face and womanly curves.

'Where are you going?'

'Only Leytonstone,' she said.

'I could give you a lift,' said Christopher, resting his hand on the roof of the car.

She looked at the Daimler and her eyes widened for a second, but then she shook her head. 'No, it's all right. I'll walk.'

'What in those,' Christopher laughed, indicating her high heels. He put on his most charming smile. 'Look, I'm William Smith, Will to my friends and I could have you home and in the warm in two shakes of a lamb's tail. What do you say?'

She studied him for a moment, then smiled. 'All right and I'm Rose.'

'Right then, Rose,' he said, opening the passenger door. 'Jump in.'

Tucking her skirt under her, she climbed in.

Christopher shut the door, then went around to the other side of the car.

'This is nice,' she said, casting her gaze around as he settled in beside her.

He smiled.

'Take a cigarette if you want,' he said, taking his Rothmans from his pocket and offering it to her.

'Ta very much,' she said.

'And light one for me while you're at it,' he said, handing her the lighter too.

He turned on the ignition and pulled away. As they reached the T junction at the bottom of the road, she handed him the cigarette.

'Thanks,' he said, gripping it between his lips.

'Oh, no,' she said, as he pulled on the steering wheel and the car turned right. 'Leytonstone's the other way.'

'I know,' said Christopher, pressing down on the accelerator. 'But I thought we could take the scenic route.'

Chapter Thirteen

'Would you like another cup, Mrs Wheeler?' asked Mattie, as she got to the end of the row.

Stan's mother, sitting huddled by the fire all bundled up in shawls, nodded. 'Thank you, my dear, that would be lovely.'

It was the third Thursday in February and Mattie was sitting in Cathy and Stan's front lounge. Despite Stan's disapproval of Cathy 'helping the war effort', her sister had, in fact, signed up for the Women's Voluntary Service and was at her weekly meeting. Stan, as ever, was out at one of his so-called peace meetings but as he didn't like his mother being alone for too long, Mattie had volunteered to keep Mrs Wheeler company until one or other of them returned.

It was also three days since her argument with Christopher and she hadn't seen him or heard from him since and, to be honest, she couldn't have cared less. She was actually glad there'd been no Valentine card sitting on the kitchen table when she'd come down that morning as it meant Christopher would not be around later and she wouldn't have to tell him again they were finished.

He was handsome enough, of course, with a good job, and he gave the impression of being a polite well-spoken young man but, after having to fight him off on Christmas night and his constant bullying about going away for the weekend, she found herself wondering why she hadn't given him the heave-ho weeks ago. But she knew why; going out with Christopher was her feeble attempt not to fall in love with Father McCree. It hadn't worked and every time she saw him the ache to have him kiss and caress her was almost unbearable. She had to face the fact, futile though it was, that she was in love with her parish priest.

Putting aside her sister's knitting, Mattie stood up and took Mrs Wheeler's cup from her.

'I thought he'd be home by now,' the older woman continued as Mattie rested the strainer on the top.

'I'm sure he's fine.' Mattie poured the old woman's tea and set it in front of her.

'And with all these dirty foreigners flooding into London,' said Mrs Wheeler. 'You hear such dreadful tales.'

'I'm sure they'd rather be at home in their own country than having to flee for their lives,' said Mattie.

Mrs Wheeler gave her a sceptical look. 'That's what they say but how would we know when they talk gibberish all the time? They might be plotting to murder us all in our beds.'

Mattie didn't reply.

An old tune came on the wireless and Mrs Wheeler started humming along. Mattie took up the needles again and, winding the lemon wool of the expected baby's matinee coat around her finger, slipped the right needle behind the left.

Mattie was just about to start her third row when the front door rattled.

'I'm home,' Stan called from the hallway.

'In here, dear,' Mrs Wheeler called back.

Stan strolled in bringing wisps of river fog with him. He crossed the room to his mother and planted a kiss on her forehead.

'I was getting worried,' old Mrs Wheeler said, her bony fingers plucking at the tweed of his jacket.

'The train was late, that's all,' he replied.

'I thought you were at the Catholic Club,' said Mattie, winding the wool around the needles and putting the knitting back in the bag.

'Not this week, it was the London regional meeting at a hotel near Charing Cross,' said Stan.

'And what was it about?' asked Mattie. 'Hitler's friends, the Soviets, bombing neutral Finland or HMS *Exeter* being blown out of the water by a U-boat?'

'No, more general stuff,' Stan replied, not meeting her gaze.

Gripping the arms of the chair, Mattie stood up. 'Well, now you're back, Stan, I'll be off home.'

'Thanks for sitting with Mum,' said Stan.

'We've had a nice time, haven't we, Mrs Wheeler?' said Mattie, raising her voice so the older woman could hear.

Stan's mother nodded and she shivered.

'Are you chilly, Mum?' Stan asked.

'Yes, could you put some coal on the fire and get my shawl from upstairs,' Mrs Wheeler replied.

'If you tell me where it is, I'll get your shawl while Stan stokes the fire,' said Mattie.

'It's on the end of my bed,' said Mrs Wheeler.

Leaving Stan to tend to the fire, Mattie ran upstairs.

Mrs Wheeler's room smelled faintly of moth balls and lavender. Every surface was filled with an abundance of cheap seaside knick-knacks and faded photos. An image of a very much younger Stan stood in pride of place on the dressing table next to a pot of Pond's face cream. The porcelain tray of the dressing table set had antique costume jewellery in it while the old woman's single bed was covered with an expensive-looking pink lace counterpane on which lay a baby blue knitted shawl.

Crossing the room, Mattie picked up the old woman's wrap and was just about to retrace her steps when her foot struck something under the bed.

She looked down to see the corner of a cardboard box sticking out. She bent down to shove it back under the bed when she caught sight of the contents. Mattie reached in and took out an identical leaflet to the one that had been shoved through the Wisemans' letterbox. Glancing quickly over her shoulder, Mattie dragged the box out and flipped open the lid. The box was three-quarters full of the same hateful pamphlet.

Her mouth pulled into a hard line. Irrefutable evidence, Father McCree had said, and now Mattie had found it.

'And may the blessings of Our Lady be upon your house, Mrs Ware,' said Daniel in his holy voice as he made the sign of the cross over the old woman standing in the doorway.

'Thank you, Father,' said Mary Ware, her lined face wrinkling in a soft smile as she looked up at

295

him. 'It's kind of you to keep Wilf company for an hour.'

It was just before nine-thirty on a Thursday evening and Daniel was finishing his last pastoral call of the day.

'It's what I'm here for,' Daniel replied.

Her gnarled hand reached out to close over his. 'And I'm thankful for your dropping by, too.'

'I'm glad my visit has given you both comfort,' Daniel replied, feeling a little pious in spite of himself.

'Yeah, cos it stops the old bugger fecking moaning about all his piles,' Mrs Ware replied. 'Good day to you, Father.'

She shut the door.

Smiling to himself, Daniel turned, intent on returning to the rectory for his overdue and solitary supper.

Father Mahon was away until tomorrow evening on a Lenten retreat so Mrs Dunn had taken the opportunity to visit her sister in Romford, leaving a lamb stew on the back of the stove for Daniel to re-heat at his leisure. However, to be honest, having had a large plate of steak and kidney pud, potatoes and peas forced on him at the Flanagans' at midday followed by at least three slices of cake during the course of his afternoon visits, he'd probably just make do with a bit of toast with his Horlicks later. Contemplating a leisurely evening in listening to the wireless, Daniel headed for home. However, just as the rectory honed into view, Daniel saw Mattie hurry across the street towards the Catholic Club.

The aching yearning that gripped him every

time he saw her tightened around Daniel's heart.

The chance to spend some time with her without that bastard Christopher hovering around was too good to miss so, with a decided spring in his step, instead of turning into the rectory, he continued past the gate towards the large building beyond.

With images of Mattie in his head, Daniel took the steps two at a time and headed for the main bar upstairs. Pulling down the front of his jacket and smoothing his hair, Daniel put his hand on the brass plate, pushed open the door and strolled in.

He cast his eyes over the dozen or so men having a quiet drink and frowned.

'Evening to you, Father,' said Pete Riley from behind the bar as he wiped the inside of a beer mug. 'Are you after someone in particular?'

'Good evening, Pete,' said Daniel. 'And I thought I might catch Paul Wells.'

'He's not been in,' the barman replied. 'Shall I tell him you're looking for him?'

Daniel shook his head. 'It's not important. I'll catch him tomorrow.'

He left and re-traced his steps down to the main hallway and casually popped his head around the door of the committee room to find Sister Ethel and some members of St Mary's Guild sitting around the table, knitting.

Sister Ethel, the nun attached to St Bridget and St Brendan's, although well into her eightieth decade, was as bright as a sparrow and blessed with infinite patience and a never-ending smile.

'Good evening, Father,' she said, turning aside

from her task. 'To what do we owe this pleasure?'

'Oh, nothing in particular,' replied Daniel. 'I heard you were down here so I thought I'd say hello.'

The elderly nun gave him a very curious look. 'Did you?'

'Yes,' said Daniel, feeling like a grubby-kneed boy under her amused scrutiny. 'Well, hello, and I'll see you at Saturday prayers, Sister.'

Giving the matrons of the parish a little smile, Daniel backed out of the door just in time to see Mattie crouching down as she climbed through the half-size door in the main corridor that gave access to the space under the hall's stage.

Wondering what she was doing crawling about amongst the cobwebs and dust, Daniel started after her but he'd only taken a few steps when the main door swung open and people surged out at the end of the weekly Britons for Peace Union.

Daniel stared after them for a moment, then a cold hand clutched around his heart.

He'd told her to get irrefutable evidence and that was just what Mattie was doing; by hiding under the stage so she could eavesdrop on Stan's so-called committee.

Fear gripped him. If they were to discover her!

Forcing down his near panic and maintaining a hallowed expression on his face, Daniel shouldered his way through the horde and into the main hall. Glancing across he saw that Stan and his chums were already there, setting out the chairs in front of the stage ready for the committee meeting which followed. Keeping his head down and using the crowd to shield him from view, Daniel headed for the stairs at the side that led up to the stage and slipped in between the grey drapes and scenery at the back of the stage.

As the Catholic Club's main hall went quiet, Mattie shifted her position and tried to get comfortable.

Although, she dreaded having her suspicions confirmed, since she'd discovered the box of leaflets under Mrs Wheeler's bed the week before, she'd been determined to find out what her brother-in-law was really up to, which was why she was now crouched under the stage.

Small shards of light shone through the cracks between the wooden planks, but it wasn't enough for Mattie to see properly. She pulled out her torch from her greatcoat pocket, flicked it on and balanced it on top of a tea chest stacked with crockery. Mattie pulled out her notebook and pen from her pocket and set it on her knees. Closing one eye, she peered through one of the large gaps between the boards at the table and the men sitting around it.

'OK, now that lot's gone, we can get started,' said someone to the right of her field of vision. 'Where are we going for our next lot of business?'

Brushing a cobweb from her hair, Mattie grasped her pencil and started to take down all the details of what was being said.

'Shoreditch, I hope,' said someone with a deep voice. 'Lots of fat Yids who think just cos there's a whole bunch of them, they won't get a seeing-to like their mates did down here.'

'If it were me,' said yet another with a slight

299

lisp, 'I'd stick petrol through all the ground-floor letterboxes in that stinking Rothschild Building and torch it.'

'I'm with you, Bob,' laughed another man. 'Singe some of those Nancy ringlets they have around their ears. What'd you say, Stan?'

In her grimy hiding place, Mattie's mouth pulled into a hard line.

'Me?' said her brother-in-law. 'I say fry the fucking lot of them. But I want to deal with the rubbish on our own doorstep first.'

'Wot, down Hessle Street, Stan?'

'That's right, Harry,' Stan replied. 'It has to be done. Having them there, just off Commercial Road, is an affront to us all and even though the press don't report it, there's been little kiddies been taken away by Jews. So, for the sake of our own nippers, we need to put our local Kites in their place.'

'Too true, Stan.'

'Plus,' continued Stan. 'We're getting a bit of reputation amongst the London brotherhood of patriots for being hard and I'd like to make sure we live up to that.'

Everyone laughed.

'Too bloody right we should,' Harry replied, as Mattie scribbled down the names as she heard them. 'Eh, Teddy?'

'I wouldn't be surprised if Mosley himself don't ask for us to join his Black Shirts when he takes over,' Teddy said.

'I bet we could show those Hitler's bloody storm-troopers a thing or two,' said the man sitting right in front of Mattie.

'Yeah, the Bermondsey crew reckons them-selves the top Jew-worriers, but they're a piece of piss next to us,' said Teddy.

Everyone laughed again.

'Right, I've not got all night,' said Stan. 'Let's get on with it. We need more petrol and old rags to start with, plus I thought we might have a bit of fun with some builders' pitch and a couple of old feather bolsters and—'

Mattie heard the main doors swing open and someone marched into the hall. As the newcomer approached, chairs scraped on the floor as the men sitting around the table stood up.

'Oh, oh, th … this is a b … bit of a surprise,' stut-tered Stan. 'Not that you're not welcome or any-thing, but… Oi, Ted, get another chair for Mr—'

'What did I say about you and your committee keeping your head down, Stan?'

Something akin to ice water washed over Mattie.

With her heart thumping in her chest, Mattie pressed her eye to the slit between the panels of wood to see Christopher, dressed in the same navy suit he'd worn when he'd called for tea with the family two months ago, looming over a self-confessed gang of fascists.

'Wot you mean?' asked Stan, the slight waver in his voice giving away his unease.

'Last week in Cable Street,' Christopher said in an icy tone. 'Shoving dog shit through letter-boxes.'

The men muttered amongst themselves and shuffled about.

'Oh, that,' Stan forced a casual laugh. 'It were

just a bit of fun, that's all. Putting the wind up a couple of Jew boys, that's all–'

'Now, you listen to me,' cut in Christopher, stepping forward. 'I don't give a damn if you round up every Jew in London and make a bonfire of them all in the middle of Wembley Stadium but, as I've told you before, the British Union and the Right Club didn't send me down here to make you better Jew-baiters. My job is to make sure you're ready to move when Germany's spring offensive starts.'

'What, is Hitler finally coming to join us?' said someone.

'Yes, he is,' said Christopher.

'When?' the gang asked in unison.

'I don't know, but when the balloon goes up you must be ready to mobilise the masses, which is why you're supposed to be getting involved in the Civil Defence, so you can glean information for the Abwehr, not larking about in the streets like a bunch of school boys.'

Nausea rose up in the back of Mattie's throat as the ground under her shifted. Putting her hand out to steady herself, she knocked against the tea chest and her torch fell off.

'What was that?' asked Christopher as all sound in the hall ceased.

Mattie held her breath as sweat sprang out between her shoulder blades.

'Sounded like something under the stage,' said Teddy.

'A rat, I shouldn't wonder,' said Stan. 'We're pretty close to Limehouse Basin and they get in through the drains.'

'Perhaps,' said Christopher. 'But best to take a look, don't you think? Just in case. There's a trap-door on the stage so we can take a shufty.'

With mounting panic, Mattie heard footsteps crossing to the stairs then on the boards above her.

She pushed her way through the old theatre props, broken furniture and tea chests as silently as she could, desperately trying to think of a way to escape. Then she remembered the old access door at the back of the stage. Shoving her note-book and pen in her pocket and grabbing her torch, Mattie fell onto all fours and crawled through the mouse droppings, dust and cobwebs towards it.

Above her head, the trapdoor creaked open.

'Anyone got a torch?' asked Christopher.

Someone must have given him one as a shaft of light cut through the darkness.

With her heart pounding in her chest, Mattie scurried behind some canvas scenery. Searching with her fingertips, she located the hatch but then realised the catch was on the outside.

'Can you see anything?' a male voice shouted behind her.

Frantically she tore a Kirby grip from her hair and, straightening it out as best she could, she poked it between the door and the frame. Wriggling it upwards, she reached the catch and, with the sound of shifting boxes behind her, Mattie tried to force it up with both hands.

It didn't budge.

The men drew closer and, with beads of per-spiration springing out on her forehead, Mattie tried again. For a second it remained fixed then, just as a torch's beam highlighted the wall behind her, the catch gave way and the door opened.

'Over here,' shouted Stan.

Without pausing, Mattie rolled through and closed the door behind her, flicking the catch back in place. She lay motionless for a moment as the door she'd just escaped through rattled a couple of times, then the sounds of searching moved away.

Shaking like a leaf, she scrambled to her feet. Before she could move, a hand closed over her mouth and pulled her behind the long grey stage curtains. The steel-like arm of her assailant around her waist pulled her tight against his hard body.

'Don't make a sound, Mattie,' a voice whispered, his breath warm on her neck.

Mattie's eyes flew open. Unbelievable – for the second time that evening she recognised the person speaking.

In every dream Daniel had ever had about taking Mattie into his arms, he'd never imagined it would be quite like this.

Holding her close to him in the darkness, the heavy drapes around them, he savoured the moment and hoped that they would live long enough to tell their children about their first embrace.

The crashing about under the stage had subsided but, as the door to the main hall swung open again and Christopher, Stan and the others stormed back in, Daniel knew they weren't out of danger yet.

Knowing she wouldn't cry out, Daniel removed his hand from Mattie's mouth. He felt her relax and allowed his own arm to slacken, although he kept it anchored around her waist.

'See, I told you it were a rat,' said Stan as the so-called committee returned to the table.

'Maybe,' said Christopher, not sounding completely convinced. 'But you can't be too careful, especially not with so much at stake, which is why if I hear any more about your stupid antics, I'll make sure the powers that be, including Mosley, get to hear about it. Do you understand?'

'Course,' said Stan. 'I ain't bloody stupid.'

'Well then, stop acting like it,' said Christopher.

There was no reply except the sound of heavy footsteps marching across the sprung dance floor.

The main door swung open and back.

There was a long pause then, in mutters and mumbles, the committee of the East London Branch of the Britons for Peace Union concluded their business and also left the hall.

As the lock turned in the hall doors, Mattie twisted out of Daniel's embrace and turned to face him, confusion and hurt on her lovely face.

She opened her mouth to speak but swayed instead. Daniel caught her in his arms and she leaned into him, her soft body moulding itself into his.

'Don't worry, my love,' he said, enjoying the feel of her closeness. 'You're safe now.'

Annoyed that her legs still didn't quite feel as if they were doing her bidding, Mattie gripped the banister tightly as she made her way down the stairs to the rectory's ground floor.

As she stepped onto the third step from the bottom, the lounge door opened and Father McCree stepped out.

'Oh there you are,' he said, gazing up at her. 'I was getting worried about you.'

She'd been upstairs for the last half an hour washing of the grime from her hands and face and combing the cobwebs from her hair. While she'd been upstairs, Father McCree had taken off his dog collar, unfastened his top three shirt buttons and rolled up his sleeves, showing his muscular forearms with their covering of smooth dark hair.

'I'm fine,' said Mattie, forcing a smile. 'I was trying not to wake Father Mahon...' She stepped down, but her foot slipped as she put it down.

Father McCree dashed up and caught her, taking her weight as if she were made of down.

'I'm sorry,' she said. Her heart quickened as his strong arms enfolded her.

'You've had a shock and Father Mahon's away for a few days,' he said, gently helping her down the last few steps. 'Now come, I've put coal on the fire and made you a cup of strong tea.'

'I'd rather have a drink,' said Mattie.

He squeezed her hand. 'I'll see what I can do.'

Mattie allowed him to lead her into the parlour.

Settling her on the sofa, he went to the sideboard and opened the cupboard.

'Jameson's?' he asked, pulling out a bottle.

She nodded.

He uncorked the bottle and poured whisky into two tumblers and picked them up.

'There you go,' he said, handing one to her and taking a swig of his own.

Putting the glass to her lips Mattie swallowed a generous mouthful then, closing her eyes, she let her head rest back as the warm liquid spread through her stomach. For a moment there was silence, then she sat up and looked at him.

'So, Father McCree,' said Mattie coolly. 'Would you mind telling me what the hell's going on?'

He gave her a quirky smile and, taking another mouthful of his drink, sat down on the other end of the sofa. 'I will, as long as you start calling me Daniel.' Seeing the look on her face, his expression became serious and he explained what she'd witnessed in the hall.

'So I was right,' said Mattie, half an hour and two glasses of scotch later. 'It was Stan and his thugs who shoved that mess and leaflets through the Wisemans' letterbox.'

'I'm sure it was,' Daniel replied. 'And I suspect Stan and his gang are also responsible for a number of arson attacks on Jewish premises and several serious assaults too, along with the vile slogans and the leaflets that are cropping up everywhere.'

'So why did you stop me going to the police?' asked Mattie. 'And why were you snooping around at the back of the stage?'

'Actually, Mattie,' he took a deep breath. 'I've got something to tell you and it might be a bit of a shock. You see, I'm not actually Father Mc-Cree. In fact, I'm not actually a priest at all. I'm Captain Daniel McCarthy and I work for MI5 and my mission in East London is to infiltrate the fascists' national organisations.'

Mattie stared open-mouthed at him.

'You're a spy!'

He gave her that crooked smile again. 'We prefer the title field operative.'

'So is there a real Father McCree?' asked Mattie.

'Yes,' Daniel replied. 'He's an IRA sympathiser and is under lock and key at his majesty's pleasure at the moment.'

'What on earth do the Irish Nationalists have to do with the British Union of Fascists?' Mattie asked.

'The IRA, as you probably already know, don't recognise the Anglo-Irish agreement and have vowed to fight to unite the whole of Ireland. One of their number, Tom Barry, has links with Germany and persuaded the IRA leadership to seek an alliance with Germany on the understanding that when Hitler takes over Britain he would return the six counties to Dublin's rule,' said Daniel.

'But the IRA don't trust the Germans,' said Mattie.

'They certainly don't,' he replied. 'Which is why they sent Father McCree—'

'As their contact with the Germans,' said Mattie.

'Precisely,' he replied. 'And, more importantly, some of the IRA council members have close contacts and are cooperating with German Intelligence; they sent McCree to be their go-between for the upcoming operation.' Leaning his forearms on his thighs, Daniel drew closer still and Mattie's eyes flickered briefly down the front of his shirt again. 'I haven't got all the details yet, but from what I've gleaned so far from the information German Intelligence has asked for, they are hatching a plan they are calling Operation Holiday, to have German undercover agents slipped into the country via London Docks so they can subvert the capital's local and civil defences prior to any land invasion.'

'How?'

Daniel bit his lower lip. 'I don't know but my superiors have ordered me to get closer to the big players in the fascist movement to keep an eye on them.'

'But surely the police are already keeping people like Mosley under surveillance,' said Mattie.

'They are,' he replied. 'But there are others: lots of others who haven't put their heads over the parapets yet but will line up behind the British Union of Fascists and the other like-minded once Hitler makes his move.'

'Invade, you mean?'

Daniel looked grave. 'I'm afraid all the intelligence we have coming back from MI5 operatives working undercover in Germany and France indicates that it's only a matter of time.'

Mattie took another sip of drink as she let everything Daniel had said sink in. She looked up again.

'So who is Christopher, really?'

'The East London organiser for all the pro-Nazi organisations who are working together to aid our enemies,' Daniel replied. 'We think he became a follower of the Nazis while he was in Berlin ten years ago with his cousins; Otto, who is one of Himmler's aide-de-camps, and Gunter, a captain in the Waffen SS. Christopher's late father was British but his mother is German and lives in Baden-Baden with her brother and family. We suspect Christopher also went to Spain, with Otto, as part of Hitler's delegation to Franco,' he continued. 'What he was up to after that is a bit of a mystery. Then he popped up again as the head clerk at City and Country Bank in Northampton in '34. It was there he first came to our attention when he became a prominent member of the Link, the umbrella organisation for all the fascist groups, and we've been keeping an eye on him ever since. It was when he moved to London, just after war was declared, that MI5 set about getting a man on the inside. That opportunity occurred when we intercepted McCree on the ferry from Ireland. It took a bit of doing but, in the end, the archbishop agreed that, as it was in the national interest, I could assume Father McCree's identity and go under cover.'

'That's why you didn't take mass or hear confession,' Mattie said, forcing her eyes back onto his face.

Daniel gave a wry smile. 'I don't think the pope himself would sanction that.'

She forced a smile. 'No, I don't suppose he would.'

'So perhaps now you'll understand why I couldn't let you go to the police.' He shifted forwards and Mattie's eyes flickered onto the spray of dark hair showing between his open shirt front.

'I'm really sorry, Mattie. It must be a bit of a shock to find out that the man you're involved with is a fascist traitor.'

'I *was* involved with,' corrected Mattie. 'He was in such a foul mood the last time we went out that I told him it was over.'

Relief flashed across Daniel's face.

'Thank God. Christopher might ooze charm but underneath he's both violent and dangerous,' he said, raking his fingers through his hair. 'You don't know how I've been out of my mind with worry over you since Christmas and I wouldn't burden you with this but, for your own safety, you need to know that Christopher is very dangerous. He raped and almost killed one of our female agents who'd infiltrated the Right Club a few months ago and one of my colleagues who was tracking him in Northampton ended up under a train so, until Christopher is safely under lock and key, I want you to be on your guard against him. And, no matter what, never, never be alone with him.'

The sofa she was sitting on seemed to tilt sideways and she put her hand over her eyes to steady herself.

'My goodness,' she whispered.

The alarm she'd felt fending Christopher off on Christmas night flashed through her mind as she realised his assertion that he didn't take no for an answer wasn't just a figure of speech.

Seeing the look on Mattie's face, Daniel stood up and crossed the space between them in two steps and hunkered down in front of her.

'He hasn't hurt you, has he?' he asked. 'Because if he has, I swear I'll–'

'No, no he hasn't,' she replied, warmed by the concern on his face. 'It's just that I took him to meet my parents, and...' She covered her face with her hands. 'I feel such a fool not to have seen through him.'

Gently, Daniel took hold of her hands and Mattie looked up.

'Believe me, Mattie, you're not.' He hooked his finger under her chin and raised her head.

He smiled and Mattie smiled back.

'And, Mattie, another thing,' he continued, looking at her intently. 'I'm sure you realise, but everything I've told you is top secret. In fact, if it was found out I'd told you any of this I'd be up on charges, and if Christopher ever discovers who I really am, I'm a dead man.'

'So why have you told me?' asked Mattie.

'Because I trust you with my life, Mattie, and...' Smiling, he reached out and repositioned a stray lock that had come adrift. 'Because I love you.'

Mattie's heart did a backflip, then a double step, then shot off Heavenward singing at the top of its voice.

Mattie's gaze slowly ran over every inch of the face she loved.

'So, just to be clear,' she said. 'You're *not* an ordained priest?'

He shook his head.

'Or avowed to the church in any way?'

A smile tugged at the corners of his mouth 'No, Mattie, I'm not.'

'Well then, Daniel,' she said, gazing deeply into his dark eyes. 'You won't mind if I do this then, will you?'

Reaching out, she wound her arms around his neck and then, as she'd dreamed of doing for so long, pressed her lips onto his.

There was a moment of perfect stillness, then Daniel's arm enfolded her and with a low moan he crushed her mouth under his.

Feeling as if her bones were made of liquid, Mattie opened her eyes and saw Daniel's face just a few inches away from hers. The dark bristles on his chin were clearly visible in the dim light from the bedside lamp. He had his eyes closed, a small smile lifting the corners of his lips as his hand rested lightly on her bare hip. He, like her, was naked and they were entwined together on his narrow single bed with just the top sheet half-draped across them. The room was chilly but, moulded into Daniel's hard body, Mattie was warm.

Careful not to disturb him, Mattie's eyes travelled over his chest, lingering on the tangle of curls before following the narrow line of hair as it continued down across his taut stomach and beyond. Images of the last hour's exertions and its breath-taking finale caused a wave of pleasure to roll through her.

What a night and she didn't just mean their bold and explosive love-making.

In the last three hours she'd found out that not only were her suspicions about her brother-in-law right but, alarmingly, until a month ago she'd actually been walking out with a facist murderer, rapist and traitor. If that weren't enough to scramble her brain, she'd gone from being in love with a man who she thought could never be hers to having him crying out her name in love as they were entwined together.

Daniel shifted and Mattie's gaze returned to the

face that, if she lived to be a hundred, she'd never tire of gazing upon. She stretched up and kissed his cheek, enjoying the feel of his bristles on her lips. His smile widened and he opened his eyes.

'Hello, you,' he said, love pouring out of his eyes as they held hers.

'Hello yourself,' she replied, casually smoothing her hand back and forth over his chest, disturbing the dark curls with her fingers.

Daniel smiled and she smiled back.

'Oh, and by the way,' he said. 'Just in case I didn't say, I love you.'

Mattie laughed. 'I think you mentioned it a couple of times.' Wriggling out from under his arm she shifted up onto one elbow. 'But now you've ravished me, Daniel McCartney, perhaps you'd be kind enough to tell me a bit more about yourself.'

Daniel gave her that quirky smile of his. 'If I remember rightly, Mattie Brogan, it was you who kissed me but, since you asked, I'm twenty-eight and I come from a place called Little Crosby, just north of Liverpool, where my parents still live. My father was a headmaster and my mother is French and was a Red Cross nurse and they met when my father was brought into her field hospital in Arras with shrapnel in his leg. He's from Belfast, so I can thank him for my Irish accent, and she's from Strasbourg on the French German Border, which is why I speak French like a native and German like a Frenchman. I had my first communion in St Mary's Church and went to the attached school until I was eleven, then I attended Seafield Grammar School and then on to Cambridge to study History and Humanities.

That is until '37 when I signed up for the British Battalion in the International Brigade.'

Mattie's eyes stretched wide.

'You fought in Spain?' she said, remembering avidly reading about each and every twist of the bloody conflict.

He nodded.

'From the siege of Jarama.' He pointed to the scar disturbing the smooth hair on his left thigh. 'Through to Madrid.' He ran his index finger lightly along the indentation under his jaw. 'Then across the ruins of Aragon, to our gasping retreat across the Ebro and our last farewell in Barcelona when all hope of defeating Franco and his fascists was gone,' Daniel replied, his voice tinged with deep-rooted pain.

They lay still for a few moments before Mattie spoke again. 'So did you return to Cambridge?'

Daniel shook his head. 'Although we were defeated, we received a heroes' welcome when we pitched up at Victoria Station and, after a drunken week saying goodbye to my comrades in London, I went home for Christmas. When I returned to Cambridge in January, I was approached by my old commander, Francis Lennox, who is now one of the senior officers in MI5 and I signed up. They sent me off to Aldershot to learn proper soldiering and after some intensive firearms and combat training, I was sent to work undercover for a travel company. I was there from April to the middle of August last year, supposedly sorting out travel and hotel arrangements for the English there who were trying to return to England but I was really monitoring Nazi sympathisers in Berlin.'

'Did you meet Christopher there?' asked Mattie.

'No, he'd already returned, which is just as well or he'd have known that I wasn't the real Father McCree.' Daniel's eyes darkened and, in a swift movement, he rolled her over onto her back. 'I know we've put the cart before the horse a bit,' he said in a low voice, nudging his hardening penis against her hip. 'But will you marry me?'

Mattie slid her hands around his neck. 'Do you even need to ask?'

She pressed her mouth onto his and his tongue darted in, sending excitement coiling through her. Running her hands over his muscular shoulders, Mattie let her head fall back.

'I'm pleased to hear it,' he murmured as he kissed slowly down her throat. 'But I'm not really in a position to make an honest woman of you just at the moment—'

'Because you're posing as a Catholic priest and in the middle of an undercover mission to flush out Nazi traitors, I can see how that might be a bit difficult,' laughed Mattie.

'But I will,' he said. 'I'm afraid I don't know when that might be or how long we'll have to wait but, as soon as this mission is over, I'll apply for a special licence and we'll be married within a week. I promise.'

'I know you will, Daniel,' she whispered, enjoying the feel of his hair-roughened legs resting against hers and the touch of his hands on her skin. 'I know you will.'

Daniel gazed lovingly down at her for a couple of heartbeats then, closing his eyes, he lowered his lips and his body onto hers again.

Chapter Fourteen

'Right,' said Mattie, pulling the reef knot of the strapping firmly. 'This casualty is stable enough to be transported to the hospital.'

The bomb victim, her head bandaged, arm in a sling, and with her casualty note pinned to her threadbare coat, took a roll-up from behind her left ear.

'Anyone got a light before I go?' she asked, grinning up at Mattie and the two auxiliary ambulance men standing ready with the stretcher.

It was the first Monday in March and Mattie, along with at least two dozen other CD personnel, was standing in the Memorial Hall in Devonport Street.

It was also exactly eleven days since she'd spent a breathless night of joy and discovery in Daniel's arms.

Their patient, Olive Grimwood from Shadwell Terrace, wasn't really a victim of the Luftwaffe but a volunteer for the Civil Defence exercise Mattie had organised.

'There you go, luv,' said one of the ambulance men, flicking his lighter and holding the flame for Olive.

As the elderly woman puffed on her fag, the stretcher bearers scooped her up, deposited her on the canvas then, taking an end each, carried her out to the waiting transport.

Mattie stretched and wiped the sheen of sweat from her brow with the back of her hand.

The Victorian hall she was standing in, which had been erected in honour of some British victory or another in the last century and usually played host to community activities, was today serving as a casualty station. Instead of sequence dancers gliding over its polished floorboards, there were two dozen truckle beds set up hospital style next to stainless-steel trollies loaded with bandages, both rolled and triangular, splints, pressure pads and bottles of surgical spirits, iodine and smelling salts. On the stage, where the Stepney Amateur Dramatic Society usually performed, Cyril Potter sat at a desk with three telephones in front of him, a pile of casualty forms beside him and two blackboards with the details of the wounded chalked on them placed behind him. There was also a further blackboard leaning against the stage wings with all the emergency contact numbers of the local hospitals, the gas, water and electricity boards and the police, along with the relevant officers on duty at the control centre at the town hail. Pivotal to the efficient running of the whole operation were the WVS, who were busily doling out cups of tea and jam tarts to the volunteers and Civil Defence personnel alike.

'How many's that?' asked Brenda, who was manning the first-aid station next to Mattie.

'Seven,' Mattie replied. 'One crushed leg, two head injuries and couple of minor casualties, plus the one that's just gone which was a fractured pelvis and a fatality.'

She nodded across to where Paddy Collins,

who'd drawn the black ticket that morning, was drinking tea while waiting to be taken to the temporary mortuary.

'What about you?' asked Mattie, laying a fresh sheet on her trolley.

'A severed leg, two broken arms and a pregnant woman who'd gone into labour,' said Brenda. 'So I sent her through to the midwifery station in–'

Brenda's gaze shifted to a point behind her.

Mattie turned to find Christopher, dressed in his civilian suit, standing behind her.

As Mattie looked up at him, Christopher smiled.

'Hello, sweetheart,' he said, forcing a contrite expression. Her eyes travelled sharply over him and then she returned to her task without replying.

Irritation fizzled through him.

Although it irked him to admit it, since Mattie had stomped off, he'd not been able to get her out of his mind. He didn't take a rebuff from any woman, let alone from the likes of Mattie Brogan, and his blood boiled every time he thought about it. It was clear that the quicker he got her into bed and purged himself of this lunacy, the better.

Christopher held his smile. 'I was hoping to have a word with you, Mattie.'

'Can't you see I'm busy?' she replied, not looking up as she set up the trolley for the next mock casualty.

'It won't take a moment,' Christopher said. 'I'm sure your friend here can manage without you for a moment or two.'

He gave the brassy-looking woman beside Mattie his most charming smile.

'Go on, luv,' she said. 'I'll hold the fort.'

Mattie hesitated, then looked at her friend who gave a little nod.

'All right,' Mattie said, putting down the kidney bowl she was holding. 'But come and get me, Brenda, if more casualties arrive.'

Christopher stepped back.

Mattie walked past him and headed for the doors. Christopher rushed ahead and opened the door for her. She walked through without a glance or a word of thanks.

As he stepped outside, she spun around.

'So what do you want to say?' she asked, folding her arms tightly across her.

'Look, sweetheart,' he said. 'I know I had one over the eight and was a bit off with you at the pub that night, but...' He summoned up his most ingratiating smile. 'I'm sorry.'

Mattie's chilly expression didn't waver. 'Firstly, Christopher, I'm not your sweetheart. Secondly, you didn't just have one over the eight, you were drunk and, lastly, you weren't a bit off, you were downright rude and nasty.'

'For God's sake, Mattie, I'd had a hell of a day.'

'And that gives you the excuse to behave like a pig, does it?' She glared at him.

'No, but perhaps we should put it behind us. After all...' He formed his face into a remorseful expression. 'I think perhaps it's time I spoke to your father. What do you say?'

'Don't bother,' she replied. 'I wouldn't marry you if you were the last man on earth.'

Christopher grabbed her arm. 'But why?'

'Because I don't want to see you any more,' she said, looking coolly up at him.

Pulling free of his grip, Mattie turned to go back through the doors, but Christopher blocked her path.

'Well top of the morning to you both,' said McCree's all-too-familiar voice.

Damping down his fury, Christopher looked around and, fighting the urge to smash his fist into the priest's face, forced a smile onto his face.

'Good morning, Father, doing your bit for the war, I see,' he said, indicating the painted blood on the priest's forehead.

'Aren't we all? Miss Brogan put a notice up in church asking for volunteers, so I thought I'd pop along.' McCree's attentions shifted onto Mattie. 'Would you mind showing me where to report?

'Not at all,' said Mattie, smiling for the first time since Christopher had arrived.

McCree looked from her to Christopher and back again. 'That's of course if you've finished chatting.'

'We have,' said Mattie. 'In fact, I was just going back in.'

She gave Christopher a meaningful look.

As Christopher didn't want McCree to witness him eating more humble pie, he stepped aside.

The priest opened the hall door and, giving Christopher a cursory glance as she passed, Mattie went through the door with McCree a step behind.

With his nails digging into the palms of his hands, Christopher watched her go but before the door swung closed, he spoke again.

'Remember what I said, Mattie,' he shouted after her. 'I won't take no for an answer.'

'Are you all right, Mattie?' Daniel asked as they walked back into the hall.

Although her heart was still hammering painfully in her chest, Mattie forced a smile. 'I'm fine, honest—'

She started to tremble as the rage and latent violence she'd seen in Christopher's face swept over her again. She realised that instinctively she'd always known it had been there, hidden beneath his smooth smile and persuasive words. It scared her but, now, having seen him at the BPU meeting, Mattie knew she would do everything in her power to help Daniel stop him.

'Where's your station?' Daniel asked, his firm voice reaching through her tumbling thoughts and steadying them a little.

Mattie pointed to an empty truckle bed with afresh trolley next to it and a number 3 pinned on the screen behind.

'Excuse me, Father,' Cyril's voice cut in. 'But if you're taking part in our exercise as a casualty, you're to report to me first.'

'I'm sorry, Mr Potter,' Daniel replied, smiling politely up at the ARP controller. 'Father Daniel McCree, St Bridget and St Brendan's Rectory.'

Taking the pen from behind his ear, Cyril scribbled on his clipboard and waved them on.

Daniel took her elbow gently and led her through the crowded room. With the warmth of his touch spreading through her and his strong presence beside her, by the time they'd reached her dressing station, Mattie's pulse had almost returned to normal.

Daniel, aware of the need to keep up appearances, hopped onto the truckle bed and their eyes and emotions locked for a second then, aware of the dozen or so people within earshot of them, Mattie pulled herself together.

'Right, Father, let's see what Gerry's done to you today.' She took hold of the label pinned to his jacket collar and turned it over. 'A laceration to the head and left forearm. I'll need you to take your jacket off so I can treat your wound.'

Daniel shrugged off his jacket and rolled up his sleeve to expose the line of red crayon that the casualty coordinator had drawn.

'What did he say?' he whispered as she reached for a bandage.

Picking up a wodge of gauze, Mattie pressed it on his forearm and repeated the conversation she'd had with Christopher.

'Thankfully you arrived or I'm sure he would have grabbed hold of me again,' she concluded.

Daniel's mouth pulled into a tight line. 'I'm so sorry I got you tangled up in all this.'

'You didn't,' Mattie replied, looking down at her task. 'It was me who discovered the truth about Christopher when I hid under the stage to discover what Stan was up to.'

Someone knocked into the screen behind them.

There was a pause and then Daniel spoke again. 'You know I love you, don't you?' he whispered.

'You have mentioned it,' she replied under her breath. She glanced up under her lashes to find him looking at her with an intensity that sent her heart trembling with longing.

Although they had contrived to see each other

323

as often as they could, it had always been either at church or in the company of others. It was better than nothing, but...

'Oh, Daniel,' she sighed.

'I know, sweetheart,' he said in the same hushed tone. 'I can't stand not being able to kiss and hold you either.'

His scorching gaze ran over her face again and Mattie's stomach fluttered.

'Perhaps there's a way,' he said.

'But isn't it too risky?' she said, trying to steady her racing heart as she tied off the bandage.

'Not if we are very careful.' He gave her that quirky smile again. 'Don't forget all this cloak-and-dagger stuff is my stock in trade.'

'Why, Father McCree, you've hardly touched your lunch,' said Mrs Dunn. 'Is there something wrong with it?'

Daniel looked up. 'No, Mrs Dunn. Nothing at all, I'm just not feeling particularly hungry, that's all. Sorry.'

She looked concerned. 'Are you feeling a bit peaky or something?'

'No, no, I'm fine,' he said, smiling at her. 'And I'm sure I'll have my appetite back by supper-time.'

Actually, he wasn't at all right, not by a long chalk, because he'd come dangerously close to destroying his mission by punching Christopher in the face.

Thankfully he'd only been blocking her path be-cause if Daniel had walked around the corner and seen the bastard doing anything more to Mattie, he wouldn't have been answerable for his actions.

When they'd got back in the hall she'd tried to make light of it but Daniel had seen how shaken she was. Instead of being able to take her in his arms to comfort her, as he was desperate to do, they had to keep up the pretence of being priest and parishioner. He just hoped to God that the bloody German Intelligence would put Operation Holiday into motion soon as he had no hope of making Mattie Mrs McCartney until they were under lock and key.

The housekeeper cast a motherly eye over him again and, satisfied she could see no hint of fever, took his barely touched plate.

'I don't suppose you'll be wanting pudding either then, Father?' she said.

'No, thank you,' said Daniel.

Giving him another worried look, Mrs Dunn bustled off to the kitchen.

'So how did you get on at the Civil Defence exercise thing this morning?' asked Father Mahon. The elderly priest was sitting at the top of the table, studying the young man intently.

'Very well,' Daniel replied.

'And were you mortally wounded?' asked Father Mahon.

'Lacerations to the head and left forearm,' Daniel replied. 'Mattie Brogan treated me.'

'Such a darling girl' continued Father Mahon. 'She looked just like a buttercup in May, she did, at mass last week.'

Putting aside his napkin, Daniel stood up. 'If you'd excuse me, Father, I'll think I'll make a start on the preparatory reading for this week's

Sunday school talk.'

'Good idea, I'm planning an hour or two with St Gregory and his thoughts on the Holy Spirit, me-self.' The old priest's sharp eyes searched Daniel's face. 'Is there something troubling you, lad?'

'Just the thought of explaining why the lions didn't eat my namesake in their den to twenty-five children on Sunday,' Daniel replied, forcing a hollow laugh.

Leaving Father Mahon, Daniel left the dining room and, taking the stairs two at a time, hurried to his room.

Unbuttoning his dog collar at the back, Daniel ripped it off and popped the top button on his shirt. Taking off his spectacles he pinched the insides of his eyes with his fingers. He studied the skyline blindly for a second, then he caught sight of the church clock opposite.

Damn!

Crossing to the door in two strides, he locked it and then switched on the small Bush radio. Hunkering down beside his bed, Daniel pulled the tan suitcase out from under his bed. Lifting it onto the desk, he opened it and quickly plugged the transmitter's flex into the socket.

While the set's valves were warming, Daniel took a pencil and a single sheet of paper – writing on a pad would leave an impression and he knew never to leave such evidence – from the shelf.

He had to check in with Meadow Rambler on a daily basis but at different times each day. On Monday it was one-thirty in the afternoon.

Forcing himself to concentrate on the task at hand, Daniel settled himself on the chair in front of the radio transmitter, then put the earphones on.

He glanced at his watch. Seeing there was still a minute to go, he took a deep breath to steady his raging pulse and stared across the rooftops towards Devonport Street.

What if Christopher had gone back to try and catch Mattie again?

Perhaps he should go back in case Christopher returned. But wouldn't that look odd? He could say he'd lost something and was searching for it. However, liar, rapist and murder he might be, but Christopher was no fool and if he ever got the slightest inclination there was something between him and Mattie it would put her in so much danger that Daniel didn't think even his steely nerve and cool head could take the strain.

He checked his watch again and switched on the radio. Turning the dial through the waveband he listened as the low hum wobbled a couple of times, then he heard the distinct voice of Meadow Rambler.

'*Dies ist Wiese Rambler, sind Sie es?*' his German contact asked.

'*Hallo, Wiese Rambler ist Hirte,*' he replied in a low voice, his mouth touching the Bakelite microphone. '*Gehen Sie voran mit Ihrer Nachricht.*'

'*Einundzwanzig, vierzig, neun...*'

Daniel wrote the numbers down until the radio went dead.

Ripping off his headphones, he switched his transmitter off, packed it in the concealed compartment of the tan case, threw his summer clothes over the top and slipped the bag back

327

under the bed.

Opening the old Bible in front of him, Daniel set about decoding the message. Writing the last word with a flourish, he stuck the pencil behind his ear and took a deep breath to steady his thundering heart. He quickly checked through again to ensure he'd deciphered the message correctly then, when he was satisfied he had, he sat back and stared at the paper for a couple of seconds. Then, putting his hands over his face, Daniel let his head fall back.

At last!

Taking a box of matches from the shelf, he lit the corner of the paper. Holding it until he could feel the heat of the flame on his fingers, he threw it in the grate. Without glancing at the Sunday school material he was supposed to be preparing, he marched out of the room and hurried out of the house.

With the rain drumming on the metal roof of the bus shelter, Daniel pretended to study the timetable under the glass of the noticeboard whilst keeping an eye on the Hope and Anchor's salon door. According to the clock suspended outside Fish Brothers, the pawnbrokers on the other side of the road, it was ten to two.

The heavens had opened as he'd left the rectory some twenty minutes ago, which suited Daniel's purpose as the heavy downpour meant people were concentrating on getting swiftly to their destination rather than looking around as they hurried by.

He was just beginning to wonder if, today of all

days, his quarry had decided to break his daily habit of having a liquid lunch when the pub's side door opened and Christopher stepped out. Turning up his collar against the rain, he started along to the street towards the bank.

Standing back for a second to avoid the spray from a passing lorry, Daniel crossed the road.

'Christopher,' he said, striding towards him and offering his hand. 'Fancy meeting you here.'

'Father McCree,' Christopher replied, eyeing Daniel warily but shaking his hand nonetheless. 'You've recovered from your injuries, I see.'

Pushing his spectacles back onto the bridge of his nose, Daniel stepped closer. 'I have instructions from Meadow Rambler but I can only tell BCCSE Council.'

Christopher opened a fresh packet of cigarettes and took one out. 'It's not that simple, especially as most of the wardens have already drifted back to their constituencies ahead of the Easter recess,' said Christopher.

'I thought Ramsay was the only member of parliament on the BCCSE Council,' said Daniel as a bus went by them.

'Officially, yes, but I think at least half of the council are MPs from both sides,' Christopher replied. 'All with an eye for a place on the new government once Mosley takes over.'

'Well then, it's even more imperative that I attend the next meeting,' Daniel replied.

Christopher chewed his lip. 'There's a London meeting in two weeks on 28th March.'

Daniel shook his head. 'No, it has to be to be with the top brass.'

'Well that won't be until 13th April at Holborn House, followed by one of Mosley's lunches at the Creighton Club,' Christopher replied. 'I'll get you added to the guest list.'

'Good, and in the meantime Meadow Rambler wants to know how many supporters you could get onto the streets,' Daniel said, relaying Francis's recent request for MI5. 'And I want accurate numbers, not wild guesses, do you understand?'

Christopher's ice-blue eyes turned glacial. 'Anything else or have you given all your bloody orders?'

'Not quite,' said Daniel. 'That incident this morning.'

'What about it?'

'I told you after that business with the dog shit not to draw attention to yourself and so what do I find when I turn the corner?' Daniel jabbed his finger at him. 'You. Threatening Miss Brogan in broad daylight.'

'I wasn't threatening her, I was talking to her,' said Christopher. 'We'd had a bit of a quarrel, that's all.'

'Well it didn't look like a bit of a quarrel from where I was standing,' Daniel replied. 'So leave her be or I'll be having something to say about it.'

A smirk spread across Christopher face. 'Quite the knight in shining armour, aren't you, Mc-Cree?'

Daniel held Christopher's mocking gaze.

'I'll drop by next week to collect the information I've asked you for,' Daniel said, flatly.

'Whatever you say.' Christopher blew a stream of smoke Heavenwards and grinned. 'And don't worry, McCree. I won't breathe a word to Mattie about you having a bit of a fancy for her.'

Despite the urge to smash his fist into Christopher's hateful face, Daniel's unyielding expression didn't waver.

Giving Christopher another derisory look, then counting backward from ten in his head, Daniel turned his collar up against the rain and strolled slowly back towards the rectory.

Chapter Fifteen

Sliding her old pram under the cafe's awning to keep it from the rain, Queenie kicked the brake on. She lifted out the shopping bag from the top. The vegetables were safe from roaming dogs but she wasn't leaving the two pounds of pigs' liver to chance.

Hooking the bag over her arm, she walked up to the half-glazed door of Kate's cafe, the name painted in an arch across the glass, and pushed it open.

The eating house in the Highway was situated halfway between St George's church and Stepney town hall and was pretty much like every other cafe around the docks, but it was the Brogan family's favourite. It was owned by Vic Watson, a stout chap with curly ginger hair everywhere but on his head, and his wife Ruby who, in contrast to her husband, was stick thin. Judging by the chipped cream tiles on the walls, smoke-blackened rafters and the disused gas mantles still fixed to the wall, the cafe had been a working man's scoffing shop for a century, if not longer.

It was the last Tuesday in March and as the midday factory hooters signalling the lunch break hadn't yet sounded, the cafe was fairly quiet with just a handful of men seated at the dozen or so tables in the front half of the shop.

Ruby was halfway through buttering a stack of doorstep-sized slices of bread when Queenie walked in.

'Morning, Queenie me love, how are you?' asked Ruby, licking a blob of stray butter off her finger and picking up another slice.

'Not so bad,' Queenie replied, taking off her gloves and unfastening the hook at the front of her fur coat. 'Although this weather is fit to baptise you, so it is.'

Ruby laughed and shoved a strand of her bleach-blonde hair back in place. 'The usual?' she asked, taking a mug from the stack behind her.

Queenie nodded and walked over to the counter. She rummaged around for a copper or two.

'There you go and on the house.' Ruby placed a milky tea in front of the older woman, waving away Queenie's thrupenny bit. 'That tip you gave us for the two-thirty at Kempton Park last week came in at seven to one.'

Queenie picked up her drink and turned to look for a free table when, much to her surprise, she spotted Father McCree sitting in the corner and staring intently out of the window.

Taking the copy of *Sporting Life* from her pocket, Queenie ambled over.

'Good morning to you, Father, on this fair soft morning,' she said, stopping next to him.

He looked up, startled. 'Mrs Brogan.'

'One and the same,' Queenie replied. 'Do you mind if I join you?'

His eyes flickered down the street again and then he smiled. 'No, of course not.'

'And it is indeed a fair soft morning,' he continued as she slipped into the chair opposite him.

'You'd think that having soaked all and everyone since dawn, it'd have the common decency to be on its way,' said Queenie, placing her tea down.

He laughed. 'You have the right of it, Mrs Brogan.'

Queenie reached for the sugar bowl and Father McCree's eyes returned to the window for an instant.

'So what has brought you out in such weather, Father,' she asked, stirring her tea.

'I'm undertaking a couple of home calls for Father Mahon,' Father McCree replied. He stretched his arm from his sleeve and glanced at his watch. 'The damp's not good for his chest so Mrs Dunn has confined him in barracks.'

'And may Mary bless her for it,' said Queenie. 'And you for taking the burden.'

'It's no burden, Mrs Brogan,' said Father McCree. 'It's the least–'

The bell above the door tinkled again.

Father McCree's head shot round and delight flashed across his face so fast if she'd blinked, Queenie would have missed it.

She followed his gaze to see Mattie in her mac

with rain dripping from her umbrella.

'Morning, Ruby,' Mattie said, in her chirpiest voice.

'Morning, dearie,' Ruby replied, stacking the last of the sandwiches she was making on the top of the pile. 'Tea?'

'Please,' she replied, taking off her hat and shaking out her hair.

Resting her elbow on the counter, Mattie casually gazed around the shop until finally her eyes reached Father McCree.

Happiness twinkled in her granddaughter's eyes for a second and then Mattie spotted Queenie. She looked startled for a second, then smiled across at them and picked up her tea.

Father McCree got to his feet and watched her as she walked over to them.

'Gran!' she said, bending down as she reached the table to kiss her on the cheek. 'This is a nice surprise.'

'For me too,' said Queenie, curious as to why her granddaughter was wearing her new Crimson Crush lipstick and expensive perfume on a Tuesday afternoon.

Mattie straightened up. 'And I see you're keeping Father McCree company.'

'Hello, Mattie, won't you join us?' he asked, pulling out a chair.

Mattie smiled. 'I'm on duty later so I can't stay long, but I … suppose if I'm a few minutes late we won't lose the war.'

Shaking out her plastic hat and folding it away, she sat down.

Father McCree resumed his seat and Queenie

noticed how he smiled at her granddaughter – who smiled back.

There was a long pause, then Mattie looked at Queenie. 'What have you been up to, Gran?'

Although Mattie's eyes remained on Queenie's face throughout her rundown of her trip to the market, Mattie's mind was clearly somewhere else entirely.

'Sounds like you've had a busy morning,' said Mattie, stirring her tea for the third time since she sat down.

'You look well today,' Father McCree said.

A blush coloured Mattie's cheeks. 'Thank you.'

'She does, doesn't she, Father?' said Queenie, watching him closely.

Mattie blew across her tea. 'I was wondering if you'd heard from your aunt recently, Father McCree.'

'Indeed I have at last,' he replied, brightly. 'In fact, I found out only today that she's in town next week so we're hoping to have afternoon tea next Thursday.'

'That sounds nice,' said Mattie, in the same bouncy tone. 'Where is she staying?'

'The Albemarle in Balcombe Street,' he replied, 'just around the corner from Marylebone Station.'

They stared at each other for a moment, then Mattie looked at the clock behind the counter.

'I better be off,' she said, finishing off the last of her tea and standing up.

Father McCree looked at his watch. 'Goodness, is that the time? I ought to be off, too.'

Finishing his tea, he also got to his feet

335

'Which way are you going, Miss Brogan?' he asked.

'Down Gravel Lane,' Mattie replied, flipping the rain hat over her head again.

'I'm going that way.' Father McCree grabbed his black umbrella leaning on the wall behind him. 'We can share my brolly.'

'Good idea.' Wrenching her eyes from his face, Mattie dipped down and gave Queenie a quick peck on the cheek. 'See you at home, Gran.'

She hurried out, closely followed by Father McCree.

Queenie stared after them for a moment or two, then picked up the priest's empty cup. Swilling the grounds around a couple of times, she emptied them into Mattie's discarded drink, leaving the leaves clinging to the side of the cup.

Peering inside, she turned the cup back and forth, studying the shape of the leaves left behind and their position.

'Oi, Queenie,' Ruby called across from behind the counter. 'Can you see what the future holds for our dishy priest?'

Laying the cup down, a contented smile spread across Queenie's line-etched face. 'God love him and bless him, Ruby, that I can.'

Pretending to be studying the artistic display of men's socks and underpants in Feltman's display, Mattie peered down Watney Street through the glass corner of the haberdasher's window.

It was almost four-thirty on a mild Friday afternoon, just three days since she'd met Daniel in Kate's cafe. Of course she'd been a little surprised to find Queenie sitting at the table with him but perhaps it was as well because had her gran not been there, Mattie wondered if she'd have been able to hide her joy that at last she and Daniel were to snatch a precious few hours together before his big meeting with the fascist hierarchy on the following Saturday.

Thinking of Daniel and what he was trying to prevent got Mattie thinking of Stan and then Cathy so, having stowed away her equipment in her locker at Post 7 some twenty minutes earlier, Mattie had decided to take a stroll through the market on her way home.

As a goods train rumbled across the railway line behind her, scattering pigeons from their girder roosts, Mattie spotted the person she was waiting for.

Adjusting her holdall on her shoulder, she stepped out from her hiding place.

'Cathy,' she shouted.

Her sister turned and waved.

She was wearing one of the dresses that Mattie had let out for her in order to accommodate her swelling stomach. With a hat perched on her head and a wicker basket over her arm, her sister looked the perfect image of a mother-to-be.

Weaving her way between prams and groups of women gossiping, Mattie hurried towards her.

'I thought Mum said you were early shift this week,' said Cathy as Mattie reached her.

'I was but got caught up with something as I was leaving,' Mattie replied. 'Where are you off to?'

Cathy laughed. 'Same as ever on a Friday afternoon; Salty Soll's, of course.'

'Blooming shift work.' Mattie rolled her eyes. 'I don't know what day of the week it is sometimes.' She slipped her arm in Cathy's and squeezed. 'Right, you two, I want two bobs' worth of cod,' said Mattie doing a passable imitation of their mother. 'And–'

'A three h'penth worth of soft roe, for Queenie,' Cathy continued, wagging her finger at Mattie as their mother used to. 'So–'

'She don't wear out her dentures,' finished Mattie. They laughed.

'Goodness,' said Cathy. 'Seems like only last week we were fetching the Friday night fish for Mum.'

'And now you're doing the same for your husband's supper,' said Mattie.

They laughed again as they continued on to Michael Solomon and his wife Lena's fishmonger stall that had been supplying the Brogans' Friday fish for as long as Mattie could remember.

Stopping two pitches along from the Lord Nelson public house, they joined the back of the small queue.

'So how is Stan?' Mattie asked.

'Oh, you know, up before dawn and off in his lorry to market,' said Cathy. 'Then on the road all afternoon, delivering all over East London although recently, what with such a cold winter and petrol rationing, he's been having to turn down deliveries to Ilford and Chigwell.'

They shuffled forward.

'Have you heard from Charlie?' asked Cathy.

Mattie nodded. 'He finished his basic two

338

weeks ago and has been posted to the Heavy Regiment Royal Artillery at Bexhill and, reading between the lines, it sounds as if he's in with a good crew. He's met a half a dozen or more fellas from Limehouse, Mile End and Shadwell and they've put together a football team. I suppose Stan will be getting his call-up any day now.'

Cathy looked surprised. 'I thought Mum would have told you.'

'Told me what?' asked Mattie.

'That Stan's been given a medical exemption,' said her sister.

Mattie looked puzzled. 'What for?'

'His asthma,' her sister replied.

'I didn't know he had asthma,' said Mattie.

'Neither did he but he had to go to the doctor for something else and was diagnosed,' said Cathy.

'I'm surprised Dr Gingold didn't pick that up before, she's usually on the ball,' said Mattie.

'No, it wasn't her diagnosed him but some doctor in Hackney one of his mates at work recommended. He's moved us off the Cable Street surgery list because Dr Gingold is...' Cathy bit her lip.

'Jewish?' said Mattie, coolly.

Her sister nodded. 'I tried to tell him that I wanted to be seen by a woman doctor but Stan was adamant and he moved us to the Hannibal Road Surgery.'

The woman in front of them tucked her newspaper parcel of fish in her basket and moved away.

'Right, luv,' said Michael, rubbing his hands

339

together as he addressed Cathy. 'What'll it be, a nice bit of cod or perhaps some eels?'

Mattie stepped aside to let Cathy choose her fish and, after her sister had pocketed her change, they fell in step together again.

Forming her face into what she hoped was a casual expression, Mattie looked at her sister. 'So if Stan's not going to be called up, is he going to volunteer for something?'

Cathy shook her head. 'He's too busy with the BPU stuff.'

'I would have thought that what with the Luftwaffe bombing Scapa Flow and the U-boats blowing up convoys in the Atlantic, even the most ardent pacifist would realise there is no hope of making peace with Germany, and...' Mattie took a deep breath. 'I'm not having a go at Stan or anything, Cathy, but with the baby on the way, shouldn't Stan be at home with you instead of at meetings every night?'

Unhappiness flitted across her sister's face.

'I wish he would, especially as his mother does nothing but worry when he's out. I've tried to bring the subject up a couple of times but he just gets bad-tempered so I've given up.' Cathy sighed. 'I just hope once the baby's here Stan will see things differently.' She tucked her arm through Mattie's and gave a girlish shrug. 'Right, enough about Stan. Let's go and have a nice cuppa at Mum's and I'll tell you about my trip to Munroe House to see the midwives as we go.'

As she set off for Mafeking Terrace, arm-in-arm with her sister, as they had done so often as children, Mattie couldn't help but think that, by the time the baby came, Stan would indeed be seeing things very differently; from behind a set of prison bars.

Chapter Sixteen

Slowly opening his eyes, Daniel gazed up at the patterns on the hotel room's ceiling and smiled. Why wouldn't he? Even with her rich auburn hair strewn across his chest and her warm body curled into his, he still couldn't quite believe that the woman he loved was actually here, in his arms.

Well, wedged against him, in fact, with her head resting in the dip between his shoulder and neck and her hand lightly resting just below his navel, already igniting fresh desire in him.

Truth be told, given all that was at stake and the deadly game being played out around them, it was madness for them to be together at all but, frankly, he couldn't have lived without just one brief afternoon together. It wasn't enough, but for now it would have to suffice. It wasn't just the sheer pleasure of their bodies entwined together, albeit that left him gasping for breath, but the time before passions arose again, when they swapped childhood memories and hopes for the future, that filled him with such happiness.

A puff of warm early April breeze lifted the net curtains in the opened window and Mattie shifted against him. Glancing down, he hooked the sheet with his toe and inched it down until it was no longer covering Mattie's hip. His eyes ran slowly over her.

God, she was beautiful.

His gaze rested on her leg draped across his, enjoying the contrast of her smooth skin against his hairy thigh. His smile widened.

Future! What a peculiar notion. He thought he'd understood the concept clearly enough, after all, wasn't that what he'd fought for in Spain and was fighting for now: the country's future? But his future had been an unformed thing until he met Mattie. Now it was a place filled with the possibility of happy laughter, togetherness, a family of their own.

Family! Daniel's gaze slid onto the unopened packet of Durex on the bedside table that they'd forgotten about in the excitement of the moment. Next time, he told himself.

Outside in the corridor a door slammed and Mattie raised her head.

Pushing her hair from her face with her forearm, she yawned.

'What time is it?' she mumbled, her hand sliding lower and stoking his rising passion.

'Just after two-thirty.'

'Plenty of time,' she sighed, rolling half onto him and resting her hands on his chest.

Daniel traced his fingers lightly up her back. 'For what?'

Raising an eyebrow, she nudged his awakened penis with her hip.

'You're a hussy, you know.'

She kissed his chest.

'And aren't you glad?' she said, giving him a

sideward look which tightened his groin further.

'I most certainly am.' He grinned. 'But the people in the next street must have had to turn their radio up to hear the two o'clock news.'

Mattie sat up, not bothering to take the sheet with her and slapped him playfully. Enjoying the sight of her curves from a different angle, Daniel didn't object to his punishment. Taking her hand, he drew her to him.

'I promise we won't always have to meet like this, sweetheart,' he said softly.

Holding her close, he laid her back on the bed and arched over her.

She smiled up at him.

'I don't mind if we meet like this forever as long as we're together,' she said, her lovely hazel eyes filled with love. They gazed at each other for a long moment, then she spoke again. 'When are you meeting Mosley and chums?'

'Next Saturday,' Daniel replied.

'You will be careful.'

'Of course.'

'Promise me?'

'I promise you I'll be careful,' he replied, shoving aside the thought of the torture and pain that awaited him if he were not.

'And once you and MI5 have caught Christopher and the BPU red-handed landing the German spies, you'll be safe,' said Mattie, running her fingers through the hair on his chest.

Daniel caught her hand. 'We'll be safe and married.'

He kissed the inside of her wrist, feeling the pulse under his lips quicken. Mattie sighed as

Daniel's mouth progressed slowly up her arm and across her collar bone.

Her arm slid around his neck and Daniel's arms tightened around her as his mouth returned to hers in a hard, demanding kiss.

As his need to make love to her again started to overwhelm him, Daniel reached across to retrieve the pack of three French letters, but Mattie's hand slid between them and down below his navel, blotting all other thoughts from his mind.

Tucked into the narrow alleyway that ran between numbers 12 and 14 Mafeking Terrace, Christopher pulled the packet of Rothmans from his jacket pocket and took one out.

Although it was still an hour or so until sunset, the sun had already disappeared behind the houses, casting the street into shadow.

He looked at his watch. Almost six-thirty. He'd been waiting for almost half an hour already so where on earth was she?

When he'd popped into Post 7 during his lunch break, that brassy friend of hers had said she'd swapped a duty to go out for the day with a girl-friend. So after an afternoon of gnawing the end of his pencil, he'd decided to hang about near her house so he could talk to her.

Of course, he shouldn't have to do this as, by rights, a girl with a bloody Irish rag-and-bone man for a father should have recognised her good fortune at having someone like him interested in her and acted accordingly, but not Mattie Brogan.

He'd expected her to fall back into his arms and

into bed when he'd offered to talk to her father, but no. So now he was forced to loiter in the dark, waiting for her to come home.

Taking another drag on his cigarette, Christopher had just settled back in the shadows when he spotted her walking towards him.

She was wearing a light blue dress with a fluted skirt which swung around her shapely legs while a squared-shouldered cropped jacket emphasised her trim waist.

A familiar hunger tightened Christopher's crotch as he watched her.

'Hello, Mattie,' he said, stepping out in front of her as she reached within a few feet of his hiding place. 'Been somewhere nice?'

Mattie stared up at him in disbelief. 'Christopher, what are—'

'I thought perhaps we could have a little chat,' he said.

'About what?' said Mattie.

'Us.'

'There is no us,' she replied. 'And I've already told you, Christopher, I don't want to see you any more.'

'Yes, I know,' said Christopher. 'But now you've had a chance to think about it, I'm hoping you might have changed your mind.'

Mattie looked puzzled. 'Why?'

'Because you see, Mattie, my sweet,' he replied, forming his face into the most doting expression he could muster. 'I seem to find myself somewhat fond of you.'

Mattie stared incredulously up at him. 'I don't—'

'I know I behaved badly,' he continued, with wide-eyed adoration, 'but can't we put that behind us?' He took her hand. 'Perhaps I should have come right out with it at Christmas but, Mattie, will you marry me?'

Gazing up at him with a look of astonishment on her face, Mattie's jaw dropped.

Christopher suppressed the smug smile that was threatening to break out.

Of course he had no intention of marrying her, not with Lord Bedlington's rolling acres on offer, but once Mosley and the rest of them were in power, he could offer to set Mattie up somewhere under his protection.

Images of how he could make Mattie show her gratitude had just started to form in his head when she snatched her hand back.

'I wouldn't marry you if you were the last man on earth,' she said. 'Now let me pass.'

She went to step around him but, as she did so, he detected another scent under the fragrance of her perfume.

He blocked her path again.

'Are you seeing someone else,' he snapped, as blackness started crowding into his peripheral vison.

She gazed unflinchingly up at him. 'Let go of me, Christopher.'

He grabbed her wrist. 'Are you seeing someone else? Tell me.'

'No.'

Something flashed across her face.

'Are you?' he demanded, twisting her arm further.

She tried to pull free but he turned his hand further and she flinched.

'You're breaking my arm,' she said, angling her shoulder to reduce the tension.

With the pulse in his temple pounding, Christopher let go of her wrist and grabbed her around the throat, pushing her hard into the wall.

Mattie's eyes flew open as terror flashed across her face. Fired by her palpable fear, Christopher's fingers tightened.

'If you think for one minute, sweetheart,' he ground out, small white flecks of spit landing on her face as he spoke, 'that I'm going to stand by and let some other bastard get into your knickers after all the money I've lavished on you, then you're very much–'

Searing pain shot up from his groin to the pit of his stomach as Mattie's knee connected sharply with his balls.

Clutching his injured genitalia, Christopher staggered back. 'You bitch!'

Mattie's hand stung his cheek and slapped the words from his mouth.

She shoved him aside and Christopher crashed into the wall.

'Clear off,' she said, giving him a look of pure loathing. 'And if you bother me again, Christopher, I'll call Old Bill.'

She stepped past him and carried on down the road.

Trying to ride the wave of nausea that swept over him, Christopher regained his balance and started after her.

'I won't be treated like this, do you hear?' he

shouted after her. 'And if I find out you've been having it away with some bastard, I'll make both of you wish you'd never been born.'

Chapter Seventeen

It was Saturday 13th April, a month since receiving Meadow Rambler's message and ten days after he and Mattie had spent the afternoon together. Daniel was in the opulent meeting room on the first floor of Holborn House, which was a favourite venue of the British Council for Christian Settlement in Europe. Like every other man in the room, Daniel was dressed in a morning suit because once this extraordinary meeting was over they would all be taking taxis to the Criterion Club to attend one of Sir Oswald Mosley's famed gala lunches.

Daniel was sitting at the far end of the table, ready to deliver his message to the men surrounding him, men who could be best described as the dregs of the British establishment. Many were already well known to MI5 as they were, if you like, the establishment face of Britain's pro-Nazi and patriotism organisations, like the Nazi apologists Greene and Beckett. However Daniel had discovered that there were several other members of the group who the authorities viewed as being peripheral to the organisation but who were, in fact, clearly embroiled in the plot to depose the legitimate British government.

For the past hour, Daniel had been diligently memorising their names and designation so he could report back to Francis.

The famous, or infamous, depending on your viewpoint, man himself, Sir Oswald Mosley, was enthroned, like a well-groomed medieval monarch, at the head of the table. With his fine-boned hands splayed on the polished surface and his head turned to show off his best side, the matinee idol of every fascist in the country wasn't so much sitting as posing. Dressed in an immaculately fitting suit and with a diamond pin anchoring his silk cravat into a debonair whirl at his throat, Oswald Mosley looked like a man who believed his destiny was on the brink of being fulfilled.

Of course, as well as the men who hoped to form the first British fascist government, the meeting was also attended by a handful of the knuckle-duster, knife-wielding and fist-smashing underbelly. Men like Jock Houston, who was chairing the meeting and, of course, Christopher, who was sitting just a few seats down from Daniel on the right.

Christopher had come good on his promise to get Daniel access to Mosley and his trusted lieutenants so, after changing into his morning suit, which he'd deposited in Left Luggage at Liverpool Station two days earlier, Daniel had met with Christopher outside Farringdon Station and they'd walked the five minutes to the hall in silence.

'So let me summarise the message from Abwehr High Command,' said Daniel, resisting the urge to hook his finger into his winged collar

349

to ease it from his Adam's apple. 'At a date yet to be decided upon, a small craft will slip up the Thames and land up to six members of the Brandenburg regiment.'

'*Das Brandenburgers?*' Mosley said, in a perfect German accent, his slicked-back hair shinning in the light from the window. 'For those of you who aren't aware, the Brandenburg are Germany's elite Special Forces brigade. They were instrumental in snuffing out resistance when Hitler annexed the Sudetenland and when he went in to Poland to reclaim Eastern Prussia.'

'I believe they are in Norway at the moment to prevent Britain and its bolstering up the government,' said Daniel. 'And they did a good job softening up Poland before Hitler made his move so I imagine their orders on this mission will be to blend in and lay low until the invasion starts, then assassinate those members of the government who advocate putting up a fight, like Churchill and his war-mongering cronies, thereby easing the transfer of power to your members, Sir Oswald.'

Mosley regarded Daniel coolly for a moment, then shifted his gaze to the plaster architrave as a thoughtful expression furrowed his smooth, aristocratic brow.

Those around the table glanced at each other uneasily but no one spoke. After what seemed like an interminably long time, Mosley's gaze returned to Daniel.

'In addition, Meadow Rambler asks that in order to facilitate their mission our German friends be lodged in pairs near Westminster and Whitehall,' Daniel continued, adjusting his glasses and casting his eyes over his notebook.

An incredibly thin chap near the far end of the table stubbed out a cigar. 'Surely one central location would suffice. After all, it's not as if Gerry will know any better.'

'They will if their hand-picked troops are all captured together,' said Daniel. 'And I, for one, wouldn't want to be the one who sent that news to Himmler.'

The colour drained from several faces around the table, showing they wouldn't relish being the conveyer of that message either.

Mosley turned to the slightly built man beside him who was taking the minutes. 'Do as our Irish friend asks, will you, Wilton?'

'Most certainly, Sir Oswald,' replied Wilton, Mosley's long-standing family retainer, lowering his head deferentially.

Mosley surveyed the dozen or so men around the table again. 'Who is in charge of welcoming our friends when they arrive?'

Christopher sprang to his feet.

'Me, sir,' he said, standing tall like a schoolboy who knew the answer.

Mosley looked him over. 'And you are?'

'Joliffe, Christopher Joliffe,' he replied. 'In charge of the East London BPU. As instructed, my boys have already identified several sites which might be suitable locations for our German friends to slip ashore but, on balance, I think the best of these is Wapping Stairs. As soon as McCree gives us the nod, we'll put our plans into action.'

'And what are your plans?' asked Mosley.

'My suggested landing place is off the main

351

thoroughfare but, even though it's hidden from view, we will post look-outs at both the east and west of the high street. Depending what time of day they land, we can either walk our friends along the shoreline or around the back of the warehouse. One of my boys will have his delivery van which will be parked around the corner so we can take them to their lodgings. In case we're stopped along the way, I'll arrange to have false papers in the van.'

'Good,' said Mosley, with a munificent smile.

His attention returned to Daniel and his pencil-thin moustache lifted at the corners. 'So you're our radio man.'

'Indeed I am,' Daniel replied.

Mosley drew on his cigarette and blew the smoke towards the twinkling cut-glass chandelier above. 'I have to confess I was a little surprised to hear that the IRA's undercover man was in fact a Roman Catholic priest, especially as some of Hitler's closest advisors aren't too fond of your kind.'

'I was an Irishman before I was ever a priest,' Daniel replied.

Flicking his ash in the heavy lead-crystal ashtray in front of him, Mosley studied Daniel thoughtfully. 'I wasn't convinced when I met Tom Barry and O'Donovan in Germany a few years back and he suggested it might be profitable to our patriotic cause to offer a hand of friendship to you Republicans, but you seemed to have proved me wrong.'

'My thanks, sir,' Daniel replied. 'And I assure you that all patriotic Irishmen and women will be praying for you to remember it when you come into your own.'

Mosley gave him a sharp look. Taking his gold hunter from the fob pocket of his waistcoat, he flipped the watch open.

'Any other business?' he asked Jock.

Houston shook his head, as did the others around the table.

'Very well, I just want to remind you all of my one-day conference next month which will be held in Vauxhall. It's for district officials.' Mosley cast his aloof gaze over the assembled company. 'I'm particularly keen to have rank-and-file members there as I am going to explain the concept of "street leadership" and "street call-out" to galvanise our support. It worked very well for Röhm and his Brown Shirts in Berlin and will for us, too, I'm sure.'

A mutter of enthusiastic agreement ran around the room. Mosley let it rumble for a few moments, then snapped his watch shut and returned it from whence it came. 'Well, gentlemen, I suggest we call this meeting to an end and head off. I don't know about you but all this excitement has made me hungry.'

Christopher surveyed the Criterion Hotel's grand ballroom and couldn't resist feeling a little smug. He had finally been invited to Oswald Mosley's private luncheon and here he was, dressed in his new made-to-measure morning suit from Savile Row, blending in with the good and the great.

At the far end of the room, surrounding Mosley, were the leading lights of the movement, including Christopher's old friend Captain George Drummond from Northampton.

Of course, after all the service he'd given the cause over the past ten years, he had more right to be here than any come-lately aristocrat or politician who, now they could see which way the wind from the east was blowing, were suddenly fervent for the fascist cause.

From the other end of the bar a rumble of male laughter caught Christopher's attention. He turned to see McCree with a drink in his hand talking to Jock Houston and a dozen or so of his cronies. Christopher's mouth pulled into a hard line.

Of course he would have enjoyed his first invitation to join Mosley's elite circle a great deal more if he hadn't had to share the occasion with that bastard bog-trotter.

'There you are, Joliffe,' said a voice behind him.

Christopher turned to find Lord Bedlington standing behind him.

'Good afternoon, my lord,' said Christopher, offering his hand.

The portly aristocrat waved his words away and took his hand. 'Algie, please. How's the Daimler going?'

Christopher smiled. 'Very well thank you. How are you, Algie?'

'Capital, old man, capital, and yourself?' Lord Bedlington took a fat leather cigar case from his inside pocket and offered it to him.

'Never better,' said Christopher, taking one.

Lord Bedlington selected his and a waiter offered them a light.

'I should really take you to task, Joliffe,' Lord Bedlington said, puffing on his cigar.

Drawing on his own smoke, Christopher raised an eyebrow.

'Yes I should,' continued the aristocrat. 'Because, since you visited at New Year, I haven't heard the bally-end of how much Lady Bedlington and Cissy enjoyed your company.'

Christopher laughed.

'It's Christopher this and Christopher that morning, noon and night, and that's just her ladyship.' The earl glanced conspiratorially over his shoulder. 'Cissy would skin me alive if she knew I'd told you this but I know my daughter and I think it's fair to say she's more than a little bit fond of you.'

Christopher blew a stream of cigar smoke from the corner of his mouth. 'I'm wondering if I may be so bold as to suggest that, as your wife and daughter enjoyed my company so much on my last visit, I might visit them again some time?'

The earl's eyes lit up with delight. 'What a capital idea. We're having a little soirée next weekend, nothing fancy, you understand, just a few close friends, but I'd be delighted if you cared to join us.'

'Sounds delightful,' said Christopher.

'Good. I'll tell her ladyship. She'll be delighted.' Something behind Christopher caught the lord's attention. 'Will you excuse me, I've just seen–'

'Of course,' said Christopher, smiling graciously. He stepped aside and Lord Bedlington scurried off.

Christopher turned back to the bar and raised his hand to call the waiter. He was just about to order a double scotch when someone shoved into him from behind.

He spun around.

'What the?' A beam spread wide across Christopher's face.

'I see they are letting in any old riff-raff now,' said the man behind Christopher, with just an echo of a German accent.

'Ernst!' He thrust out his hand and it was taken in a firm grip.

Ernst Holnstein Von Notzing was about Christopher's height with corn-coloured hair and clear pale grey eyes. He was impeccably groomed, as always, with his collar crisply turned and his cravat tied just so.

Christopher had met Ernst through his cousins Otto and Gunter and they had become firm friends after the four boys had spent the long, hot summer of '32 and '33 together hiking in the mountains and sampling the local beer and fresh-faced fräuleins while they stayed in Christopher's uncle's house high in the Bavarian Alps. Like Otto, Ernst had joined the Nazi party and worked his way up in the Third Reich's government before being sent to London as an undersecretary to Von Ribbentrop, the German ambassador, in '36.

'What are you doing here?' Christopher asked, grasping his friend's elbow and having his gripped in return.

'A bit of business for Goebbels.' Ernst tapped the side of his nose. 'But do not let MI5 know.'

Christopher laughed. 'How's your family?'

They exchanged family news.

'And Gunter asked me to send you his regards, if I saw you,' said Ernst. 'And to tell you that he looks forward to seeing the look on your face when he marches up Whitehall alongside Himmler.'

Christopher laughed again.

'What about you?' Ernst asked. 'Are you still at your little bank?'

Christopher nodded. 'For now, but my prospects are looking decidedly rosy.' He gestured at Lord Bedlington, who was hovering around Mosley's wife, Diana, one of the Mitford Girls;

'You speak of the bald, dumpy chap bursting from his suit?' asked Ernst.

'His only daughter, actually,' Christopher replied. 'Who'll inherit half of Essex along with a grandiose pile in rolling countryside when old Algie snuffs it.'

'Good-looking is she?'

'In the same way the winner of the Cheltenham Gold Cup is,' Christopher replied. 'But I can turn the light out.'

An image of Mattie with her pleasing curves and flashing eyes flitted through his mind causing the sting of her refusal to succumb to all his blandishments and rejection to sting afresh.

Ernst slapped him on the back. 'Well, then let us drink to your coming nuptials.'

He clicked his finger and ordered them both a double scotch.

There was another burst of rowdy laughter from the gathering around McCree and Christopher's sour expression returned.

'You were right about the riff-raff,' he said, looking hatefully at the man holding court at the other end of the bar.

Ernst's gaze followed his. 'What is he doing here?'

'You mean that jumped-up Paddy McCree?' Christopher replied, lighting his cigarette with the bar lighter. 'The Irish Republicans have sent him over to show *solidarity* with our cause. I tell you though, Ernst, when I've finished with Father Daniel McCree he'll wish he'd never crossed the bloody Irish sea.'

Ernst gave Christopher a studied look, then threw back his drink. 'Get us both another, I won't be long.'

Strolling down to the end of the bar, Ernst greeted someone in the huddle around McCree. The man Ernst was talking to introduced him to Daniel and they exchanged a few words before the German casually ambled back to his friend.

Christopher handed him his replenished drink and Ernst took it.

Taking a long sip, he looked up and gave Christopher a crooked smile. 'That's not Father Mc-Cree, that's Daniel McCarthy, an MI5 operative.'

'So, did they?' asked Francis, cutting across Daniel's jumbled thoughts.

Daniel looked at his friend sitting across the table from him. 'What?'

Francis gave him an exasperated look and leaned forward a little. 'Did Mosley and his bloody lot swallow your story hook, line and sinker?'

'Of course they did,' Daniel replied. 'Why wouldn't they? It was exactly what Meadow Rambler had told me.'

It was nine o'clock in the evening and the

Wednesday after his meeting with Mosley's inner circle. He and Francis were sitting in the Unicorn, a small pub tucked away in an alley just off Fleet Street. Judging by the low oak-beamed ceiling and the lead light windows, the pub was probably two hundred years old and seemed to have survived mainly because it was propped up on either side by Edwardian office blocks built from solid Portland stone. As with every other watering hole in town, the place was packed with service personnel but, given its location, there were also some chain-smoking news hacks with inky-fingers seated amongst the uniformed clientele.

'And what about the coordinates?' his friend continued. 'Are you sure Meadow Rambler doesn't suspect you're sending him incorrect locations?'

'Of course I am,' Daniel replied, forcing his mind back to the task at hand. 'Why else would Meadow Rambler be asking me for grid references for specific targets if the Germans are suspicious? Of course it won't matter if the moon's out because the Luftwaffe won't bother with navigation as they can just fly up the Thames and find us.'

'The top brass know that,' said Francis. 'Which is why the powers that be in Whitehall are running around like nuns in a brothel trying to get the capital's ack-ack guns in place before Gerry's on the move again.'

Daniel picked up his glass. 'Pity someone didn't think it might be prudent to get them in place *before* we were actually at war.'

'That's what I said to the chief,' said Francis.

'But, apparently, while the government was trying to negotiate a peace, they didn't want to look too aggressive. I know,' said his friend, seeing the exasperation on Daniel's face. 'But politics, old chap. You know politics.' Daniel's mouth pulled into a hard line but he didn't comment.

An image of Mattie dressed in her ARP uniform, desperately trying to get people to safety while fire engulfed the streets and houses, loomed in Daniel's mind. His chest tightened painfully.

Francis gave him a considered look. 'What's eating you, Daniel?'

Daniel forced a laugh. 'What do you mean?'

'Well, for a start you've done nothing but bite my head off since I arrived,' said Francis.

'Nothing.'

'If there's something that might impact on the operation, then–'

'It's nothing to do with the operation. It's Joliffe,' said Daniel. 'He's an utter bastard.'

Francis raised an eyebrow. 'Of course he is but why is that gnawing at you?'

Daniel regarded his old comrade for a moment, then put his drink down. 'Well if you must know there's this girl, and...' He told Francis about Mattie, relieved to be telling someone at last.

'...so perhaps you understand why I'm a bit overwrought,' Daniel finished, looking up at his commanding officer.

Francis stared at him for a moment or two and then spoke again. 'So in the middle a mission that could affect the future of the nation, nay, the future of the world, you embark on an affair with the girlfriend of the leader of the Nazi cell you've been sent to infiltrate?'

'No,' said Daniel. 'I fell in love with Mattie Brogan, who happened to go out with Joliffe a couple of times before breaking off their relationship.'

'How do you know he didn't rumble you and sent her to sleep with you so he could keep an eye on you?' asked Francis.

'He didn't, and she's not,' Daniel replied.

'But how can you be cert–'

'Let me be clear about this, Francis,' cut in Daniel, holding his senior officer and long-standing friend's incredulous gaze. 'I'm not having an affair with Mattie. I love her and, as soon as this is over, I'm going to marry her. Furthermore,' he continued, as Francis opened his mouth to speak again, 'I trust her with my life.'

The two men eyeballed each other for a moment, then Francis picked up his drink again.

'Very well, you know the stakes are high but... Well, you've never let me down, so we'll leave it at that.' He took another mouthful. 'However, you do know that when this is all over Uncle Vernon will be sending you off on another operation somewhere.'

'Of course,' Daniel replied.

'And for national security reasons if you do decide to marry it will have to be in secret, no big white wedding and all that,' said Francis.

'I know that,' said Daniel.

Francis sighed. 'I hope for your sake, Daniel, that she understands that, too.'

Mattie's lovely hazel eyes flashed through Daniel's mind and he gave his friend a wry smile.

361

'So do I, Francis, so do I.'

Finishing the last mouthful of his Guinness, Daniel rose to his feet and headed for the door. Francis had left the pub some fifteen minutes earlier and now, at ten to ten, Daniel judged it was safe to follow. Settling his hat on his head, he squeezed his way through the bar to the door.

As was his routine, he'd left his clerical clothes in Liverpool Street Left Luggage so he needed to catch a number 9 or 11 bus back to the station but, as he passed the end of the bar the hairs on the back of his neck rose. Casually glancing around, he noticed a thin-faced man wearing a tweedy jacket sitting at the corner. As Daniel's gaze skimmed over him, the man shook out his newspaper and turned a page.

Maintaining his nonchalant expression, Daniel continued on but, as he stepped aside to let a sailor carrying two drinks walk past, he glanced at the wall mirror behind the bar and saw that the man in the corner had put away his newspaper and had stood up.

After holding the door open so that a young couple could come in, Daniel left the pub. The sun had set two hours before, but it was a clear night so the street was partially illuminated by the waning moon.

The street was alive with vans hurrying the next day's newspapers to the four corners of London. Daniel paused at a newsstand to buy a copy of the morning's edition of the *Sketch* and strolled on.

He stopped at the bus stop at Ludgate Circus and, casually leaning against the stop sign, opened the newspaper. Pretending to read the headline story about the Allies landing in Norway, he glanced back along the road.

The hairs on the back of his neck prickled as he saw the man in the tweed jacket stop and light a cigarette.

A bus loomed into sight and Daniel waited until the handful of people around him had stepped on before moving forward. Out of the corner of his eyes he saw the tweedy jacket man walking briskly towards the bus stop.

Jumping on as the conductor rang the bell, Daniel headed upstairs and swung into the empty seat at the back above the bus's platform. He waited but no one came up the stairs after him. Pulling aside the leather concertina blind a fraction, Daniel glanced out of the window at the empty street.

In the shadow of the back seat, Daniel's mouth pulled into a hard line. He might be imagining it, of course, but...

The conductor came up and took the fares and the bus trundled on around St Paul's Cathedral and up towards London Wall. Pretending to read the newspaper, Daniel watched everyone get on and off until he reached Moorgate then, tucking his newspaper under his arm, he made his way down the stairs.

Bouncing along on the platform as the bus approached the next stop, Daniel glanced along the bus's lower deck and saw the man in the tweed jacket three seats back on the right. Although he was facing away, instinct told Daniel he'd watched him come down from the deck above.

As the bus slowed, Daniel leaped down from the platform, noticing the tweed jacket rise from his seat.

As his feet touched the pavement, Daniel turned and, keeping to the shadows, walked off in the opposite direction to the one the bus was travelling. He'd only gone a few yards when the sounds of footsteps echoed behind him.

Ducking into an alley, Daniel pressed himself against the wall. The footsteps came closer and then stopped.

With his eyes fixed on the passage entrance, Daniel held his breath as the man in the tweed jacket walked past and on towards City Road. Daniel waited for a few minutes then, satisfied the man in the tweed jacket wasn't coming back, walked back to Moorgate. Cutting through Finsbury Circus, he reached Liverpool Street within minutes and slipped into the station by the goods entrance at the side. After retrieving his suitcase containing his clerical clothes, he disappeared into the men's toilet and re-emerged dressed as Father McCree a few moments later. From behind his plain glass spectacles, Daniel surveyed the concourse and noticed the man in the tweed jacket looking at the departure board.

Positioning himself behind a porter pushing a barrow loaded with travel trunks and suitcases, and with his hat pulled low over his face, Daniel retraced his steps to the goods entrance. Keeping in the shadow of the building, he walked briskly down to Bishopsgate, then turned into Middlesex Street.

Slowing his pace, he carried on until he reached

Whitechapel High Street where, mercifully, a number 15 was waiting at the bus stop. Leaping on to the back board as the bus trundled off, Daniel swung into the nearest seat. Only then did his pulse start to return to normal.

Of course it could have just been a coincidence that the man who'd left the pub in Fleet Street happened to get on the same bus and then happened to get off the same stop to cut through to the Liverpool Street Station, but ... Francis had said the stakes were high and they'd suddenly got a whole lot higher.

Chapter Eighteen

Lying very still, Mattie stared at the fringe on the lampshade as it fluttered in the early morning breeze and prayed for the wave of nausea to subside.

Her early morning struggle to keep her stomach contents had been going on for over a week now. For the first couple of days she'd put the bouts of queasiness down to something she'd eaten but when her breasts had started to feel tender, the reason for her morning nausea was obvious. Although they'd never been particularly regular, the last time she'd had her monthly visitor had been on Palm Sunday, almost ten weeks ago and two weeks before she and Daniel had spent the afternoon together in the hotel.

Outside, the rattle of bottles accompanied by

the steady clip-clop of horse's hooves and the sound of heavy boots marching over cobbles told Mattie that the first day of the working week was just about to begin. As ever, her first waking thought was of Daniel and the time when she would wake up beside him.

Turning her head carefully, she looked past her sleeping sister at the bedside clock. Five to six. As her father would be at the yard, her mother would be just finishing her cleaning job and her gran would be fetching the family's bread from the baker's, Mattie could get to the privy in the yard without anyone being any the wiser.

A billow of cool air from the half-open window drifted over her. Mattie took a deep breath then slipped quietly out from under the covers.

Shoving her feet in her old shoes, she grabbed her dressing gown from the end of the bed and shrugged it on.

Mattie walked slowly down the stairs so as not to worsen the feeling of nausea but, as she reached the kitchen, the smell of her mother's geraniums filled her nose and her stomach rebelled.

Clapping her hand over her mouth, Mattie ripped open the back door and tore across the yard. Bursting through the rough-hewn door of the privy, Mattie only just got her head over the hole cut in the wooden seat before her stomach heaved up what was left of last night's supper.

Taking the handkerchief from her dressing gown pocket, she coughed then wiped her mouth. She pulled the chain but, as she took a breath, she caught the acidy whiff of the Vim tub on the small window sill.

For the second time, she doubled over.

The lavatory door squeaked open and she looked up to see her mother standing there, glaring at her.

'Well there's no prize for guessing what's wrong with you, is there?' Ida snapped.

Mattie held her mother's angry eyes for a second or two and then retched again.

'How far gone are you?' asked her mother, her voice echoing around the enclosed space of the privy.

'Three months, as far as I can tell,' Mattie replied. She straightened up and wiped her mouth.

Her mother studied Mattie's face for a second or two, then turned.

'I thought you were supposed to be the clever one of the family,' she called over her shoulder as she marched back across the yard.

Pulling the chain again, Mattie followed her.

Her mother had already re-lit the kettle by the time Mattie walked into the kitchen and was spooning tea into the pot from the caddy.

Sinking into the corner chair, Mattie slumped with her elbows on the table and her head in her hands as a wave of sickness threatened to rise up again.

Her mother ran the tap for a moment, then thrust a cup of cold water in front of Mattie. 'Take a few sips and it might help.'

Mattie raised her head and smiled wanly. 'Thanks, Mum.'

Her mother huffed by way of reply, then returned to her task of getting the family's breakfast. The kettle whistled. Mattie watched her mother fill the pot and collect the cups from the dresser.

'I suppose that's why he skipped off like he did,' said her mother, setting the crockery down ready for the rest of the family.

'Who?' asked Mattie.

'Christopher,' snapped Ida. 'Who do you think I mean?'

'Oh, him,' Mattie replied. 'He didn't skip off, as you put it, Mum, because I broke up with him.'

'Well, now you'll have to un-break up with him, won't you?' said Ida, returning to the range. Grasping the wooden spoon sticking out of the pot, she gave the porridge a stir. 'Unless you're going to tell me you've been having a bit of slap and tickle with someone else.'

Taking a mouthful of cool water, Mattie let her head rest back against the wall but didn't reply.

'They're all the same,' her mother continued after a moment. 'Once they get what they're after they're not interested in what happens to you. I can't even begin to imagine what your dad will say when–'

'You mustn't tell Dad,' cut in Mattie, as fear gripped her.

'Tell him what?' asked Queenie as she strolled in through the back door with her shopping basket hooked over her arm.

Ida gave Mattie a sharp look. 'Go on then. Tell her.'

Mattie forced a smile. 'I'm in the family way, Gran.'

'I know you are,' said Queenie, closing the door behind her. 'And by the look of you I'd say you're about three months or so.'

'About that.' Mattie took another sip of water.

Pulling up a chair, Queenie sat down beside her granddaughter and placed her gnarled hand over Mattie's. 'How are you, me love?'

'Sick,' Mattie replied.

'Well that's good,' Queenie replied. 'It shows the baby's anchored good and proper.'

A little bubble of happiness rose up in Mattie and, without thinking, she placed her hands on her stomach.

'And it's not as if you're the first young woman to find herself in such a position.' Amusement played across Queenie's thin lips. 'After all, your mother had to carry her bouquet high when she walked down the aisle.'

'Queenie!' A scarlet flush spread up Ida's throat. 'That was different.'

'Was it?' Queenie replied.

The two women glared at each other for a minute, then Ida thrust her arms back into the sink.

'Even so,' she said, wiping the dish cloth over a plate. 'Her dad will have to–'

'Soft now, Ida.' Stretching forwards, Queenie repositioned a stray curl on Mattie's forehead. 'Mattie's carrying tight-in so I'm thinking we should bide awhile yet and give the father a chance to do as he should.'

Feeling her cheeks burn, Mattie forced herself to hold her gran's bright eyes.

'If you ask me, he's done enough already,' Ida replied. 'But I suppose a week or so won't matter, after all, people are getting married so fast these days I don't suppose anyone will think anything of it if our Mattie does, too.' Licking the porridge spoon, Ida jabbed it at Mattie. 'But don't you worry, Mattie, your dad will make sure that Christopher does the right thing by you.'

Shoving the spoon back in the pan, Ida crossed to the parlour door.

'Jo! Billy!' she screamed. 'Get up, the both of you, or you'll be late for school.'

Jo bounced into the kitchen wearing her uniform and with her thick night plait draped over her shoulder.

'Morning, Gran.' She saw Mattie and looked confused. 'I thought you were on early duty.'

'She is but she's a bit feverish so she came down for an aspirin,' Queenie replied, rising to her feet. 'So she's going back to bed for a while.'

Mattie raised her eyes and smiled. 'Thanks, Gran.'

Placing her hand back over hers, Queenie squeezed it and they exchanged a fond look.

Leaving Jo to her breakfast and her mother haranguing Billy to dress himself for school, Mattie made her way back upstairs.

Slipping under the covers, she placed her hand on her still-flat stomach and imagined the little life growing there. She and Daniel had talked about how many children they would have and she knew he would be as thrilled as she was when she told him. And she would tell him but not now, not yet. It wouldn't be fair to him, given the danger he was facing, to add to his worries. So, just for now, in the still of the early morning and in the familiar comfort of her bed, she would be happy and enjoy the fact she was carrying Daniel's baby. However much she ached to tell him the happy news, she would keep it to herself just for now. After all, with all the other deadly balls he was keeping up in the air at the moment, Daniel didn't need to have his mind filled with anything else.

'Stop writing and put your pens down,' said the man in the baggy hopsack suit at the front of the classroom.

Mattie put the top on her pen and sat back as the three dozen or so exam candidates sitting at the desks around her did the same.

It was the last Friday in May and she was sitting in the main hall of St Katherine's Junior School which was a few streets back from St Katherine's Dock. The Victorian school was attached to St George's Church on the Highway and although it was now a mixed infant school, it had once taught the girls and boys separately, as evidenced by the antiquated sculptures of a girl in a white pinafore and mop cap and a boy wearing a tasselled hat, frock coat and breeches stationed above the two respective school entrances.

Mattie had finished the Joint Matriculation and School Certificate History paper, the last one of her exams, twenty minutes ago, but she had been reading through her answers to make sure she'd crossed the 't's and dotted the 'i's.

She was reasonably satisfied with her answers although, to be honest, she'd found it difficult to concentrate on 'how the harnessing of water power influenced the British eighteenth-century textile industry' with everything else going on.

Her mother had asked her why she was bothering with her exams. Her mother assumed that the baby Mattie was carrying was Christopher's and that once he was acquainted with the fact, he would do the honourable thing or Jerimiah would make him. Either way, as far as Ida was concerned, by the time the Civil Service exams came around in September, Mattie would be a married woman with a house to run and a baby on the way.

Actually, when September came around, Mattie hoped to be a married woman but, as her fiancé was a MI5 operative, she could equally be facing life as an unmarried mother.

Married or not, one thing she did know was that by the time their baby was born, Daniel, like thousands of other men, would be away serving his country. By the same token, she, like thousands of other women, would have to manage on her own and it would be a whole lot easier to do that on a civil servant's salary than as a piecework machinist.

As the invigilator took her paper, Mattie put her pens, pencils and sharpeners into her pencil case and slipped it into her satchel.

Wishing her fellow students the best of luck with their results, she stood up, unhooked her rain mac and umbrella from the wall peg and made her way out of the school.

Standing in Royal Mint Street, she opened her umbrella, then glanced at her watch. Eleven o'clock. It wouldn't take her more than twenty minutes to reach Kate's cafe so, as she was just a few minutes from the Tower of London, Mattie decided to take the long way round and stroll down to the river to catch a breath of air before meeting Daniel at eleven-thirty as they'd planned.

Keeping to the inside of the pavement to avoid being splashed by passing dock traffic, Mattie turned right and walked down the road until the grey stone of the Tower's outer wall came into sight. Tower Bridge was up so the traffic in the Minories was stationary. Weaving between the idling cars and trucks, Mattie walked under the roadway. However, as she emerged onto the cobbled pathway that ran below the fortress, she found herself surrounded by people all pressing towards the river.

Securing her bag on her shoulder, Mattie wriggled through the crowd until she was up against the railings. Grabbing the ironwork with both hands, she looked down to see dozens of tug boats, pleasure cruisers, ferries and a couple of motor boats along with half a dozen river police patrol boats, coastal haulage ships, pilot boats and even a paddle steamer belching black smoke, all heading downriver towards the estuary.

'Do you know what's happening?' Mattie asked a garrison soldier in his khaki battle dress with his rifle over his shoulder, who was watching the flotilla along with everyone else.

'I'm not at liberty to say, miss,' he replied, as those around Mattie gathered closer.

'Come on, chum,' said a squat chap at the back wearing the hard flat cap of a market porter. 'We read the papers, you know, and can put two and two together as good as those buggers in Whitehall. Them boats there are off to Belgium, ain't they?'

Of course the papers were full of how the British Expeditionary Force and their French allies were standing firm on the Maginot Line but rumours around the docks were rife. Added to which, the king had announced on a special broadcast the night before that the coming Sunday 24th May had been designated as a national day of prayer, and you didn't do that if you were on the offensive.

A flush coloured the young soldier's neck and he ran his finger around the inside of his collar. 'As I said, I'm–'

'Three cheers for our little boats,' cut in a woman standing behind Mattie. 'Hip, hip!'

'Hurrah!' bellowed the crowd.

'Hip, hip!' yelled someone further down the line.

'Hurrah!' the crowd roared back, waving their hats and handkerchiefs.

'Hip, hip,' shouted yet another voice.

As Mattie stared across at the armada of little boats bobbing along in the warm summer sunlight, excitement and dread mingled together. With the German army sweeping across Europe the Phoney War, as the newspapers were calling it, seemed to be over. Although she didn't relish what the country had to face, perhaps now Hitler had given up his play-acting, she and Daniel would be able to do the same, too.

Taking the peg from her mouth, Cathy pinned the last of her husband's shirts up on the laden washing line. It was one of his new white ones that he liked to wear for his BPU meeting each week. As the chairman, he had to look the part and had even bought himself a new double-breasted navy suit in the January sales and Cathy had to admit he looked very dapper in it, too. However, it was just a pity each time he got togged up in his new gear it was to attend a blooming Britons for Peace Union meeting and not to take her out.

She couldn't remember the last time they'd spent an evening together and he always seemed too tired for...

Cathy felt her cheeks warm. She sighed. She shouldn't complain about his commitments to the BPU, after all, if it wasn't for that BPU chum recommending that doctor in Hackney, he'd never have found out about his asthma. At least now when the baby came he would be here, not twiddling his thumbs in some army camp miles away.

Putting aside all thoughts of her patchy love life, Cathy pushed her hands into the small of her back and stretched to ease the tight knot caused by an hour of turning the mangle on a sweltering hot day.

Tilting her face upwards to feel the warm sun on her face, Cathy ran her hands over her swollen stomach. It was the first Tuesday in June and less than two weeks off her due date, the 18th June. Grasping the empty wicker laundry basket by the handle, she waddled into the house.

'Would you like a cuppa, Mother?' she called through to Stan's mother in the front parlour.

There was no reply.

Popping her head around the door, Cathy saw her mother-in-law, who despite the heat was huddled with a shawl around her shoulders, was in fact fast asleep.

She returned to the kitchen and, taking the kettle from the stove, went over to the sink.

'Yo-ho, anyone at home?' called a familiar voice from the back door.

'In here, Mum,' Cathy called back as she turned the tap off. 'I was just putting the kettle on.'

Ida bustled in with a full shopping bag over her arm, which she plonked on the table. She'd obviously been shopping straight from work as she was still in her wraparound apron and old lace shoes with a scarf tied around her head turban-style.

'Thirty minutes I had to queue,' she said, settling herself in the chair. 'Thirty minutes just to be told by the butcher's spotty lad there's no lamb chops. Offered me a bit of scraggy skirt instead and I had to part with half me week's meat coupons for the privilege.'

'Well, it's the same everywhere,' said Cathy. 'Our Sunday dinner was liver and onion this week instead of beef.'

'Well, it's a bloody disgrace, that's what I call it,' said her mother. 'Still, I did manage to get this for you.' She took a greaseproof bag from her shopping bag and slid it across the table.

Cathy picked it up and peered inside at a lump of cheese.

'Oh, Mum, you shouldn't have,' she said.

Ida waved her words away. 'It's for the baby. How's Stan's mother?'

'Seems to be sleeping a lot,' said Cathy. 'And I think she's lost weight, although that's hardly surprising as she just picks at her food, and sometimes I think she's going to cough up her lungs but she won't see the doctor. Truth be told, Mum, I think she's fading.'

'God love and bless her.' Ida crossed herself

'How old is she?'

'Sixty-six,' said Cathy.

'Blimey,' said Ida, raising her eyebrows. 'She's only four years older than Queenie. Still,' she pulled a face. 'Only the good die young.'

The kettle whistled.

Putting the cheese in the cool pantry, Cathy added a teaspoon of tea leaves to the previous ones in the tea pot, then made the tea.

'You look as if you've dropped a bit,' said her mother, eyeing her stomach as Cathy put their tea on the table.

'That's what the midwives at Munroe House said when I went there last week,' said Cathy, taking the seat opposite to her mother. 'They said it could be any day now so I've got everything ready upstairs for when Stan has to call them.'

'I expect he's hoping for a boy,' said her mother, taking a sip from her tea. 'Men always want their firstborn to be their son and heir.'

'I don't think Stan minds,' said Cathy. 'He just says as long as I'm all right and the baby's healthy, that's all he's worried about.'

Stretching across, her mother placed her work-worn hand over Cathy's. 'Your Stan's a good 'un.'

Damping down her spousal disappointments, Cathy smiled at her mother. 'I know.'

'Not like...' Her mother's chin started to wobble and tears welled up in her eyes.

'Oh, Mum, what's wrong?' asked Cathy. 'It's not Dad, is it?'

Ida shook her head. Pulling out her handkerchief from her apron pocket, she blew her nose.

'It's Mattie,' said her mother.

'She's not ill, is she?' asked Cathy.

'Oh no, she's not ill.' Her mother's mouth pulled into a tight bud. 'Quite the opposite; in fact, you could say she's blooming.'

Cathy's eyes stretched wide. 'She's in the family way?'

'Shhhhh,' hissed her mother. 'I'm not supposed to say anything and you mustn't either but I had to get it off my chest.'

'Does Dad know?' asked Cathy.

'Do you think I'd be in this state if your father knew?' her mother replied. 'I was all for telling him so he could make Christopher do the right thing by Mattie but she made me promise not to say anything.' Her mother wiped her nose again. 'I suppose she was hoping he'd come around but it's been he hasn't called. I tell you, I'm that worried. I didn't think that Christopher was that sort, you know, to take advantage of an innocent girl.'

'Come on, Mum,' laughed Cathy. 'They're all "that sort" and, to be honest, I know Christopher had a top job and all that but I always thought he was just too good to be true.'

'How could he be too good, for Heaven's sake?' scoffed her mother. 'Anyway, whatever Christopher is or isn't don't matter because he's got our Mattie in the family way so, no matter what Mattie says, I'll give him another two weeks before I send your father to go and–'

'Stan!' said Cathy, springing to her feet as her husband walked in through the open back door. 'What are you doing home?'

'I had to drop off some spuds in Salmon Lane so I thought I'd pop home and have a cuppa before I drive to Plaistow,' he replied.

'Hello, Stan,' said Ida, as a red flush crept up her cheeks. 'We were just saying how the baby could be any day now?'

'You're in luck, luv,' said Cathy, giving him a bright smile. 'There's one in the pot so take the weight off your feet and I'll fetch you a cup.'

She walked over to the dresser as Stan sat on the chair she'd just vacated.

Worrying that perhaps Stan had heard about Mattie, Cathy took Stan's big mug from the hook. Still, even if he had overheard, what harm could it do?

Chapter Nineteen

'So are we all clear then that Stan and Roger will be at Wapping Old Stairs at twenty-three hundred hours next Thursday, ready to greet our friends when they land?' Christopher asked, scanning his eyes over the half dozen men sitting around the table.

The BPU committee nodded their heads and muttered their agreement.

It was almost ten o'clock on the first Wednesday in June and Christopher was at the weekly BPU committee in the Catholic Club. McCree had contacted him the day before to tell him that Operation Holiday was set for the night of 14th June in ten days.

When Ernst had told him about McCree at the

BCCSE meeting, Christopher's first instinct was to denounce him there and then but, thankfully, he'd held back. Having spent all night and the following day running through all the possible scenarios, he'd finally decided to hold fire and wait for an opportunity to expose the bastard, but in such a way that would give him all the glory and secure a place within Mosley's tight-knit inner circle.

Ernst, who was in England posing as a Swiss English teacher attached to the Italian Embassy, but was in fact heading up a small unit of under-cover operatives on some hush-hush mission that Ernst couldn't divulge, had offered to put a tail on McCarthy and to send messages directly to the Abwehr, allowing Christopher to bypass the MI5 bastard to contact Meadow Rambler himself. Thanks to Ernst he now had a much better plan for dealing with McCarthy.

'I can't believe it's all going to kick off at last,' said Harry, grinning at the men around him.

'Although I don't know why they're bothering with all this palaver now,' grumbled Teddy. 'After all, the Frogs have caved in and Hitler's already in France so it's only a quick hop across the Channel and it'll all be over.'

'Some people don't see the true threat that the Jewish conspiracy poses to this country so there's likely to be resistance, but the German High Command's experience in Norway and Belgium has proven that it's easier to deal with any oppo-sition if there are Nationalists on the ground ready to identify and deal with insurrection swiftly,' Christopher said, repeating more or less what Daniel had told Mosley a few weeks before. 'That's why it's imperative that we keep up our guard at all times and why I need you in place and ready to get our friends from Germany away from the river as quickly as possible,' said Christopher, sternly.

'And where will you be, mate, while we're hanging around the docks?' asked Roger.

'Don't you worry about what I'm doing, you just do your job.' Christopher stubbed his cigarette out in the ashtray. 'Now, if there's nothing else?'

The men looked from one to another and shook their heads.

'Good, then I suggest we call it a night, but remember: be vigilant and don't tell anyone. Not even your own mother,' continued Christopher. 'If those bloody MI5 buggers get even a whiff of what we're up to, we'll all be dangling from the end of a rope.'

Chairs scraped back as the men stood up and drifted away until only Christopher and Stan were left. Stan shuffled the papers into a pile and then straightened them again, casting the odd furtive look at Christopher as he did so.

'Something on your mind, Stan?' asked Christopher, as he shrugged on his lightweight summer blazer.

'Sort of,' Stan replied, shoving his hands in his pockets and jingling his loose change.

'Is there a problem with one of the chaps?' Christopher asked.

Blinking rapidly, Stan shook his head. 'It's my wife.'

'What about her?' asked Christopher.

'It's Mattie really.' Stan shifted his weight from one foot to the other then back again. 'I'm not supposed to know, but I overheard my Cathy and her ma chatting in the kitchen the other day and well... It seems Mattie's in the club. Don't worry, her old man don't know or he would be after you by now but I thought I ought to give you the nod.'

Christopher stared incredulously at him for a moment and then he smiled. 'So Mattie's pregnant, is she?'

Stan let out a long breath and nodded.

'You won't say I told you, will you?' said Stan, shifting about again. 'I mean, my mother-in-law has a tongue like a razor and–'

'Don't worry, I won't say a word,' Christopher replied, tapping the side of his nose.

Stan's shoulders relaxed.

Picking up his hat, Stan flipped it onto his head and winked. 'You old dog. I didn't think anyone would get themselves in Mattie's knickers this side of the altar.'

Laughing, he strolled across the stage, trotted down the handful of steps and left the hall.

Alone in the space, Christopher stood stock-still, staring at the clock above the half-glassed doors. A red mist hovered in his peripheral vison and his temples pounded. He stared blindly into the empty hall for a moment then, snatching up his coat, dashed out.

With his brain pounding and images of his hands tight around Mattie's slender neck dancing in his mind, Christopher ran down to Chapman Street towards Mafeking Terrace.

Bitch! After all the bloody money he'd spent on

her and this is how she paid him back. Well, he'd show her; show them both when he found out what bugger she'd been opening her legs for.

Turning into Mafeking Terrace, Christopher pelted down the darkening street towards the Brogans' front door. He stumbled on an uneven paving slab and kicked a milk bottle off a doorstep. It went skidding away and set a dog barking in one of the back yards.

Christopher slowed his pace and slipped into one of the alleyways that ran between the houses.

Standing in the shadows, he looked at his watch and saw that it was almost ten-thirty. Chewing the side of his thumb, Christopher took a couple of deep breaths and reconsidered the situation.

His fingers itched to throttle the name of the bastard out of her but, as the red rage in his mind cleared a little, it occurred to him that if he dashed into her house now, he'd be the one who came off worse.

If Jerimiah didn't yet know that his little girl was pregnant, him charging into the house in the middle of the night demanding to know who'd got her in that condition wasn't such a good idea. And was she even at home? They were working double shifts at the police station so she could just as likely be on ARP duty.

Stepping out from the shadows, Christopher retraced his steps to Chapman Street and, cutting down Library Alley, headed for the telephone box opposite the Britannia Pub. Wrenching open the door, he stepped in. Taking out a handful of coins, he placed them on the shelf above the telephone directories.

He picked up the receiver.

'Operator, how can I help?' said a young woman at the other end of the line.

'Can you put me through to ARP post 7, please,' said Christopher.

'Just putting you through,' said the voice.

The pips went and Christopher shoved in three pennies and was connected.

'Post 7, Supervisor Potter speaking, how can I help?' asked the ARP post's senior warden.

'I'm wondering if I could have a word with Miss Brogan, if she's on duty,' said Christopher.

'Well, she is on duty tonight but she's out on blackout patrol,' Potter replied. 'Who's calling?'

Christopher replaced the handset. Pushing the door of the phone box open, he stepped out into the street.

Taking out his lighter, he flicked the flame to life and looked at his watch. Five to eleven.

She would be halfway through her late blackout patrol. He knew she walked east to the end of her patch, then worked her way back so she would now be heading west along the Commercial Road.

Overhead, the barrage balloon creaked and strained against its mooring in the night breeze as Christopher, with a smile lifting his lips, headed off towards the north perimeter of Mattie's ARP area. Hurrying between the empty stalls in Watney Street Market, he reached Commercial Road just as Christ Church clock struck the hour.

There were a couple of trucks from the docks travelling along the road and a few people making their way home after last orders but, otherwise, it was quiet. Crossing the road, Christopher secreted himself in a shop doorway and peered down the street in the direction of Limehouse. Taking out a cigarette, he lit it.

A night bus heading for the Haymarket trundled by, followed by a police car with its bell ringing, then Christopher spotted Mattie walking towards him on the other side of the road.

Thinking he would wait until she reached him before accosting her, Christopher waited. However, as Mattie reached St Bridget's and St Brendan's church, she turned down Sutton Street.

Flicking his cigarette away, Christopher strode across the road and down the side street after her, just in time to see her disappear through the side gate of the rectory.

Daniel's lips left hers and Mattie's mind started to drift down from the cloud it had been on for the last five minutes.

'Oh, Daniel,' she sighed, pressing herself against the hard muscles of his chest.

'I love you,' he whispered, before lowering his mouth onto hers again.

They were tucked in the dark recess between the coal bunker and the garden shed in the rectory's back garden and had been for the last ten minutes. Mattie was dressed in her ARP uniform and was on her second blackout check of the evening and Daniel was in his clerical shirt but without his dog collar as he was supposed to be making his bedtime cocoa. He'd slipped out under cover of darkness, as he always did when she was on a late or night duty.

She tore her lips from his. 'We shouldn't be

doing this.'

'I know.' He kissed her hard, anchoring her against the shed wall with his body, pressing his thigh between hers.

'It's too dangerous,' she gasped.

'Yes.' He covered her mouth with his.

She grabbed a handful of his hair and pulled his head back. 'Someone might see us.'

'They might,' he murmured, before capturing her lips again.

She kissed him hard and Daniel returned it with a heart-pounding intensity.

Tightening her hold around his neck, Mattie pushed herself against him and gave herself up to the exquisite excitement pounding through her body. They stood locked together for a long moment then, moving her hands to rest on his chest, she gently pushed him away.

'I ought to get on,' she sighed.

'And I ought to go to bed,' he replied, gathering her back into his embrace. 'With you.'

They kissed briefly.

'Soon, I promise.' His teeth flashed white in the pale moonlight. 'If all goes to plan in two weeks I'll be getting that special marriage licence.'

Mattie twirled her finger in the curl resting on his forehead. 'I know.'

He pressed his mouth onto hers again.

Blotting from her mind what might happen to Daniel if things didn't go to plan, Mattie gave herself up to his pulse-racing kisses for a moment, then pulled away.

'Oh, Daniel,' she said. 'You will be carefu–'

He stopped her words with his lips again.

'Of course, sweetheart,' he whispered when he finally released her. 'Now, you'd better go before I forget who I'm supposed to be and carry you upstairs to my bed.'

Reluctantly, Mattie stepped out of his embrace.

Hand in hand, they walked to the side gate and Daniel slid back the bolt and opened it. Mattie squeezed his hand and let go but, just as she was about to step back into the street, his arm wound around her again as he pulled her back for a final embrace.

As he watched from the shadows, fury cut through Christopher so forcefully that, for a second or two, he lost the sight in his right eye.

Although the urge to dash across and beat them both to a pulp almost overwhelmed Christopher, he forced his feet to remain where they were. Balling his hands into tight fists, he focused on the pain of his nails as they bit into the palms of his hands, bringing his brutal thoughts into order.

With his jaw aching from his tightly clenched teeth, Christopher watched Mattie step out of McCree's arms and back into the street.

Pulling down her jacket and repositioning her knapsack, she switched on her torch again and continued her patrol along the street.

Christopher waited until she was almost at the bottom of the street and then, with a mirthless smile lifting the corner of his mouth, he started after her.

She and McCree would pay for this, and pay dearly, but perhaps he could ensure he got his revenge in a way that would make it impossible for Mosley to leave him unrewarded.

With the warmth of the brief time together glowing through her, Mattie lowered her dimmed torch towards the pavement and continued along the road.

Turning into Cable Street she headed for the air-raid shelter at the east end of the street but had only gone a few feet when an unsettling sensation tickled the spot between her shoulder blades.

She turned and looked back down the darkened street but saw nothing. Smiling at her over-active imagination, she carried on until she reached the brick-built structure opposite Glasshouse Street Yard.

Stepping through the white painted entrance she stopped when she realised that the shelter wasn't empty. 'Warden!' she called out, to give the occupants some notice of her intent to enter.

She smiled and waited until the muttered voices and frantic scuffling had stopped, then, removing the filter from her torch, she walked into the damp cavern.

'Sorry, chaps,' she said, as her torch highlighted half a dozen or so courting couples with mis-buttoned clothing and dishevelled hair sitting on the wall benches. 'But regulations are regula–'

Caught in the beam of light, Mattie saw her sister Jo. She was dressed in her candy-striped summer dress and, apart from the smudged lipstick, looked the picture of innocence. But what really stopped Mattie in her tracks was the fact that Jo was sitting next to Reggie Sweete's younger brother, Tommy. He was wearing a well-fitting chocolate-coloured suit with cream stripes and had an imprint of her sister's lips in Cherry Crush red on his cheek.

He gave her a lazy smile. 'Hello, Mattie, long time no see.'

'Hello, Tommy,' Mattie replied. 'I didn't realise they'd let you out.'

'Yeah, me and all the other buggers with less than three months to serve.'

'Tommy was telling me he's going to sign up,' said Jo.

'Is he?' said Mattie.

'Yes,' her sister continued, fastening a heart-shaped bodice button that seemed to have come adrift. 'If he volunteers before he gets the call-up, he'll be able to pick which service he goes into.'

Mattie looked at Tommy and held his amused gaze for a couple of seconds, then she shifted her attention back to her sister. 'I thought you were round your friend's house doing your homework.'

'I finished it,' said Jo.

'Then you'd better get home then.' Mattie pulled open the door. 'Before Mum wonders where you are.'

Jo looked back at Tommy. 'I'd better go.'

'That's all right, luv, I'm going to head off now,' he replied, standing up and smiling at her.

Giving Mattie a defiant glance, Jo stood up and gave him a peck on the cheek.

Rubbing the spot thoughtfully, Tommy bowled past Mattie, giving her a casual salute as he passed.

'Don't forget to say goodbye when you get posted,' Jo called after him.

Quickly checking that the shelter's emergency fire buckets were full of water and that the grill cage containing the stirrup pumps, axes and shovels was still secure, Mattie took hold of Jo's arm and, leaving the other couples to pick up where they'd left off, she walked her sister out of the shelter.

'What do you think you're doing, Jo, hanging around with one of the Sweetes?' asked Mattie as they headed along Cable Street towards Mafeking Terrace.

Her sister ripped her arm out of Mattie's grip and glared at her. 'His name is Tommy.'

'Yes, Tommy Sweete, younger brother of Reggie Sweete, who has his finger in every dodgy pie between Aldgate Pump and Bow Bridge. The same Reggie Sweete who smashed up the Fiddle and Flute and slashed the landlord's face, plus put two policemen in hospital when they tried to arrest him.'

Jo's lower lip jutted out. 'I know Tommy's just come out of Borstal but, honestly, Mattie, Tommy's not like that.'

'Perhaps he's not,' said Mattie, her severe expression softening a little. 'But what do you think Mum would have to say about–'

Fear flashed into Jo's eyes. 'You won't tell her, will you?'

'Is he really signing up?' Mattie asked.

Jo nodded. 'As soon as he can get Reggie's consent.'

Mattie considered her younger sister, who was walking beside her.

Tommy was a good-looking chap so she could

very well see why he'd turned Jo's head and, to be truthful, although his brother was an out-and-out villain, Tommy himself had come to the local Old Bill's attention more for his connection to Reggie than because of his own wrong-doing and, having just been enjoying Daniel's embraces, she couldn't be too hard on Jo for doing the same with her young man.

'Well, in that case, it's not worth upsetting her for nothing so I won't,' said Mattie as they walked the last few yards home.

Jo threw her arms around Mattie's neck. 'Thanks, Mattie.'

Mattie hugged her back and then released her as they got to the corner of their street.

'Off you go then,' she said. 'But don't go sneaking about with Tommy Sweete again or it might not be me that finds you.'

Jo smiled and gave her sister another quick peck on the cheek. She hurried off but after she'd gone only a couple of steps, she turned back.

'But you know something, Mattie?' she said, looking her sister straight in the eye. 'You're all wrong about Tommy and, one day, I'll prove it to you all.'

Mattie waited on the corner until her sister disappeared into their house then, switching on her torch, she continued along Chapman Street to check the ground shelter in Cannon Street Road. As she reached Anthony Street, she felt a prickling sensation start between her shoulder blades. Turning, she shone her light down the street, startling a cat that ran across from the shadows and disappeared in to the darkness again. She swung the muted beam onto the parked market stall but, again, nothing stirred.

Chiding herself for being so skittish, Mattie lowered her torch and was just about to resume her patrol when a voice spoke out of the darkness.

'Hello, Mattie.'

With her heart crashing in her chest, Mattie flashed her beam up and onto the face of the person behind her.

'For the love of Mary,' she laughed as she found herself staring into Brenda's grinning face. 'You near "frit the spirt from me" as my gran would say. What you doing here?'

'Frank's missus has gone into labour so he's gone home so, as his area's next to mine, I said I'd do his rounds. What about you?' said her fellow warden.

'Found my sixteen-year-old sister canoodling in a shelter so I walked her home,' Mattie replied.

'Tell you what,' said Brenda. 'Old Cyril's gone over to number 3 post for some meeting or other so why don't we do our blackout patrols together just for once?'

Glancing over her shoulder, Mattie gazed down the deserted street for a moment, then turned back and smiled at her friend.

'Why not?' she said, shoving aside her uneasiness. She slipped her arm in Brenda's. 'We can have a natter.'

Chapter Twenty

'This is the part of the film where we came in,' whispered Francesca, as the opening sequence of the Pathé News they'd watched when they slipped into the row an hour and a half before started again.

'Yes it is, let's go' Mattie replied.

Holding their seats to prevent them banging as they swung up, and ducking down so that people behind them weren't disturbed, Mattie and Francesca side-stepped their way out of their row. Keeping her eyes averted from the couples smooching in the back row, Mattie made her way towards the exit, past the two usherettes whispering to each other at the back.

Pushing open the heavy glass door, the two girls emerged from the cinema into Mile End Road.

It was 10th June, the second Monday in June and, since the evacuation of Dunkirk, the whole of the ARP had been on high alert so, as this was her first day off in over two weeks, she and Francesca had decided to make the most of it. After some deliberation, they'd decided on an evening at the ABC cinema on Mile End Road watching *Gaslight,* a new film that had just opened. Coming out into the darkened street, Mattie was surprised to see that although it was late and the green night buses had already started to run, the street was full of people wandering up and down, energetically debating with each other.

Waiting to ensure there was a gap in the traffic, Mattie and Francesca hurried to the other side of the road just as a crowd of drinkers spilled out of the Hayfield public house on the corner of Hannibal Road.

'What's happened?' Mattie asked a man wearing a flat cap with a roll-up dangling from his lips.

'Ain't you 'eard?' he spat out. 'Fucking Wops have declared war on us, too.'

Francesca gasped and covered her mouth with her hand.

'When?' Mattie asked, squeezing her friend's arm reassuringly.

'It was on the ten o'clock news just now,' the man replied. 'That Mussolini bugger did one of his speeches in Rome.'

'And talk about the bloody fifth column!' said a ginger-haired man standing behind him. 'How many of the greasy bastards have we got here already?'

'Lock 'em all up, that's what I say,' the first man chipped in to murmurs of agreement.

'I have to get home,' said Francesca.

Turning their back on the crowd outside the public house, Mattie and Francesca hurried past the men and women spilling out of their houses in Jamaica Street and headed towards Commercial Road.

'Look!' shouted Francesca as Tony's baker's shop at the corner of Stepney Way came into view.

Mattie followed her friend's terrified gaze to see Mr and Mrs Rizado, the elderly couple who'd been selling locals their morning loaves for almost a quarter of a century, huddled on the pavement while a mob of their angry neighbours threw bricks and mud through their shop window.

Francesca stood staring at the scene for a moment then, skirting around the mass of people, dashed off down the street.

Mattie caught up with her as she reached Commercial Road. Across the road from them an angry crowd milled around outside Romano's barber shop and someone had already daubed 'String them all up' across his front window in red paint.

The two girls turned eastwards and ran on but, even before they reached halfway, they could see the baying mob besieging the Empress Fish bar.

Francesca screamed and tore forward, with Mattie close on her heels.

As Mattie reached the onlookers at the back of the melee, she saw Francesca's brother Giovanni, sleeves rolled up and fists raised, standing in front of his father who was crumpled on the floor with blood on his forehead.

Elbowing her way through the crowd, Francesca ran to her father and crouched down beside him.

'What's happening?' Mattie shouted at Giovanni as she pushed her way to the front.

'Bloody mob rule, that's what,' he yelled back.

A man in the front swung a punch and Giovanni fended him off. The crowd growled its disapproval and shuffled about.

'Sod off, the lot of you,' bellowed Giovanni.

'Bloody turncoats,' screamed a woman at the back. 'Selling us down the fucking swanny to your chum Hitler.'

'We ain't got nothing to do with Mussolini,'

Giovanni shouted back. 'Now clear off or I'll call the rozzers.'

'Call 'em,' shouted someone. 'They can lock you and your spy family up.'

'Let's get him inside,' Mattie shouted, pushing through the crowd and taking Enrico's arm.

With insults and taunts flying over their heads, Fran and Mattie helped the old man to his feet. They were just about to re-enter the shop when a handful of market lads, carrying a bottle with a rag dangling from it, shoved their way forward. The leader took a lighter from his pocket, set fire to the taper and lobbed it at the shop window, shattering the glass.

There was a moment of silence then, with a whoosh, the interior of the shop burst into flames. A cheer went up from those around them and all hell broke loose.

Lunging at the man who'd just destroyed his home, Giovanni grabbed him by the throat and punched him.

The mob surged forward, pushing Mattie, Francesca and her father back towards the blazing shop.

'Bloody Ities,' screamed the mob, and Francesca's father covered his face with his hands and sobbed.

A blast ripped out from the shop. Instinctively everyone ducked as heat roared from the shattered window, charring the wooden frame on the way through. Someone grabbed Francesca's brother but he smashed his fist into their face and they crumpled to the floor.

Enrico had slumped on the pavement again so,

hooking their arms in his, Mattie and Francesca moved him to the side and out of the line of fire. Ignoring the heat, Mattie took her clean handkerchief from her pocket and pressed it to the gash on Mr Fabrino's forehead.

Several police whistles blasted out as half a dozen of Arbour Square's finest bobbies dashed in and started laying about with their truncheons.

The crowd drew back leaving Giovanni and a couple of the petrol bomb gang slogging it out. Francesca's brother was just about to land a knock-out blow when two policemen grabbed him.

'All right, chum, that's enough,' said the larger one as they dragged him off.

'What about them?' yelled Giovanni, lunging at the gang leader who was nursing his pulverised nose.

'Never you mind about them,' said the section sergeant, a red-faced man with a bushy moustache. 'It's you and your old man we're interested in, so if you'd like to come with–'

'But they've done nothing wrong,' shouted Francesca, grabbing the officer's arm.

'Now, now, miss,' said a tall constable with prominent front teeth as he stepped between her and his superior officer. 'There's no need to get upset, is there?'

'Upset?' cried Francesca. 'Those thugs set our home ablaze.'

'And the fire brigade will be here in a moment,' the officer replied. 'And no doubt you'll be able to salvage something when they're done.'

'And Mr Fabrino needs to go to hospital,' said

Mattie, indicating her blood-stained handker-chief.

'The police surgeon can take a look at that at the station, miss,' said the sergeant. He turned to Giovanni, who was still being held firmly by two policemen. 'Now, are you both going to come quietly or—'

'What about them?' shouted Francesca, jab-bing her finger at the crowd gathered around. 'Are you going to take them to the station too for setting light to our home and assaulting my father?'

The sergeant's eyes narrowed for a moment, then he looked over Francesca's head at Mattie. 'If I were you, miss, I'd take your friend home.'

Mattie put her arm around her friend. 'Come on, Fran,' she said softly.

'But I—'

'Go with Mattie, Sis,' said Giovanni as the police officers clamped the handcuffs on him. 'And don't worry, I'll look after Papa.'

'In you go,' said Mattie, ushering Francesca into her kitchen some thirty minutes later.

Woodenly, her friend stepped over the threshold. Shutting the door behind them, Mattie guided her to a kitchen chair and sat her down.

Giving her a quick hug, Mattie took the kettle to the sink and held it under the tap. Just as it was full, the parlour door opened and her mother walked in.

Swathed in her dressing gown and with her curlers in, she'd clearly been in bed and looked relieved when she saw Mattie.

'Thank goodness you're home,' she said, her down-at-heel slippers scuffing over the lino as she shuffled in. 'Dad was telling me there's been trouble on the streets.'

'I know, Mum,' said Mattie, indicating Francesca who was hunched in the chair, staring dumbly into space.

Her mother gave her a questioning look

'They've taken Giovanni and Mr Fabrino into custody,' Mattie explained.

Her mother's mouth drew into a hard line. Pulling up a chair, she sat next to Francesca.

'Now then, luv,' she said, putting a motherly arm around the young woman's slender shoulders. 'You tell your Aunt Ida all about it.'

Mattie made them all tea and, between bouts of crying Francesca recounted the events of the evening.

'And not only is the shop gone but my home too,' Francesca concluded. 'The fire brigade arrived as we came away, but the shop's already gutted so we've lost everything, including the things Mum left for—'

Francesca covered her face with her hands and sobbed. 'What will we do?'

'Well, first off,' said Ida, 'you're going to drink your tea and get yourself up to bed. You're staying with us for now and we'll worry about everything else once your dad and brother are let go.'

Francesca looked up. 'Are you sure?'

'What a question,' said Ida, waving away her words. 'You'll have to put up with Mattie's snoring, mind, but–'

'Thank you, Mrs B.' She enveloped Ida in a

grateful hug.

Ida gave her a kiss on the forehead and stood up. 'I'll leave Mattie to find you a nighty and you can borrow some of her bits and pieces until we can sort something out.' She yawned. 'I'm up in six hours so I'll say goodnight.'

Ida left.

Mattie downed the last of her tea. 'You finish your drink while I go and get you some night-clothes.'

'Thanks,' said Francesca, giving her a plucky little smile.

Mattie left her friend sipping her bedtime cuppa and tiptoed upstairs to her bedroom. Opening the door carefully so as not to disturb Jo, Mattie crept in and over to her chest of drawers. Kneeling down, she found the bits Francesca needed, closed the drawer, then retraced her steps downstairs.

Francesca looked up and smiled as Mattie walked back into the kitchen.

'There you go,' Mattie said, offering her friend the nightclothes and Cathy's old dressing gown. 'You can have a wash in the sink before you turn in if you like.'

While Francesca used the last of the water from the kettle to give herself a quick wash, Mattie downed the rest of her bedtime drink. After her friend had combed and plaited her long ebony-coloured hair, Mattie refilled the kettle for the morning and then tidied away their mugs.

Sliding in next to Jo, Mattie shuffled over so Francesca had enough room. After whispering goodnight, they lay together in the dark, listening to the sounds of the nighttime street. She was just drifting off, imagining Daniel's joy when she told him of their baby, when she felt Francesca start to shake.

Rolling over, Mattie hugged her friend as she wept silently.

'Oh, Mattie,' she said in a hushed tone. 'When the war's over I wonder if any of us will be the same again.'

'I wouldn't think so,' Mattie replied in the same soft manner, 'we've only been at war for nine months and already we're very different people.'

'So you see,' said Christopher, as he stubbed out his cigarette in the over-flowing ashtray. 'He's not Daniel McCree, the priest and IRA operative, but Captain Daniel McCarthy, MI5's undercover agent.'

'MI-bloody-5,' ground out Wilf Hall, the man in charge of the south side of the river and who liked to be known as the 'scourge of Bermondsey'.

'To the core,' Christopher replied, allowing a self-satisfied smirk to spread across his face.

It was the day after their glorious ally Mussolini had finally found his balls and declared war on Great Britain and just three days before the German spies were due to land. He was sitting in the upstairs room of a grubby little pub called the Drovers' Arms which was situated around the corner from Smithfield Market in Farringdon.

Surrounding him were half a dozen of the BCCSE London area wardens, well, those of them who hadn't been scooped up by the police purge on the Right Club, the Link and the British People's Party after the fiasco at Dunkirk.

It didn't really matter, of course, as Hitler would be here soon enough but had General Rundstedt not held his Panzer Division back, it would have all been over by now.

There were murmurs of 'bastard', 'pig' and 'Jew-lover' around the table.

'So, what are you going to do?' asked Jimmy Willis, the sallow-skinned chap who ran Hackney, Islington and Haggerston. 'I mean, about our friends coming up the Thames in three days?'

'Nothing,' said Christopher.

Roger Pilchard, a thick-set individual with a brow so low it almost obscured his vision, looked puzzled. 'But McCree, or whoever he is, will have told his bosses at MI5 where our German friends are landing.'

'Of course he bloody has,' Christopher replied, not bothering to keep the contempt from his voice. 'But I've sent a message to Meadow Rambler via a friend to tell the spies to land at Coldhouse Wharf instead of Wapping Stairs as originally planned.'

'But won't MI5 come looking for you when they get to Wapping Stairs and don't find no one,' asked Jimmy.

'Oh, they'll find someone all right,' Christopher replied. 'Stan and his man will be there and I'm sure arresting and questioning them will keep MI5 busy while I deal with that bastard McCree.'

Wilf chewed the inside of his mouth. 'I don't know, Christopher. After all, Stan and his men are a good bunch and I don't like the idea of selling them down the swanny. Wouldn't it be better to just bump him off now and save all–'

'No!' snapped Christopher, rubbing his temples lightly with his fingers to ease the throbbing. 'I'm the one who's been led a merry dance by this bugger and I'm going to be the one who finishes him, do you understand?'

The men around the table glanced at each other uneasily.

'Perhaps we should run it by them up top first,' said Jimmy. 'You know, just to get their say-so–'

'Who are you going to ask, Willis?' cut in Christopher. 'Mosley and Ramsey are under house arrest, Houston's left the country with his bit of skirt and Domville is rumoured to be in Wandsworth, along with Drummond.' Rising to his feet, Christopher placed his fingertips on the table. 'As our leaders have been detained by those who seek to prevent our glorious fascist revolution, I am taking sole charge of the operation. Would anyone like to say otherwise?'

His icy gaze travelled slowly over the assembled company.

The men around the table lowered their eyes and shook their heads.

'Good.' Christopher slammed his fist on the table. 'From now on, we're doing things my way. Do you hear? My way.'

Sipping the froth of his bitter, Daniel skimmed the Ministry of War advert appealing for able-bodied men to sign up as Local Defence Volunteers.

It was the second Wednesday in June and close to eight in the evening. Daniel was sitting in the bar of the King of Corsica on Berwick Street, Soho. He was surrounded by costermongers wetting their whistles after a long day in the market and gangs of fresh-faced, closely shorn conscripts on leave after completing basic training, who were skylarking about before going on to one of many strip clubs in the area. There were also, as you'd expect in the capital's unofficial red light district, a number of overly made-up young women draped around the bar.

Needless to say, given the location, Daniel had abandoned his clerical garb and was dressed in worn cords and a saggy tweed jacket with a workman's cap rolled up in the pocket.

He took another sip of his drink and had just turned the page of his newspaper to the report on how the Royal Navy were ruthlessly hunting down every U-boat in the Atlantic when a shadow fell across the page.

He looked up to see Christopher standing next to him. He was clutching a pint of bitter and had a half-smoked cigarette in his mouth. Like Daniel, he'd ditched his usual attire and was dressed in a pair of grey flannels and a rough jacket.

'I hope I haven't kept you waiting?' he said.

'About ten minutes,' said Daniel.

Christopher sat down on the chair opposite. 'Is it still on?'

Daniel nodded. 'I contacted Meadow Rambler at lunchtime and they have a green light their end. Are you and your men ready?'

'Don't you worry about us,' Christopher took a long drag on his cigarette. 'We'll be there.'

Something caught his attention.

Daniel looked over his shoulder and saw a young woman dressed in a low-cut satin gown, her blonde hair piled high, tottering across from the bar on a pair of impossibly high heels.

''Ello 'andsome,' she said, as a waft of cheap perfume overpowered Daniel. 'Got a light?'

Picking up the box of matches, Daniel struck one.

The young woman leaned forward and, cupping her hands around his, lit her cigarette, giving him the benefit of her abundant cleavage.

'Thanks,' she said, giving him a slow, lavish look and running her hand along his shoulder. 'I'm Gina. I've got a little place around the corner if you fancy a bit of company? You can take as long as you like.'

'No thank you,' Daniel repeated, removing her hand.

Gina shrugged and shifted her attention to Christopher.

'What about you?' she asked, bestowing her voluptuous charms on him.

'I'm busy at the moment, luv, but why don't you get yourself a drink?' Rummaging in his pocket, he pulled out a shilling and gave it to her.

Gina took it, blew him a pouty kiss, then swayed back to the bar.

A smirk lifted the corner of Christopher's mouth. 'I'm surprised you turned her down or perhaps you're one of those God-bothers who fancy choir boys. Or perhaps you favour brunettes,' he paused, 'like Mattie.'

'I'm a priest,' Daniel said placidly, as alarm bells sounded in his head.

'You might wear your collar the wrong way round but I can tell by the way you look at Mattie

405

that your trouser tackle's still working.' A hard glint appeared in Christopher's eye. 'I suppose you know she's pregnant.'

Despite the chaotic thoughts racing around in his head, Daniel managed to force a mildly surprised expression on his face.

'Why would I?' he asked, truthfully.

'I thought perhaps she whispered through the grille of the confessional box,' Christopher replied, stubbing out his spent cigarette and taking a packet from his pocket.

His eyes searched Daniel's face, but Daniel maintained his dispassionate façade.

'Stan overheard her mother and sister talking,' he said, taking a fresh cigarette from the pack and lighting it. 'Apparently, her family thinks it's mine.'

'Isn't it?' asked Daniel, already knowing the answer.

'No,' Christopher replied. 'I never got so much as my hand on her ha'penny, let alone poke it with my old man.' He smiled across the table at Daniel. 'I don't suppose you have any idea who the father might be?'

Sweat sprang up the length of Daniel's spine.

He forced a regretful smile. 'Sorry. I don't.'

He locked gaze with the Nazi for a few seconds, then Christopher looked away and took another drag on his cigarette.

'No matter.' He blew a series of smoke rings towards the nicotine-stained ceiling. 'I've got myself fixed up with some toff's daughter, so even if it was mine the best I could offer her is a couple of quid to have it hooked out somewhere.' He smiled. 'Still, with six members of the Brandenburg Regiment landing at Wapping Old Steps in two days, perhaps we should focus on that rather than worry about that slut Mattie.'

Mastering the almost overwhelming urge to smash his fist into Christopher's traitorous face, Daniel swallowed his last mouthful of beer and stood up.

'If there's any change between now and Friday, I'll let you know, otherwise stand ready at twenty-three hundred hours.'

Christopher raised his glass.

'Heil Hitler,' he mouthed silently.

Daniel regarded him coolly for a moment, then marched out of the pub.

Closing her eyes, Mattie tilted her head back and, heedless of the inevitable freckles, soaked up the warm June sunshine bathing her face. Somewhere in the branches of the plane tree above her a wood pigeon's coo competed with the chirp of a couple of sparrows. She took a deep breath and the sharp fragrance of the newly cut grass filled her nose.

She was sitting on a bench facing the boating lake in Victoria Park. Mattie knew the irregular-shaped Victorian Garden, which sat between the Regent's Canal and Hackney Wick, like the back of her hand. She'd spent many happy hours in the park as a child, feeding the ducks, splashing in the lido and enjoying an ice cream while her parents lounged in deckchairs by the bandstand listening to a Sunday afternoon concert.

However the park was rather different now

from when she'd visited as a child. The crocuses, red-hot pokers and delphiniums that normally grew in the carefully tended herbaceous border had been replaced with rows of cabbages and onions. The bowling lawns had been ploughed into corduroy stripes of dark earth ready for sowing and a WVS mobile canteen surrounded by Civilian Defence personnel was now parked in front of the boarded-up ice cream booth. On the lawn that ran up towards Mark's Gate there was a forest of khaki tents with soldiers milling around them, and on the East Park area there was a battery of ack-ack guns pointing skywards.

Pleasant though it was to spend her day off relaxing in the balmy summer air, the real reason Mattie was in the park was because she had accompanied Fran as she visited her brother and father, who had been taken away two days previously after their home and business had been destroyed. Across the road from Mattie, a hastily erected corral of metal fencing topped by barbed wire surrounding some tin huts had been built and this was where Giovanni and Enrico, along with other men of Italian extraction, were now prisoners of war.

Mattie watched as a platoon of the newly formed Home Guard, with armbands over their civilian clothes and shouldering broom handles and garden forks because their equipment hadn't arrived, marched past. On the other side of the gravel thoroughfare, dozens of women, many with bewildered children gathered around their skirts, were clutching onto the fence of the compound as they spoke to their menfolk, and Francesca was amongst them.

Mattie saw Francesca turn towards her and wave her over.

Picking up her handbag, Mattie stood up and walked across.

Giovanni, who had dark circles around his eyes and three days' worth of stubble, looked through the wire at her as she approached.

'It was good of you to come with Fran,' he said, as she reached the fence. 'And thank you so much for having her to stay with you.'

'Don't be silly.' Mattie slipped her arm through her friend's. 'How's your father bearing up?'

Pain flitted across Giovanni's handsome face. 'Not so good. I managed to get some breakfast down him this morning but he refused to leave his bed when they served up the midday meal and now he's lying in the tent with the blanket over his head.'

'Perhaps he'll perk up a bit when you tell him I saved Mama's painting and some of her other things from the fire,' said Francesca.

Mattie and her father had gone back to the shop the day before with Francesca to see what they could salvage. Although the front had been totally destroyed, thanks to the fire brigade's timely arrival the rear of the property had suffered only some charred timbers, smoke and water damage. Treading carefully up the scorched staircase, the three of them had gathered what remained of the Fabrino family's personal items, including a suitcase of Francesca's clothes and some of Giovanni and Enrico's too. Fran had brought the men's clothes with her today and, after they'd been checked for weapons, the soldier had assured her that they would be passed on to her father and brother.

'I'm sure he will,' Giovanni replied, in a tone that indicated otherwise. 'But I know he'll be relieved to know you're staying with Mattie, Fran.'

'She's not staying with us, Gio,' said Mattie, putting her arm around her friend's shoulder. 'She's living with us and will be until you and your father come back.'

Giovanni raked his fingers through his coal black hair. 'God only know when that will be. There's a rumour started this morning that we're being shipped to some island off the coast up north.'

Tears suddenly gathered in Francesca's eyes.

'Oh, Giovanni,' she gripped the wire. 'I can't believe this–'

'*Vieni ora sorella*,' Giovanni whispered, his long fingers closing over his sister's delicate ones.

He said something else in Italian and pulled a comical face. Francesca gave her brother a heartbreaking smile and nodded.

'All right, that's enough fraternising with the enemy,' shouted a weedy-looking soldier, taking the gun from his shoulder and jabbing it through the wire towards Fran and Mattie.

Francesca stepped back but Giovanni spun around to face him. 'Don't you threaten my sister,' he yelled, raising his clenched fists.

Other men who were standing by the fence started to gather around Giovanni.

Beads of sweat sprung out on the soldier's forehead.

Gripping his gun tighter, he pointed it at Gio-

410

vanni's chest. 'Get back or I'll–'

'It's all right, Private Trotter, we don't want no trouble,' said an older man with deep-set eyes, putting a restraining hand on Giovanni's arm. 'We'll get back, won't we, lad?'

Although his enraged expression remained, Giovanni stepped back.

'That's better,' said Private Trotter. 'And don't go trying to sneak secrets to your Wop family in future.'

Giovanni started forward, but his older friend grabbed his arm again and both men glared at the private as he marched away.

'You'd better come,' said his friend. 'Your father's a bit distr–' His eyes flickered onto Francesca for a second. 'Upset.'

Giovanni slapped him affectionately on the upper arm. 'Thanks, Bennie.'

Bennie nodded and then strolled back towards the Nissan huts at the far end of the compound.

'*Dio benedica la sorella*,' Giovanni said, placing a hand over his heart.

Francisca crossed herself. Her brother's attention turned from his sister to Mattie. 'Thanks again.'

He hurried after his friend.

Mattie put her arm around Francesca's slender shoulders and led her away.

'I think Fergus and the Kerry Boys are playing in the Catholic Club later so do you fancy popping along for a quick drink?' said Mattie, as she and Francesca turned into Mafeking Terrace an hour later.

Her friend forced a smile. 'Yes, if you like.'

They'd sat in silence on the bus ride home and Francesca had hardly spoken for most of the short walk from Commercial Road, which wasn't surprising given what her poor friend had been through in the last few days. Mattie understood her anxiety completely. After all, in less than two days, God willing, Daniel's mission would be accomplished, and they could be married. Although the Germans might still swamp the country, at least after Friday, if everything went to plan, she and Daniel could face the future, whatever it was, together.

Mattie could hear the 'Children's Hour' signature tune drifting out of an open window, indicating it had just turned five, and the men who worked in the dock were already trudging home. As it was a balmy night, a handful of girls sat on the kerb playing gobs with chalk cubes while the boys were darting between bollards, lampposts and open doorways as they fought to wrest control of the street from invisible German stormtroopers.

Like most of her neighbours, her mother had left the front door open to let what little air there was cool the house so, instead of slipping around the back as she usually did, Mattie and Fran stepped over the whitened step and walked into the parlour.

'Yo-ho, we're back—'

She stopped dead at the sight that greeted her.

Her mother and Jo were standing almost toe to toe and glaring at each other while Queenie, who was standing next to her youngest granddaughter, looked on uncertainly at them both. Billy was standing by the window staring glumly out and sucking his thumb, something he hadn't done for a long time.

As Mattie walked in, they all turned and looked at her.

Francesca touched her elbow. 'I think I'll put the kettle on.'

Leaving the Brogan womenfolk regarding each other warily, Fran hurried through to the back of the house.

'What's happened?' asked Mattie, as the kitchen door closed.

'Me and Billy are being bloody evacuated,' screamed Jo. 'And it's all your fault.'

Mattie was confused. 'Mine?'

'Yes, you,' sobbed her sister. 'You said you wouldn't tell Mum and you did and now she's sending me away to the poxy country with Billy.'

'I didn't tell her,' said Mattie.

'Tell me what?' asked Ida.

Jo wiped her tears away with the heel of her hand. 'Then why am I being sent away?'

'So you can look after Billy,' said Ida.

'I don't believe you.' Jo jabbed her finger at Mattie. 'You told her.'

Mattie crossed herself. 'I didn't say a word.'

'Say a word about what?' asked Ida.

'Yes you did,' screamed Jo. 'I know you did. I hate you. I hate you all.'

With tears streaming down her face, Jo dashed past Mattie and out of the house, slamming the door behind her.

Mattie, her mother and grandmother stared after her for a moment, then Ida's expression

413

crumpled. Covering her face with her hands, she slumped into the nearest chair.

'Why couldn't she just stay away?' she sobbed.

Mattie gave Queenie a puzzled look.

'Her bloody sister, the Devil take her,' her grandmother explained, giving her daughter-in-law an uncommonly rare sympathetic look. 'Swanned in here an hour ago and said if your mother didn't send Billy to safety before the end of next week, she would tell Billy everything and take him back with her.'

'So why is Jo going?' asked Mattie.

'He's too young to go by himself,' said Ida.

Mattie pulled a face. 'He's almost ten, Mum, and there are children half his age travelling alone.'

'He's got a sensitive nature,' her mother remarked as Billy squashed a fly trapped between the glass and net curtains with his thumb. Pulling a handkerchief from her sleeve, she blew her nose loudly. 'Jo's going and that's an end to it.' She gave Mattie a sideways look. 'And what was it you were supposed to have told me?'

Chapter Twenty-one

'Is it time?' Mattie asked him for the fifth time in as many minutes.

'Almost,' whispered Daniel, savouring the feel of her in his arms.

It was just past ten-thirty and he was standing in the shadow of the rectory with the woman he loved in his arms, as she had been for the past twenty minutes. She was on duty so was wearing her ARP uniform and he was in his clerical shirt with the top two buttons unfastened.

He would have to put on his dog collar and Father McCree's persona again soon, but not just yet. Not before he seared the feel of Mattie's head resting on his chest and the touch of her mouth under his into his brain.

'You will be careful,' she said.

'Of course,' he replied, the feel of her hand resting lightly on his chest, firing his emotions.

Memories of a bullet pitting the plaster behind his head, a knife slicing within inches of his cheek and the sickening crunch as his fist broke an assailant's nose flickered through Daniel's mind.

Each time he'd faced death he'd been afraid, of course he had and, in truth, he wouldn't be here now if he hadn't. Fear set your heart beating and put your senses on high alert so you saw movements and changes in your enemy's demeanour in a blink of an eye. But tonight was different. He wasn't just fighting for the future of king and country, he was fighting for his future with Mattie and their unborn baby.

'And, don't worry, I'm sure everything will be fine,' he added, confidently.

In the dim moonlight, Mattie scrutinised his face. 'What's wrong?'

'Nothing,' he said, shoving the image of Christopher's smirking face from his mind. 'Nothing at all.'

Daniel tickled her waist but she didn't laugh. Instead, her mouth pulled into a firm line.

'Daniel?'

He held her gaze for a second and then let out a long breath.

'I'm just fired up, that's all,' he said, nonchalantly.

A lump of anxiety settled on Mattie's chest. 'Oh, Daniel, I'm so scared–'

Cupping her lovely face gently in his hands Daniel smiled down at her.

'Francis has armed soldiers all along the river and three police patrol boats disguised as Thames dredgers are ready to apprehend the spies. There are also armed members of SOE hidden in warehouses and wharfs overlooking Wapping Stairs, plus the local constabulary is acting as backup. Everything will be fine. I promise. And tomorrow, once Christopher and his Nazis are locked up, we can make plans.' His lips touched hers briefly. 'That is, of course, unless you've changed your mind about becoming Mrs McCarthy.'

'I certainly haven't.' She gave a low laugh as some of the tension went from her body. 'So you just make sure you come back so you can carry me over the threshold.'

With the boom of the barges on the Thames echoing around them, Daniel closed his mouth over hers again for a heartbeat, then released her.

'I'll see you tomorrow,' he whispered.

'Until tomorrow,' she replied, picking up her ARP helmet and kitbag.

As he watched her disappear into the shadow at the side of the rectory, Daniel imagined his child growing snug within her.

When Christopher told him about the baby in

the Soho pub, Daniel had wondered fleetingly why she hadn't told him about the baby, but then he understood. She hadn't told him because she knew it would distract him. And it did. Why wouldn't it? He was going to be a father. However, the real conundrum Daniel faced about Mattie and their baby was whether Christopher had really mentioned Mattie's condition just by chance.

Fighting the urge to rush back and throw herself into Daniel's arms for one more embrace, Mattie forced her feet to walk down the rectory's side entrance.

Repositioning her tin hat and anchoring her bag across her, Mattie unhooked the latch and went back into the blacked-out streets. Taking her muted torch from her pocket, she shone it at her feet and made her way back up the street towards Commercial Road. With her mind full of Daniel, she hurried on, anxious to get home. Concentrating on following the white lines painted along the side of the road, she didn't hear the footsteps behind her. Then, as she passed the paintworks, a hand closed over her throat and she was dragged back into the side alley. With her voice choked off, she kicked back but her heel met nothing solid. Mastering her rising panic, Mattie twisted away from the hand blocking off her air but something hard jabbed into her spine. She stopped struggling instantly and her arms fell to her side.

'Yes, that is a gun, Mattie, my dear,' Christopher's voice said, his warm breath feathering over her neck. 'Now, let's take a little walk.'

417

Buckling his gun holster across his chest, Daniel stowed the Browning revolver deep within it, then turned to face the mirror. He fixed his dog collar in place. Taking his jacket from the back of the chair by his desk, he slipped it on and pulled it down over the holster.

He looked at his watch. Ten to eleven. He had time yet as it was only a short walk to Wapping Old Stairs. Standing stock-still, he stared out of his bedroom window and summoned up a picture of Mattie standing beside him as his wife. He ran that image through a couple of times, added a visit to his parents to the mix and then fast forwarded to a snug little home with children's toys dotted about the cosy parlour. The church clock striking the hour brought his mind back to the job in hand. He checked his watch again and then looked out of the window but, this time, his mind ran through the plans he and Francis had made earlier that week. Nothing was left to chance, so nothing would go wrong. That was the theory, at least. He just prayed it would be so in practice.

He checked his revolver was still secure and then, adjusting his jacket again to obscure the additional bulk, Daniel took a long, slow breath and walked out of his bedroom.

Trotting down the stairs, he'd just reached the bottom step when the telephone in the hall rang. He picked it up.

'St Bridget and St Brendan's Rectory, Father McCree speaking, how can I help?' he asked, glancing at the hall clock.

'I'd like to speak to Daniel McCarthy,' said a man's voice.

418

A cold hand gripped Daniel's heart. 'I'm afraid there's no one of that name here.'

'Pity,' said the voice. 'I've got his sweetheart Mattie Brogan with me.'

Terror shot through Daniel. Christopher! He knew in his guts he should have got Mattie away somewhere safe after Christopher had told him about the baby. And if he knew who Daniel really was, where did that leave Francis's carefully crafted plan to capture the German spies landing in little over an hour?

Actually, he didn't care. He didn't give a damn about Francis, MI5, Hitler, the German Panzer division sitting on the other side of the Dover Straits or even his own life. All he cared about was getting Mattie and their unborn baby away from Christopher.

'What do you want, Christopher?'

'Coldhouse Wharf, Siam & Burma Trading Co. Come alone and come quickly,' Christopher replied. 'One whiff of your MI5 chums and I'll put a bullet through her head.'

Daniel sprinted the half mile to the wharf next to the Limehouse Basin in ten minutes flat, coming to a halt just outside. His first instinct had been to call Francis, but he would already be in position a mile away at Wapping Stairs. Christopher was no fool. He knew that even if Daniel could summon help, it would take too long.

Drawing his gun, Daniel pushed open the small watchman's door set in the massive double gates that secured the entrance to the wharf. The door creaked open and he slipped through. Once in-

419

side, and keeping to the shadows, he tried to get his bearings. The wharf was lined on both sides with two-storey brick-built warehouses which housed various import and export traders. Sending up a small prayer of thanks for the clear night and full moon, Daniel cast his eyes down the row of buildings and spotted the Siam & Burma Trading warehouse at the far end, next to the river.

Ducking in and out of the shadows, Daniel headed swiftly towards the building until he got to the front doors. Hoping to better the odds, Daniel scouted down the side of the building on the off-chance there would be an unsecured window or fire escape which might give him some edge. There wasn't.

He returned to the front of the building and, jamming his gun firmly back in the holster, pushed the door open and stepped in.

'I'm here,' he shouted, his voice echoing around the cavernous storage area.

'Say hello to your lover then, Mattie darling,' said Christopher from somewhere at the far end of the vast empty room.

'Daniel, don't come any nearer,' Mattie screamed. 'It's a—'

Her voice cut off abruptly.

Somehow, Daniel conquered the urge to dash forward into the dark.

'She was going to say trap,' mocked Christopher's disembodied voice. 'In case you were wondering.'

'Let her go, Christopher,' said Daniel, trying to make out the other man's form in the gloom.

'Wondering where we are, are you?' asked

Christopher, his voice echoing around the rafters above Daniel's head.

There was a burst of light which momentarily blinded him, but as his eyes focused he saw Christopher holding Mattie like a shield in front of him, the barrel of his gun pressed against her temple.

She was standing motionless in Christopher's grip with her arms hanging loosely at her side. Although her face was expressionless, as their gazes locked, Daniel saw the panic she was struggling to keep in check.

A primeval urge rose up in Daniel so violently that, for a split second, his mind was filled with nothing but the visceral need to protect her, but he held it in check. If Mattie and the baby were going to survive, he'd have to find a more cunning way to defeat Christopher.

'It will be all right, Mattie, I promise,' he said, looking intensely into her eyes and willing her to believe him.

She forced a little smile. Daniel held her gaze for a heartbeat, then shifted his focus to the man holding her.

'Doesn't he look brave?' asked Christopher, his mouth close to Mattie's ear. 'Is your little heart beating faster, thinking your knight in priestly armour is going to save you from the nasty man? Or perhaps,' his mouth pulled into an ugly shape, 'perhaps it's beating faster because you're remembering him getting it up you.'

Without thinking, Daniel took a step forward.

'Ah, ah, ah.' Christopher jabbed the gun harder into Mattie's temple.

Daniel froze and forced himself to stay calm.

421

'There. Isn't that the way it ought to be between friends?' said Christopher, his contemptuous voice cutting through Daniel's chaotic thoughts. 'We all know you're not the IRA's man, Father McCree, but a MI5 operative. I'm working to have a fascist regime installed in England and you and Mattie have been sneaking away to hotels for a tumble in the sheets. And now everyone knows Mattie is having your baby.'

'So what now?' asked Daniel, refusing to rise to the bait.

'I'll be coming to that in due course,' Christopher replied. 'But I know you've got a gun, so take it out slowly.'

Daniel reached inside his jacket and grasped the revolver's handle.

'Slowly, remember,' Christopher said, jabbing the butt of his own gun against Mattie's temple.

Daniel inched his gun free of the holster and spread his arms.

'Very good.' Christopher grinned. 'Now, throw it as far as you can towards the barrel over there.'

Without taking his eyes from Mattie, Daniel flung it aside and heard it clatter on the concrete floor as it landed.

Christopher's shoulders relaxed a notch.

'He's right, Mattie, my love.' Christopher pressed his mouth against Mattie's cheek. 'Everything's going to be all right: for me.'

Swinging the gun in his hand, he smashed the butt of it against Mattie's head and she sank to the floor without a murmur.

Looking at her lying at Christopher's feet in a crumpled heap, Daniel decided, even if it took the last breath he had in his body, he would one day watch Christopher dangling at the end of a rope.

One thing Mattie had learned from listening to doorstep gossip as a child was that when a man hit you, you stayed down. Although she had stars bursting at the edge of her vision and her head throbbed like it was about to explode, Mattie lay unmoving and feigned unconsciousness.

Opening her eyes a fraction, she saw Christopher's polished brown brogues level with the top of her head, which meant he was facing away from her. She cast her gaze around. The warehouse was empty, apart from some lengths of ropes and a few broken packing cases. As her eyes focused and she began to see more clearly, she also spotted several lengths of rusty chain and a broken docker's hook, but what caught her attention was the two-foot-long forked-ended jemmy, used for prising open crates, which was partially hidden under a pile of dusty sacks just six inches away from her right foot.

'So I'm guessing the plans to land the German agents has changed,' Daniel said, somewhere beyond her field of vision.

'Indeed it has,' Christopher replied.

Keeping herself pressed to the ground and her eyes on Christopher's shoes, Mattie inched her body back towards the sack.

'So where's Stan and his crew?' asked Daniel.

'At Wapping Stairs,' Christopher replied. His shoes scuffed her hand as he stepped sideways. 'You see, when I realised who you were, I contacted Meadow Rambler and changed the spies' landing place, but I had to keep up the pretence that it was business as usual, so Stan and his merry men are a decoy to keep your chums at MI5 busy.'

Mattie closed her eyes and took a long breath to steady her thundering heart.

'So they are to be sacrificed for the cause, are they?' said Daniel in a conversational tone.

'Indeed,' said Christopher. 'But they will be imprisoned only for a month or two until this misguided government surrenders,' said Christopher. 'Then they will be released and decorated as heroes.'

'Or hanged as traitors when England fights on,' said Daniel.

There was silence. Mattie heard the sound of a lighter being flicked and then an empty packet of Rothmans landed on the floor next to her.

'I suppose you want me to tell you where my friends are actually landing,' continued Christopher, as the smell of cigarette smoke drifted down.

'You're going to anyway,' Daniel replied. 'You megalomaniac master-race types are always desperate to show off how bloody clever you are.'

Christopher started forward but then stopped.

Taking her courage in her hands, Mattie tilted her head back slightly and looked up.

Although Daniel hadn't moved, Christopher was now two feet in front of her, which meant she was out of his line of vision.

'Very clever, McCarthy,' laughed Christopher, as Mattie shifted across and grasped the jemmy. 'Trying to provoke me, but it won't work. However, I will satisfy your curiosity. I can tell you that this warehouse, which is owned by a fellow

424

devotee of the fascist cause, has direct and secluded access to the river. My German friends will be arriving shortly and, as they are all very familiar with London, they will be making their way to their lodgings alone. I, on the other hand, will be travelling back to France to assist German High Command with Operation Sealion which, in case your deciphering boffins haven't worked it out yet, is the Führer's glorious plan to invade England. Not only will I be lauded as a hero of the Reich and as one of Mosley and the BCCSE's most-successful area coordinators in London, I'll probably get promoted to a major-general. At least I will when I pitch up with an MI5 officer and his pregnant girlfriend, who will no doubt be invaluable to the SS as a means of persuading you to divulge the names of all SOE and MI5 operatives in France, Belgium and Holland, along with all the relevant codes.'

'You bastard,' Daniel ground out as Mattie pulled the jemmy clear of the sacking. Tightening her grip, she took a long breath and waited.

'Yes, aren't I.' Christopher laughed.

He stepped back.

Flexing her arm, Mattie grasped the cold metal in both hands and, using every ounce of strength, swung the jemmy at Christopher's ankles.

The hard iron connected with the bone with a sickening crunch, he screamed and a shot rang out.

Mattie scrambled to her feet. Christopher was half-lying, half-sitting on the floor holding his leg with his hand, his lips pulled tight back, showing his clenched teeth.

'The gun,' Daniel shouted.

She looked across to where Christopher, his foot dragging behind him at an unnatural angle, was now crawling across the floor towards the weapon. Gathering her wits, Mattie dashed across and snatched it up just as his fingers touched it.

Christopher fell back, exhausted with the effort and let out a string of expletives that would have made a docker blush.

'Mattie, fetch it here,' said Daniel.

Gripping it firmly in one hand and carrying the crow bar in the other, Mattie ran to where Daniel was leaning against an upright beam.

'You bitch,' Christopher bellowed, hunching himself into a sitting position and inspecting his shattered ankle. 'You'll both suffer for this.'

They ignored him.

'Are you all right, sweetheart?' Daniel said softly as she handed him the gun.

She nodded.

'My head feels like I've done ten rounds with Joe Louis but I'll live, what about you?' she said, noticing with alarm the tight lines around Daniel's eyes and his grey pallor.

'I'm fine.' He flexed the gun in his hand and winced.

Daniel sank to the ground.

'You've been shot,' she said, as her eyes fixed on the blood oozing from his left shoulder.

'It's just a graze,' he replied, resting his head back on the pillar supporting him.

Mattie dashed to her ARP bag. Falling to her knees in front of Daniel, she flipped the top open. She rummaged around and found a wound pad.

'Hold this firmly over it,' she said, tearing the paper wrapping with her teeth and pressing the gauze onto the wound.

Daniel winced but did as she said. Taking a bandage, she quickly wrapped it around his upper arm, but by the time she'd tied it off, bright red blood was already seeping through.

Daniel knew that the bullet wound in his shoulder was more than a graze. But that wasn't his main concern.

'Leave it,' he said, as Mattie turned back to her bag to find another bandage.

She frowned. 'But it still–'

'Go to Wapping Stairs to fetch Francis,' he interrupted, forcing himself to sound firm rather than breathless.

'But you're injured.'

'How touching,' shouted Christopher. 'Say goodbye to dear Daniel, Mattie darling, because he'll be dead before you get back.'

Mattie's eyes flew open and she delved into her bag again, but Daniel grabbed her arm. 'Mattie, please,' he said, fixing her terrified eyes with a steady gaze. 'We haven't got much time.'

To his relief, this time she didn't argue. Throwing her bag aside, she stood up.

'I won't be long,' she said, bending down to kiss him briefly on the lips.

Ignoring the throbbing in his arm, Daniel forced a smile.

'I'll be here. And, Mattie,' he said softly. She looked at him. 'Look after that baby.'

Giving him a brave smile, she ran out of the warehouse.

427

He ripped off his dog collar and unfastened his top button then, grasping the gun in both hands, levelled it at Christopher's chest. He glanced at his watch. Ten to twelve.

'How you feeling, old man?' asked Christopher.

Daniel didn't respond. It took energy to speak and his was ebbing away fast.

'I'm guessing that the bullet shot through an artery,' Christopher continued. 'Damn unlucky that as if it had only been an inch or two higher, it would have missed you completely.'

Taking a deep breath, Daniel focused on steadying his heart. Mattie's pressure bandage had slowed the haemorrhaging, but only temporarily. It would take her ten minutes to reach Wapping Stairs and if she located Francis quickly, they could be back in twenty. He might have enough time, perhaps...

A grey mist started to form at the edges of his mind, but Daniel forced it back and stretched open his eyes.

'Feeling sleepy, are you?' asked Christopher.

Daniel raised the gun barrel a fraction in response.

'It's just a matter of time you know, before you pass out and I put you out of your misery,' said Christopher.

There was a long silence, then Christopher spoke again. 'I wonder what it is? A boy or a girl?'

Grief gripped Daniel's chest.

'I guess even MI5 operatives have a heart, so yours must be breaking in two by now,' Christopher went on. 'Knowing you're never going to see your child. Still, I'm sure it'll have a father eventually, after all, a pretty girl like Mattie's bound to find some chap to take her on and your sprog will be calling him Daddy...'

Daniel's eyelids started to droop as blackness crowded his vision.

There was a shuffling noise. Daniel forced himself back to consciousness to find Christopher had moved closer.

Although it felt like a lead weight, Daniel raised the gun. He glanced at his watch. Five past.

'How long they been gone now?' asked Christopher. 'Fifteen minutes? Well, I reckon you've got about another five, chum, and then you'll be out.'

He was probably right, thought Daniel, willing the gun in his hand to remain level, but at least Mattie and their baby would be safe.

His eyes started to droop again. Daniel tried to force them open but, this time, he couldn't over the ringing in his ears, he heard Christopher shuffle forward. He tried to respond but couldn't. Christopher laughed. An image of Mattie smiling at him floated into his mind for an instant, but then the blackness took him. A gust of air flowed over him as the Holy Spirit arrived to gather his soul to eternity and then everything went blank.

Mattie was just two steps behind Francis and the half a dozen MI5 and CID officers who burst into the Siam & Burma warehouse as the clock chimed quarter past midnight.

Mercifully, she'd reached Wapping Stairs just as the local constabulary were loading Stan and his gang into the back of a Black Maria. After she'd given a breathless explanation of the events at the Siam & Burma trading wharf, Francis, whose Oxbridge accent was quite at odds with his working man's disguise, had commandeered a police car, rounded up a handful of men and, with Mattie squashed in alongside, they'd sped back along Wapping High Street, scattering rats and stray cats as they tore along.

While Francis and his men pounced on Christopher, Mattie ran straight to Daniel, who was slumped grey and lifeless beside the pillar. Throwing herself on her knees next to him, she grabbed his lapels.

'Daniel!' she screamed, shaking him.

There was no response.

Pulling a crate over, Mattie propped Daniel's legs on it and felt for his pulse. With relief she could feel a thready beat and a little colour returned to his face, although he didn't move.

Leaving his men to drag the prisoner away, Francis came over to join her.

'Daniel, wake up, you stupid bugger,' he yelled, stripping off his coat and tucking it firmly around Daniel. He turned to Mattie. 'The ambulance will be here soon but we have to get some fluid in him now.' He shouted at a plain-clothed officer who was searching through the debris. 'Get me a pint of something to drink. I don't care what it is – beer, gin, dishwater – but something. And quick, damn you.'

The officer hurried off and returned a moment later carrying a kettle. 'It's all I could find and I've filled it with water from the outside tap.'

'Good work,' said Francis, snatching it from

him. 'Now go and look for that bloody ambulance.'

The officer ran off.

'Right, my dear,' said Francis, in a brisk tone. 'Lift his head and I'll pour.'

Kneeling down behind Daniel, Mattie raised his head and rested it on her lap.

Francis placed the rusty spout in Daniel's mouth and tipped it up but the water just dribbled out of the side of Daniel's mouth.

'Come on, you bloody fool, drink!' bellowed Francis, rubbing his friend's breastbone with his knuckles.

'Daniel, wake up,' shouted Mattie, slapping his cold, clammy cheek. 'I love you. We're going to be married. We're having a baby. Wake up, Daniel McCarthy. Jesus, Mary and Joseph, will you wake up and drink.'

Daniel lay motionless for a second, then his eyes flickered. He spluttered and then swallowed as the frantic tone of an ambulance bell cut through the night.

Father Mahon had often assured his flock that there was no suffering in Heaven so, as he came back to consciousness, the throbbing pain in Daniel's left shoulder told him he was still amongst the living.

Lying still, he ran his fingertips across the starched sheet beneath him and then, reassured by the astringent smell of disinfectant and the sound of the soft tread of rubber-soled shoes, he opened his eyes a fraction and his world was complete.

Mattie, still in her ARP dungarees, was curled up

431

asleep in the chair beside his bed, a blue hospital blanket half-draped over her shoulder. With happiness threatening to burst his heart, Daniel let his gaze run slowly over her. Instead of being neatly caught back from her face, her hair looked like a lopsided brunette birds' nest. Her mascara had smudged, as had her lipstick. Her right cheek was swollen to twice its normal size and there was a livid mauve bruise on her forehead where Christopher's gun had struck her. However, as the early morning sun from the window bathed her in soft copper tones, Daniel thought she'd never looked so beautiful. And now he knew she was carrying his baby, even with a bullet in his shoulder, it was the happiest day of his life.

Mattie stirred. She blinked the sleep away and her large hazel eyes opened and fixed on him.

Daniel smiled. 'Hello, you.'

'Hello yourself,' she replied, smiling back.

Unfolding herself from the chair, she moved closer and took his hand.

He squeezed it. 'How are you?'

'I've got a head fit to burst, a crick in my neck and I swear I could sleep for a week.' She lowered her head and pressed her lips to the back of his hand. 'But you're alive.'

'And the baby?' asked Daniel.

'Tucked away safe and sound,' Mattie replied. 'It seems it will take more than being held at gunpoint, smashed in the head and running a mile in the moonlight to dislodge this little McCarthy.' She gave him a wry smile. 'I'd say he was a chip off the old block already.'

Daniel grinned and, ignoring the pain, stretched

out his hand and laid it on her still-flat stomach. Mattie wove her fingers in his as they rested on her and they smiled at each other.

The door opened and Francis marched in wearing what looked like a second-hand barrow boy's outfit complete with oily leather cap.

'Glad to see you're awake,' he said, dragging across a chair and settling himself down on the other side of the bed. 'Thought I'd bring you the good news myself. That blaggard Joliffe is where he should have been long ago, behind bars, along with his gang of gorillas who we nabbed at Wapping Stairs.'

Daniel shifted a little to relieve the numbness in his rear, then promptly wished he hadn't as a sharp pain shot down his arm.

'What about the German spies?' he asked, trying to keep his mind above the pain.

A smile lifted his commander's thin moustache. 'Well, it transpires we weren't the only ones on our toes last night. Thames Division Police launch picked them up at Barking Creek just before they reached the Royal Docks. Silly buggers had disguised their craft as a Medway craft but had painted Charham instead of Chatham on the stern. The floating bobbies had become suspicious and hailed them. The Jerrys made a dash for the estuary and got themselves stuck in a mud bar at Barking Creek. They're sitting in the cell next to Joliffe and his crew in Scotland Yard awaiting transfer to…' His pale blue eyes flickered across at Mattie. 'Other facilities.'

'So the operation was a complete success,' said Mattie.

'Indeed it was, Miss Brogan,' agreed Francis, 'due in no small part to your skilled use of a crowbar. Perhaps we should think of recruiting you for future operations.'

Mattie laughed. 'I'm flattered, but I'm going to have another job in about six months, which will keep me fully occupied.'

'Until the war's over and I come back,' said Daniel. 'Because then she's off to university.'

Francis's eyebrows rose almost to his hairline, but he didn't comment. Resting his hands on his thighs, he rose to his feet.

'Well,' he said with a sigh. 'It's been a long night and I'm off to catch up on some shut-eye and I suggest you both do the same.' He looked at Daniel. 'Doc says you'll be as right as rain in six weeks, so I expect to see you in my office in three, McCarthy. After you've married this young lady of yours, of course.'

'Yes, sir,' Daniel replied.

'Good man. We may have Mosley and his Nazi chums like Joliffe behind bars but there are hordes of them sitting on the other side of the Dover Straits, so we need all hands on deck.' Francis marched to the door but, as he reached for the handle, he turned. 'You had a bit of a close call that time, McCarthy. Don't do it again or I'll have you up on a charge.'

Daniel grinned. 'No, sir.'

Francis's pale gaze ran over Daniel again and then he marched out.

'You'll never be fit enough to report for duty in three weeks,' said Mattie, looking anxiously at him.

'It'll only be to debrief and to make a statement for Christopher's trial,' Daniel replied.

'But, Daniel–'

'Have I told you how much I love you, Mattie?' he cut in, giving her an extravagantly adoring look.

She held her furious expression for a couple of seconds and then let out a long sigh 'All right, but don't think you'll always get round me that easily.'

He smiled and she smiled back.

'How bad was I?' Daniel asked after several heartbeats had passed.

'Three pints of blood and a torn axillary artery,' she replied. 'If you'd lost another half a pint, your kidneys would have collapsed. Thankfully, they took you straight into surgery and after two hours on the operating table winkling out the bullet and stitching you up, the surgeon said that as long as there's no other complications, you can be out in three or four days.'

'Just as well,' said Daniel, 'as I've got to have a serious word with your father.'

Chapter Twenty-two

As Daniel stepped off the last tread of the rectory stairs, the kitchen door opened and Mrs Dunn walked out, pushing the trolley loaded with afternoon tea.

'You, Father McCree, look as if his spirit was about to fly to Heaven,' she said, giving him a disapproving look. 'And shouldn't you be resting in bed, not gadding about the house.'

It was Tuesday and about three-thirty in the afternoon. After a four-day stay in the London hospital, Daniel had been discharged from the Charrington Ward just two hours before.

'I'm fine, Mrs Dunn,' Daniel replied. 'So I thought to save you the walk upstairs, I'd join Father Mahon for tea.'

'Very well,' she replied, not looking at all convinced. 'But I've given you an extra round of sandwiches to build up your strength a bit.'

'Thank you,' Daniel replied.

'But mind you don't go stepping out in front of motorbikes again,' she added, face lifted in a motherly smile. 'You might have more than just a cracked collar bone next time.'

Daniel nodded.

Stepping in front of the housekeeper, he opened the study door and she pushed the trolley in, the crockery rattling together as she passed.

Father Mahon was sitting in his chair by the fire with his glasses on the tip of his nose and his Bible open on his lap. He looked up as Daniel walked in.

'You're out of bed then, lad,' he said, as the trolley came to rest beside Father Mahon's chair.

'Yes, Father,' said Daniel. 'I've had enough of lying about in bed so I thought I'd keep you company.'

'If you ask me,' said Mrs Dunn, pouring drink into both cups. 'He ought to still be in–'

'Thank you, Mrs Dunn,' cut in Father Mahon, giving the housekeeper a sweet smile.

Giving the elderly priest a tight-lipped look, Mrs Dunn left.

'Tea?' asked Daniel, picking up the pot with his good hand.

'I'd rather a scoop,' said the elderly priest.

Daniel smiled and, crossing the room, took a bottle of Jameson's from the sideboard.

He brought it back and, prising off the cork, poured an inch or so in two teacups.

Daniel sat down in the chair opposite the old man and raised his glass. *'Adh mór.'*

'And yourself.'

The old priest knocked back his drink in one gulp and so did Daniel, feeling the warm spirit spread down his throat.

'How are you, lad?' asked Father Mahon, putting his cup down.

'A bit sore, but I'll live,' Daniel replied, picking up the teapot to fill their cups.

Although his shoulder was healing well, it hurt like billy-o. The painkillers the nurse had given him to take hadn't touched it, but the Jameson's was starting to.

Daniel handed the old man his tea and glanced at the sheet of headed notepaper lying on the side table at Father Mahon's elbow. 'I see you've got the bishop's letter.'

'Yes, it arrived this morning,' said Father Mahon. 'So you're off to join the Royal Army Chaplain Corp.'

'I am,' said Daniel. 'I wanted to tell you myself first before it arrived, but...'

'You found yourself in hospital,' said Father Mahon.

'That I did,' Daniel replied.

'It was lucky Mattie Brogan was on duty that night and found you,' said Father Mahon, 'and a kindness to pop in on you each day so we knew how you were faring.'

'Yes, wasn't it?'

A warm glow of happiness enveloped Daniel.

Mattie had been at his bedside, ARP duties permitting, for the past four days but, as his undercover operation was subject to the Special Powers Act, they had maintained the pretence that she was just a concerned parishioner. Unfortunately this meant she couldn't accompany him back to the rectory. However they would be meeting later.

'When are you off?' asked Father Mahon.

Daniel took a fish paste sandwich from the plate. 'Next Monday.'

'So soon,' said the old priest, looking concerned. 'Will you be fit enough?'

'I'll have to be,' Daniel replied.

Father Mahon sighed. 'Well, I suppose needs must when the Devil sits at Calais.'

Daniel finished his mouthful and picked up his cup.

The two men ate their afternoon refreshments in silence but, after Father Mahon drained his cup, he spoke again.

'Now, I don't want you to be taking this the wrong way, lad,' he said, putting it back in the saucer. 'And you've done a grand job in the parish and no mistake, but I'm not so surprised you've decided to serve God by enlisting because I've been thinking for a while now that perhaps the Good Lord hasn't called you to be a parish priest.'

Daniel laughed. 'You may well be right, Father.'

'You'll be in my prayers, of course,' continued the elderly man. 'But if there's anything I could assist you with—'

'Actually,' said Daniel, putting down his cup and rising to his feet. 'There is something.'

Francis had given permission for Daniel to reveal his true identity to Mattie's family but no one else. However, out of courtesy, respect and his fondness for Father Mahon, Daniel felt the elderly priest should know what had been going on beneath his roof and, luckily, he could do this without committing treason.

Taking a step forward, Daniel knelt down in front of the elderly priest and, crossing himself, he bowed his head.

'Forgive me, Father, for I have sinned,' said Daniel in a hushed tone. 'It's been many years since my last confession and I—'

Twenty minutes later, having recited the whole story about himself, Mattie and Christopher, Daniel waited with his hand clasped in front of him and his head bowed.

It had been almost half a decade since he'd knelt to receive absolution and probably the same length of time since he'd regarded himself as an unbeliever. Truthfully, in the face of all the cruelty and suffering he'd seen in Spain and the cruelty and suffering he would see again before Hitler was defeated, he still wasn't sure how he felt about an almighty being. However, with Mattie's love holding his heart and the joyful prospect of fatherhood, Daniel felt perhaps he'd give God another chance.

Stretching out his gnarled hands, Father Mahon laid them on Daniel's head. *'Ego te absolvo a peccatis tuis in nomine Patris et Filii et Spiritus Sancti,'*he said quietly.

'Thank you, Father.' Daniel crossed himself and raised his head.

'Well, that explains a few things,' said Father Mahon as Daniel stood up and returned to his chair. 'And, of course, what is said in the confessional is sacrosanct and I can't tell you how relieved I am about Mattie, for it's been as plain as the nose on your face that you've been in love with the girl for months.'

Daniel gave a wry smile. 'Was it that obvious?'

'Only to me,' said Father Mahon. 'Although, given the circumstances of me thinking you were in holy orders, I'll confess the knowing of it has caused me some worry, I can tell you.'

'I'm sorry, Father,' said Daniel.

'Well, it's of no mind nor matter now, is it? After all, you wouldn't be the first man of the cloth to get involved with one of the girls in the parish, but...' An odd emotion flickered across the priest's aged face. 'At least you're in a position to make an honest woman of her.'

'I'm applying for a special licence tomorrow,' Daniel replied. 'I want to wed before...'

'Before you're sent on your next mission,' said Father Mahon.

Daniel nodded. 'It's not the best way to start married life but, as you say, Father, needs must. We will have to tie the legal knot in secret but Mattie and I would be honoured if you would conduct a nuptial mass afterwards, if we can

440

arrange for it to be done.'

Father Mahon smiled. 'I'd always hoped, if God in his good grace allotted me the years, to see the Brogan young uns happily wed. I'd be as happy as a man with two donkeys to bless you both.'

Daniel laughed and so did Father Mahon but, as the old man smiled at him, Daniel suddenly knew who Jerimiah Brogan reminded him of. The same person who had known Queenie Brogan as a young, barefooted girl in Ireland and who had entered the Catholic seminary just before Queenie married Seamus Brogan.

Thirty minutes later, having recovered from the shock of discovering Queenie Brogan's secret, Daniel took his leave of Father Mahon and left the rectory. Although it was only a ten-minute stroll to Chapman Street, it took him considerably longer as everyone he met along the way wanted to ask after his injury, which meant he arrived at Jerimiah's scrapyard at almost a quarter to five.

Straightening his dog collar and adjusting the sling supporting his left arm, Daniel crossed the cobbled street that ran along the side of the Tilbury to Minories railway arches.

As he stepped through the open gates, Jerimiah was just settling Samson in his stable for the night. Mattie's father looked around as Daniel walked in.

'Good afternoon to you, Father,' he said, throwing the bolt across the door of the horse's stall. 'And how are you after losing your argument with a motorbike?'

'Well, thank you, Jerimiah,' said Daniel. 'I won-

441

der, have you got a moment as I'd like to have a word with you?'

'Now, Father, if it's about me not going to mass, then I–'

'It's not about your church attendance, Mr Brogan,' Daniel interrupted. 'Perhaps I could stand you a Guinness at the club while we talk.'

'So Father McCree isn't Father McCree at all,' said Ida, looking across the kitchen table at Mattie.

'No, Mum,' said Mattie. 'He's Captain Daniel McCarthy, an undercover officer working for MI5.'

It was just before six in the evening. Knowing that Daniel was going to see her father to explain a few things, when Mattie had found her mother and gran preparing the evening meal when she'd returned from her shift at Post 7, it had seemed the perfect opportunity for her to do the same. So rather than nipping up to get changed, she'd decided to tell them everything before Francesca arrived home.

That was an hour and three pots of tea ago and she'd finally finished.

'So he wasn't run over by a motorbike?' said Ida.

Although she'd taken off her scarf turban, her mother, like Mattie, was still in her working clothes which, in her mother's case, was a colourless dress that was at least as old as Billy, covered by a wraparound overall.

'No, he was shot in the shoulder,' said Mattie.

'And he's the father of your baby and not

442

Christopher,' said Ida, her bare elbows resting on the table as she held her cup in both hands.

'Yes,' said Mattie.

'And Christopher is a–'

'For the love of Mary,' interrupted Queenie, also swathed in a vintage pinafore. 'Mattie's Daniel works for you-know-who and pretended to be a priest to flush out a bunch of fascists who Christopher was in charge of. Mattie and Daniel, God bless them, fell in love and now Mattie's in the family way. And I sincerely hope at your time of life, Ida, I'll not have to explain to you how that happened.'

Ida gave her mother-in-law a sharp look. 'Of course not, it's just a lot to take in, that's all.'

'Well,' said Queenie, folding her arms across her slender chest. 'Didn't I know all along what was going on between Mattie and Daniel?'

Ida raised a sceptical eyebrow. 'I suppose you saw it in the tea leaves, did you?'

An innocent expression spread across the old woman's face.

'Don't be daft,' she said. 'I saw it in their faces.'

Her gran winked and Mattie laughed.

'I suppose Christopher will be had up for treason?' said Ida, picking up the pot and pouring the last of the tea into her cup.

'I expect so,' said Mattie.

'What about Stan?' her mother continued. 'Cathy was in a right state, I can tell you, and so is his mother. They were down the station six hours being interrogated. Six hours!'

'I know,' said Mattie, feeling more than a little guilty about her sister's situation.

Stan, along with the rest of his crew, had been arrested at Wapping Stairs but the first poor Cathy knew about it was when the police burst through her front door and searched the place. After she and Stan's mother were released, Cathy had tried to find out what would happen to Stan but the police weren't very forthcoming. However Mattie had spoken to Francis, who had told her that Stan was being held in Pentonville prison under Section 1 of the recently passed Treachery Act for 'intent to help the enemy'. Due to the serious nature of the charges against him, neither Cathy nor Mr Wheeler was allowed to visit

'I'm not surprised she went into labour after such a shock,' concluded her mother. She pressed her lips together and shook her head. 'You know, I still can't believe it. Stan helping the Nazis? It don't seem possible. Not Stan.'

Mattie didn't reply. Francis had already warned her that she would be called to give evidence in both Christopher's and Stan's trials. Although she knew categorically that Stan was guilty of the crimes he'd been charged with, she still didn't relish being the one who might send him to the gallows. However, in Christopher's case, she had no such qualms.

Her mother looked at her. 'Have you told Cathy about Daniel?'

'Not yet, and I'm going in to the hospital tomorrow to tell her, so I'm counting on you not to tell her when you visit later, Mum, or speak to anyone else about what happened and who Daniel really is,' said Mattie, looking meaningfully at her mother.

Her mother bristled. 'I hope you're not implying that–'

'I'm just saying we're not to talk about what Daniel really does outside the family,' said Mattie.

'Well, people are bound to ask,' said Ida, 'especially with you having a baby.'

'Daniel's speaking to Dad now so we'll be getting married in the next couple of weeks, quietly though with no fuss,' Mattie explained. 'So if anyone asks, I can just say I got married as soon as my new husband got his call-up papers, after a whirlwind romance, which is the absolute truth. He'll be going off to fight like thousands of other men and, just like thousands of other new wives, I'll have to make the best of it.'

As Mattie said her last words, the back door opened and her father strode in with Daniel just a step behind.

Daniel's gaze immediately fixed on Mattie. Although he was still dressed in his clerical attire, the expression in his eyes was anything but saintly and Mattie's heart squeezed with happiness.

'Well, Mother,' said Jerimiah, putting a hairy muscular arm affectionately around Daniel's shoulders and beaming at his wife. 'It seems we're to have another wedding.'

Stretching out her hand, Mattie smoothed a crease from the blue hospital blanket covering her nephew.

'He's so lovely,' she said, looking at her sister, propped up in bed.

'Yes he is,' Cathy replied, gazing adoringly at her three-day-old son.

Mattie was on the Marie Celeste ward in the London hospital. She had been almost the first visitor through the door at 2 p.m. and that was half an hour ago.

The night of Stan's arrest, the police had taken Cathy in for questioning and had just told her she could go home when her waters broke. An ambulance was called and, ten hours later, she delivered Peter Jerimiah Stanley in the early hours of the 15th, four days early after his father had been charged with treachery.

Peter sneezed and woke himself up.

'Can I give him a cuddle?' asked Mattie.

'Of course.' Cathy glanced at the clock at the end of the ward. 'He's overdue his two o'clock feed but I suppose as sister's not on the ward it won't matter.'

Slipping her hands under the stretching baby, Mattie lifted him up and tucked him into the crook of her arm.

'He is just so lovable,' said Mattie, imagining herself cradling Daniel's son in her arms.

'I know and he looks just like his...' Cathy's eyes filled with tears. 'Why did he get mixed up in all that Nazi stuff?'

Mattie didn't answer.

'I know he never had a good word to say about Jewish people, but lots of people are like that,' Cathy continued. 'You know they grumble about the Jews owning all the shops and businesses but when the police showed me those horrible leaflets they found under his mother's bed and told me he'd confessed to being part of a conspiracy to get German spies into the country, I nearly fainted.'

'You weren't to know,' said Mattie.

'But you think I'd have noticed something,' her sister continued. 'And how will I face all our friends and neighbours once they read in the papers that my husband's a traitor?'

'The trial will be in secret so no one will know except the family and we won't tell, will we?' said Mattie.

Peter started wriggling in Mattie's arms and rooting around.

'I think it's time for his feed,' Cathy said, sitting up. 'Hand him to me.'

Mattie gave Peter to her sister, who opened her nightdress and settled him on her breast. Cathy watched her son feeding for a few moments, then looked up.

'The police asked me lots of questions about Christopher.'

'They would, because...'

Mattie told her about Christopher's involvement with Stan and the BPU.

'Oh my goodness,' said Cathy when she finished. 'So we're in the same boat.'

'Not quite,' said Mattie.

Cathy's blue eyes stretched wide with astonishment as Mattie told her sister the rest of the story, including Daniel's role.

'Mum never said anything when she came yesterday,' said Cathy, changing her son onto the other side and not meeting Mattie's gaze.

'I told her not to as I wanted to tell you myself,' said Mattie.

'So you're getting married,' said Cathy.

'Yes, probably on the 1st July,' said Mattie.

'Daniel's getting the special licence now. We'll be getting married in secret as I'm only allowed to tell close family about Daniel.'

'But you won't have a lovely dress or a do after,' said Cathy.

Mattie smiled. 'No, I won't, but I'll be Daniel's wife and that's all I care about.'

Having finished his afternoon feed, Peter had fallen asleep in his mother's arms. Cathy gazed at him for a moment, then looked up at Mattie.

'Odd isn't it that by Christmas both of us will have a baby,' she said. 'I wonder if you'll have a boy or a girl?'

A glow of warm contentment spread through Mattie but she cut it short and looked at her sister.

'I wish there was some other way, for your sake, Cathy,' she said sombrely. 'But you must understand I will be a witness for the prosecution at Stan's trial.'

Tears formed in Cathy's eyes. 'Will he hang?'

'I don't know, Cathy, but he might.'

Cathy pressed her lips lightly on her son's downy head and then her eyes snapped open and she looked at Mattie. 'So you were right then, weren't you, Mattie, about Stan wasting his time with the BPU?'

'Only because I didn't think trying to talk peace with Hitler would get us anywhere. It was only after I saw Stan running away from the Wisemans' that night that–'

'For God's sake, Mattie,' Cathy cut in, tears running down her cheeks. 'Why couldn't you have just turned a blind-eye?'

448

Mattie stared helplessly at her sister cradling her newborn son in her arms and weeping uncontrollably. Reaching across, Mattie placed her hand on her sister's, but Cathy snatched it away.

'It's all right for you, isn't it?' Cathy snapped. 'No doubt your bloody husband will have a medal pinned to his chest and be able to tell his kids how he won the war whereas my poor Peter will never know his dad.'

Peter woke up and started whimpering. Rocking back and forth, Cathy hugged him closer and continued to sob.

Feeling the chasm growing between them, Mattie spoke again. 'Cathy, I–'

'Just clear off, Mattie,' Cathy shouted, glaring at Mattie through red-rimmed eyes. 'Clear off and leave us alone.'

Aching to take Cathy in her arms and comfort her, as she had done when they were children, Mattie stared at her for a few moments, then she stood up.

'I can't undo what's happened,' said Mattie. 'But you're my sister, Cathy, and I'll always love you. No matter what, if you ever need me, I'll be there.'

She studied her sister's golden curls as they cascaded over the baby in her arms then, with her heart feeling like lead in her chest, Mattie turned and walked off the maternity ward.

Chapter Twenty-three

As the Castle Rock Hotel's hall clock chimed two o'clock, Daniel rolled onto his back and kicked the top sheet down. Mattie didn't blame him. Even though the hotel where they were staying was high on Hasting's East Cliff, the sweltering heat of the day had barely dipped overnight. Hoping to catch the breeze from the sea, Mattie had left the curtains drawn back and the window open, but the room was still too hot for her to sleep.

Turning on her side and tucking her hand under her head, Mattie's eyes ran slowly over her husband as he lay peacefully beside her. Love and happiness surged up so forcefully that tears pinched the corners of her eyes.

Daniel had applied for the special licence to marry the day after he came out of hospital and they were married in Caxton Hall two weeks later, on the 1st July, with Francis and Francesca as their witnesses. They weren't alone as there were at least two dozen other young couples eager to tie the knot before the husband reported to duty. As the registrar pronounced them man and wife, the air-raid siren went off so, instead of a celebratory drink, the four of them huddled in the hall's damp basement for an hour.

Because of the imminent threat of invasion, all unnecessary travel had been strictly prohibited to allow the swift deployment of troops. However

Francis had managed to twist a few arms in the Ministry of Transport and had obtained a permit for Daniel's parents to travel down from Liverpool. This meant that both sets of parents, plus Queenie, were present when Father Mahon conducted the nuptial mass in the bishop's private chapel three days after they were legally married. Although both Mattie and Daniel would have liked the church's sanction on their marriage to have taken place in St Bridget and St Brendan's, it was too dangerous as the congregation had already been told that Daniel had left to join the army.

So, for Mattie, there was no white wedding dress lovingly stitched over weeks, no bridesmaids, no wedding cake or buffet and no family other than her mum, dad and gran. Charlie was, God only knew where, waiting to repel the Germans, Jo and Billy were in Suffolk billeted with Miss Piggot and her unmarried son and Cathy wasn't speaking to her so had refused to attend. Daniel's brother, like Charlie, was with his squadron while his sisters weren't free to come at such short notice.

Now, lying in their hotel room, after just eight short glorious days of married life, Mattie knew that Daniel would soon be gone. Although she could feel her eyes aching for sleep, she forced them awake. In the dim moonlight she lay watching her husband sleep and tried to imprint in her mind every detail of their last night together. She refused to believe that she would never see him again but there was no knowing when he would return from his next assignment so these precious hours, minutes and seconds were all she would have of Daniel until he did.

Mattie's gaze travelled from the sheet that skimmed Daniel's hips, up the line of hair in the middle of his stomach to the mass of curls across his chest before continuing onto the puckered skin of the bullet wound on his shoulder.

He wasn't really fit for what he was about to face, but then was anyone? With the Germans sitting just twenty-three miles away across the Channel he, like his fellow countrymen and women, would have to find the strength to protect his country.

Downstairs, the hall clock chimed the quarter of an hour and Mattie leaned forward and kissed her sleeping husband's forehead. He opened his eyes.

'Is it time?' he asked. Reaching up, he moved a stray lock of Mattie's hair from her forehead.

Unable to speak, Mattie nodded.

They lay motionless, gazing into each other's eyes for several heartbeats, then Daniel threw off the sheets and, swinging his long legs out of bed, walked over to the chair with his clothes draped over the back.

Mattie sat up and tucked the sheet around her. Resting back against the padded headboard, she watched her husband of a week and a day dress in a moth-eaten sweater, canvas trousers and scuffed boots.

Shoving the set of French identity papers that MI5 had created for him into his pocket, Daniel returned to the bed. Kneeling beside her, he took her in his arms, crushing his mouth onto hers in a deep kiss. With the heady scent of his skin sur-

rounding her, Mattie tried to imprint the rough-
ness of his early morning bristles into her mind
as she clung to him.

Too soon, much too soon, his lips left hers.

Mattie released him and then wrapped her
arms around herself to stop herself reaching for
him again.

Laying his hand on her gently swelling stomach,
Daniel closed his eyes for a second, then opened
them and looked down at her. 'Kiss our baby for
me if I'm not back.'

With tears pressing the back of her eyes, Mattie
forced a smile.

'I will,' she whispered.

His gaze ran over her face once more, then he
stood up and strode to the door.

Grasping the handle, he paused and turned
back. 'I love you.'

Their gazes locked for a heartbeat and then he
marched out.

Mattie stared at the door until she could no
longer hear his footsteps on the stairs, then she
got up. Retrieving the shirt he'd discarded yesterday, from the floor, Mattie went back to bed.
Pressing her face into the crumpled cotton, she
curled into a ball and wept.

The cool early morning breeze from the sea
ruffled Mattie's auburn hair as she sat hugging her
knees on Hasting's East Cliff Green. She was
wearing the new summer frock that Daniel said he
liked her in and was sitting on her rain mac. To her
right was the tumbled-down Norman castle and
vernacular Victorian lift while on her left were the

caves that had been the centre of the town's smuggling trade but were now air-raid shelters. The English Channel stretched before her. Mattie stared at the misty outline of France on the horizon, where Daniel now was.

The first golden streaks of the July morning were just colouring the sky when Mattie had taken up position above the Cinque Port's old town two hours ago. Now the sun had broken through and it was a fine, clear day. As her eyes strained across the shimmering body of water in front of her, she noticed something high in the few wispy clouds that peppered the bright blue summer sky. Shading her eyes from the glare of the low sun, Mattie studied the thin forms shooting towards her. The aviation spotters in their turret noticed them, too, and sprang into action. The wail of the air-raid siren cut across the stillness of the beautiful English morning as dozens upon dozens of Luftwaffe Messerschmitt shot over her head, sunlight sparkling on their wing tips.

As the enemy's engines roared overhead, Mattie felt the baby inside her move for the first time. Placing her hands protectively over her stomach, she swung round to follow the planes' lightning progress northward. In the distance she could see a lone squadron of RAF Hurricanes flying out to meet their challenge.

The Battle for Britain, it seemed, had begun.

The publishers hope that this book has given you enjoyable reading. Large Print Books are especially designed to be as easy to see and hold as possible. If you wish a complete list of our books please ask at your local library or write directly to:

Magna Large Print Books
Magna House, Long Preston,
Skipton, North Yorkshire.
BD23 4ND

This Large Print Book for the partially sighted, who cannot read normal print, is published under the auspices of

THE ULVERSCROFT FOUNDATION

THE ULVERSCROFT FOUNDATION

... we hope that you have enjoyed this Large Print Book. Please think for a moment about those people who have worse eyesight problems than you ... and are unable to even read or enjoy Large Print, without great difficulty.

You can help them by sending a donation, large or small to:

**The Ulverscroft Foundation,
1, The Green, Bradgate Road,
Anstey, Leicestershire, LE7 7FU,
England.**
or request a copy of our brochure for more details.

The Foundation will use all your help to assist those people who are handicapped by various sight problems and need special attention.

Thank you very much for your help.